Detective Cummings displayed the photos. The single flash-bulb hadn't done much to enhance the beauty of the bathroom. But neither had the body. And neither did the face—chalky, eyes staring, mouth agape in a parody of awe, lips drooling red.

"You know this man, Mr. Sweeney?"

"We went into the CIA together. We did a lot of things together."

"Tell me, Mr. Sweeney: Why would an old associate, dying of an advanced case of bullet holes, pull himself across yards of sand, up a long flight of stairs, across a lawn, over a deck and breeze-way, through a door he unlocks with a years-old key, so he can do his dying on your bathroom floor?"

Sweeney shrugged. "Maybe you can suggest a reason."

"You're not telling me something, Mr. Sweeney. There's something you know you're not telling me. I feel it in my police-man's bones."

SWEENEY'S RUN

"A genuine edge-of-the-seat, page-turner of a novel."

—*News Journal* (Wilmington, DE)

"A pool of danger, intrigue and ambiguity . . . Captivating."

—*Florida Times-Union* (Jacksonville)

"The action is fast-paced, the plot shifts like quicksand."

—*Folio*

"Enough twists and turns to keep you on your toes. And just when you think it's all over, Hunter grabs you with a hammerhead stall leading into a spinning spiral before landing you solidly on the last page."

—*Compass*

Tor books by Jack D. Hunter

Potsdam Bluff
Sweeney's Run
Tailspin

A TOM DOHERTY ASSOCIATES BOOK
NEW YORK

This is a work of fiction. All the characters and events portrayed in this book are fictitious, and any resemblance to real people or events is purely coincidental.

SWEENEY'S RUN

Cover art by Larry Selman

A Tor Book
Published by Tom Doherty Associates, Inc.
175 Fifth Avenue
New York, N.Y. 10010

ISBN: 0-812-51339-8
Library of Congress Catalog Card Number: 92-20968

First edition: September 1992
First mass market edition: May 1994

Printed in the United States of America

0 9 8 7 6 5 4 3 2 1

SWEENEY'S
RUN

39° 27′ N

76° 02′ W

The gusts were out of the northeast, chill and damp and stirring the shallow Chesapeake headwaters into a nasty chop. But the rental boat, a 22-foot cabin-type runabout with twin 60 horsepower outboards, kept its poise, even under reduced power amidst winds astern and a tidal current from broad on the port bow.

Nageler had cleared the yacht basin late in the afternoon and made way directly down the Susquehanna Flats to the nun buoy west of Turkey Point, where he turned the bow to the weather and dropped anchor—thus becoming, to the casual eye, no more than a lone fisherman riding out what promised to be a temporary unpleasantness.

The lowering sky brought an early twilight, and the weather—contrary to the forecast, which was for a general clearing and abating winds—not only persisted but worsened. The water became more turbulent, and a misty rain began to swirl, dimming the evening lights of Havre de Grace and Perry Point and the gaggle of bridges between.

The anchor rode tautened, and the stern wanted to swing—a rotten development, for violent yaw reduced the efficiency of the laser-guided videomagnifier. To better his chances for clear pictures and static-free audio, Nageler allowed the boat to settle back firmly on the anchor, making fast when the proper scope had paid out; then, easing on the power and playing the rudder, he kept the anchor line taut and in sight until it was abeam. He hurried forward and threw in the second anchor, then dropped back and adjusted both rodes so that they established equal scope at a 45-degree angle. The swinging fell off importantly, and he began to feel a little better about things. The videomagnifier, along with the other hardware in his kit, was touted as being aloof to erratic motion, but experience had taught him not to trust supply officers' hype. A stable platform never worked a hardship on anybody, doing anything, with anything.

Which he'd learned one night during the Starnberger Turnverein festival two decades ago, when he and Gerda von Reichling had waded ashore from a disastrous attempt to make it in a canoe.

He smiled in the darkness, caught up in nostalgia.

Gerda.

A wonderful girl, by any measure. Smart, warm, funny.

God, where had his life gone? What had happened to all those great people?

The nostalgia made a quick, bitter turn into loneliness, and, as always when memory or circumstance caused his soul to bleed, he applied the tourniquet of physical activity. He broke open the kit—a suitcase-size, stiff-sided bag with airport casters and digital locks—and pulled the magnifier tube and seven-inch video screen from their packing snaps. He affixed the video box to the dash just behind the boat's windscreen and flipped its acuity-test switch. A nice clear pattern, amber on black. The receptor tube and its laser aiming barrel, each in its weather hood and both nestled in the gyro-mount, were made fast to the gunwale with butterfly clamps. A trial shot brought the Perry Point Veterans' Hospital onto the screen with surprising clarity. Despite the foul weather, he could even hear the tires chirp as a car rounded the turn to the exit gate there.

Not bad. But he'd have to do better here. Much better.

He fine-tuned the video knobs and punched in the audio booster. After a bit of scramble the screen held on the face of the man at the window of the hospital gatehouse.

"Jesus, what a lousy night," the man said to someone in the room behind him.

"Even the birds are walking," the someone agreed.

A test of the camcorder delivered a perfect replay.

Satisfied, Nageler activated the radio, set it on the garble mode and called in.

"Achtung, achtung. Wienerschnitzel, am Apparat."

The acknowledgement came in, tinny. "Hier Apfelstrudel. Was geht?"

"Startbereit. Alles in Ordnung."

"Gut. Du hast vier Stunden."

"Abgemacht."

"Rufe an, eh?"

"Selbstverständlich. Ta-ta."

He switched off the set.

Now all he had to do was wait.

Nageler was at the wheel, full of beef sandwiches and thermos coffee, listening to the wind and feeling the sly tugging at the anchors. His gaze wandered ashore to Turkey Point's wooded hills, seeking the dim white dot that was the house, left to Tom Sweeney by doting parents.

A good man, Sweeney.

Sharp, quick, gutsy. Honest.

Which was why Sweeney was sure to be among those canned in the Defense Department cutbacks, he thought, wryly amused. Brilliance and honesty are rarely appreciated in any royal court of any era, but they were downright feared and detested in the contemporary Washington hierarchy, which was fashioned of manifold layers of mediocrity and dissemblance. Even so, there were a few exceptions. Sweeney was one of them. Sweeney had risen to the top, like cream. Or, as Sweeney himself had put it in one of his many press interviews, "like the fat in gravy."

Nageler smiled again.

At the end his mind was not, contrary to folklore, on a fast-forward replay of his life. It was, rather, racing with self-reproach—an angry embarrassment over his lack of preparation for betrayal.

He had been bent over the panel box, making final adjustments to the receptor, and so there was no way he could have seen the swimmer's rising from the noisy seas. The first he knew was the slamming of the knee in his back, with the swift looping and closure of the garotte.

The swimmer was large and powerful—and a bit unlucky. He had closed expertly from the rear, but the tossing, slippery deck betrayed his footing, slowing the snap of the noose by a microsecond. So Nageler, although benumbed by shock, pain and giddiness, found it possible to insert his left hand between his throat and the garotte and to turn his right hand behind him and seize the man's scrotum, an unguarded lump in the sleek nylon racing trunks. There was a yelp—a brief scream—and the wire loosened, a tiny slippage that enabled Nageler to break, pivot and land a crushing kick against the attacker's knee. A follow-up lunge sent the man staggering backward in what suggested a mad tap dance, and then he was gone, flailing and screeching, over the motor mount and into the surging seas.

Nageler punched the starter button, and the twin motors thrummed. As the boat leaped forward, he swung his knife and cut away the anchor rodes, nearly rolling overboard in the effort. But he made it to his feet and was able to steady the wheel and swing the bow toward the Turkey Point beacon, which was fast disappearing in the swirling rain.

He groped, caught up the microphone. "Achtung, achtung! Hier—Wiener—schnitzel!"

Silence.

"Achtung Wiener—schnitzel—Die begierige—Königin hat—uns—beschummelt! —Schnell—mit ihr quitt—zerschlage ihre—Büchse!"

Silence.

From the starboard rear quarter came the stuttering of a machine gun. The air was filled with a crazy crackling, and hammers pounded him, and the windshield and instrument panel dissolved in a cascade of glass and splinters.

"Apfelstrudel! Why don't you—answer? Where—are you— What the—hell's—going on? Apfelstr—this is—answer—for— crissake—"

"Hello, there, Weenie-schnitzel. Sorry to report that apple stroodel is out for a long lunch. Eh? Ha-ha."

New pain, new shock, and the understanding that the betrayal had been complete.

Gasping, struggling, his eyes blurring and stinging from wind and tears, he caught sight of the other boat and the winking of its gun. His left hand clawed for the microphone, which had fallen away and now swung on its cord, just beyond reach. But still another burst tore along the length of the boat, and he went down, legs beyond control.

Eventually the wind and seas and nightfall united in his defense. The gun sounds dwindled, and he managed to pull himself sufficiently erect to maintain a heading and beat the ebb tide to the muddy flats below Sweeney's house.

Later, lying on the tile in the final moments, when the sorting of memories and images was still possible, he listened to the wind and rain against the house, the way he had all those years ago in boyhood autumns in the Tyrol.

He was aware, too, of disappointment—a vague annoyance at having been at the short end of the stick. The Sweeney thing again. Sweeney had always made him feel as if he were missing something important.

A voice. Not a voice. A gurgling. Somewhere in his head: "This one's on me, Sweeney. The mushrooms are my treat."

Was that laughter he heard?

He reached out through a gathering gauze, straining to lift and push. Then he fell back, curious: as the pain diminished, the cloudiness brightened . . .

CHAPTER 1

As usual, Randolph Ridenour was moderating "Sundown Symposium." Today his panelists were those other phonies, Thomas Barlow, Lewis Murray, and Carmelita Delgado, whose manner suggested that God had brought them to the studio in his limo, briefing them en route on his plans for the world. Even so, their revelations, delivered in that pseudo-Oxonian drawl currently chichi among network pundits, amounted to no more than a rephrasing of what the less godly already knew: the world was a stinking mess and would likely remain so.

Internecine war was raging among the no longer unionized socialists of the Soviet republics. Post–Castro Cuba sought to become a protectorate of Japan, the fat cat, increasingly smug superpower. Germany's economic and political health was worsening daily, thanks to the staggering cost of unification and an explosive surge of neo-Nazism in key population blocs. Middle East theocrats, traumatized by their recent Saddamy, concocted vengeful conspiracies against the American Satan. China was torn by new riots. The United States, in the morning-after of its Gulf War bacchanal, was assigning its remaining pocket change to the battle against declining, but still-epidemic narcotism.

Sweeney sighed and flipped the remote off-switch. He pushed himself free of the swivel chair and left the desk for the window wall, where he stood for a time, regarding the rain-washed Georgetown street below. The impeccably dressed strawberry blonde, who was reputed to be the mistress of Senator Riggles, came out of No. 20, snapped open her hundred-dollar umbrella, tiptoed through the puddles to her red BMW, and drove off in a swirl of exhaust. Philip Bridgewater, the economist, appeared briefly in the doorway of No. 24 to scowl at the sky, and moments later a cab dropped off What's-His-Name, Something Something Anderson, the poet who lectured at the university and was said to hold seances in No. 28.

With this, the street returned to its rainy-afternoon somnolence.

An expensive neighborhood.

A most unlikely neighborhood for his line of work.

Which, after all, made it the most likely neighborhood.

He was considering this irony when the intercom sounded its polite warble.

"Yes?"

"Mr. Richter's office buzzed, Mr. Sweeney. He wonders if you might find a moment to drop by."

As secretaries went, Irma Landrey was competent. But her oiliness was the pea under his office-time mattress, an insignificance which, perhaps because it was Civil Service and therefore everlasting, had become a major annoyance.

"I often wonder about that myself, Irma."

"Sir?"

"I'm on my way."

He entered the corridor—a hushed, carpeted gangway lined with Chippendale, parchment-shaded lamps and elegant art in gilded frames—which led from Operations, housed in No. 21, to the abutting No. 23, where Aaron Richter, as director of Special Intelligence Initiatives, nested behind a second-floor redan composed of Administration and Central Coding.

Sweeney stood for a moment, listening to the far-off, muted computer clackings with a sudden uneasiness. Something was up. Richter never called meetings this late in the day. Gathering himself, he headed for corridor's end and the highly varnished, gatelike doors bearing the brass plaque: DIRECTOR'S SUITE and, in a kind of parenthetical, equally elegant but smaller font below, ADMISSION BY ELECTRONIC KEY ONLY.

In gentler times, Richter's office had served as a corner bedroom. It was now a mellow melange of book-lined walls, draped windows, polished mahogany and red leather.

"Hello, Tom." Richter, seeming diminished and somehow forlorn behind the mammoth desk, waved at the wing chair. "Have a seat."

"Thanks. It's been a long day."

Richter turned slightly in his chair to regard the evening taking form beyond the streaming windows. His face, in profile, suggested a weathered Remington range rider—craggy, self-sufficient, made pensive by isolation and loneliness. "I have an unhappy duty, Tom."

"How so?"

Richter cleared his throat, his gaze still on an unspecific distance. "I'll move right to the bottom line: your voluntary withdrawal from SII is being requested. The budget cuts require an across-the-board reduction in force, and since your post is very high level and, on paper, at least, somewhat redundant to my own, you're a sitting duck—hopelessly vulnerable in the eyes of the bean-counters. Naturally, the Department would like to circumvent the costly, time-consuming Civil Service procedures governing dismissals, and so your resignation would be a big help. I hate to lose you, but requesting your resignation is the only card I can play in this rotten hand I've been dealt."

Sweeney smiled wryly. "Why is it that I'm so unsurprised?"

"You should be surprised. You're one hell of an intelligence handler. None better, actually. And with all that fast-lane field experience, from Nam to Panama, with all your years of German and Central European experience, the Secretary is out of his mind to release you."

"Well, that's show biz."

"I'm trying to arrange the most liberal possible severance payment—plus whatever paid vacation time and other benefits you've accrued—to carry you while you're looking for something else. And I'll do everything I can personally to help you relocate, of course."

"Appreciate that."

"Do you have any ideas? Any angles you might exploit?"

"Window-washing. Since nobody does windows anymore, there might be a buck in it."

Richter smiled dimly. "It's good that you can still make jokes."

"Hell, Aaron, what's to cry about? It's only a job. I'll find another one. Meanwhile, getting serious about your question, I think I'll just take the car and roam the country for a couple of months. No special itinerary, no timetable. See some old friends here and there, do some hiking and climbing in Colorado, look at Wyoming between the ears of a horse. That kind of thing."

"Sounds good."

"There'll be some doubling up around here, obviously. Who'll handle my stuff?"

"I'll have to, I'm afraid. Nobody's as good as you are in dealing with the Germans—me especially. But I'm all we've got at this point."

"You'll do great. The boys at the Nachrichtendienst have a lot of respect for you."

"Well, it's going to take some doing. The Germans are very unpopular with the American people these days, and I don't have the patience you've shown. Your reports—your position papers—have been models of official lip-biting. Especially after that silly ass von Zoll shot off his mouth the way he did. I can't imagine what the man was thinking."

Sweeney considered that. Officially, the government of unified Germany gave lip service to "our American friends," but Mann-in-der-Strasse TV interviews revealed a disdainful condescension among younger Germans and a readiness of older Germans to forget the Marshall Plan and the Berlin airlift and to see themselves as sole authors of their nation's dazzling recovery from "that 1940s incident." Things had taken an angry turn when Hugo von Zoll, most outspoken member of the plutocracy that decreed from glittering towers in Berlin, Frankfurt and Munich what Germans would eat, drink, read, watch, own and think, had grumped on "Sundown Symposium" that, with the imminent U.S. economic meltdown, "The Yankee Doodle wastrel will simply be getting what he has deserved for so long." A noisily gathering horde of P.O.-ed Yankee Doodles was looking for ways—in the words of syndicated columnist Billy Rupert—to "tell the German sheiks to stick their dazzling recovery where the sun don't shine."

Sweeney sighed. "Von Zoll made things about as bad as they can get. That's for sure."

"Any suggestions as to what I can do about it?"

"Well, you have to hold on to the fact that there's a silent majority of Germans who are really good people. People who are decent, hardworking, and, after all's said, quite clear in their minds that the United States has been—and remains—the best foreign friend they have. All the recent nastiness has derived from media scare stuff on clandestine German arms traders and that sort of crap. There's trading, all right, but nowhere near the scale Randolph Ridenour and some of the other news types have been wailing about. And, as I've been reporting all along, the German government has been badly hampered in its efforts to enact and enforce military export bans. Von Zoll's vocal and very rich right-wing legislative minority sees to that—a fact that gets very little publicity because von Zoll's claque includes the German media barons."

"Your reports never seemed to give any credence to the neo-Nazi stuff, the return to the Führer Prinzip and all that it implies."

"Von Zoll's group is too slick for that. They simply have abiding, long-range plans to control the pan-German government and its decisions regarding business."

"I wish I could be as sure of that as you are."

"When you're working with the problem on a daily basis, I think you will be. Germany has once again become a world-class pain in the ass, sure enough. But you won't see any more goose-stepping Sieg-Heilers. Bad for business."

CHAPTER 2

When the melancholy little meeting and its strained, overly correct dialogue ended with the ritual handshake and pat on the back, Sweeney left, picked up his briefcase, turned off the office lights and went straight to his apartment in Alexandria. He knew he would have to relocate. At best, the severance cash—Richter's sanguine promises notwithstanding—and his savings and CDs could carry him through January. Then, failing gainful employ, he'd be forced to fall back on some piddling interest income and a pension which, in these digs, would pay for no more than every second Tuesday.

Staring into the bathroom mirror, he tried to be depressed about all this. But the relief was akin to that felt by a schoolboy on Saturday morning. Aaron Richter, earnest and funereal with pseudoconcern, had cut through Sweeney's waffling and set him free.

He made his face all solemn in a parody of Richter's, and then he laughed outright. *Wild West, here I come.*

The phone rang.

"Long distance, calling a Thomas F. Sweeney." The man's voice was stilted.

"Speaking."

"You the owner of the place called Overlook, down in the state park at Turkey Point?"

"Yes. Who is this?"

"Detective Lieutenant Cummings, Cecil County Police, in Elkton, Maryland. There's been some trouble at your place and we wonder if you could run over here and answer some questions, and like that."

"What kind of trouble?"

"One of our patrol car crews passing your place saw a light. The house had been dark for weeks, so they investigated. There's a dead man in your downstairs bathroom."

"Oh, God. Another one?"

"I don't follow you, Mr. Sweeney—"

"This is the second one in two years. Beach bums. Park drifters. They break in to get out of the weather, to get something to eat, to rip off the stereo and drink the booze. Sometimes to die under a roof."

"You don't seem to be very upset."

"Upset? Why should I be upset? Half the world is killing the other half. People are dying on steam vents and in alleys right here in town. Two of my neighbors have checked out on overdoses in the past six months. My God, man, I'm supposed to be upset because I have another break-in and the luckless klutz died in my john? Come on."

The official voice became more brittle. "Well, we still have to talk to you."

Sweeney sighed, suddenly ashamed of himself. "Of course, you do, Lieutenant Cummings. I apologize. But I've had a sort of stressful day today, and I didn't need this."

"Sure," the man said, unforgiving.

"Where did he break in? Window? Door?"

"There are no signs of a break-in."

"Well, if he had a key and let himself in, then died, you'd have found the key, wouldn't you?"

"How soon can you get here?"

"Where's here? At your headquarters; at the house?"

"Make it the house. I'd like you to tell me if anything seems unusual, out of place, different."

"Where am I supposed to look at the body?"

"I have Polaroids. If those don't do it, we'll take you to the medical examiner's."

"What was it? Heart attack? DTs?"

"The medical examiner hasn't said yet."

"The weather's getting worse down here. Can you give me until, say, seven o'clock?"

"All right. See you then."

He decided to take the Bay Bridge route. It was looping and indirect compared to I-95, but it cut out Baltimore and, once free of the Annapolis clutter and into 301's northern sweep toward the Delaware underbelly, it was much less traveled. The bad weather persisted; low, fast-running clouds the color of charcoal seemed barely to clear the trees, and a wind-whipped rain rattled heavily against the car's flanks and turned the highway into a mirror that doubled the glare of approaching headlights.

He drove mechanically, setting the cruise control on the fifty miles per hour federally mandated by the recently established Energy Conservation Program. Once, when the car rocked in the swirls of filthy mist left by a passing scofflaw ten-wheeler, he was tempted to revert to old times and teach the trucker a lesson by flooring the accelerator and leaving him to grope in the backwash. But it wouldn't be wise to taunt the jockey of a semi with a Mercedes—even an antique one like this; the idiot might be one of those German-haters with a magnum to match. So he stifled the urge and settled into the long, monotonous drive into the night.

It was an American Gothic farmhouse—a rambling white clapboard thing with a tin roof, tall windows, slim chimneys and filigreed porches. It sat on a hill in a wedge of oak forest, surrounded by state parklands and overlooking a hundred-mile sweep of the bay and its distant western shoreline. Sweeney had been born here in 1951, the only son of Big Jim Sweeney and his beloved Adrianne, married in Dijon after the Hitler War. They had chosen to settle in this remote and beautiful place because Big Jim, having made the transition from the old OSS to its successor, the CIA, was almost always out of the country anyhow, and Adrianne, daughter of a Normandy coastal resort owner, craved a return to her childhood privacy and wide-water views. Big Jim, killed on some obscure mission in South America, had long been no more than a little-boy memory, and

Adrianne was now in a Wilmington nursing home, drifting in a silent unreality while awaiting her turn.

Sweeney felt the poignancy of this as he turned into the long arc of driveway. Only when it was too late had he realized how great it had been to see that dear woman standing expectantly under the porch light when he came home from college, or the Army, or wherever. These days it hurt especially much, knowing that she still existed behind those staring eyes, in that shrinking, medicine-stained wreckage.

Ah, well. One pain at a time, Sweeney . . .

The storm was quite heavy now, with the rain rushing horizontally before the wind, the trees tossing, the surf booming in the darkness at the foot of the hill. A solitary unmarked Ford sat in the parking circle, lights blinking, radio muttering. A man in a yellow rain slicker waited in a corner of the breezeway.

Sweeney pulled his car to a stop beside the azalea beds. Lowering the window a crack, he shouted into the gale, "I'm Tom Sweeney. Are you Cummings?"

"I'm Sergeant Ames. Lieutenant Cummings is in the kitchen. He'll talk to you there." Ames followed Sweeney in.

Cummings was short and lean. His eyes, dark and heavy-browed, moved restlessly, as if it hurt them to linger too long on a single subject. His speech had a peculiar cadence, and Sweeney couldn't decide whether it was an impediment or an accent. He settled for impediment, since the man's idiom was unredeemably Urban-American.

"Could I see your driver's license, Mr. Sweeney?"

Suddenly annoyed by the detective's faintly insolent manner, Sweeney said, "Sure, if I can see your badge."

This time Cummings's glance held. "You understand that I have to be sure who I'm talking to, don't you?"

"Certainly. And, since all you power-company meter readers look the same to me, you can return the favor."

Ames, a tall redhead who wore the kind of tinted, gold-framed glasses that competition shooters favor, snapped, "Don't get cute with us, pal."

Cummings gave Ames a cautioning glance, then produced his badge case. "No need to be unpleasant, Mr. Sweeney. We've all got our burdens."

"Like I told you: I've had a heavy day, and it wasn't helped by a three-hour drive under Niagara Falls."

Cummings pocketed his notebook and became cautiously polite. "Would you please walk with me through the house and tell me if anything's missing, anything's out of order, or whatever?"

"Sure. You think the guy was a burglar?"

"No. I think he was murdered."

Sweeney gave him a sharp look. "Murdered? You mean here, in the house?"

"I'll get to that. Let's look around first."

"You've done all your fingerprinting?"

"All we need. I got to warn you, though, that the downstairs bathroom is in pretty bad shape. You have somebody who can clean it up?"

"My caretaker, Sam Alger, will take care of it in the morning."

Cummings glanced at his partner. "You'd better go back to the car and monitor the radio, Ames. There might be a call for us."

They completed their tour and returned to the kitchen within five minutes. "It all looks normal. I don't leave much around. Certainly nothing of real value."

Cummings gave him a sidelong glance. "I noticed that the bathroom didn't get to you too much."

"I've seen a lot of blood in my time."

"But not in your house."

"That's right. Not in my house. And not when somebody writes somebody's initials on the wall in his own blood. You say you have pictures?"

The detective nodded toward the breakfast nook. "There. On the table."

The single flashbulb hadn't done much to enhance the beauty of the bathroom. But neither had the body, sprawled as it was between the towel closet and the toilet bowl. And neither did the face—chalky, eyes staring, mouth agape in a parody of awe, lips drooling red—the face of Heinrich Ludwig Nageler.

"Jesus to Jesus."

"You know this man, Mr. Sweeney?"

"Heinrich Nageler. Everybody called him Hank. I met him in the Green Berets. We went into the CIA together. We did a lot of things together. Nam. Europe. South America. The Middle East. I haven't seen him in ten, twelve years."

"You considered him a good friend, then?"

"Not really. We were professional collaborators in some high-risk stuff." He shook his head slowly. "God. From these pictures, somebody was very annoyed with him."

"He was hit at least nine times by Nato-caliber bullets in the lower body and legs. The neck also showed signs of attempted strangulation. He apparently was attacked—then shot—down on the beach somewhere last night."

There was an uneasy pause. Then Cummings said, "It would take a hard man to make that distance with all that lead in him."

"Hank was one tough chunk, all right."

"Any idea why he would work so hard to get up the hill and into the house?"

"No." Sweeney pointed to the photo. "And I don't know what the hell he was trying to do with those three letters. *H, L, Z*. Or, maybe, *H, C, Z*. Or even *H, L, N*. Hard to tell. They sort of slant down."

Cummings peered at him carefully. "Are you certain that they don't mean anything to you?"

"Not really. Unless Hank was trying to write his own initials—*H. L. N.*—as a kind of attempt to identify himself, or something. What did his wallet show? What name was on his driver's license?"

"Albert F. Parsons."

"See what I mean? He was obviously working on something undercover, and when the opposition caught up with him, he wanted to regain his identity."

"You don't really believe that, do you?"

"No. But I can't imagine why he wrote those letters."

"You say you last saw him about ten, twelve years ago. Where?"

"In a whorehouse in Munich. He and I were there to intercept a KGB letter drop, and there was a fuss, and I got my ticket punched. He said he would come to see me in the hospital, but he didn't. I never saw him again. Until—this."

"You are sure he had no access to the house? A key you might have loaned him?"

"If he had a key, it was no loan."

"How about some office pal, say, who might've come down from D.C. for a weekend he didn't want the wife to know about, or like that?"

Sweeney gave him a wry glance. "It's against my religion to have office pals."

The detective cleared his throat. "Well, Mr. Sweeney, we did find a key, as a matter of fact. It was in the breezeway door. It had blood on it."

"Hank's blood?"

"We're checking that."

"Why didn't you tell me this in the first place?"

"I wanted to try you out."

"Try me out? For what? Am I a suspect?"

"Let me put it another way: I didn't want to influence your comments by telling you everything up front."

"Why is it that I resent your trying me out?"

The detective shrugged, indifferent.

"May I see the key?"

Cummings drew a plastic evidence bag from the pocket of his tweed jacket. "Leave it in the bag, please."

"This is an old key, sure enough."

"Did Nageler ever visit you here?"

"Only once. Years ago, before Munich. I threw a party for some army acquaintances. He was among them."

"So he could have found a key, say an extra one on a bureau or something, and taken it with him. As a souvenir or something, right?"

"I suppose. Hank was like that. He would squirrel things away for what he called 'days of deluge.' Maybe he thought this house would turn up handy someday."

Detective Cummings nodded and made another note.

Sweeney said, "Now that I'm here, I'd like to stay for a couple of days. Is there any reason why I shouldn't?"

"No police reasons. We've got all the latent prints, the samples, the pix, the sketches. We're trying to locate next of kin. Any ideas?"

"I never knew about Hank's family. They were Austrian, I

think. He came to the States as a kid, was brought up by an aunt or something. Try the CIA in Reston. Or the Pentagon. He should have records there."

"All right." Detective Cummings snapped the black book shut, scooped up the photos, glanced around the kitchen one more time, then went to the door. Pausing there, he said, "Tell me, Mr. Sweeney: Why would an old associate, dying of an advanced case of bullet holes, pull himself across yards of sand, up a long flight of stairs, across a lawn, over a deck and breezeway, through a door he unlocks with a years-old key, so he can do his dying on your bathroom floor?"

Sweeney shrugged. "Maybe you can suggest a reason."

"You're not telling me something, Mr. Sweeney. There's something you know you're not telling me. I feel it in my policeman's bones."

"I know a lot of things about a lot of things. But what I don't know is exactly what, among all those things, could be of any importance to you."

Cummings sighed, the sound of weariness and frustration. "I'll be getting back to you. Meanwhile, don't discuss this case—don't even mention it—to anybody but me. You get any new thoughts, hold them until I call you." He stepped into the night and closed the door behind him.

Finally alone, Sweeney made a pot of coffee and sat at the breakfast table, sipping from a mug and staring into the storm raging over the bay.

He had a major problem.

A dilly of a problem.

Before dying on the bathroom floor, Hank had used a years-old signal to warn him that the team members were in extreme danger and should run for cover.

But there had been only three team members in Munich.

Nageler, Sweeney, and Leonardi.

Nageler was now dead.

So what warning should Sweeney send, and how should he send it?

Of what danger should he warn an old pal, Richard D. Leonardi, currently in his first term as president of the United States?

CHAPTER 3

The secret emergency meeting was set for 11:00 A.M. in the penthouse hospitality suite of the Eldorado, one of the glitzy high-rise motels on the rim of Baltimore's international airport. Aaron Richter had chosen the time and place for its convenience and logic. Brandon McKell, vice president of the United States, was to be guest of honor down the hall at a noon luncheon of Delmarva Enlightenment, a teachers' political action group, and nobody was likely to give much importance to the Veep's sitting around a hospitality suite, chewing the fat with a couple of Administration types who happened to be at the motel; it was, after all, a watering hole popular among the area's more muscular politicians. Major polls consistently placed McKell near the bottom of the list of Washington's most influential insiders—Will Edwards, dean of the Press Club's wags, cracked that, by President Leonardi's second term, McKell's charisma and clout might have improved to the point where he'd command a cover-story in the *Petunia-Raiser's Gazette*—and so the print and electronic troops rarely kept watch on his daily comings and goings. Moreover, those few newsies assigned to provide him routine coverage were virtually guaranteed to see higher priorities elsewhere once they learned that the teachers expected him to deliver a few remarks, because it was universally agreed that each minute of Brandon McKell's impromptu oratory was as soporific as a metric ton of phenobarbital.

Richter was almost as anonymous as McKell, but for vastly different reasons. Richter's official, lawful function was to direct Special Intelligence Initiatives, a tiny but autonomous agency, which, like the CIA, was answerable directly to the National Security Council, and which *Time* had described as "a mysterious and menacing box in the U.S. dirty-tricks attic." His duties made him a truly powerful man in the Washington context, and he was calculating, erudite, suave and articulate—characteristics ideally suited to his delicate work.

McKell likewise represented the ideal, archetypal vice president, the cliche in gray flannel cardboard, the airhead fashion plate and ribbon-cutter whose bland good looks and uncompelling manner provided fodder for the funny-boy columnists and whose public utterances caused no problems for the president or the capital's power elite. Which in fact made him a slickster in dumbbell's clothing, since, as Colt had grumped in the limo on the way over, "Compared to McKell, Machiavelli was a summer-camp practical joker." Richter readily agreed, but reminded Colt, "Don't knock it. Our beloved Veep has dealt us in on the caper to end all capers and has invited us to join him on the road to stinking-richhood."

McKell's secret persona was known only to a few like Richter and Colt, and like Jenny Malone, the silver-haired matron with endless party credentials who served as Leonardi's chief of staff. Jenny Malone shunted all matters she considered too malodorous for presidential nostrils quickly and most privately to Brandon McKell for disposition as he saw fit. Thanks to a conscience made malleable by his years in local and national politics, McKell had no difficulty with outright payola, rationalizing that, as a diligent member of the Administration, his transcendant obligation was to help the president govern, and he did this best when—most discreetly and with the tacit understanding that he was acting in the president's stead—he led citizens through the government labyrinth to emotional relief, economic reward, or both. The fact that these citizens were very few, very rich, very grateful and themselves very discreet had brought McKell his own relief and reward, including the Vail condominium, the Porsche, the vacations in Acapulco, and the million a year in artfully laundered birthday and Christmas cash.

At 10:02, Richter and Colt sat at a coffee table in the Eldorado's glass-walled rooftop palace, spooning sugar and stirring cream as a means of avoiding eye contact during the ritual of McKell's opening monologue, which always reminded Richter of the surgeon's general's warning on a pack of cigarettes: *Caution! The president must be kept absolutely sanitary. There must be no suggestion—not the tiniest inference—that he's involved. He must be protected at all times from any possible connection with what we're doing here. And remember, I, too, am at very serious personal risk. So watch your P's and Q's, you two.*

And, as always, once McKell's stock speech had concluded, Richter delivered his stock assurances. "There's no need for you to be concerned, Brandon. Look at us: Covertly you have almost as much to say about how this country runs as President Leonardi himself. Colt, here, wields unequalled influence with the Colombians and the Peruvians and is a world-class expert on clandestine warfare. And I, as a ranking intelligence chief, know as much about the national defense mechanism as the Joint Chiefs of Staff—probably more, in some ways. We are the varsity, Brandon. We have not become so by being unwary, or inept." The words, the syntax would vary from session to session, but the rite itself was as pro forma as reveille at an Army camp.

McKell's cold gray gaze followed the rise of a Delta airliner that sparkled in the sunny morning and rumbled in the distance. "Well, schemes take on life of their own sometimes, and I don't want this one to get away from us. There's too much riding on it."

"Yes, sir." The obligatory prologue thus dealt with, Richter turned his gaze toward Colt, a mustached, cadaverous man in a vaguely blue suit of discount polyester. "I've called this meeting, Mr. Colt, to deal with a pronounced disruption of our plans by a purely coincidental turn of events the night before last. I'd like to have you bring the vice president up to speed on developments to date—your plans for the Cartagena meeting next month, and so on—but right now it's important that we deal with this unforeseen twist."

Colt waved a hand, a lazy invitation to proceed.

Richter knew that the trick would be to throw the best possible glow on what was undeniably a very dark cloud—an incident that should have had more prep time in the silver-lining department before being allowed to drift through McKell's already too-goosey disposition. "The Audio-Patrol Network in Harrisburg picked up some rapid radio traffic, on garble, that seemed to emanate from the Havre de Grace area. They put a de-scrambler team on it and came up with some German conversation from a boat anchored off Turkey Point. Just bits and pieces which themselves seemed to be encodements. So Aberdeen sent out a patrol boat. The weather was rotten, and, as the patrol boat was being launched, there were sounds of heavy shooting out on the bay. The patrol found nothing, and, since the Aberdeen command is under orders to report all security incidents directly to me, I was informed immediately. I called Cummings at once, since he has people in that area, and he agreed to investigate. After daybreak, park police found the intruder boat, which had been rented from a marina in the town of North East, on the beach in the state park area, badly shot up and with no trace of its occupant." He paused.

McKell said icily, "I think I know the answer already, but I'll ask anyhow: So what's the catch?"

"According to the police, the boat was carrying some very sophisticated portable surveillance gear. From their description, it was state-of-the-art stuff."

"Let me guess: German stuff, right?"

"Yes, sir, it would seem so."

"Where is it now?"

"In an evidence locker at the Elkton police station."

"Can we get it?"

"We're working on that."

"The Dienst is on to us, sure as hell."

Richter disagreed. "I don't think so. If they were on to us, why would they have played around with a small surveillance mounted by a mercenary?"

"Mercenary? What in hell do you mean?"

Richter, his own testiness growing, said, "Cummings, much more sophisticated than those country cops, followed tracks from the boat and finally found the intruder's body. It was ID'ed as Hank Nageler."

"*The* Hank Nageler? The guy who got thrown out of CIA five years ago?"

Richter decided to get it over with. "And this is where our problem begins. There was a hitch, and the hitch is why I called this meeting."

"What kind of hitch?"

"The body was found in Tom Sweeney's vacation house."

McKell actually rose from the sofa to stand in a kind of half-crouch, his face a study in astonished anger. "Tom *Sweeney*? Sweeney has a *vacation* house—?"

"Near Turkey Point. The family homestead. He was born there, grew up there."

"Good God almighty. If Sweeney gets involved in this—even in the most indirect way—we could have a disaster on our hands. That son of a bitch is a tiger. A holier-than-thou, self-righteous, jingoistic pain in the ass. If he gets one idea—"

"Easy, Brandon. I think I've taken care of it. Ironically, I fired him the very day of the incident. He and Cap O'Brien and several other specialists had to be let go due to the budget cuts. Sweeney's no longer with the government. Finis. Over and out."

McKell sank back on the sofa, seeming to be near apoplexy. There was a silence in the room as the others waited out his struggle to regain composure. Eventually his normal pallor returned, and he gave Richter a long, evaluating stare. "Need I remind you that only you, Jenny Malone, Colt, Cummings, Corbato and I are in on this operation? That's only six people in the whole world. But now, just because that idiot, Nageler, chose to die in Sweeney's house, the number stands to rise to seven, because the seventh is a clenched teeth, all-American zealot. Oh, God—this can't be coincidence."

"There is a link. Hank Nageler and Tom Sweeney had served together in the military. While they weren't exactly buddies, they did share some hairy assignments in the Cold War days."

McKell was unimpressed. "They were buddies enough for Nageler to do his dying in Sweeney's house. He must have gone there to—Jesus: Did he leave any *messages*?"

"Not that we know of. Apparently Nageler, fatally wounded, beached the boat and crawled to Sweeney's house for help. But the house was unoccupied, and Nageler died alone. Two of

Cummings's trackers found his body in the Sweeney place. After making Polaroids, they deep-sixed the body in the Elk River shipping channel before the sheriff or state police could find it. Cummings, naturally, personally searched the house and grounds for any messages Nageler might have left, but found nothing significant. Nageler had written his own initials on the wall in his own blood, but Cummings dismisses that as a dying man's whim, a statement like the 'Kilroy was Here' of the World War Two days. Just to be on the safe side, though, Cummings, playing cop, called Sweeney down there for questioning. He found no indication that Sweeney has the faintest idea as to why Nageler did what he did. Even so, Cummings wanted to shut Sweeney down at once, but Cummings—because he isn't familiar with all the nuances, with the forces at work here—thought he ought to check it out with us first. So that's why we're here, gentlemen. What do we do about Sweeney?"

Colt stirred in his seat and spoke, his voice like creaking rope. "It seems to me the solution is easy. First we find Sweeney. Then, since he's such a hotrock and now is in obvious need of employment, you persuade him to join us. What's an out-of-work guy going to do—say no to a couple of million?"

"Even if Sweeney were that kind of man, that could be pretty difficult," Richter said. "He told me he was leaving immediately for a couple of months of driving around the country, visiting friends, hunting and fishing and climbing. And, since he thinks he already talked to the cops about the Nageler incident, he's probably somewhere west of Pittsburgh by now. But all that aside: Brandon's right. Sweeney isn't that kind of man. He's an uncommonly straight arrow, and that's the very reason I never asked him to help us on this thing. He would have had terrible ethical problems with all of it."

McKell's stare was direct and angry. "Can you swear that Sweeney is really out of things? He's such a goddam terrier. He's always made me nervous."

"Well, hell, Brandon, I can't guarantee what will happen in any part of this sad old world of ours. But I do know Sweeney, and I'll bet he's so traumatized by his dismissal he won't do a thing. He's mad, he's hurt, and he never thought much of

Nageler anyhow. I'm sure he'll say the hell with it and remain on a long, pouting vacation."

McKell was unconvinced. "That's not good enough. Even when Sweeney was working for you, when we had ways to keep him busy on other things so he wouldn't tumble to our thing, he was a source of possible trouble. But now—" McKell spread his hands in frustration. "Now that he's got nothing to do, nothing but retirement, he'll try to figure out who broke into his house, and why, and then he'll learn about the shot-up boat, which the police and insurance adjusters and God knows who else have most certainly examined by now, and he'll start asking questions, and when he doesn't get any answers—Well, he could quickly turn into a big problem."

Colt nodded philosophically. "That says it, all right. Richter says he didn't place Nageler out there and had nothing to do with his being wasted. Cummings said he, likewise, had no knowledge of Nageler's being out there—nor would he have killed him, if he had. It would have been much more useful to question the man. So what we have here is a known agent-for-hire spooking around a locale that's fundamentally important to our thing, and none of us has the slightest idea why he was there or who set him up for killing and why. Nageler, gents, is a mystery to us. And now he's also a mystery to Sweeney, whose greatest joy, apparently, is to solve mysteries. And if Sweeney solves this mystery, we ourselves will be in the deepest of doo-doo."

Richter shrugged. "We'll find him before he does, though. I've already got a national all-points on him, and when we find him I'll keep a constant round-robin watch on him. If he tumbles to anything sensitive—something he can act on—we'll know at once."

McKell snapped, "Well, just see to it. And the quicker the better."

There was an interval, and Richter, sensing it to be time to move on, said, "Shall we hear what Mr. Colt has to report, Mr. Vice President?"

"Why not? My day's already ruined."

Richter rested back in his chair, and nodded at the large, somber man in the cheap suit.

Colt set his cup and saucer carefully on the table, and his deep-set eyes made a slow traverse of the room before his gaze, oddly oblique, seemed to settle on McKell. "We have Julio and Manuel lined up. Corbato says they haven't said no to our proposed price. He thinks they'll want us to sweeten the overall deal a bit, but we're close."

McKell shifted on the sofa and, with the touch of an immaculate forefinger, tested the centrality of the knot of his hundred-dollar silk tie. "That gives us five of the seven major entrepreneurs, right?"

"That's right. We're trying for a grand slam, of course, but if Mendez and Santos don't come along, Corbato will, as part of his deal with us, shut them down."

"By that, you mean—"

"Shut them down."

McKell's lips tightened slightly, and he watched another airplane for a time.

Richter knew that McKell was having trouble with the leadership thing again. This special sensitivity to others and their motives was, for Richter, the classic combination of blessing and curse, and it had told him early on in this weird relationship that McKell served as a prime specimen of the Be-The-Boss-But-Cover-Your-Ass Syndrome—an obsession evinced by all too many Washington denizens, in which the chronic need was to get everybody else to do the work or take the risk, so that if there was success, you would automatically be given the credit, and in case of failure, well, hell, you weren't really involved in the first place. Ostensibly the alpha and omega of this so-called "Operation Lorelei," McKell had shown that he was in fact unable—or unwilling—to take direct command and deal with the grubby realities that the creator of such an epochal undertaking had to confront. The "shutting down" of a pair of recalcitrant Andean narcotics tycoons, would obviously involve the routine purchase of murder, demolition and arson—a workaday business cost, like typewriter ribbons, or paper towels for the washrooms at Amalgamated Smithereen Company. Yet McKell's question, his taut lips, certified a squeamishness that was symptomatic of a larger inability to put himself on the line when sweaty, negative choices must be made. McKell, obviously, had no difficulty with the immoralities themselves; it was simply that he had a debilitating fear of being identified with them.

God help us, Richter groused in silent, controlled anger, *if this man ever becomes president of the United States.*

"If we have to knock heads," Colt was saying, "it will be pretty easy to disguise it as merely one more large-scale raid on the narco-cartel's support structure. The machinery is already in place—the Southcom commandos out of Quarry Heights, the Special Forces mercenaries, the Florida National Guard and its picket balloons and air surveillance, et cetera, et cetera. It'll be just another part of the ongoing drug war and that kind of six o'clock news crap."

"Besides, Brandon," Richter put in coolly, "the participating entrepreneurs won't complain. With the two Peruvians out, their slices will be all the bigger."

McKell glanced at his expensive watch. "All right. But I want to be notified immediately if there are any glitches. Contact me through the Chevy Chase cutout, and allow me an hour's reaction time."

"You got it."

"About those mercenaries," McKell asked. "Are we making any headway on recruitment?"

"Yeah," Colt said. "As of yesterday, General Reynolds has pipelined to Corbato four hundred and thirteen skinheads virtually handpicked out of the soldier-of-fortune type magazine want-ads. Every damn one of them an unthinking, hard-ass bullet-sprayer. And every damn one of them, by the way, amounting to an upheld middle finger to General Wallace and his staff, who have been screaming that if troops are to be recalled they should be the best of the best from Special Forces, and like that."

"Well," McKell said, "I admit it's rather blatant, but General Reynolds and I managed to sell the Pentagon the idea that this was just messy, mop-up kind of stuff and we should be conserving our Special Forces talent, not wasting it in a South American barroom brawl."

Richter smiled. "You mean they actually bought that?"

McKell shrugged. "The budget-cuts have spooked them. Even the best people don't want to ask questions for fear they might turn out to be dumb questions."

Richter glanced at Colt. "The mercenaries are being sent to that camp in the Everglades, right?"

"Mm. For organization and equipping. Some training together, so we can identify and jettison whatever really smart ones might have slipped through the Reynolds screening. Then the remainder will be shipped to the Cartagena Zone for integration into the Lorelei thing."

There was a pause, each giving these things thought.

Richter coughed dryly. "You people want to hear about the Hammerhead tryout?"

"Of course we do," McKell snapped, as if there hadn't been anything more important on his mind.

Colt put in, "Rumor says it's one hell of a machine."

Richter looked bleakly out the large window. "The rumor's right. General Reynolds managed to sneak one of the prototypes through the godawful jumble at Wright-Patterson. It was trucked to Aberdeen Proving Ground last Thursday, and one of our contract crews attached it to a twin-engine Piper Something and wrung it out. It not only performed credible maneuvers but also gave a persuasive counterfire. It gives every indication of being just what we've been looking for. It's—"

"Are you sure?" McKell interrupted.

Richter completed his sentence. "—said to be temperamental as hell, and it sure ain't cheap. But in the tests we loaded the plane to capacity with deadweight, and in two hours it had flown to Norfolk, made a U-turn and was back over Aberdeen, doing its thing without a single detectable hitch."

Presumably because he felt he was expected to, McKell reacted. "So that's good, eh?"

"If it does as good every time out, we've solved one of our major problems."

McKell asked, "So where does that leave us?"

"I've got a contract laid on for two of them," Richter said. He glanced at Colt. "They could be very attractive to your German buyers in Delaware."

"Will they be delivered in time to be attractive?" McKell asked.

"Yes. Our electronics people expect to have completed four more by the end of the month."

"Sounds pretty slow to me," McKell said.

"Remember, these people are working in a vendor lab. They just can't take over Wright-Patterson and work around the clock in front of God and everybody."

McKell delivered a non sequitur. "The German government is getting nosier by the minute. Three top agents of the Nachrichtendienst have shown up in the German embassy in the past two weeks. Have we infiltrated the Dienst to any helpful degree?"

If Colt was uncomfortable, he didn't show it. "We're having trouble with that one. But we're working on it."

"Well," McKell said irritably, "all the mercenaries and fancy planes, all the wheeling and dealing in Munich, all the arrangements in the Andes won't be worth a fig if the Dienst tumbles to what we're up to."

"As I say, we're working on it."

McKell glanced at his wristwatch and stood up, adjusting his tie again. "I've got to go now. If there's anything else, tell Jenny, and she'll get word to me."

At the door, the vice president paused. "Remember, Richter: top priority to finding Sweeney. We can't afford to have him running around unchaperoned."

"Yes, sir."

"Hello?"

"Cummings?"

"Yes."

"Are you on scrambler?"

"I'm always on scrambler, Mr. McKell."

"The Sweeney thing worries me terribly."

"As it should."

"Well, find him and fix him. I want him out of the way—completely and irrevocably."

"Good thinking. Consider it done."

"Stiegel and Company, Public Relations, Miss Fitzgerald speaking."

"Warren Stiegel, please. Aaron Richter calling."

"Yes, sir. One moment, please."

"Hello, Mr. Richter. What can I do for you?"

"Are you on your secure line?"

"Of course."

"I told you about the Sweeney incident."

"Mm."

"I want you to find him. At once. Whatever the expense. It's absolutely imperative that you find him and put him into maximum security until I can handle him further. Do you understand me?"

"Yep. No wet stuff?"

"Not until you have him in hand and I can make a decision under the current circumstances. I don't want anything impetuous, or impulsive, or gangland style. I want this handled surgically. It's a most delicate matter."

"Okay. I'll put Zimmermann and Pollock on it. Top priority all the way. We'll find him for you."

"Get Sweeney out of the way."

"Consider it done."

CHAPTER 4

Sweeney was shaving in the upstairs master bathroom, thinking hard about Hank Nageler's warning and wondering yet again what he should be doing about it, when a discordant sound interrupted the rustlings of wind and leaves in the sunny woods outside. It had been the careful shutting of a car door. And his curious glance from the window picked up at once the patch of dark blue in the forest's autumnal tones. A moment given to reflex—the quick stab of alarm and the pressing in of panic—and then the old familiars, the habits, the automatic modes and rhythms of the seasoned warrior, began to assert themselves.

As he toweled away the soap, his mind posed the base questions. Was there any workaday reason why two guys might be parking in the woods, smoking cigarettes and watching the Sweeney house? Were they tourists? Lovers? Doing drugs? Enterprising realtors? Was Thomas F. Sweeney, unemployed spy handler, simply overreacting?

None of the above. Konglike men do not sit in dark blue Dodges in state parks to admire nature, or to contemplate the verities.

Time for consultations.

He went into the bedroom, picked up the phone and, despite his instructions, dialed the number.

"Sheriff's office."

"Lieutenant Cummings, please."

"Lieutenant who?"

"Cummings."

"You sure you got the right number, sir? There's nobody by that name works here."

"Badge number: Four Thirty-eight."

There was a moment of silence. Then: "Sir, would you give me your name, please? And where you're calling from?"

Sweeney hung up, hearing, as he did, a tiny prefatory clicking.

Shee-it.

Not only was he under surveillance, his line was tapped.

Next question: What should he do about all this? Call 911? Scream and run?

Neither. He would try for the school solution, which would be to identify the men and learn what they were after. He finished dressing and hurried downstairs, through the kitchen and utility room and into the garage. Moments later he was in the car, out the driveway, and heading north on the state road—not too fast. He wanted to give the boys time to back the Dodge around and catch up.

The Dodge following, he drove directly to the village of North East, where he turned north on Route 40 and made for Freddie Dilworth's Discount Religious Bookstore and Believers' Auto Repair.

Freddie, the representative American entrepreneur, had contrived to serve both God and Mammon by catering to a down-home clientele much given to inspirational paperbacks and dyspeptic pickups, vans and campers. His marketing strategy, for all its modesty, was apparently on the mark, since the premises were usually sprinkled with born-again book-browsers whose disheveled vehicles awaited attention in the potholed and weedy adjacencies.

"Mr. Sweeney," the big bald man hailed from his stool behind the cash register. "Good to see you."

"Hi, Freddie. Are you alive and well?"

"Medium rare. That old Mercedes of yours suffering a relapse?"

"No, it seems to be in pretty good shape."

"Surprised you're still drivin' it, the way people are down on anything Kraut these days."

"That car is an heirloom, made by Black Forest elves in the Middle Ages and handed down through many generations of Sweeneys. I'm not about to give it up because a few contemporary Germans are acting like horses' asses."

"S'pose not." Freddie paused, taking in Sweeney's fly-and-lure-spangled hat. "Going fishing, then, eh?"

"Nope."

Freddie tried again. "It ain't likely you want something to read."

"Your books are a bit over my head."

"Mine, too. All them thee's and thou's and verily's." Freddie waited again, polite, expectant.

"I'd like you to do me a favor."

"You name it, you got it."

"If I leave the Mercedes as collateral, would you rent me a car for a week or so?"

"A car? What kind of car?"

"Anything you can spare, so long as it runs pretty good."

Freddie's eyes showed puzzlement. "I don't get it. You can rent a car that's a helluva lot better than anything I have without putting up yours as collateral. All you need is a credit card."

"It's a bit more complicated than that. There's something else I need that the agencies can't handle."

"Oh?"

"I need you to put on this fishing hat and this jacket and then go out and get into the Mercedes and drive it to Jamison's Restaurant outside Elkton. Park it in the lot there, then go inside and hang the hat and coat in the men's room. Leave the place by the side door and walk to the cabstand at the corner, hire a hack and come back here."

The puzzlement had become wariness. "You in some kind of trouble?"

"I'm trying to break loose from some people."

"What's that mean?"

"I have a lady friend in Washington whose former boyfriend is very jealous. He's hired a hood to work me over, and the two of them have been following me today, looking for the time and place. I want to lose them."

Freddie nodded slowly. "A hood, you say. That means I better not let them catch up with me, either. Right?"

"That's why I picked Jamison's. It's a dark place, and when you go in the front door out of the sunlight it's hard to see anything for a minute or two. That'll give you the advantage. You can leave the hat and coat and be out the side door before they can even see the maitre d'."

"Meanwhile, you'll be driving back to Washington in my car. And if they come back here to my place to pick up your trail, I play dumb, telling them that all I know is you left in your Mercedes"—he glanced at the wall clock—"sometime before noon. Right?"

"You got it."

"What are those yuks driving?"

Sweeney nodded toward the front window. "See that dark blue Dodge parked by the VW bus out there? The driver's wearing a checkered jacket. The other's in a raincoat."

Freddie's stare turned sly. "Sure this isn't some of that secret intelligence crap you're such a big shot in? I seen you in the tabs, on the talk shows—war hero turned spymaster, all that shinola."

Sweeney feigned elaborate innocence. "Whatever do you mean, Freddie?"

"Ha. I thought so. Girlfriend, my ass. We're talking spies here, ain't we."

"You're even smarter than I thought, Freddie."

The big man looked pleased. "I been around."

"That's why I came for your help."

Freddie, even more pleased, said, "And also because I got an illegal souped-up Pontiac that'll get you to the moon and back in four minutes flat."

Sweeney took out his wallet and drew two bills from it. "Here's a couple of hundred to cover the rental and your cab fare back from Elkton. If you need more, I'll settle later."

"Won't be no rent. The Pontiac's my personal car. The insurance is okay if I lend it to a friend, but not if I rent. Follow me?"

"So I don't rent, I just give you two hundred because you're so gorgeous, eh?"

Freddie laughed softly. "Nobody's more gorgeous than me."

"One other thing: Hang the Mercedes keys on that nail beside the electric meter on your garage. You might not be here when I want to pick them up."

"All right. You want I should leave the car on the Jamison's lot?"

"That's the other reason I chose the place. The restaurant is a twenty-four-hour operation and that mall is major, with cars around it all the time. The Mercedes won't stand out there in the crowd for a day or two."

Freddie slid off the stool and eased his bulk around the counter. He called into the other room, "Hey, Tillie."

His daughter, a reed-thin brunette in her twenties, peered through the archway. "What's up?"

"I got to be gone an hour or so. Watch the store, eh?"

"Sure, Pop."

Freddie headed for the back hallway. "Come on, Mr. Sweeney. The back door's this way."

As they traded car keys in the blue shadows of the rear porch, Freddie said, "I ought to be paying you for this."

"Say again?"

"I been bored outa my eyes. Now here I am, running interference for a secret agent. Are you sure I don't owe an entertainment tax, or something?"

And so now, here he was—behind the wheel of Freddie's illegally souped-up Pontiac sedan, parked in a far corner of the lot at Jamison's Restaurant, watching the watchers watch his Mercedes.

Eventually they tired of the game, presumably deciding that he would not be returning to the car. The Dodge backed around and entered the northbound highway, and he trailed, keeping the Pontiac well buried in the traffic pack. At Route 896 they turned west, slowing to a stop at the new Avis office, and the raincoat went in to ask some questions of the blonde at the counter, who shook her head a lot. Next came the Hertz, the National, and the Budget shops, with essentially the same scenario. With nobody remembering a client named Sweeney, the beautiful couple at last headed back to the bookstore, where

Freddie, too, could be seen shaking his head and hunching his shoulders and managing to look bored.

With nothing left to do, the raincoat man made a call from a Route 40 phone booth, obviously describing his unrewarding day to whoever he worked for. Then they all took I-95 back to Washington, where the boys parked the blue car in front of a tacky D.C. hotel bearing the legend *Radimore Arms* and Sweeney checked into a Holiday Inn near the Beltway.

His first move was to punch up two thousand dollars in twenties and fifties at one of his bank's prime customer auto-teller stations. Next he visited Allenby's Men's Shop in the Capitol Mall and bought underwear and socks, a half-dozen shirts, a pair of dress oxfords and a pair of deck shoes, two ties, some denims, two pairs of slacks and a tweed sports jacket. He wore the jacket and slacks under a new topcoat, and the rest he carried out in two suitcases. After picking up some chicken and fries at a fast-food shop, he returned to the motel, where he sat on the bed and put in a call to Tim Schachtel at the CIA in Reston.

"Sorry to bother you so late in the day, Tim, but I need an assist that can't wait."

Schachtel's tone was not entirely friendly. "So what's up?"

"I want a make on a D.C. registration for a blue 1993 Dodge four-door." He checked his notepad and recited the numbers. "Could you buzz your cop pals for me?"

"Well, the cops are getting a bit spikey about this kind of thing—"

"Come on, Tim. Just because I'm out of a job doesn't make me a close encounter of the rotten kind. You ought to know I have a good reason for asking."

"Hell, Tom, you worked for Richter, and you're both sort of, ah, controversial, and I could get my ass in a crack."

He felt the stirrings of resentment. "I know that. But I also know that you're not the kind of person who'd let a little flak stand between you and someone who remembers a certain night in a Juarez brothel."

Schachtel coughed, an uneasy, unhappy sound. "Hey. No need to go hardball, Tom. I'll get your make for you. Where should I call you?"

"I'll call you."

"Are you in some kind of trouble?"

"Just identify the car for me, will you, please?" Exasperated once again with the shifting treachery of Washington's sands, he hung up.

Weariness settled in, a palpable weight across his shoulders, a stickiness in his eyes. Falling back on the bed, he stared at the twilit ceiling, feeling a sudden and terrible loneliness.

Memory.

(What had De Quincey written? *It is notorious that the memory strengthens as you lay burdens upon it, and becomes trustworthy as you trust it.*)

A memory, long unused and suddenly heavily burdened, had swung out of a darkened corner of his mind to send him running—to paraphrase the poet—from he knew not what to he knew not where.

Nageler.

Nageler had put him to crazy flight.

Nageler, sprawled in grotesque disarray on the smeared tiles, had spoken, as surely and directly as if he had been leaning on a bar and suffering one of his seizures of tedious, curiously dated oratory. Nageler had loved to talk, seeming to fall into glazed-eye pleasure when delivering a hard-guy soliloquy derived from many hours spent with Hammett and Chandler. But with death at hand, when he might have been expected to achieve true grandiloquence, Nageler, poor wretch, had been compelled to leave his last message to—of all things—a toilet seat.

Lying in the gathering darkness, Sweeney probed memory for the sound of Schroeder's voice, for the nuances and beats as Hank might have told it:

"Leonardi and Sweeney and me—we were a team working the Munich dark side in the early eighties. We'd set up shop in an apartment in Schwabing. We took turns being anchor man, meaning the one always on duty in the apartment, either tending the radio or questioning informants or like that, while the other two were out beating the alleys for the stuff needed Topside.

"There was a powder room at the end of the hall. If the john door was left open, you could see the hopper through the glass trim at the foyer door. We had a code. If the john door was closed, all was normal—in the apartment and wherever the outside guys were working that day. If the door was open and hopper lid and seat were down, it meant an interrogation or some other business was in progress inside. If the lid was up, it meant stay out and watch your ass—there was trouble on the informant network. If lid and seat were up, it meant that all hell was breaking loose and team members should dive for any cover they could find.

"So now I been shot all to hell and I'm bleeding all over Sweeney's fancy bathroom, and the only way I can tell the son of a bitch to run is to put the goddamn lid and seat up. Let's hope the dumb bastard doesn't think I crawled umpteen yards up a hill with nine slugs in me just to go toity—"

He slept.

When he awoke, night had darkened the room. He turned on the bedside lamp and, suddenly hungry, stood up and crossed to the writing table, where he had left the food. But the chicken had gone cold and the fries were like lard, so he called room service for a hot pastrami on rye and a bottle of beer. While waiting, he took a shower, then dressed in the denims and deck shoes.

His watch told him that it was after hours, so he put in a call to Schachtel's place in Arlington.

"Hello."

"Did you get my make?"

"Oh. Yeah. The blue Dodge is registered to a Herman Zimmermann, the Radimore Arms on Connell Street."

"What else?"

"What else could there be on a registration?"

"Don't get cute, Tim. I'm not in the sparring mood."

Schachtel cleared his throat. Then: "Zimmermann, who calls himself a traveling salesman, has a laundry list of suspecteds with the D.C. police and the Maryland State Police. Several arrests on suspicion of armed assault, but the pinches have never made it to court."

"How come?"

"Very expensive lawyers."

"Where does a hood who lives in the Radimore Arms get the money for very expensive lawyers?"

"My source says he knows for a fact that Zimmermann is a dirty-tricks pistoleer working under a vengeance contract for some Colombians with long memories."

"I have trouble with that. The cartel boys would be very unlikely to hire an outside shootist. They run a closed shop. They call in their own to do their chores."

"Then why would my very well placed source lay such an unequivocal report on Zimmermann?

"A very good question, Timothy. One I might better answer if I knew your source."

"Now that's something you know I *won't* do for you. There's just no way I'll tell you who my source is."

"Relax. I'm not asking."

"Well, then—"

"Do me another favor, Tim. Don't mention this chat to anyone. You haven't heard from me. Right?"

Schachtel sniffed. "Oh, boy. Now *that's* something you don't have to worry about, believe me. SII types, and you in particular, are in very ill repute around the CIA these days. And you *know* how this town is when it comes to guilt by association."

"Do I ever. That's why nobody will ever know that I've been talking to you, either."

"What? What's that supposed to mean?"

Sweeney hung up.

Chew on that awhile, you simpy bastard.

CHAPTER 5

The sky was brilliant, its blue so intense, so unbroken by lesser hues, it seemed fake, like one of those heavily retouched Coney Island postcards. Below, sparkling and green in the October noon, the Chesapeake Bay wheeled in slow majesty as Cap gentled the biplane into a turn.

She felt the machine around her—the subtle tremblings, the engine's happy burbling, the soft sighing in the brace wires—and it was a kind of intoxication. Even the exhaust, an aromatic wash of hot oil and spent high octane, suggested an incense marking rites in high, holy places.

Staring off through the propeller's glittering arc, she gave a moment to that idea. When she was a child, her mother had dressed her starchily and plopped her into Sunday school as a superstitious offering to whatever force might rule the cosmos. Disappointed with heaven's failure to celebrate the gesture with angelic choirs and lights in the sky, mother had retired to the bottle, leaving daughter to struggle on alone with the question of Just Who is God, and What's on Her Mind, Anyhow? No answers were forthcoming, and eventually, when childish mysticism had melded into adult pragmatism, she'd dismissed religion as man's organized attempt to organize the unorganizable. Yet it hadn't remained that simple. A fleeting perception of the spiritual side of her nature and an impulse to capture it, to give it substance, to freeze-frame it, would often obtrude on her times aloft. So, in its way, aviation had given her an appreciation of what the world's religionists seemed to be groping for.

She was feeling it now.

Exalted, she nudged the stick and toed the rudder, and the Stearman went into an obedient, lazy roll to the left. Another roll, this to the right, and then, the excitement gathering, she began a routine: snap-rolls left and right; two full loops, followed by an Immelmann turn; a hammerhead stall, which she guided into a steep, whining spiral with a chandelle and snap-roll follow-up. Then a climb to nine thousand, where, after throttling back and nosing into a stall, she allowed the ship to fall into a wild, giddy spin—five moaning revolutions in which the sky and bay and the distant Pennsylvania hills became an amalgam of rushing colors and dazzling patterns.

Bringing the Stearman to heel, she headed for the field, her breathing fast and near laughter, her eyes teary behind the goggles. And later, as the ship settled, its wheels kissing the grass, she patted its fabric flank and shouted into the wind, "I love you, you beautiful son of a bitch!"

Sammy came to help her tie down the plane. As she shrugged off the parachute and swung down from the cockpit, he said, "You got a visitor."

"Oh?" She pulled off the helmet and ran a hand through her hair, then turned to peer toward the office. "Who?"

"Didn't give me his name."

"What's he want?"

The little mechanic hunched a shoulder. "I don't know. I just work here."

"Not very hard, you don't."

Sammy sounded a soft little raspberry. "You got the greatest flying machines in the world, thanks to me."

She winked and tapped his chest with her forefinger. "I won't argue that, pal."

"The guy looks familiar. But I don't know why."

"Check the right tire, will you? I think it's soft."

"I don't think I like him."

"And gas her up. I'll have another go this evening, before the sun goes down."

"He looks like a cop. One a them smoothie detectives on the TV shows."

"Not to worry, Sammy. Maybe he wants flying lessons."

She strode off toward the office, squinting in the sun's glare and feeling the need of lunch. She rounded the corner of the toolshed and saw that a dirty green Pontiac sedan had been parked on the gravel pad directly behind her immaculate Mustang, a juxtaposition that inexplicably offended her. The annoyance became surprise when she saw that the man beside the Pontiac was Thomas F. Sweeney.

"Hello, Veronica. How are you holding up in these dark days of forced retirement?"

"Mr. Sweeney," she said, carefully polite. "I'm overwhelmed. You're interested in aerobatics?"

"Like I'm interested in macrame." He looked around, his cool eyes taking in the hangar, the office shack, the sunny meadow. "You actually run a flying school here?"

"Not really. I'm certified as an instructor in performance flying. I teach pilots—people who are already licensed."

"I see." He considered the biplane, thoughtful. "I knew, of course, that flying was your hobby, but I didn't realize you were a regular Red Baron."

"Chartreuse Countess, actually."

He smiled, and there was a pause, an awkward interval in which the breeze whispered, a door banged somewhere, the wind sock fluttered. She had never before seen him in denims—Ivy League suits, silk neckties and glossy brogans had been de rigueur in the SII and its tendril operations—and it was a shock of the kind one would feel when coming across a picture of Abe Lincoln wearing a tanktop. She asked the natural question: "If you're not interested in flying lessons, Mr. Sweeney, may I ask why you're here?"

"To ask for your help. As a former colleague. As one who has blazed a trail into the world of the unemployed."

"What can I do?"

"For starters, let me live with you."

It was his manner that made the difference. She had always been impressed by the ease with which he wore command; when he was in charge, he seemed simply to assume that his people would do precisely what he expected them to do. And they would, usually without complaint; first, because they knew he was working harder than they were and, second, because he was quick and lavish in rewarding excellent performance. Moreover, it was his way to say or do outlandish things to ease difficult situations—she'd seen him lighten up a tense staff meeting with one of those Groucho Marx nose-and-glasses sets, or awake his drowsy audience by breaking into a mad Sid Caesar German accent while explaining some dreary process. So his proposition wasn't altogether out of character; she could hear him suggesting something equally grotesque at, say, a budget meeting. What was different now was the anxiety in his eyes, the soft seriousness in his voice. She had never seen him confused or worried, and she was now willing to bet the Stearman that he was both.

Still, she decided, he would be expecting her to play his game, so she gave him a lingering, frosty stare.

"Are we on 'Candid Camera,' or something?"

He waggled a hand to show he was kidding. "Let me rephrase: I'd like to rent a room in your house."

"Why?"

"I'm in trouble. I need a place to put up. I need a friend. You're a friend, and you have a house hereabouts. I remember you telling us about it at an office Christmas party. How you planned to come back here and aviate if and when you left government."

She was surprised again, and again she tried not to let it show. They had never been friends, in the usual sense. Mutually considerate. Coolly affable. But he'd never shown any inclination to find and press her friendly button. And she hadn't thought for a moment that he would remember her mention of the Maryland house.

"Well, I don't mean to sound inhospitable, Mr. Sweeney, but why me? You were a pretty good boss, as bosses go, but I never had the idea we were old pals, or like that."

He shrugged. "That's part of being a good boss, the way I see it. I always tried to treat all my people the same: friendly, without being the kind of friendly that gets in the way of business."

She nodded. "I'll give you that. You didn't play favorites."

"So, see?" he said, spreading his arms in confirmation. "We're friends."

"You haven't answered my question. A successful man like you—a military hero—a hot-stuff intelligence chief, a confidant of the mighty—is pretty likely to have made a few real pals who'd put you up. So why do you come all the way to the Eastern Shore to rent a room from an out-of-work GS-14 you never treated like a favorite?"

"Because those few I'd be likely to stay with are probably staked out."

"Staked out? Like in police? Are you in trouble with the law?"

"I don't know who I'm in trouble with. Someone I worked with on the dark side a long time ago apparently got himself murdered in my Turkey Point house last Sunday, and the cop I talked to about it turned out not to be a cop—was probably the killer, trying to see if I'd be a threat to him. And I've picked up a tail. A couple of Neanderthals in a blue Dodge who are definitely not policemen."

"Apparently. You said apparently murdered. Didn't you actually see the body?"

"No. Only some Polaroids."

She thought about that. Then: "You think they killed your friend and hid the body and now they're trying to kill you?"

"Yep."

"Why?"

"I suppose they suppose that my friend told me something I shouldn't know."

"What was the guy's name?"

"Hank Nageler."

"That CIA klutz? What was he doing in your house?"

"A good question. Knowing him as I do—did—and listening to my giblets, which are usually a reliable source, he was trying to tell me that something huge is going down. Something representing a humongous threat to the national security."

"He left you a note, then?"

"No. He wrote his initials on the wall, a kind of weird good-bye, but the important thing is that he raised both lid and seat on the bathroom hopper. It was a signal we used in the old days."

"The original latrine telegraph, eh?"

"Something like that."

"A lovely business you're in, Mr. Sweeney."

"Was in. And you ought to know. You were in it with me for several hundred years."

"Strictly as office help. And I never said it was enjoyable."

There was an interval, during which she confronted and weighed the obvious. Squinting at the sky, she said, "If I rent you a room, I'll be putting myself in the line of fire, right?"

"I'll try to see that doesn't happen."

"Sure. And I'll try to fly the Stearman to Mars."

"I mean it. I plan to keep a very low profile. But if they pick up on me, I'll stay away from your place. I'll do everything I can to keep the heat off you."

She gave him a sidelong glance. "So where are the Neanderthals now, Mr. Sweeney?"

"Watching my car in the parking lot of an Elkton mall."

"I don't pretend to understand that. But I tell you straight out: Wherever they are, they scare the hell out of me. And I don't see why I should get involved. After all, you and I don't owe each other anything."

She had given words to Sweeney's own dour assessment. He had made a list of those who would be willing and able to help him, but those who were likely the most willing were also the least likely to be able. Veronica O'Brien represented the converse; she could help him but he wasn't at all sure she liked him enough to take the risk.

And worse, his pitch, rehearsed aloud during the drive from Elkton, was going badly. He had turned into a stammering schoolboy, entirely unprepared to deal with her astonishing good looks.

That she was handsome he'd known from the morning she reported to SII as general administrative assistant, poised, cool, groomed to shining and wearing a month's salary's worth of understated, precisely right, suit, blouse and pumps. Perceiving her attention to detail and her coolness under pressure, Richter had eventually appointed her to the epicentral post of supervisor of documents and interagency communications, and so, when he wasn't in the field, Sweeney saw her almost daily. But it was as if she were a mannequin in a department store—a background presence, so precisely dressed, so unchanging in persona, she never jiggled the needle on whatever meter it is that measures gonad tremors. And now here she was, squinting in the sun glare, tousled, her nose smudged, her coveralls spotted with grease, her suede ankle boots scuffed. It was revelation: she wasn't handsome and neutral, she was gorgeous and vital, and he had been made suddenly clumsy and confused by that truth.

"Well," he said, "I admit that's what almost persuaded me not to come here. I don't have any right to expose you to what could be—problems. But—"

"But you came anyway."

"I've seen you handle problems. More important, though, you're one of the few people who really give a good damn about our country."

Her smile was faint, skeptical. "Come now, Mr. Sweeney. Surely you're not going to use recruiting-poster language with me, are you?"

"No. But I am going to admit that I know your secret. You're a closet patriot."

She sniffed. "What's that supposed to mean?"

"You cover it pretty well, but you're sort of sentimental about the good ole U.S. of A. You're a Molly Pitcher in Guccis."

"Wherever did you get that idea?"

He played his trump. "I eavesdropped that day when the recruiter from Banzai Industries phoned to ask if you had had a chance to consider his offer. First you told him never to call you again—especially while you were on the job—and then you gave him a little speech about your job and what it meant to you."

Her cheeks reddened and her remarkable eyes glittered. "How did you know that guy had made me an offer?"

"It was my job to know what was going on around me. I was a government-issue, card-carrying know-it-all."

"Horsefeathers. You're just a plain old sneak, aren't you, Mr. Sweeney."

"There's nobody sneakier, I guess."

He had meant the words to be airy, disarming. Instead they had sounded like a sigh, an involuntary vocalization of a sublimated self-contempt. What was this woman doing to him? He'd never been this off-balance. Had her face, so reminiscent of some of his best years, triggered a recurrence of the ambivalent pain-pleasure of his firing? Or was it rotten coincidence, a moment of bizarre reunion occurring at that specific moment in the maturing process when youth's cocksureness ends and middle-age's diffidence begins? Yesterday—hell, just an hour ago—he'd had a strong appreciation of exactly who he was and why; now, standing here in the sunlight and wind with this beautiful, familiar stranger, there was a sense of lostness, confusion. Of time running out.

Whatever it was, it must have been obvious enough to trigger some kind of change in her, too. He thought he saw a softening in her eyes—a fleeting alteration of the dark colors there that suggested an ebbing of her catlike wariness. The impression was confirmed when she nodded toward the cars and said, "If you'll get that green clunk out of the way I'll drive us to The Orchards for lunch."

"The Orchards?"

"That's what I call my little house. It sounds sort of snooty and upscale, don't you think?"

"Is it in an orchard?"

"Heck, no. But it does stand on a nice little point, with a gorgeous view of the bay and the Elk River."

"Is it private? Pretty well hidden?"

She shrugged. "My father, a career waterman, was an expert at hiding from the world. He built the house after World War Two because privacy was exactly what he wanted. He willed it to me."

"How about your mom?"

"She died when I was six. I don't remember much about her and Pop never talked about her. Hurt him too much, I guess."

"How do you know that?"

"I used to see him brooding over her picture. Poor dear. He always seemed so—lost, sort of."

"My kind of fella."

She gave him one of her cool looks. "You were never lost in your life, is my guess."

"Well, don't bet The Orchards on that."

They had lunch on a brick patio shaded by ancient oaks.

The house was low-slung, built of weathered brick, with a cedar-shingle roof, three gables, two squat chimneys and casement windows.

"You say your pappy built this?"

"Practically singlehanded."

"He had taste."

"Yep. He was a very talented gent in lots of ways."

"You liked him, eh?"

"You better believe it."

"And I bet he liked your chowder, too."

"Sure. He taught me to cook." She glanced at his cup. "More coffee?"

"No, thanks."

They watched a blue heron circle for a landing on the far end of the dock. She broke the silence with a question. "Can you tell me what all this is really about?"

"I'd tell you if I knew myself. A long time ago, Nageler, the man who was killed, was one of a three-man espionage team. I was another member, and Richard Leonardi was the third. I'll spare you the details. But the bottom line, I think, is that Nageler was trying to tell me that Rick is in danger."

She gave him a quick, surprised look. "You mean *our* Leonardi? Richard D.? The president?"

"It was years ago. Before Rick got into politics."

"My God. When you get in trouble it's in wide-screen Technicolor."

"Ain't it the truth."

"So what are you going to do?"

"The only route open to me is a reconstruction. I've got to figure out what Nageler was working on, and then I might understand what danger Leonardi is in."

She shook her head slowly. "That's going to take some doing. You're out of government. You have no resources, no files, no access."

"Tell me about it."

"I'm serious, darn it—"

"So am I. I think the one thing going for me is that Nageler was out of government, too. That means he was working for private or foreign interests. There's bound to be some cracks in whatever wall was around him. Nothing is ever hermetically sealed—even the tightest, most carefully planned government security. So I have to find and peek through the cracks left by Nageler and his employers."

There was another pause. The heron, bored, took off in a lazy flapping of wings.

"So what can I do to help, Mr. Sweeney?"

"The first thing you can do is stop calling me Mr. Sweeney. It makes me feel like a high school principal. My name is Tom, to you."

"You don't look like a Tom."

"So call me Sweeney. Everybody else does."

"Call me Cap."

"Cap?"

"Pop had a hell-for-leather pal named Cap who served with him in the Big Red One in the push across France in forty-four. Pop began to call me Cap when I proved to have a strong streak of tomboy in me. It's one of those dumb family things."

"Who calls you Veronica?"

"You."

"Nobody else?"

"The Reverend Norton. My Aunt Hazel. That's it."

"How come I never heard Cap around the office?"

"Because you insisted on the female staff being addressed as Miss or Missus. Remember?"

"Oh, yeah."

"You could be awfully stuffy sometimes."

"It's my main thing."

She smiled faintly. "So I call you Sweeney. So what else can I do?"

"Call Lou Simon, my lawyer in Washington. Tell him to use his power of attorney or whatever to set up a bank account in the name of, say, John Meyers and send me the things I have to sign. He has a list of my assets and he can use those as collateral for the money he'll lend me and put in the Meyer account. And I want you to keep a running, itemized tally of what I owe you, too. Payment from the Meyers account at the end of each month." He paused. "You need to take notes, or something?"

"I have a tape going in the kitchen. The mike's in the flower arrangement in front of you there."

He gave her a startled, narrow look. "Say again?"

"It's *my* main thing. I tape visitors whose conversation I want to remember."

"That's illegal as hell."

"So sue me."

It was his turn to smile. "You learned some bad habits, hanging around the SII."

"Yep."

He leaned forward and told the daisies: "Have the post office change my home address to a D.C. box number and have Lou's secretary pick up my mail daily. Then try to get me a copy of the marine police report on the history of the boat Nageler rented and ask the Cecil County Police for a list of the things found in the boat's wreckage. Use the freedom-of-information law if you have to."

She put in, "I'll call the chief. I taught his son to fly, and he used to hunt and fish with Pop."

"Whatever."

"Anything else?"

He hesitated, considering her thoughtfully. "I'd like to sneak copies of the Joint Chiefs' daily briefing sheet. And also the DEA drug war communiqués. And Wilson Boles at CIA: he writes a hell of a good daily wrap for the various intelligence directors. But now that I'm ex officio and on the lam, all that might take some doing. I want you to think about ways we might get our hands on those items. You got a fax here?"

She shook her head. "Only an IBM computer primed for word processing. The world's slowest daisy wheel printer. That's it."

"All right. See what you can do to improve that picture, too." He stood up and pushed his chair neatly under the table. "Meanwhile, I'm going to the motel to pick up my things." He spoke into the flowers again. "Thanks for the great lunch, Cap."

"Know something?"

"Vot's dot?"

"I didn't even vote for Leonardi."

"Neither did I. It's hard to take a president seriously when you've rassled him to his room and thrown him on his cot, drunker than hell."

CHAPTER 6

Sweeney drove to Elkton and parked among the junkers at the edge of a car parts lot, which was on a rise that offered a panoramic view of the Jamison's Restaurant mall. The Mercedes, dusty and forlorn, was flanked by a Winnebago with Missouri plates and a Taurus station wagon filled with pillow-fighting moppets and a happily barking Labrador. A car-by-car survey eventually confirmed the absence of the blue Dodge crew or anybody remotely suggesting the hardcase hit man. Either Herman Zimmermann and his flat-faced pal had given up the watch or they'd been replaced by a crew disguised as housewives, raggedy-ass teenagers, and retirees in bubba hats.

He would have to move the Mercedes soon, but just how and where was something he had yet to work out.

Twilight was coming early these days, and the shadows were long when he swung off Route 213 onto the pockmarked, weedy blacktop with which the Happy Hour Motel welcomed its nightly gaggle of failing salesmen and low-budget trysters.

He had taken the room that morning, using the name Flugel and leaving his luggage in the closet. Before retrieving his bags and paying up, he ducked into the front office to see what newspapers might be in the coin racks there. The local paper was sold out, so he bought a copy of the neighboring *Wilming-*

ton News Journal, which would probably carry anything gaudy that might develop in these Cecil County parts.

As he turned for the door, folding the paper under his arm, he made eye contact with the clerk, a wan Juan with a shiny pompadour and cheeks as pocked as the parking apron outside. Their gazes locked briefly, then the man blinked and began a serious study of the countertop, as if Secrets of the Ages were being revealed on its flyspecked vinyl.

A bad sign.

Motel clerks regularly witness all levels of human depravity, expecting the worst of everybody, unruffled and smug when bleak expectation becomes grim reality. It is, in sum, difficult to shock a professional hotelier, so Sweeney saw it as a discord when this clerk could be flustered by a guest whose only notable transgression had been to leave his luggage in a closet all day.

He went to the Pontiac, lifted the trunk lid, and unclamped the jack handle, which he placed under his arm with the newspaper. Then he climbed in, started the motor, set the brake, and left the car idling as he made for his room.

Sliding the key into the door lock, he made a deliberate fuss, as if having trouble with the mechanism.

Through the thin paneling he heard the soft sounds of quick footsteps.

Dropping the newspaper, he held the blade end of the jack handle with the fingertips of his right hand. With his left hand he turned the knob and lunged, throwing the weight of his body against the door as it swung inward and to the right.

A sharp intake of breath and a yelp sounded as the man behind the door took the full impact. In the same instant, Sweeney dropped to the carpet, and the nasty snick of a silenced pistol shot tore the air above.

A tall man in a Madison Avenue topcoat came out of the dark bathroom in a half crouch, swinging an automatic whose tube silencer looked only slightly larger than a mainline sewer pipe.

As the man lined up for his second shot, Sweeney, on his knees now, threw the jack handle with all the force he could manufacture. The steel bar went through two lazy tumbles and then made its entry, blade-end on, slightly to the right of the nose. The man, his topcoat a gray blur, reeled backwards into the bathroom, where he disappeared in the crashing collapse of the plastic shower curtain.

Rolling to his back, Sweeney raised a foot and launched it into the crotch of the other man, who was staggering from behind the door. But the kick was faulty, and the man was suddenly all over him with karate moves.

One of the blows connected solidly. Sweeney's ears rang, and he saw dazzling lights, and there was the taste of blood in his mouth. Another strike, and the room's murkiness deepened, and the sounds of cursing and raling diminished, falling away as sounds do in a fever. But then there came a moment of clarity, and he saw that the man was the redhead with shooter's glasses, the erstwhile Sergeant Ames, reeling above him, pointing an enormous revolver at his left eye.

Sweeney watched, dimly curious, as a large fist came out of nowhere to slam Ames below his right ear. The sound of the blow seemed faraway, soft, almost irrelevant. The revolver spun across the carpet, bouncing, and Ames went into a kind of pirouette that ended when he staggered out the door into the evening.

Hands hauled him erect.

"Are you all right, Mr. Sweeney?" Soft, urgent.

"Freddie?"

"We better hurry. My car's behind the motel. We got to go out the bathroom window. A crowd's gatherin' out front, and the cops'll be here in a minute."

"What the hell are you doing here?" Sweeney worked his jaw back and forth, testing.

"Come on—out the goddam window."

"The clerk—I have to tell the sumbish—"

"I already talked to him."

"He'll tell the cops about me."

"Relax. I got him believin' you look just like Calvin Coolidge."

Freddie Dilworth shoved Sweeney into the passenger seat of a maroon Ford and they were on the highway and headed south just as sirens sounded in the distant north. Nothing was said until they had cleared the high-rise bridge at Chesapeake City.

Then Freddie glanced away from his driving to give Sweeney an amiable scrutiny.

"That's a pretty cute trick you have with jack handles, buddy. Where did you learn that?"

"I've got a better question. Where did you learn to set up such a good tail?"

Freddie laughed, delighted. "You never spotted me, did you. I'm pretty good, wouldn't you say?"

"You're the greatest."

"I got a book on police procedures awhile back. I been practicin'."

"I'll say. If I had a medal I'd pin it on you."

"You want to go back to Cap's house?"

"You know Cap?"

"Sure do. Her pappy and I fished together a lot."

"Well, get me back there as fast as you can. She and I have a large problem we need to work out."

"So do you and me. Our old friends in the dark blue Dodge are tailin' us."

Sweeney stared out the rear window. "Damn."

"Never fear, Freddie's here. Ha-ha."

"How come they didn't join the fun in the motel room?"

"They were just pullin' into the motel parking lot when you and me were bustin' out. They got tied up by all the people millin' around. Now they're catchin' up."

"You got plans to ditch them?"

" 'Less you want we should stop and tangle with 'em."

"Come on, Freddie, get real. I can hardly stand up as it is."

"So then, watch this."

Freddie slammed on the brakes and the Ford, careening, tires screaming, slowed to a smoking halt. The Dodge, already too close, swerved wildly into the northbound lane of the two-lane highway as its driver sought to avoid a rear-end collision.

But Freddie had timed his move to coincide with the arrival of a thundering, smoke-belching northbound ten-wheeled tractor-trailer combination, and the Dodge's driver, with nowhere else to go, continued his leftward lurch, and the blue sedan disappeared in a cloud of splinters, leaves and spray as it plowed through a honeysuckle hedge and into an adjacent duck pond.

"Cool, Freddie. Did you get that out of a book, too?"

"Nope. Made that one up myself. Neat-o, eh?"

30° 08′ N

80° 02′ W

The setting sun was at their backs, and the sea was a glassy green directly below, blending farther on into a deep aquamarine, and eventually into royal blue where it met the eastern sky. The airplane, glinting dully in the day's last light, was in full sight now, skittering northward across the vastness, tiny and remote, like a purposeful gnat traversing a pond.

"There he is, Skipper. Ten o'clock, very low. You got him?" Coleman's intercom voice was deliberate and drawling, a not entirely successful attempt, Romelo thought, to hide uneasiness and—What? Guilt?

"Yep. What's your screen say?"

"Single-engine Avio. Altitude four hundred thirteen feet, speed one-two-six, heading two hundred seventy three degrees."

"Registration?"

"The scanner's locked on, magnifying and computing." Coleman integrated with the master computer at Homestead. The wait, a full thirty seconds, was filled with the thunder and clacking outside and the soft, almost intimate hiss of the intercom circuit. The big chopper tilted gently as Captain Romelo brought the compass around to a 273 heading.

"Ah. Here we are. The computer says it's a Model Ten, built at Avio's Caracas plant and certified in 1980."

"Still another antique, eh?"

"Sure enough."

"What kind of a dummy would try a hop to the States in something that ancient?"

"A dummy who hopes to be a rich dummy."

"You couldn't pay me enough to climb into that sumbish, let alone expect me to fly it to Georgia, or wherever."

"I'm not being paid enough to climb into this frigging hee-lee-o-copter, either. So what am I doing here?"

"You are an intrepid American flying ace, Lieutenant Coleman. You are a Weekend Warrior, one of the brave many called to serve in our beloved nation's war against the drug barbarians. Paid? You really ought to be paying for the privilege."

"All due respect, Captain, but may I suggest that you go pee up a fugg'n drainpipe, sir?"

"Suggestion received, considered and rejected." Romelo punched up his Pilot's Area Survey Display and the escorting jets appeared as a luminescent wedge at the upper right. They were at fifteen thousand, and descending, preparing to serve their function as witnesses.

Coleman, hunched over his Weapons and Information Control Console forward of Romelo's command seat, raised a gloved hand and waggled the forefinger. "Achtung, Herr Chopperdriver. Homestead is serving us up some history on yonder flying machine."

"Let me have it."

"The screen says the Avio was registered to Angelo Survey Company in the year of certification. Later sold to Signa Aero in Mexico City, with Mexican registration. There's a list of subsequent owners, most of them Mexico-based small-time commercial, and then the registration was retired when the plane was lost and presumed destroyed in a storm on a flight to Guatemala two years ago."

"Who owned it when it was lost?"

"Pancho Mining Company, Santa Maria."

"So now we have a resurrection, eh?"

"Looks as if."

"Well, let's start making like soldiers. I'm activating ship's combat recorders, so keep your language clean."

"Before you punch on the tapes: You want rocketry and full electronics, or do you prefer to do the Red Baron thing?"

"No missiles. The chain gun should suffice. But let's do it by the book. You need practice. Lots of practice."

Coleman blew a raspberry into his mike.

"Recorders running."

"Weapons Control to pilot: Arming now."

"Roger. Descending to five-zero-zero. Accelerating to one-four-five miles per hour, IAS. What's the Avio's frequency?"

"Computer reads eleven-thirty-five, B Channel."

"Activate major-languages warning tape, leading off with English and Spanish, both to be repeated at end."

"On automatic, and tracking."

"Notify Homestead Situation Room."

"Notification sent."

Captain Romelo switched to the escort frequency. "Top Hat One, this is Little Boy. Over."

"Roger, Little Boy," the Air Force flight leader crooned. "Top Hat One here."

"Top Hat One, Little Boy. We are closing for visual examination of suspect aircraft. We will attempt to signal pilot to follow us. Failing that, we will destroy, per Standing Order Thirty-two-slash-Baker."

"Roger, Little Boy. We are circling at eleven thousand and have you on our boards. Camcorders running. Advise if you need assistance."

"Roger, out."

Romelo made a course adjustment, and the Avio, close ahead now, shone golden against the lavender sky. The sea rushed below, a dark, forbidding smear.

"I've heard no answer to the challenge, Weapons Control. What's your screen say?"

Coleman was all business now. "Negative, sir. The suspect aircraft remains silent."

"He's not maneuvering, either."

"No, sir. He's steady as a rock."

"Activate starboard camcorder. I'm pulling alongside."

"Roger, sir. Camcorder running."

Conversation ceased and the intercom resumed its whispering as Romelo jockeyed the helicopter into position. Twilight had settled in, and the Avio's bright red trim had turned black in the diminishing glow. There was something melancholy about the plane, drumming along, solitary and dark against the coming night. Romelo raised his visor and peered hard at the pilot, a dim figure behind the Avio's wheel.

Romelo waved, pointed a finger at the airplane, then traced an arc to the west. He repeated the gesture three times, without apparent effect. "Come on, pal. Show me a reaction. Any reaction."

"Weapons Control to pilot: the pilot is ignoring us, sir."

"Can you see him?"

"Not clearly, sir. But I can see he's paying no attention to us."

"All right. I'm falling back to trail at five hundred yards. Top Hat One, Little Boy. Suspect aircraft refuses to acknowledge. We are positioning for chain gun attack."

"Little Boy, Top Hat One, we are recording. Over, out."

"Begin countdown, Coleman."

"Roger. Thirty seconds, and counting."

"The target is yours, Coleman."

"He's in the reticle and chain gun is charged."

An interval. Then: "Countdown complete, sir."

"Fire at will."

There was a kind of hellish burp and a surrealistic halo flickered around the canopy as a full loading of 320 thirty-millimeter rounds roared out from the helicopter's chin.

The Avio disintegrated. The left wing folded back, then tore free. The tail assembly collapsed. The fuselage buckled amidships, like a man bending with stomach cramps, and a wheel fell away. Then, as the jumble began a mad cartwheeling, a sheet of flame—incredibly bright and punctuated by internal explosions—enveloped the whole and traced an incandescent arc down the sky and into the darkening sea. A tower of spray lingered briefly, and the business was done.

"Target destroyed, sir."

Coleman's voice, Captain Romelo noted, held no trace of its earlier smart-aleck sound.

As for himself, there was the usual nausea.

CHAPTER 7

It was after six when Brig. Gen. Harvey M. Wallace arrived in St. Augustine and nearly seven o'clock by the time his driver pulled the staff car into its niche behind the Government House on the King Street plaza. To escape the tourist traffic on I-95 they had taken Route 1—a mistake, thanks to the lava of tin and plastic that erupted from the tin and plastic industrial parks in Jacksonville's Southside and oozed, turgid and stinking, all thirty miles to the Ancient City Beltway, completed last year as the solution to the very problem it now compounded. Bad had become worse as they entered town; the Bridge of Lions was undergoing one of its "rush-hour renovations," with work gangs holding its draw spans out of alignment by an infuriating eleven inches. Government House was on the mainland, so he had no need to cross the bridge, which made it all the more exasperating to be immobilized, a mere five blocks from his office, among the suppertime thousands bound for Anastasia Island.

It would have pleased him to get out and walk, but he had brought three briefcases filled with classified papers, which he could neither leave in the car nor comfortably carry, so he resigned himself to what would probably be another ten minutes of exhaust fumes and honking horns. He used the time to consider questions that would surely be asked in the interview.

Randolph Ridenour was not one of his favorite TV news types; he seemed a pompous nerd who was so crazy about himself he could barely stand it. But the man was a UBS network biggie with a hell of a following and, according to Barney Coombs, public affairs director of the ANCF, it was a very muscular status thing to be the subject of one of Ridenour's "Sundown Symposium" inquisitions. Even Millie, who hated personal publicity and had declined Ridenour's invitation to appear briefly as "Mrs. Drug-War Commandant," thought it was a great opportunity to emphasize the importance of a strong Armed Forces Reserve Corps—and it might inch him toward another star.

Even so, Wallace had misgivings. Ridenour had something of the charlatan about him.

At Government House a small crowd was waiting in the anteroom: Ellie Dumas, his secretary; Fred McIntyre, Florida's adjutant general, and Pete Loomis, his senior Army advisor; Bud Dix, the Coast Guard's Southeast Area DC; George Cannon, UIF air operations chief; Bill Dirk, Army Special Forces liaison; and Alice Richards, UIF staff PIO. A man in blue jeans was waving a light meter, while another made sightings with a shoulder-held camera and muttered unintelligibly to a scruffy woman who scowled and made notes on a clipboard.

"Sorry I'm late, everybody," Wallace said. "Rotten traffic tie-up in the village." After giving the briefcases to Ellie for placement in the office safe, he glanced at Richards. "Where's Mr. Ridenour?"

"Waiting in your office, General. He said he wanted to be alone awhile."

Wallace pushed through the connecting door and was instantly but silently furious. The room was clogged with electronic read-panels, and the network biggie was slouched in the high-back leather chair, feet propped on the glistening mahogany desk whose lack of clutter was the Wallace trademark.

"Hi. You're General Wallace, I take it."

"And you're Randolph Ridenour, I take it."

The man laughed softly. "A wag, eh?"

"I don't follow you—"

"My face is pretty well known."

Wallace refused to give him an inch. "All that makeup makes

people look different off camera. Do you mind if I get at my desk? There are some things I want to check out."

"We're ready to begin taping." Ridenour, his annoyance showing, unfolded himself and rose from the chair. "You've already put us behind schedule."

"My apologies. I'll be just one moment."

Ridenour called through the door, "Everybody in here."

Wallace made a slow business of going through his desk drawers. Actually he was looking for the notes he'd made for this session, but he was just angry enough to be in no hurry about it. The other officers filed in and stood about, looking uncomfortable, while the little woman with the clipboard went into another mysterious conference with Ridenour, the blue-jeans beauty, and the cameraman.

"All right," the woman said finally, "you military guys take those chairs there along the wall. You, the tall one, in the middle. And you with the bald head, don't sit too close to that lamp. Your head lights up." To Alice Richards and Ellie Dumas, she said, "We don't need you two, so you can tootle on."

Wallace, feeling heat in his cheeks, said, "I want them to stay. I want them to record what's said here."

The woman looked at Ridenour, and Ridenour looked at the general. Everybody was becoming truly peevish.

"No need for that, General," Ridenour said sourly.

"The media have paraphrased me inaccurately and edited me out of context too many times. I've learned to keep a record of what I really say."

"I'm not the media," Ridenour snapped in his Englishy way. "I am an essayist, a presenter of think-pieces."

"Ellie, get the recorder."

The transformation was remarkable. When the camera's little red light blinked on, Ridenour, the snappish prima donna, became within a millisecond the suave, silver-haired, avuncular president of the universe. Seated in an easy chair beside the bookshelves, legs crossed casually and hands clasped around a knee, he peered into the camera, eyes level and sincere, and drawled in cathedral tones, "I'm Randolph Ridenour." (Dramatic pause.) "We are in the office of one of the most powerful chieftains in the nation's tragic, seemingly endless war against the narcotics pestilence. We are about to meet this man and his staff. We are about to take a Ridenour Ride with him through the labyrinthine organization that has been established to bring the drug interests to their knees. But first, a word from those gifted people at—"

He paused, the camera light went out, and the clipboard woman said, "We'll redo that. This week's sponsor is Hygiene, Incorporated, and 'gifted' doesn't seem to fit with people who make condoms and douche solutions."

Ridenour made a sour expression and cracked, "Anybody who can get a three-billion-dollar return out of somebody else's screwing is as gifted as hell in my book."

General Wallace, vastly irritated now, broke in. "I suggest that you not talk that way in the presence of these ladies."

Ridenour, no less testy, sniffed. "This is the real world, General. We aren't at the VMI Christmas cotillion."

"This is my office, Mr. Ridenour, and while we're in it, I decide the nature of the real world. Now if you truly want to interview me and my people, you will cooperate. If not, then I urge you to return to your own real world."

Alice Richards, face pale, her public relations blood curdling, tried to save the situation. "Please, gentlemen, we're all trying to realize some benefit from this. Let's take a few minutes to compose ourselves."

"Bug off, sister," the clipboard woman barked. "I'll decide who composes what in this little do."

General Wallace stood up, his face incandescent. "I think we've all had enough of this. Please clear my office at once."

There was an electric moment in which the television people traded glances. Then, waving a hand, the clipboard woman said, "All right. We've all got too much invested to let ourselves get pissed off like this. Let's get back in our places, and we'll take it from the top."

The five officers turned their eyes toward Wallace. After a protracted interval given to the cooling off within him, he motioned them to their chairs with a nod.

Ridenour repeated his opening, and this time "gifted" became "ingenious." Then, reading from the scroll-panel trundled about and operated by Blue-Jeans, he went on:

"So where do we Americans stand in the drug war today? What are we doing—and what remains to be done—to halt the cataclysmic social degeneration caused by the narcotics blight? The questions can't be effectively answered without first considering the historical, political and economic mosaic into which the drug problem fits.

"The Soviet Union is wracked by the Cold War's bitter legacy—civil war and hunger riots. The United States teeters on the rim of insolvency due to an onerous deficit, massive defense cutbacks, and decades of decline in competitive capability. Germany struggles with its unification burden and a resurgent Nazism. Japan dominates legitimate world trade and calls the political tune in the Pacific and Eurasian spheres. China is the sole remaining subscriber to the Marx-Lenin political philosophy, while Cuba wallows in the chaotic limbo left by the former Castro regime. Third World nations continue their spiral into catastrophe, and the Central and South American countries subsist on a bare break-even basis, except for Colombia and Peru, which remain pivotal to what has become the six hundred-billion-dollar-a-year narcotics manufacturing and distribution business.

"The Department of Defense, after huge reductions in mainline Army, Navy and Air Force expenditures, has concentrated on 'small war' capabilities, and the resultant streamlined Special Forces—particularly naval and airborne—are being used on a broad scale in the interdiction of the drug traffic between the South American production centers and their mainland U.S. distribution nets. It is, in fact, very close to formal warfare, now that treaties permit U.S. naval forces to blockade coastlines and U.S. combat aircraft to overfly drug production centers between the Rio Grande and the Andes."

God, Wallace thought, shifting in his chair, *won't the pompous ass ever get to the interview?*

"For all their complexity and expense," Ridenour drawled on, "considerable progress is being made in the military and diplomatic offensives against the drug barons and their armies. President Leonardi, especially in his recent State of the Union message, has made much of the decline in domestic drug availability and the concurrent growth of federal treatment centers for the nation's eleven million addicts, who will inevitably be forced into abstinence by the crunch between the scarcity itself and the runaway inflation it brings to street prices."

The blowsy woman held up a hand. "Cut there. Hold. Now in this next passage, Randy, give me some emphasis around the quotes. Don't just read, let us hear the quote marks."

"Damn it, Petey, I've been doing this shit for years. I know how to make a quote."

"You've been dropping them lately, goddammit, and I want you to stop it. Now pick up at 'The president.' "

The red light went on. Ridenour's scowl changed to an affable knowingness, and he picked up:

"The president is also enthusiastic about the recent announcement of a consortium of anonymous Japanese businesses—alarmed by the faltering U.S. markets—that it will provide America, in a kind of reverse Marshall Plan, a special emergency fund of ten billion dollars a year to educate its unskilled and rehabilitate its skilled who have been impaired by narcotics. A like announcement, promising another two billion dollars annually, has been made by an association of U.S. defense-related businesses. Leonardi praises the groups' beneficence as what he called 'the epitome of international private sector cooperation in meeting a primary international need,' adding that, 'Between the advances made in the drug war and this major nourishment of our ailing education system, America is very much back on the road to national health and vigor.'

"Congressional reaction, of course, reflects the public's skepticism. The consensus is that it will take a lot more than a modest Band-Aid from a gaggle of self-serving tycoons to stop the drug-induced hemorrhage in the labor force and, deficit be damned, the federal government must do the job right, whatever the cost. The Administration, predictably, argues that such a solution is actually no solution at all, since it most certainly would serve as the coup de grace for a job-creating investment community already suffocating under a lethal tax load."

Ridenour paused again, recrossed his legs, and folded his hands once more. His eyes became even more earnest, confidential. Sharing.

"At the strategic level, the drug war is being fought under the direction of the Allied Narcotics Control Force, formed following the 1993 Treaty of Acapulco and now headquartered in Panama City. At the tactical level, operations are conducted by special small forces assembled by the treaty's signatory nations and placed under the direction of a combat command called the Unified Interdiction Force." (Pause, a rearranging of the legs and hands.)

"With me today is the commander of the UIF, Brigadier General Harvey Wallace, until his appointment earlier this year, a Florida industrialist and an officer of the U.S. Army Reserve. His headquarters are in a beautiful building erected by Spanish colonizers in St. Augustine—the oldest city in the United States. This puts him only a few blocks from the ancient arsenal where the Florida National Guard, itself a key element in the UIF tactical forces, has been traditionally headquartered. The effort involves all branches of military service, of course, but their coordination at the Florida tactical level is the business of my guest, General Wallace"—the camera began to pan along the line of chairs—"assisted by these officers, whom we'll introduce later." Turning, he crooned, "General Wallace, just how did your responsibilities evolve? I mean, how is it that you, a part-time soldier and crony of Governor Gomez, were named to head such a critical military operation, when so many highly skilled, professional career military officers are sitting on the sidelines these days?"

The camera was on him, and Wallace, as always, felt the flutter of panic. Was his hair combed? Was his tie straight? Was, for God's loving sake, his fly closed? Then, as was his way under pressure, he picked a point to stare at while reminding himself just who he was—a mature adult, very skilled in his profession, who really didn't have to apologize for breathing. In this moment he picked Randolph Ridenour's silvery widow's peak.

"Well," he said evenly, "first I want to make it clear that I'm not a part-time soldier. I am a soldier a hundred hours every day. But to answer your question, I suppose I was named to the job essentially for the same reason your bosses picked you to do your job. They decided that you knew your stuff and could handle the responsibility."

Ridenour had been caught off guard by the answer, but he recovered quickly. "Ah, yes," he said condescendingly. "But I was recently doing one of my programs on location outside

Cartagena, and I interviewed Manuelo Corbato, one of the mightiest of the drug lords. He was openly contemptuous of your appointment as chief of UIF. He himself pointed out that there are many high-ranking Academy-trained Regulars who, ah, can see and deal with the panorama, while you, a mere one-star general sponsored by a politician, are without experience at truly high-level management, the kind of management so sorely needed in a military operation of this scope. So, again, why you?"

What's with this guy, anyhow? the general wondered. *He's come all the way to Florida to do a number on me, sure as hell. Well, whatever his reason, I'd better flip his switch right now.* "I also disagree with your assertion that I have no high-level management experience. If you had read my personal history sheet, you'd have seen that I was chairman and CEO of Harrison and Caldwell, with thirty-two plants and offices in two dozen cities. I retired from that post when I was asked to become UIF commandant. I was asked, as that same personal history sheet would have shown you, because of my extensive military schooling and practical experience as a noncom and officer at leading combat troops in Korea, Europe, Panama and Saudi Arabia. Moreover, the governor did not choose me for the post of Tactical Commander, Unified Interdiction Force. General Reynolds, head of the Joint Chiefs administrative staff at the Pentagon, chose me."

"Well, General," Ridenour put in, mildly triumphant, "General Reynolds himself tells me that he would have preferred a more experienced officer but that Governor Gomez persuaded the president, as commander in chief, to recommend you for appointment, a recommendation General Reynolds was understandably loath to ignore. And it is widely known that since your appointment you have been openly dependent on the daily suggestions made to you by Vice President McKell."

Wallace felt the blush of anger rising again. " 'Daily' is outrageous hyperbole, Mr. Ridenour. The vice president calls me on occasion, but he hardly has time or the desire to confer with me daily. Moreover, I resent the assertion that I am dependent on a political leader for assistance in making my military decisions. That, of course, is grossly untrue." His words accelerating, he added, "And I continue with my earlier comparison: No doubt the executives of your network enjoy their high rank because of their great experience, their ability to decide and act on what they see in the television industry's panorama. I'd guess that none of them would want to work below their capabilities by, say, doing what you do—merely bouncing around here and there, asking presumptuous, off-the-wall questions of strangers. You're good at what you do, I'm good at what I do. That's why our bosses, infinitely more broad-scale than we are, have us doing what we're doing."

Ridenour was having difficulty disguising his fury. "So what is it you're doing, General?" he grated.

"The organization of the nation's antidrug effort has gone through many evolutions since the late 1980s." The general's mouth felt tacky. "The Drug Enforcement Agency was in charge at first, of course, and soon began to receive assistance from certain military support mechanisms when the scope of narcotics smuggling grew exponentially. The Coast Guard, the Air Force, some naval units, National Guard engineers and port surveillance teams—these kinds of units became quite active and were directed by the DEA out of Washington. Following the Gulf War the problem grew so large there was a basic reorganization of the regular military establishment, a redesign that took key elements of the Army, Navy, Air Force, Marines and Coast Guard and put them under a single command, the Unified Interdiction Force, based here in Florida. Then, when almost all of the Western Hemisphere nations signed the Treaty of Acapulco—permitting overflights and offshore blockades of the signatory nations by the ANCF—the United States, in effect, made Florida virtually an armed camp with me in charge. What I do, Mr. Ridenour, is decide where and when the hundred thousand men and women of the UIF strike out against the drug cartels and their operations in those portions of the Western Hemisphere that lie within the rectangle Miami–Los Angeles–Lima–Rio. It's a very responsible job, and I give it my very best shot—daily, hourly, always."

"Mm. Yes. But back to Governor Gomez for a moment. Is it true that your appointment really derives from your support of his election campaign and from his close political ties with certain South American governments?"

"Not only is your suggestion poppycock, but I fail to see its relevance to what is a military matter."

Ridenour's redness was sudden and spectacular. "This is my program, General. I'm Randolph Ridenour, and I decide what is relevant. You are a supporter of Governor Gomez. He, it is asserted, persuaded the Leonardi Administration to name you—most reluctantly and over the heads of many better-qualified officers—as head of UIF. And I have decided that this is most relevant. You—"

General Wallace stood up, smoothed his tunic, and squared his shoulders. "Correction, Mr. Ridenour. You decide nothing when it comes to me. You are in charge of your program, of course. But I am in charge of me. And I'm now withdrawing me from further participation in your program."

"Wait a minute, pal! You can't kiss me off—"

"Oh, can't I, now. Please get out. At once."

"You need me, you asshole. You need me bad—"

"I need you to get out of here before I call the guards and have you thrown out."

The clipboard woman jumped up and down. "Cut! Cut! Cut, goddammit! What the hell's everybody so sore about?"

General Wallace nailed her with his battlefront glare, born to a corporal in the Pusan Perimeter. "I am sore, young woman, because I was led to believe that this interview was about drugs and what we're doing to halt their flow into this country. But I can see that Mr. Ridenour is really trying to use me as leverage for some political thing he must be planning. I will not be party to any media harrassment of Governor Gomez, a fine gentleman, an astute political leader, and a personal friend of mine. If you want to do a program on the governor, see the governor—don't sneak around me."

"Governor Gomez is a Latino squid and you are a phony who can't go to the bathroom without checking first with Vice President McKell, and—"

Wallace pointed a forefinger. "One more word out of you, you supercilious creep, and I, personally, will throw you out that window there." The finger traversed, like a machine gun, to the clipboard lady, who was about to shriek again. "And that goes for you, too, you foulmouthed little wretch. All of you: out of my office at once. I have a war to fight."

* * *

Near midnight, he turned off the desk lamp and, aching and stiff, rose from his chair and went to the windows overlooking the plaza green, the regal bridge beyond, and the distant, measured flaring of the Anastasia lighthouse. Restless clouds were coming in from the sea, low and fast, laden with rain, and he watched them, dealing with an unspecific sadness.

There was a tapping, and Ellie Dumas looked in from the doorway. "I'm packing it in for tonight, General. Anything you need before I go?"

"No, Ellie. I'm heading out myself."

"Well, then. I'll see you in the morning, sir."

"Ellie?"

"Sir?"

"I really blew it with the Ridenour thing."

She came into the room slowly, her thin face thoughtful. "Well, I'm not so sure, General. The man has a lot of reach, certainly, and there are important people in the Pentagon who are friendly with him. But it was pretty clear that he was getting ready to box your ears."

"But why?"

She shrugged, the small, unhappy reflex of a chronically unhappy woman. "I couldn't say, sir. He's an evil person. That's plain enough to anybody."

"But you think I was a fool to tell him off, don't you."

"Well, sir, if anybody ever needed telling off, that man sure does. And, although I've seen you do some foolish things in the course of our long association, a fool you aren't. You're one of the kindest, most decent men I've—I've—ever—"

Her voice broke then, and she hurried from the room, her head bowed, a hand to her mouth.

Astonished, slightly embarrassed, he said aloud, "That poor woman needs a vacation."

He was writing a note to himself about this when George Cannon tapped on the door casing.

"Hi, George. Doesn't anyone go home around here?"

"I just got a computer message from Homestead, sir. There's been another interecpt."

"Oh?"

"A plane. Jets out of Homestead picked it up and shadowed

it to a point at sea off Jacksonville, where they recorded its destruction by one of our National Guard muscle choppers."

"No resistance?"

"No, sir. Not even a paper wad."

"Why don't they ever fight back? Or simply surrender?"

"As you've said many times, sir, that's our puzzle."

"We're patrolling for wreckage? Bodies, clues?"

"The radio traffic indicates some sea trash. But nothing revealing."

"Well, we'll keep at it. Sooner or later we'll find something. Sooner or later there'll be something that tells us why the hell we're having such grossly lethal success at air and sea-level interdiction."

"Yes, sir."

"It's creepy. Absolutely creepy."

"Well, sir, I'm off. 'Night. And hello to the missus."

"Good night, George."

"Jenny, it's Dolf. Just checking in."

"Hi. Still in Augustine?"

"We come back to Washington in the morning."

"How did it go today?"

"Terrible, that's how. A complete bust."

"Poor baby."

"Wallace is a creep. A Neanderthal."

"Well, you're going to take care of him, so don't fret."

"What are you doing?"

"It's late, pal. I'm getting ready for bed."

"Wish I were there. Can we have dinner tomorrow night?"

"No. The president is entertaining some Hollywood hotshots and he wants me there. With no first lady, he sort of depends on me to balance the table seating."

"Hardly. He depends on you to make the conversation, if the truth were known. Socially, he's a real wet smack."

"Why don't you come by, say, around eleven? We'll have a nightcap together at least."

"I can't wait. I miss you very much. You're the only—tenderness—in my life."

"You're sweet, Randolph. You haven't mentioned our relationship to anybody else, have you?"

"I never mention you out of my job context, darling. What we have going is strictly between us."

"I'm crazy about you, and I'd love to have the world know, but I don't think it'd fly too well with your network bosses and some of your fellow media critics. After all, you're supposed to be covering the Administration, not sleeping with it."

"Ha."

"So get some sleep, dear. I'll see you tomorrow."

"Around eleven. Good night."

CHAPTER 8

"SII. Miss Dryer speaking."

"Mr. Richter, please."

"May I ask who's calling, sir?"

"A friend of his, passing through town. My name is Robert Fresca, of the International Services Company."

"One moment, please."

"Mr. Fresca?"

"Yes."

"Sorry to keep you waiting, sir. But Mr. Richter is in conference right now. May I ask where he might buzz you?"

"The Radimore Arms, Room Seven."

"Thank you, sir. Mr. Richter will call you in a very short time."

"Hello?"

"Mr. Fresca?"

"Yes."

"Mr. Pepsi here."

"I didn't want to bother you at your office, but I think we should talk."

"It's all right, Colt. The damned budget thing has me in meetings about when to hold meetings. What's up?"

"Are you on your secure phone?"

"Of course. Why?"

"Why didn't you tell me you found Sweeney?"

"Well—"

"But now that you have, I'd like to know the scoop."

"Scoop on what?"

"I never got the idea at our meeting that you planned to kill the bastard. But obviously you have, and I'd like to know the details."

"Tell me what you know and I'll be able to talk more sensibly."

"All I know is that two hoods—I'm assuming they were yours—made a move on Sweeney in an Elkton motel. Well, he killed one and the other got away."

"Damn. This is all news to me."

"Obviously you need better communications with your hired guns."

"Obviously. So what happened?"

"Apparently it wasn't Sweeney alone. It seems he's picking up friends. He and another guy shut down your troops, then drove south in a maroon Ford. They were followed by a second car with two guys in it, a blue Dodge. Nobody got the tags on either car."

"Who was the dead man?"

"Cop friend of mine tells me it was Charles Boyle, a gun-for-hire out of Philly with a record that goes from here to there. Witnesses say the other guy was a tall redhead with tinted glasses who jumped into a tan Chevy and disappeared toward Elkton."

"Not to worry. There's absolutely no way those two can be linked with me—with us. But just to be sure, I've already planted a story to explain Sweeney's wipeout whenever it occurs. It says that Sweeney was under a vengeance contract assigned by Colombians who were hurt by Sweeney a couple of years ago. And there's no way that story can be traced. Certainly not with the Colombians, eh?"

"So what's your next move, Richter?"

"I'm giving priority to finding out who those pals are Sweeney's picked up. As you know, I was hoping that Sweeney was away on a six-month tour of the States. Well, obviously he's not—he's reverted to type and is trying to solve another one of his beloved goddam mysteries. Which is bad enough. But if he's gathering a crew in the process, he could give us some really bad times."

"Yeah."

"Anything else, Colt?"

"That's it for now."

"McKell wants me to accompany him to Camp David this weekend. Leonardi's holding talks with the Mexican bigwigs. I'll be out of touch until Monday."

"Well, maybe you'd better check in with me whenever you can. Make a Mr. Pepsi call at, say, noon, or as close to noon as possible, on Saturday and Sunday."

"Okay."

"But for God's sake, Richter, you've got to do better on Sweeney. We simply can't afford him. He's the most dangerous thing there is: a man with principles.

"Stiegel and Company, Public Relations, Miss Fitzgerald speaking."

"This is Aaron Richter. Is Warren Stiegel in?"

"Hi, Mr. Richter. You're in luck. He's about to leave for Baltimore. Hold on a sec, please."

"That you, Mr. Richter?"

"Can I talk?"

"Sure. I'm alone in my office."

"Why didn't you call me about that mess at the Elkton motel last night? I just heard about it from somebody else."

"Because I'm still trying to find out what went on myself, Mr. Richter."

"Where the hell were your guys Zimmermann and Pollock when all that was going on? And who the hell was it who elbowed in to help Sweeney?"

"Here's all I've got up to now: Zimmermann and Pollock had located Sweeney by checking all the motel registers in the area. They set up a watch from a nearby gas station. But they ran into a bad break. They happened to be at a gas pump, refueling their Dodge, when Sweeney showed up at the motel. As soon as he went through the door, all hell broke loose. By the time they were able to break clear, the guy named Boyle was dead, his pal had disappeared, the road was filled with gawkers and cars, and

Sweeney and his backup got away. And I have absolutely no idea who Sweeney's backup was because Zimmermann and Pollock never got a look at him. That's all I know right now. But I'm going to work over the motel deskman. He may be able to put more light on things."

"I'm paying you a bunch to deal with Sweeney in exactly the way I say. I don't like this sloppiness."

"Don't worry, Mr. Richter. We'll straighten everything out and we'll be completely on track in a day or two."

"Well, see that you are. Sweeney's very heavy cargo in this game I'm playing."

CHAPTER 9

Cap had gone to Elkton to talk to her police friends about the file on the shot-up boat. Later, she would check on things at the airfield.

The morning was warm and dry, but the sky was neutral, uncommitted either to overcast or haze, and there was a general inertness; trees stood motionless and the bay lay flat and glittering, like sheet metal. Sweeney left the house and stood on the dock for a time, tossing crumbs to the swirling gulls and staring into the water, as if it might contain words, or designs, or motions that would explain how and why he was in this alien idyll, aching in body and troubled in soul.

As a product of the American military and its John Wayne ethos, he had always tried to let on to others that close calls were something to joke about—just one of the job's many vexations and a good excuse for a bit of restorative whiskey-drinking when the heat was off. In clinical actuality, a peculiar inner calm would prevail during the crisis itself, but in the aftermath, in the quiet time, there would be a fluttering in his stomach and a tendency to retch, a need to pace, and a depressing awareness of his vulnerability in an uncaring and whimsical universe.

That night in Nam, when his chopper had been sieved by small-arms fire and was windmilling into the trees, his mind had raced with vows of vengeance against Farley Tremaine, the English teak merchant who had betrayed him with assurances that the contact area was Cong-free. After the crash, on his trek to the delta, plans for Tremaine had eventually been lost in persistent nausea and a trembling that resembled the racking of malarial fever.

Sweeney was older now, and time presumably had brought changes in the way his body reacted to violence and fear. There had been calmness in the midst of the motel action, as always before, but this time there had been virtually no delay in the onset of gagging and trembling. His stomach had churned even as the car careened from the motel parking lot, and the coldness and quivering had remained through the night, by dawn diminishing to the vague uneasiness he now felt.

He was returning to the house when the maroon Ford purred down the lane and came to a halt in the parking circle. Freddie Dilworth swung from behind the steering wheel, looking ten feet tall in his bubba hat, blue jeans and sunglasses, and made straight for the patio. He was carrying a manila envelope.

"Hi, Freddie," Sweeney called from the dock, "are you still poking your nose into my business?"

Freddie grinned. "There he is: the Jackhandle Kid."

"Nice to see you. But not nearly as nice as it was last night at the Happy Hour Motel."

"I bet. Have you seen today's papers?"

" 'One killed, another injured in shootout at Elkton motel. Two others being sought.' Three paragraphs in the second section."

"Elkton's turning into a fast-lane town, eh?"

"I owe you a big one, Freddie."

"No way. I'm having the time of my life. But I really would like to know where you learned that jack handle trick."

"I did some heavy-breathing in my boyhood. Airborne infantry. Then Special Forces. Then CIA's Dirty Tricks Department. That's where I learned jack handles."

"Cool, man. Will you teach me?"

"Consider it done."

Freddie held out the envelope. "Cap's doing some work on the Stearman, and she asked me to bring this stuff to you. It's police file stuff she says you want to look at."

"Wow. She doesn't waste any time."

"Her old man was real popular around the county. Him and the police chief hunted a lot. So Cap sort of has a lot of influence in these parts."

"For a guy who liked privacy, Mr. O'Brien sure did build up a social following, is all I can say."

"Good fella. Tough. Honest. Self-reliant. Matter of fact, Cap's a lot like him."

"Well, thanks for bringing this stuff over."

"Sure. Anything else you need?"

"One thing you might give me a hand on. I'd like to get my Mercedes out of that parking lot before it's towed away. Moved to a safe place. Do you think you can arrange that?"

"Piece of cake. I'll pick it up this afternoon."

"No. There's another angle. That tall kid with the pimples who works around your garage—can he do it?"

"Sure. But why?"

"I want you parked where you can see the whole lot. When the kid gets the car, keep your eyes open. There may be a new tail team watching it. I'd sure like to have you tell me what they look like, if that's the case."

"Right. We'll stash the car in the horse barn at my Cecilton farm and bring you the keys."

"You're a good soul, Freddie. Are sure you haven't been reading those holy roller books you sell?"

Freddie grinned, climbed into the Ford, waved a hand, and drove off.

Sweeney sat at the patio table and went through the envelope. First he dealt with the contents of Nageler's wallet—a rather impressive selection of driver's licenses, Social Security cards, concealed weapons permits, and credit cards. Two dry-cleaner receipts, the boat rental receipt, and a health insurance ID. There were two photographs—one of an unidentified woman, a pretty face, smiling against an Alpine backdrop, the other, curiously, a color shot of a storage cabinet. A built-in storage cabinet, painted ivory, with blue trim and black wrought iron drawer-pulls. He then turned to the chewier, more interesting stuff, but the more he read the more depressed he became. Hank Nageler had died while going first class.

According to the investigation report, signed by a Detective Ruggles, a man who gave his name as Albert F. Parsons had paid Hogarth Boatyard a thousand dollars cash, in advance, for a week's rental of a 22-foot Seabird runabout with twin 60 outboards and complete instrumentation, with dropoff at rental's end at any licensed marina on either shore of the bay between Havre de Grace and Crisfield. He also put down five hundred as a returnable deposit against damage to the boat's "esthetics and/or mechanical systems."

The boat, Ruggles wrote, had been recovered the following day, beached on the Northeast River side of Elk Neck about a quarter-mile south of the state park main entrance. The boat was badly damaged by gunfire and there was no trace of Parsons. Heavy rains the night before had washed away whatever blood or other clues there might have been.

The rest of Ruggles's report made it clear to Sweeney that Nageler had been planning a lot of sophisticated reconnaissance and eavesdropping. The list of items recovered from the gunshot hulk included a device—described in Ruggles's awkward police language—that simply had to be a Jagdmeister 500, the absolute state of the art in electronic surveillance gear, so new and so advanced it had been taken over from the German developer by the Nachrichtendienst and held under the strictest security. Sweeney knew this because he had organized SII's theft of the 500's blueprints—a coup that had ticked off the entire American intelligence apparatus, from CIA to CIC, which had never been fond of him anyway, thanks to his reputation, especially around the White House, as a loose cannon.

The 500 was a narrow-focus, long-distance audio-visual machine that was part television, part radio, and part telescope—all of it carried in a hardside satchel no larger than a salesman's sample kit. It was a marvel of compactness and simplicity, a battery-operated computer that controlled a telescopic, laser-aimed receptor tube and a miniature videocassette recorder. It could find, display and record the time on a watch dial on any line-of-sight horizon and, while screening out ambient noise, could select and record specific sounds from as far as ten miles. With a 500 mounted on any stable surface on Turkey Point, an agent could watch the hive and listen to the drone of bees across the bay in Havre de Grace. When he felt like it, he could play it all again, precisely as he saw and heard it the first time. And with its auxiliary modem, a companion piece that performed spectro-analyses, he could, while in replay, determine the chemical structure of the honey.

As of this date, only the Germans had working copies of the 500, and they weren't about to lend them to free-lancers. Sweeney knew exactly how much time, effort, money and manpower had been required simply to steal the blueprints; Nageler, working alone, couldn't have stolen one of the machines in twenty years. Which meant, then, that Hank had to have been working for the Germans, directly under the Nachrichtendienst.

So then the next step was a two-step.

First, he'd confirm the German involvement. Then, with luck, he would have a clue as to why Hank had been grubbing about Turkey Point and what he'd been looking for there.

The inventory included a DKK 77 portable shortwave radio with integral scrambler of the kind favored by Central European security services. Why would Nageler have brought that along unless he had someone to talk to on a special, prearranged frequency? A helper ashore, say. If he had transmitted—and it was certainly likely that he had when his boat had come under a shooting attack—there would be an audio copy and a written text on file at the National Communications Agency's CI registry.

Ah-ha.

But how to get a copy?

Ah, yes. Lover-boy Schachtel again.

He reached for the phone and dialed the airfield.

"Hello?" It was Cap's voice.

"Good morning. I want to thank you for getting the police report for me."

"Freddie's been there, then, eh?"

"It was one of life's pleasant surprises to discover that you and Freddie are an item."

"An *item*? He's just an old friend of Pop's—"

"The way he talks about you, I can see he's madly in love with you."

"You're a piece of work, you are."

"Seriously. He admires you O'Briens a bunch."

"He tells me there was a scene at the motel. Are you all right?"

"Scene is the word. And yes, I'm okay."

"I was going to ask you about it this morning before I left. But I heard you snoring, so I didn't knock."

"Impossible. I do not snore."

"Then there was a local thunderstorm in your room."

"The police report on the Nageler incident helps. But it also tells me I need something else."

"Like what?"

"I'd like Polaroids of the items recovered from Nageler's boat. The most important one is a case, sort of like a large typewriter case, now stored in the victims' personal effects locker at county police headquarters. With it will be another, smaller case, which I'd also like to have pictures of. And photocopies of each page of the charts and Nageler's notebook. Please see if you can get those for me, too."

A moment of silence followed, filled with her doubt. Then: "Chief Delaney is a real dear, and he's already gone out on a limb for me. Personal effects and investigation reports are one thing, but messing around with evidence—that's a bit much."

Sweeney pressed in. "Does Delaney know you were working with Intelligence in Washington?"

"Well, yes—"

"Tell him you're doing some deep-dish special work for DOD and you need those things."

"That would be lying."

"The hell it would. Whether you like it or not, you're now up to your buns in deep-dish DOD stuff. It just isn't official, that's all."

"Well—"

Sweeney sighed. "And it's also true that the owners of those cases will be moving to get them back at all costs—even if it means burning down Elkton. So give it a whirl, eh?"

"All right. I'll go up there right away."

"Appreciate it."

She called back within the hour. He had just finished a shower and was dressing when the phone rang.

"Hello."

"I can't get the pictures—"

"What's the matter? You sound awful."

"I—Well, first—"

"Are you all right? What—"

Her voice, strangled, liquid, formed the words. "First, I found that a couple had come and claimed to be Nageler's relatives. An aunt and uncle. They took all his effects with them, including the typewriter case and like that. They were from Austria, or some such place. And—"

"Hey. Relax. Don't take it so big. We'll find another way. Besides, I'm not surprised. I sort of expected this."

He could hear her struggling for control. "I was leaving the station when—" A long pause.

"When what? Is something wrong?"

"There was all this commotion. Cops hurrying to cars, and sirens and things. I asked Chief Delaney what happened and he said—" Another silence.

"Said *what*?"

"There'd been an explosion. At Elkton. In the Jamison's mall parking lot. A Mercedes blew up. A man was killed."

Sweeney sat on the bed, speechless himself now.

"The chief said it was Chuck Vernon—"

Sweeney managed to find his voice. "He was picking up the Mercedes for me."

"Chuck's dead. He was only a boy. I know his family."

"I can't tell you how sorry I am."

Her words came rapidly. "I don't want you to tell me how sorry you are. I want you out of my house at once. I want you to get as far away from me and my friends as you can get."

"Cap—"

"I don't want to hear any more, do you understand? If you don't leave, you are going to get us all killed."

He took a deep breath, struggling with shock. "You didn't even have to ask. I'm already out of here."

"It's terrible—The violence—"

He kept his voice calm. "I think you'll be all right. They haven't connected you to me yet. If anybody comes asking questions, play dumb. You'll be okay."

"But Freddie—"

"They've dismissed him as a guy who takes care of my car. They already know about Freddie."

"Well—"

"So long, Cap. Thanks for everything."

He had just hung up when the phone rang again.

"Yeah?"

"This is Freddie, Mr. Sweeney. I got some real bad news—"

"I know. Cap just called."

"It was terrible."

"I know how much you liked the boy, Freddie."

"Yep. A good kid. I tried to warn him, Mr. Sweeney. I really did. But I couldn't catch his attention in time. He just hopped into the car and—well—"

"You tried to warn him? About what?"

"I was watchin' from a used-car lot across the road, like you asked me to. And just before the kid got to the Mercedes, I spotted that tall redheaded guy, the one who was workin' you over at the motel. He was in a black Toyota, watchin' the Mercedes, too, and when he saw Chuck fiddlin' with the Mercedes' door lock, he started up and hauled ass. I got a real fast hunch, a feelin' of danger, sort of, and I honked my horn and yelled at Chuckie, but, it—didn't do no good."

"Will you be all right, Freddie?"

"Sure. How 'bout you?"

"Cap's asked me to leave. I can't blame her. She might be next. And if you know what's good for you, you'll get out of my life, too, Freddie."

"Where you goin'?"

"My house at Turkey Point, I guess. Where else?"

"Well, be real careful, hear?"

CHAPTER 10

The staff limousine dropped General Wallace at the Potomac River entrance, where, attaché case swinging, he took the steps in an easy lope. The autumn sun and Washington's legendary humidity were in an intense collaboration this day, seeming determined to melt the Pentagon and turn its parking acres into molten lagoons. Across the river, the skyline of distant domes and spires and lacy trees appeared to float in a motionless haze, and he paused to consider this briefly, his gaze thoughtful. Then, after giving his uniform a quick, final inspection, he pulled open one of the tall doors and stepped through the first infrared inspection beam.

The stony-faced Marine sergeant on duty at the visiting officers' desk examined his MID card and travel orders, then initialed and time-stamped a For-the-Day-Only building pass. "Thank you, General," he said cheerlessly. "You know the drill, I'm sure."

"Through the metal detection booth over there, then follow the ring to the Area Security desk, where I show my orders and sign the log."

"Yes, sir. But they've added something since your last visit. Personnel entering the Joint Chiefs Area are required to pass voice and handprint IDs. Talk to the CPO there. He'll fix you up for this and subsequent visits."

General Wallace tried for a light tone. "I remember the days when all I had to do was show my green card. Now that we have a stupendous peace going, a drastic reduction in the military, we're all of a sudden getting supercautious. How come?"

"I wouldn't know, sir. When you leave the building, by whatever exit, for whatever purpose, please return your FDO building pass with the duty NCO at the exit location."

Wallace, trying not to feel rebuffed, gathered his documents, then pushed on.

At the entrance to the Joint Chiefs Area the effects of the military budget reduction program became dramatically apparent. The central corridor, flanked by cubicles and glass-walled section rooms, was only dimly lit, because the vast steppe of desks, worktables and computer terminals was devoid of humanity. Only in distant corners, where detail maps hung and key-installation message center traffic was on-screen, was there animation—a cluster of company-grade officers staring into glowing VDTs and sipping coffee from paper cups. In other, presumably normal times, the four hundred officers who attended to the daily chores of the Joint Chiefs had made a mannerly Babel of this place—a huge, GI newspaper city room was what had always come to Wallace's mind—but now it was a nothing, a mere furniture warehouse.

He was considerably depressed by the time he arrived at the large office of his drug war boss, Lt. Gen. Donald F. Reynolds, special assistant to the chairman and head of the newly formed Special Contingency Command, to which UFI reported for administration. Even the perky Captain Laura Simms, the general's aide, failed to dent his mood with her welcoming weather-and-sports small talk, a ploy that was supposed to help visiting firemen "relax before the ax," as inside idiom put it.

A buzzer sounded, and Captain Simms said, "General Reynolds would like you to come in now, sir."

Wallace pushed through the heavy connecting door and found that Reynolds was not alone. Seated around the room in various attitudes of casualness were Hoff, Benson, Donnelli, and Grubb, the officers who composed the chairman's informal brain trust and whom the cognoscenti jokingly called—very much behind their backs, of course—"the JCs' Jaycees."

Wallace saluted, but Reynolds made it clear at once that this was a bull session, not a meeting, by waving at a chair and smiling his prim smile. "Welcome, Harve. Take a load off. We're kicking some things around, and we'd like you to give us some of your ideas. Coffee?"

This was not at all what Wallace had been led to expect of this day in Washington. Worse, it was a singular departure from the norm, a discord that made him instantly uneasy. Working to hide his surprise, he shook his head. "No coffee, thank you, sir." Glancing about affably, he added, "It's good to see you all again."

"Likewise, Harve," Reynolds crooned. "How's your lovely wife? Well, I hope."

Wallace knew for a fact that Reynolds and Millie were considerably less than fond of each other, and so the question represented a faint taunt. Her dislike had been given words one night after a Reserve Officers' Association ball in Bethesda, when Millie sputtered, "That man never remembers my name. You'd think a Regular Army officer of his rank and position would at least remember names." Wallace had gained no brownie points by kidding, "Especially a name attached to a little number like you, eh?" He'd meant it as a compliment, but it had sounded as if he'd seen her annoyance as wounded female vanity, and she'd gone into a real snit. As for Reynolds, some radarlike sensitivity had enabled him to pick up her antipathy and, while he had never said as much, it became clear that he saw her as just another bitchy Army wife.

"She's fine."

Donnelli, a major general who served as the chairman's special liaison with the Atlantic, Pacific, European and Southern unified commands, was known to despise small talk. So it was no surprise when he went directly to business. "Tell me, Harve, just what the hell are you doing down there in Florida that enables you to rack up such an astonishing kill rate on incoming contraband shipments? I mean, my God, you've got a record of damned near ninety percent interceptions and destructs, both surface craft and aircraft."

Wallace's quick intuition, his single most valuable character trait, told him that this was a loaded question, designed not so much as a means of eliciting information as it was to test him—Harvey Wallace—in some arcane way. This bizarre meeting, in which four of the most powerful and influential members of the national defense mechanism had invited a mere one-star active reservist to a feet-up bull session, had as its subject, not the cosmic issues one might expect, but chitchat on local operational tactics. It simply didn't make sense. The voluminous reports sent daily from his St. Augustine office direct to Reynolds were edited and summarized by Reynolds's staff people and distributed to the National Security Council, the DOD and its JCS, the State Department, the DEA and the CIA. It was inconceivable that Donnelli, in his exalted position, would not have been at least generally informed on procedures followed by Harvey Wallace's UFI field strike forces. So why ask about them, unless it was to see how Wallace would answer? These guys were fishing, sure as hell, and the suspicion that he was their wriggling bait increased his nervousness.

"Good people, good training, and good equipment, sir. Plus a lot of latitude in their application on a daily tactical basis. We couldn't hope to be so successful if it weren't for the enlightened counsel we get from General Reynolds and his staff."

There. That should put a stopper in the smart-ass's bung, Wallace thought testily. *What was the old saying? If you're going to be bait, be slippery, Dad—be slippery.*

"Well, of course," Donnelli purred, "but I was asking nuts and bolts. Which people, which equipment—that kind of thing."

This dude's a real piece of work, Wallace thought. "It's pretty cut and dried, sir. We have no magic wands. Our federally activated Guard chopper crews, flying standard GI Super Apaches and Stilettos, follow up at-sea discoveries made by Navy AWACs and Orions, or by National Guard jet jockeys flying out of Jacksonville and Homestead. If the contraband is airborne, we signal the pilot to follow us to Jax or St. Augustine or Homestead, if need be, for landing and search. If he ignores the signal, he's shot down. If the stuff is aboard surface vessels, we order them to heave to and await Coast Guard boarding and search. If they ignore the command, we sink them. Most of them choose to ignore us, so most of them are destroyed. There's nothing very spectacular about it. In fact, our crews are showing, well, psychological trauma as a result of the fish-in-a-barrel nature of the shooting."

"Your reports say that the bastards never fight back. Do you have any idea why?"

"No, sir. None. All I can say is, we have no record of any challenged craft, sky or sea, ever putting up armed resistance. Resistance of any kind, actually. Unless you can call a weaving, evasive course a form of resistance. Because that's the most they've ever done—weave. And it's getting to some of our crews."

Hoff, who had emerged from the Korean War as an Air Force fighter ace and rarely let anyone forget it, shifted in his chair and gave Donnelli a condescending smile. "It's part of the price we pay for having our Regular Air Force on standby under the Continental Ready Command. If our father who art in the White House hadn't cut us to the bone and had put the job in pro hands, there wouldn't be any trauma, I assure you."

Benson sniffed. "Well, trauma or no, you have to admit that Harve's people are doing a hell of a job. Combined with the bombing of SAC and the on-site assaults by our Special Forces in the South and Central American drug initiating centers, we've got the goddam drug people on the goddam run. Our streets are drying up. We've got a forced drug withdrawal—a national-scale drying-out—going on. What sneaks through our combat Regulars in the drug zones is knocked off, at sea and in the air, by Harve and his people. Trauma-shmauma."

Why are they being so nice to me? Wallace wondered. He had the impression that they expected him to say something, something significant, but how could you say something significant when you hadn't the foggiest notion as to what the hell was going on? He decided to throw out a question of his own. "What about those projections we've been getting on increased narcotics flow from the Orient?"

Benson, deputy to the Marine Corps rep on the Joint Staff, shook his head. "It ain't really so. There have been a few attempts by Hong Kong wholesalers to upscale their traffic through Honolulu and Seattle, but the DEA people, in concert with the Coast Guard out there, canceled them, toot-sweet. The Asiatics and the Africans have just not been able to come anywhere near matching the production and distribution of their South American brethren because they don't have the options. The hemisphere smugglers have planes, small boats, runners, cars—the whole nine yards. But the Asiatics have to import by ocean vessel or transocean air, carriers that are quite easy for the Customs and Coast Guard folks to nail. And that's been true from the beginning."

Wallace tried a little joke. "Well, my in-box has sure been buried in teletype and fax sheets on the subject. God help us if 'it really ain't so' turns into 'hell yes.' "

There was an interval in which it became apparent that nobody had caught the joke, or, if he had, thought it was funny.

Reynolds sipped some coffee, his ice blue eyes evaluating Wallace across the mug's rim. "Those pilots and crewmen—are you rotating them enough? Do you think the same crews might be flying and shooting too much?"

"Not likely, sir. We have an excellent rotation policy, drawn up by the medics themselves, as a matter of fact."

Huff spoke next. The plans and training honcho, according to an apocryphal story he never denied, had beaten Eisenhower in a pickup round of golf at Burning Tree when he—Huff—was a mere shavetail, and had found himself transferred to the Canal Zone the next morning. He said, "Take it from me, Harve: Look hard at that rotation policy. The medics think they know a lot about troops, but they don't, really. My experience tells me that you've got a stress thing going that a revised rotation policy would fix in a jiff."

Benson nodded. "I agree. We, as Joint Staff types, can't—and shouldn't—get into a field commander's business, but, if you want advice, and that's what the OJCS is all about, then my advice is to back off on the number of sorties those boys are expected to fly. Activate some standby Guardsmen and put them in the air. That way, as a bonus, you'll be giving more crews more experience on the same budget. Synergism, sort of. See what I mean?"

"Yes, sir. I'll sure look at it."

The conversation went on, and as they tossed things back and forth—the recent reorganization of the Defense Intelligence Agency, the need for more noncoms of staff competence, the gee-whiz new hardware that would probably never see service, the heavyweight responsibilities that had been placed on the National Guard, the World Series—Wallace knew, with an inexplicable certainty, that the four generals had heard from him what they had been listening for and now had no real interest in him or what he had to say. In fact, the more casual and jolly they became the more convinced he was that they really didn't like him much. It was a subtle thing—an air of supercilious indulgence—like that of fraternity seniors chitchatting in the presence of a pledge. He was glad when General Reynolds's buzzer buzzed and Captain Simms announced that a call from General Von Kruger in Bonn was waiting on Line Three. The session broke up, but as he stood by the door, waiting for the others to leave, Reynolds called, "Just a sec, Harve. There's one more thing."

"Yes, sir?"

Reynolds reached for his phone, but before lifting it he said, "The chairman and some of the OJCS people are very upset over the way you handled Randolph Ridenour. The son of a bitch has been raising blue hell. He's called everybody, from President Leonardi to the lady who cleans my john, to protest what he calls the rotten waste of network time and resources—your inviting him to Florida, only to walk out on the interview."

"I didn't invite him anywhere. He invited himself."

"Makes no no-how, Harve. The man's a monster, yes. He is usually more wrong than he is right, yes. He specializes in humiliating people, yes. But we've got to get along with him. He has enormous influence, and if we can't have his friendship we must have his neutrality. That can't happen if you continue to treat him like a horse's ass."

"He *is* a horse's ass, goddamit, sir."

Reynolds picked up the phone and, cupping a hand over the mouthpiece, said coolly, "I want you to visit the video center down the hall and tape an apology to Ridenour. We'll have it piped to Ridenour's office in New York. The video crew is waiting for you right now."

"Sir, I can't do that."

"That's a direct order."

"Sir—"

Reynolds waved a hand of dismissal, spun in his chair, put his feet on the desk and crooned into the phone, "Otto! Wie angenehm! Ich dachte, Sie wären noch auswärts . . ."

* * *

Later, General Reynolds turned from the window, from which he had been watching the bustling on the Potomac bridges, and pressed the buzzer. Hoff, Benson, Donnelli and Grubb came in from the small staff conference room. They did not sit down.

"What do you think, gentlemen?" Reynolds asked.

Donnelli, as could be expected, spoke up immediately. "If, as you tell us, the vice president worries about him, the vice president is wasting his time. Wallace is nobody to worry about."

"Hoff?"

"I'm not so sure. We had him at a pretty big disadvantage, and I think he handled himself pretty well. He was confused, certainly, but I don't think he's a jerk. And his concern over the whim-whams his aircrews are feeling worries me a bit. He's the kind of man who would look into such matters carefully."

Reynolds nodded. "I've been in touch with McKell. He is very sensitive to that possibility himself, but he's received reassuring reports from the electronics vendors in Dayton. Tests of Hammerhead have been very positive and the system should be available to our people in Cartagena before the end of the month."

"I hope so," Hoff said. "I think that's where the crunch lies vis-à-vis Wallace and his people."

General Reynolds's gaze shifted. "How about you, Grubb?"

"I worry more about the Ridenour flap. Smaller incidents than that have ruined careers, gotten people bounced from jobs. The vice president needs Wallace where he is. He's a good officer—devoted, smart, well-trained, energetic, and therefore credible if needed as our sacrificial lamb. But he's just enough of the dilettante, buried in just enough operational turmoil, to miss seeing the real action or to misinterpret it if he does see it. And that, gentlemen, as I've been given to understand, is precisely why we have him doing all this in the first place. Wallace, as a patsy, is supervaluable to Brandon McKell, and it would be silly indeed to lose such an asset in a dumb little peeing contest with Ridenour."

"And you, Benson?"

"I don't think Wallace'll be a problem. Unless, as Hoff says, the Ridenour thing gets out of hand."

Reynolds nodded. "All right. So it's agreed that we keep him on the job down there in Florida. As for Ridenour, I've been in touch with him. He says an apology, written, taped and video'd for his exclusive use as he sees fit, will satisfy him."

There was a pause. "Any further concerns, gentlemen?"

The others stood in silence.

"Okay, everybody. Thanks. Back to work, eh?"

CHAPTER 11

Sweeney slumped in the padded cradle of the deck lounger, legs wrapped in a blanket, once again moving the night glasses through a traverse of the Proving Ground shoreline, five nautical miles to the northwest. The night was cold and starry, and the lights of Havre de Grace and Perryville sparkled, brittle and unfriendly, across the restless darkness of the bay. A persistent wind, filled with the smells of wide water and the oncoming winter, made melancholy sounds in the eaves of the darkened house behind him. The surf broke noisily on the rocks and fallen timbers far below, and the forest hissed and clacked. Baltimore's glow, beyond the southwestern horizon, offered no cheer.

Hank Nageler had been killed while doing something out there. He had been on a boat loaded with sophisticated gear, offshore from a military installation devoted to the design and testing of weapons and projectiles. It could be assumed that he had not been interested in either of the towns, small, water-oriented, with no major industries, or in the railroad and highway bridges spanning the Susquehanna River, which separated the two. Nor was it likely that he'd been interested in what might be going on underwater, since the bay's headwaters were only one to four feet deep even in the most central sweeps—called, as a consequence, the Susquehanna Flats—and even the smallest power- and sailboats held to the channels or navigated with great care so as to avoid hanging up on the bottom, which was mostly sticky mud. No submarine activity in these waters, by gum.

So what, then? What had Nageler been doing, or looking for? Why had he written those letters in blood—those double-damned, infuriatingly puzzling letters? The more thought he gave it, the more he was convinced that Nageler had not been indulging in vanity, in a "Kilroy was Here" egoism, when he'd written those initials. So, if not, what *had* he been doing? And who were his bosses? Where had he acquired all that gear? And what could be learned now, days later, by staring at a black nothing through a pair of antique, Viet-period night glasses?

It was half-past midnight now. Again, as on the previous two nights, a C-130, workhorse transport of Army aviation, descended out of the south, whistling softly, engines hushed, lights blinking, to circle wide over the distant rises of Pennsylvania and come in on a final crosswind approach to the Proving Ground airfield. Sweeney, flicking on the hooded penlight, made the entry in his log.

At 01:11, a tug pulling a trio of scows came thumping down the northeast main river channel, eventually to disappear beyond the cliffs of Turkey Point. At 01:34, a tanker, riding high in the water and lit like a Christmas tree, loomed briefly in the southern shipping lane before completing its swing into the Elk River entrance to the Chesapeake and Delaware Canal.

God, Sweeney thought, scribbling in the log, *such suspense. Such frenzied activity.*

He yawned, rubbing his eyes with thumb and forefinger.

To the north of the house, through the jittering forest, headlights flared briefly as a car came out of the state park hairpin turn and made its way down the hill.

A sodden, unhappy husband, no doubt—bound for one of the stick-and-plastic houses surrounding the Jacob's Nose inlet, where a ticked-off wife waited in a darkened living room and contemplated murder.

Sweeney snickered at his flight of fancy.

He became instantly serious, though, when the car decelerated at the bottom of the hill, turned into the driveway and came slowly toward the house, lights out, tires crunching in the gravel.

Placing the glasses and log on the side table, he threw off the robe, rolled out of the lounger and scurried across the deck for the covering shadows of the garage. Huddled there, concealed in the copse of azaleas at the base of his mother's favorite oak, he pulled the .45 automatic from his jacket pocket and released the thumb safety.

The car, a dark lump in the greater darkness, came to a halt near the breezeway steps and fell silent. After an interval, the door opened and the driver stepped out.

Sweeney, quickstepping through the shadows, threw his left arm around the driver's neck and, with his right hand, held the pistol muzzle tightly against the parka hood.

"Bang, bang, you're dead," he grated.

"Hold it, Sweeney! It's me—"

"Cap?"

"For God's sake, take that thing away from my head."

He spun her around, peering at her face in the gloom. "What the hell are you doing here?"

"I came to look for you."

"How did you know I was here?"

"I guessed."

"Guessed?"

"Would you please put that damned gun away?"

He returned the pistol to safe and slid it into his belt. "I'll open the garage door. Put your car next to mine. No lights."

"All right. But can we go in the house or something? This wind's about to freeze me."

They sat in the leather easy chairs in the library, which was lit only by the starlight and reflected glow of the far-shore towns that came through the big window. The wind had picked up, and the night outside was busy with its sounds, but the room itself was relatively warm.

"I can't give you coffee or anything," he said. "I have the power off. There's some whiskey in the cabinet there."

"Nothing, thanks."

After a strained interval, he said, "I hate to think that Freddie told you I was here."

"He didn't. I asked him where you were, but he said he'd promised you he wouldn't tell anybody."

"So you guessed."

"That's the only word I can think of. I figured that you would want to stay in the area, because this is where it all started and this is where you have the best chance of picking up threads, like. A motel wouldn't do because they're easy to watch, and their registers are easy to read. And it struck me that this place is probably the last place that anybody'd expect you to be, what with all the murdering and surveillance and whatever. It's just too obvious."

"The mantel."

"What?"

"Back in basic training four hundred years ago I was taught that if I wanted to hide something I should place it in plain view. On the mantel, say. Nobody ever looks hard at stuff that's in plain view—that's too obvious."

"Well, whatever. The main thing is, I guessed right."

There was another extended pause in which they made a business of watching a brightly lit yacht move up-channel toward North East Harbor. He was dealing with a rush of—What was it? Something subtle and complex. Something akin to the mixture of gratification and surprise he felt when, as a graduating second looie, he had squinted through the aluminum glare of a Texas summer and seen Mary Alice Gibbons watching him from the front rank of the commissioning-parade spectators. There had been little hope that she would accept his invitation, what with her snooty attitude and the implicit logistical problems, but, impelled by his unreasoning infatuation, he had asked her to the ceremonies anyway. Her prim haughtiness had proved to be a mask; in less than an hour after dismissal of troops, they were tearing at each other in the dusk of a San Antonio motel room, beginning a weekend of rutting that had reduced him first to stupefaction and then to the eventual understanding that, beyond her sexual virtuosity, she hadn't really all that much to offer. Even so, and despite the many women to follow, that initial excitement—the thrilling parade-ground realization that the beautiful, aloof Mary Alice Gibbons had seen him to be worth three days of cut classes and four hundred miles of driving—had never been equalled.

Until now.

He needed Cap O'Brien's help, to be sure. In no way did she need Tom Sweeney.

And she'd come back anyhow.

Eventually he asked the big one. "Why were you trying to find me?"

"I was ashamed of myself. I shouldn't have treated you the way I did. I wanted to apologize and offer my help."

"Ashamed? I had just caused a friend of yours to be killed. I was the one who owed the apology."

She sighed. "You didn't cause Chuck to be killed. It was—fate. Chuck was due to go."

"I have trouble with that kind of stuff."

"It's not just 'stuff.' Chuck could have fallen down stairs, or walked in front of a bus. Whatever. You didn't have anything to do with it. If you did, you wouldn't have let it happen."

"Well, this is all too deep for me. I'm just glad you don't hold it against me. And I'm glad you guessed right."

There followed another period in which they listened to the surf below. He caught Cap's scent, a trace of soap, and it pleased him in an almost erotic way.

"I like your house, Sweeney. There's—an atmosphere. Your parents must have liked each other a lot."

He gave her silhouette a sidelong glance. "Yep."

"You were lucky to live here, grow up here."

"This, from the girl who grew up at The Orchards."

"My house never had the feel of loving parents in it. And it only smelled like cigars and gun oil."

He focused the glasses on a lone tug, southbound before the wind. "Take an outsider's word for it: The Orchards is Doze-off City. And it has the feel of you in it."

"I think it would be a good idea for you to come back there. They'll put things together sooner or later and come looking for you the way I did. And you said yourself that they hadn't connected you and me. I think you'd be safer at The Orchards than you are here."

"You're probably right."

She studied his profile for a time. Then: "Are we going to be good friends someday, Sweeney?"

"Looks that way."

"I'm so sick of being lonely."

"Everybody's got the lonelies. The trick is to find somebody to share them with."

"I suppose."

Keeping the glasses to his eyes with his right hand, he reached out with his left and patted her shoulder.

"What time is it, Sweeney?"

"Three-thirty."

"Lord, I've been here two hours."

"You fell asleep about an hour ago."

"You were laughing."

"I didn't mean to wake you up."

"But you did. What's so funny?"

"I was remembering that old story about the factory worker who was a thief—always sneaking stuff out of the plant. Products, parts. The bosses suspected him but couldn't prove anything, so they played safe by putting him on the evening trash detail. He'd go out to the dump every evening, just at shift change, with a wheelbarrow full of trash, and the guards, ready to leave, would always look at the load to be sure he wasn't carrying out something hidden in the trash. Never found a thing. So they decided the guy had turned over a new leaf—"

"Until they realized he was stealing wheelbarrows."

"You heard it, then."

"No. It just doesn't take genius to see what's coming."

"You're a smug and pompous wretch."

"And you're a twelve-cylinder idiot, Sweeney, if you think that story is funny. Especially at three-thirty in the morning on a windy damned hill."

"I've been watching wheelbarrows at Aberdeen."

"Say again?"

"I've been watching the Proving Ground for most of the night. Nothing going on over there. Not one shot, not a single bang. Only some cargo planes. But the planes are the thing. The thing I wasn't seeing. They're either flying something into the base or flying something out."

"That's not really analagous to the wheelbarrow story."

"Why don't you just throttle back and go to sleep."

"I'm going back to The Orchards and do it right. I have to fly to St. Michael's tomorrow. Chuck's funeral is at noon."

"That's dumb."

"I want to go to Chuck's funeral."

"No."

"Why not? I can fly down there and be back—"

"The Others will be going to the funeral, too. Just to put a scan out for me. Chuck had gone to get my wheels. That means he might have been a friend of mine. I just might be going to his funeral."

"That's you. So what's the problem with me?"

"Your remarkable face. Somebody might remember you once worked for me. Boy gets killed picking up Sweeney's car. Beautiful woman who used to work for Sweeney shows up at funeral. Does beautiful woman know where Sweeney is now? Donnerwetter, let's find out, eh?"

"I've known his family for years. They'll be very upset if I don't show up."

"And I'd be very upset to have to go to your funeral. So take your choice of upsets."

She rose from her chair, flipped the parka hood over her head, and said, "Okay. I get it. When will you be coming back to The Orchards?"

"I don't know yet. I've got to do some running around."

"Where?"

"Washington, mostly."

"Is that wise? I mean, there are a lot of people looking for you—"

"There are things I have to do, to look at."

"Well, don't get bent."

"While I'm gone, do what you can to tap into your government sources. I want a premium-grade, unleaded flow. I want a mountain of chitchat and gossip and hard stuff—all of it. And remember those briefing sheets. I can really use them."

"All right." She went to the door to the breezeway, where she paused. "You think I'm beautiful?"

"You know you are. Any mirror will tell you."

"That wasn't my question."

"I think you're the most beautiful woman I've ever seen."

"That's baloney. There are lots of more beautiful women. As you say, I have a mirror."

"So what do you want of me?"

"Oh, to hell with it. See you back at the house."

"Cap."

"What?"

"Thanks a ragin' lot for everything."

"You're welcome."

"I mean it."

"I know you do. And I think we'll make pretty good friends."

CHAPTER 12

The briefing, that inescapable ritual the military always laid on visiting politicians, was at 1930 hours in the staff conference room of the USS *Marcus Hook*, a Blue Ridge class command ship, anchored off Cartagena. At least two dozen officers of various sizes, shapes and ranks were in attendance. This was official suck-up time. All the scrambled eggs and chesty careerists who could wangle invitations lined the table and the walls, or bulkheads, or whatever the hell the Navy called them, to wear earnest and savvy expressions while a lanky baldy named Fitz, or Fritz, described as the senior something of the Skaty-eighth Frammus Squadron, spoke of missions and strike capabilities and logistics and weaponry. Richter hated ships and the sea—they frightened him in a deeply phobic way—and he'd never understood the Navy and its peculiar nomenclatures and its people, all scrubbed and starched and so goddamed capable. He was never in a situation like this, with Navy people all around, that he didn't feel defensive and bleakly inadequate. He lived by his wits, period; these people lived by their wits—and their dedication, and their technical skills, and their traditions, and their tireless and tiresome patriotic energies. They were everything he was not, and, as a visiting Civil Servant wearing the only sport shirt in the visible universe, he felt their covert stares, their sizing up, their secret resentment of his clout—granted to him via a whim of God and assorted Pennsylvania Avenue deal-cutters—and its superiority to their own, so hard-won.

Well, screw them all.

"And so, as you can see, sir," Fitz-Fritz was saying in his crisp Annapolis baritone, "the challenge has been quite large, in that in excess of a half-million tons of coca leaves were being grown annually by more than a million farmers in the Andean Reaches of Peru and Bolivia. The leaves were carried to nearby refineries and processed into some six thousand tons of coca paste, then sent up to Colombia, where it was further refined into the nearly three thousand tons of cocaine powder smuggled into the U.S.—in small, concealable lots—aboard fleets of aircraft and ships operating out of incredibly well equipped and organized bases along the upper rim of South America. But the Combined Narcotics Task Force, peer group of the UIF formed by the legislation of two years ago at President Leonardi's instigation and accelerated by the Western Hemisphere Narcotics Treaty of the year before, has drastically altered that picture. With the blockades by U.S. Navy vessels and supporting aircraft authorized by the treaty, and with the special intervention of airborne Army Special Forces and the work of U.S. technical advisors with local governments—made possible by the same diplomacy—we have virtually stifled that enormous flow and negated the enabling mechanisms, from hillside farm plots to sophisticated chemical labs. We are confident that the drug war has been won, with only the mopping-up phase still to be completed."

Richter realized suddenly that the voice had paused and that all eyes were on him, a condition that mandated some kind of comment from him. He followed his policy: When caught off guard, or stalling for time, always ask a question. "Mopping up, you say. What's involved in this mopping up?"

Fitz-Fritz was not caught napping. He flipped back the cover of the chart board on the easel beside him, revealing a brightly colored map of the Caribbean and Pacific coasts of South America. Squiggles, dots, squares and stars were sprinkled there, and Fitz-Fritz swept an authoritative hand across the whole. "These arrows leading north from Colombia and Venezuela, sir, represent the routes generally followed by the dwindling numbers of small boats and aircraft that persist in making runs for Jamaica, the Bahamas and certain wilderness areas of the southeastern U.S.—mainly the timber and swamp areas of Florida and its adjacent states—where U.S. drug distributors maintain a network of hidden airstrips and highly mobile vehicular pickup systems. While the Drug Enforcement Agency and the Coast Guard concentrate on these locations, the Florida National Guard is—with help from the Navy and Air Force—searching out and destroying the blockade runners, both in the air and on the sea, before they reach the continental U.S. While the Guard effort is achieving spectacular intercept success, the participating governments in Central and South America have virtually snapped the spine of the industry by destroying major manufactories and export bases. However, the action still remains intense and, we expect, will continue until the cost of smuggling becomes so high and risky it will become altogether unprofitable."

The dramatic silence resumed, and Richter, still not ready for his closing remarks, asked another. "Are U.S. troops being heavily engaged in the sweeps against the refineries and warehouses in Colombia and Peru?"

"No, sir, that action is spearheaded, developed and finalized by resident troops and their strategic and tactical staffs. We have special U.S. mercenary forces available on continuing standby to assist or backstop or counterattack if the resistance becomes severe or lopsided. And even then they are called in only by the resident forces. We initiate no actions. We and our mercenaries are a looming presence—a psychological boost to the locals, an omnipresent threat to the drug barons."

Richter continued to feign innocence. "Resident troops, you say. How come the governments of Peru and Colombia and Venezuela are all so willing to commit their troops, their cooperation, to the overall drug war when for years they've dragged their feet, either out of fear of the drug lords and their violent reprisal techniques or out of resistance to America's 'outside pressure'?"

Fitz-Fritz smiled patronizingly, and Richter could feel the shocked amusement running through the crowd. (Here's this hotshot intelligence guy out of Washington, and he shows not the slightest sign of knowing anything about the economic fangs behind the Hemisphere Treaty.) "Well, sir," the officer explained smoothly, overly polite, "the United States gave them an offer they couldn't refuse. Under the Hemisphere Treaty, the participating South and Central American nations receive direct foreign aid payments, investment incentives, most-favored nation status in trade agreements, and supplies of U.S. surplus farm crops and military hardware on an at-cost, open-ended deferred payment plan. Their arithmetic shows them they'd be making a lot more money and solving many more social problems by cooperating with us than by continuing to indulge the drug barons."

Richter thought he'd better save a bit of face. "I'm aware of all that, of course, Captain. But my question was really this: the governments involved are often corrupt, participating in and/or raking in enormous slices of the drug income pie. And the producers and distributors are notorious for welching on deals, for betraying even their own mobs, for outwitting even the most stringent and effective government countermeasures. What's to keep the corrupt officials and the individual growers, lab operators, marketers and distributors from continuing clandestine operations—albeit admittedly on a much smaller scale—no matter what the official government stance happens to be? For instance, thanks to ever-higher taxes and the increasing regulation of the manufacture and sale of booze, making and selling moonshine is starting to be a darn profitable business in the U.S. these days."

The captain nodded. "Quite so, sir. And that is essentially what the mopping up is all about. To convince the individual operators that the UIF and the Combined Narcotics Task Force represent a very long arm with a powerful fist at the end of it, and that they're the ones who will continue to get punched if they persist in, as you put it, making 'shine.' What we're doing, sir, is breaking up the industry by armed force and international political-economic cooperation and thereby making it so incredibly difficult and expensive to produce illicit drugs and sell them in the States the profit to be realized won't be worth the risk and hassle. There will always be a trickle, of course, but with a dry market and an impossible overhead, the druggies will have to go into some other racket." He smiled at his own philosophical wrap-up.

"Okay. So what's being done about nailing the small boats and airplanes before they set out for the U.S.?"

Fitz-Fritz was ready for that one, too. "That's precisely where our mercenaries are preparing to do their most important work in the fight, sir. Our ground force commander ashore has just informed us that his people are striking out to the north and east—at the request of the host governments—and will in the next two months have closed down the departure points, both airfields and harbors, for what remains of the narco traffic. It is, actually, the coup de grace, and it will be administered by hired American soldiers, at the request of the various host governments."

Another pause, during which Richter decided it was time to start schmoozing. How to do it? The action seemed to be all ashore and off the Florida coast, so what would these jaspers like to hear?

"Well, thank you for your most thorough and enlightening commentary, Captain." He let his sincerest gaze pass around the room. "And thank you, gentlemen, for your courteous reception and the use of your facilities—especially the helicopter that will take me in for my interviews with our commanders ashore. As scuttlebutt has probably told you by now, I'm here to gather information at the special request of Vice President McKell, and so I have to talk to quite a few of your colleagues."

The faces remained impassive, so he turned up the heat. "Before I get out of your hair, please tell me more about this magnificent ship. It's obvious—even to a landlubber like me—that the great victory that's being won over the drug lords could not have been possible if it weren't for the coordination and oversight that emanates from this incredible vessel. I'll be leaving in a moment or two, but please, so that I might bring the vice president up to the minute, describe what you people have achieved here."

The faces lit up like light bulbs.

Fitz-Fritz beamed. "That would be our pleasure, sir." The officer glanced at a beefy captain at the head of the table. "Would you like to take over here, Captain Lewis?"

"Delighted," the man rumbled, pushing himself erect from his place behind the glistening mahogany. "The *Marcus Hook* is one of the Navy's four fleet command ships, which means it can serve the dual role of command and communications coordination center for either fleet operations or amphibious assaults. It's just under seven hundred feet long, has an eighty-three-foot beam, and draws almost twenty-seven feet, with a displacement of more than nineteen thousand tons, fully loaded. It's propelled at a top of thirty knots by a steam turbine that generates twenty-seven thousand horsepower. It's armed with surface-to-air missiles, two Sea Sparrow eight-tube launchers abaft the superstructure and two twin three-inch guns forward, plus three batteries of pompom-type antiaircraft machine guns. It also carries three helicopters, which operate from the stern pad."

Aglow, like a father describing his son, Lewis picked up speed. "The ship is a sophisticated modification of the old Iwo Jima class of amphibious assault ships. Where the originals provided hangar space, this vessel provides office space and accommodations for the seven hundred officers and men—not counting the crew—who compose the command center staff. In addition to the regular electronics carried by the modern warship—radio, radar, sonar, and so on—the *Marcus Hook* is equipped with NTDS, the Naval Tactical Data System; ACIS, or Amphibious Command Information System; and NIPS, or Naval Intelligence Processing System. Which means, sir, that we have here a small seagoing Pentagon, so to speak. And—"

"That's simply not so, Captain," Richter broke in. "You people are quick, efficient, highly organized and thoroughly reliable. The Pentagon cannot make that claim."

There was a round of delighted laughter, as Richter knew there would be, and after it subsided, he stood and passed his warmest smile to one and all. "I could listen to this for another hour, gentlemen, but I really must be going." He glanced admiringly about at the walls, or whatever the hell they were called, and said softly, "I love these things. Huge, graceful, clean and dependable. I always feel at home aboard a Navy vessel. I always hate to leave them. My congratulations to you all, gentlemen. And I'm not only authorized, but also personally highly pleased, to pass along the vice president's most hearty 'Well done.' "

"Come back and see us again, hear?" someone called out, and there followed a murmur of chucklings and approving sounds. Waving, he ducked through the hatch and followed Fitz-Fritz, who had offered to lead him to the helipad.

They sat on the veranda of the Banana Club, an exclusive watering hole patronized by the Cartagena elite and the cream of Colombian and American military establishments.

Colt, because he had been deeply sunburned and had allowed his mustache to lengthen, could have passed as a Colombian, an effect heightened by his white suit, his long cigar, and his projection of the kind of unruffled benignity to be found in a successful mortician. It was an impression he had cultivated carefully, since here, as wherever in the world duplicity was the norm, it was an advantage to look local. He now took an appreciative sip from his tall, dark glass and gave Richter what presumably was meant to be a smile but which, in fact, suggested a gas-pain leer.

"Look at that," he said complacently, sweeping his cigar across the panorama of moonlit sea, twinkling harbor lights and curving, purple shoreline. "A beautiful place, eh?"

Richter was in no mood for esthetics, stuffed as he was with Navy pomp and acronyms and anxious to get this crap over with. "So where do we stand?"

"Relax, man. You're too tense. Cartagena is a place to take out the kinks, not put them in."

"I'm on a tense schedule. I'm not the kind who can futz around when there's work to be done."

"Then you must be a real standout in Washington, eh?" Colt's shoulders moved in sync with his husky laugh.

"You're right. Washington is full of horses' asses. If it weren't, there'd be no work for people like me and no bucks for dudes like you. So count your blessings."

"My, oh, my. We are bitter tonight, aren't we?"

"I'm making you rich. Don't forget that."

"You aren't exactly hurting yourself, is my guess."

"I have more trouble keeping money than you do."

"Hey. We should talk. I got a lot of little tricks that would help you beat the laundering problem, pal."

"When all this is over. Right now I'm too busy making it work."

"Aren't you getting any help from dreamboat McKell?"

"He's the biggest horse's ass of all."

"Do tell."

"And now you sound like you're turning into one."

Colt flicked the ashes from his cigar. "Keep your cool, sonny. You tick me off and Brandon McKell's ambitions will fade into the sunset."

The pause that followed was protracted, heavy and taut. The saraband being played for the rooftop dancers drifted down, soft, muted by the moist tropical night. A woman laughed somewhere, briefly, musically.

"You'll have to excuse me, Colt. I've just spent a whole day with the clean-living U.S. Navy, and I'm up to my lobes with the resultant bad moods and impatience."

"No sweat. We all have our bad times."

"Well, there really was no need for me to get on your case. Especially after that excellent dinner."

Colt took a final draw at his cigar and then stubbed it out in a crystal ashtray on the table at his elbow. Rearranging himself in the rattan chair, he blew a stream of smoke at the starry night and said, "So back to business. Here's how it goes down. Our mercenary recruits—the pee-and-vinegar gun-nuts—have formed a protective loop around the aircraft and small boat launching sites in the Manuelo district. Nobody, nothing gets through until we say so. And to keep the pee and vinegar flowing, I've arranged to have the Colombian troop commander in Diega—a very corrupt fellow, incidentally—send out patrols under orders that guarantee a collision with our perimeter defenses. There'll be a noisy shootout that will get the Colombian patrollers trashed. Our bloodthirsty mercenaries will cream their drawers and the local population will get even madder at the narcotraficants, whom they are already blaming for all their miseries."

"How about the refineries in the south? In Peru?"

"The token stuff has been a big success. Lots of noisy shooting and general commotion for the benefit of our clean-living Regulars and Navy types sent there as gun-pointers and advisors. A spectacular falloff in the flow to and from the remaining sites. It's all straight Twentieth-Century Fox, man, and the clean-livers are eating it up in massive mouthfuls, hardly able to wait to get home and tell the little wife and the kids—and, of course, the local media—about their thrilling experiences in the war against the evil drug lords." Colt chuckled softly.

"Well, I'm glad something's going right."

Colt gave him a look. "So what's not going right?"

"Sweeney keeps giving us the slip."

"Oh, for crissake. How hard is it to find and nail an out-of-work bureaucrat?"

"Sweeney's no bureaucrat. He never was. And you damn well know it."

"So he was an A-Team leader. So he was a Ranger with icing. So he was a Company man, specializing in dirty tricks. He ended up being a deputy director in the SII, and that makes him ending up a fat-ass, over-the-hill satrap—present company excepted, of course, ha-ha. But there is nothing special about Sweeney, no matter what the legend says. It's time we do ourselves a favor and prick the bastard's legendary balloon."

"Well, I've had some very expensive professionals on his case, and all they've managed to do is blow up his car and get themselves trashed. He may not be a legend, but he sure as hell is no sitting duck, either."

"Who's on him now?"

"Stiegel and Company, of Chester, P-A."

"They're a very capable group. They'll make short work of our Mr. Wonderful."

"Well, they've been on it two weeks now, and they haven't resolved things yet."

"Patience, my boy, patience. If it was easy you wouldn't need Stiegel. Or me, for that matter. Right?"

Richter was about to comment further, but a strange thing happened. Colt rolled out of his chair.

"Down—Get down, Richter—"

A nasty cracking filled the air directly beside his right ear, and he felt a blast of hot air and concussion. There was no thought—simply a reflex drop to the flagstones, the rattan furniture spinning and bouncing. Two snapping sounds rapped from the suppresser on the barrel of the automatic pistol Colt had drawn from the folds of his white suit, now smudged by his rolling in the flower bed.

Richter, terrified, stared wildly in the direction of Colt's shots, and as he watched, a man in a tuxedo stepped out of the shadows of a jasmine bed, peered thoughtfully at the two red dots on his otherwise-faultless shirtfront, then sank to his haunches. He sighed once, then rolled onto his back, his eyes blankly regarding the stars.

Colt glanced about, catlike. Then, concealing his pistol in the white suit, he rose and quickstepped to where the body lay. To Richter, he said, "You remember where I parked the car?"

"Stall Three."

Colt threw him a key ring. "Go get it. Bring it around to the driveway beside the fountain. I'll haul this turkey down the hill and have him waiting for you."

Richter finally discovered his voice. "Who is he?"

"Get the goddam car. Quick. Before somebody comes through this part of the garden."

"You know who he is?"

"Of course I know who he is."

"Who—"

"Hurry, damn you. Let's get this body out of here."

They managed to get the dead man, a youngish fellow with a thin black mustache and an obviously rented tux, into the trunk of Colt's Cadillac. Colt drove to a secluded stretch of road beside the sea and they both carried the body across the sugar white beach and gave it up to the gentle surf. They returned to the car and drove back to town under a moon darkened by a gathering overcast.

"All right, Colt. Who was he?"

"Tomas Rosada, a hit man for Jose Lomas, the top druggist in Cali."

"You know this for sure?"

"I know."

"Why did he try to kill us?"

"Not us. Me."

"How come?"

"Lomas, until just this week, was Corbato's last remaining partner. Three days ago, Lomas was hit, and now there's just Corbato. The Lomas people know I've been, ah, instrumental in Corbato's ascendency to the lonely top. This guy was sent to do a vengeance number on me and to remind Corbato they'll be looking for him, too."

"What's it all mean?"

"It means we have even less time than we thought."

CHAPTER 13

The attempted assassination required no change in plans. Colt had scheduled the meeting with Corbato in the management conference room of the recently completed El Mercado Mercantil because, beyond its futuristic opulence and commercial amenities, it offered excellent security. And this, he assured Richter, was precisely why Rosada had chosen the dark and exclusive gardens of the Banana Club for his try. There was no way the three of them could be similarly threatened in the penthouse offices of the Mercado—even without the platoon of plainclothes gunsels Corbato could be expected to deploy in and around the building.

Richter had been badly rattled by the experience. For Colt, bodies in the surf were a way of life; for Richter, a man who grew faint over a nosebleed, the incident had been relived a thousand times during a sleepless night. Like most who had risen to the top of his trade via staff desk work, he had seen violent death as an abstraction—a mere journalistic term for the ultimate grubbiness experienced by others. Moreover, he could arrange to shut down a problem individual in a train collision in West Gismo, read the headline announcing the consequent death of hundreds, scan the photo of crumpled steel, and then turn to the sports page, munching raisin toast on the way. But to hear the slap of a bullet, to feel the concussion and heat of its passage on your very own cheek—this was to have one's sense of personal exclusiveness and immortality shattered forever. The sudden understanding: *For me, too, time is finite. Temporary is indeed the word for man. This man.*

Once such a truth is acknowledged, all else can only be anticlimactic, as the meeting itself demonstrated.

Richter had traveled thousands of miles, at the expense of the American people and under the falsest of pretexts, to trade stares and words with one of the mightiest, cruelest, most implacable criminals in the contemporary world—being nearly shot to death en route. All in all, an adventure that could be expected to quicken the blood of even the most jaded. But now, on this overcast morning in an oceanside tourist trap, in the context of a near-death experience, the mission seemed insignificant and the crime lord as fearsome as Aunt Tillie's part-time gardener.

Corbato entered the room almost diffidently. He was a short, balding man with a tatty mustache, a receding chin and eyes like wet stones. He wore a smudged tan polyester blazer over rumpled sailcloth pants, a blue shirt buttoned at the throat, dirty white canvas deck shoes and no socks. He acknowledged Colt's introductions with a mere blink.

A living goddam doll, Richter thought dourly.

"Would you mind," Corbato said in soft English bearing only a slight Hispanic trace, "if I took the chair by the window? I like a high view of the city."

"Of course," Colt said, obsequious. "There are refreshments, too—"

"Nothing, thank you."

The liquid brown eyes, opaque, emotionless, studied the panorama beyond the plate glass at his elbow, first traversing the sea's gunmetal horizon, then settling on the busy plaza below. "So you," he said, still examining the traffic flow, "are Mr. Richter, the trusted agent of Brandon McKell, vice president of the United States."

Richter traded glances with Colt, who had taken a place on the sofa across the room, and who now gave the tiniest of go-ahead nods.

"We work together, yes."

"Are you here in Cartagena in his interests, or your nation's interests, or in your own, personal interests?"

"I hope that all three are the same."

"That was a tricky answer, Mr. Richter."

"That was a tricky question."

Richter knew, only too well, his own capacity for flying off the handle in the face of condescension, and here was one of those moments, occurring in conditions that were tense, portentous, and filled with danger. He knew he must, at all costs, keep his cool. He must take no crap from this palm-tree Al Capone, but he must also not be belligerent about it.

The major problem was his special knowledge of Corbato's contempt for the Yankee.

Just three weeks earlier, in Cali, Corbato had assured elements of the Dega Group, in his soft little bank teller's voice, that he was weary of the North Americans' pompousness, their autocratic interventions, their swaggering through Central and South America. In the SII tapes he characterized the Yankee as a breed of arrogant ass that tolerates profligacy and gluttony and addiction among its own and then, when the discomfort runs too high, turns to brand others—to destroy others—as the cause of the difficulty. Corbato was, according to the tapes, sick unto death of the self-indulgent, self-satisfied, and self-congratulating imperialistic Yankee. Now, here in this room, it was his secret awareness of this attitude that worked heavily on Richter's already raveled nerves.

The brown stare came around to settle on Richter's silk necktie. "What is it you hope to accomplish this morning?"

"First," Richter said, "to confirm the basic agreement, which is that there will be only two spokesmen. More than two voices would quickly lead to confusion, a reduction in efficiency, a squabbling over turfs. My people have appointed me as their representative. It's our hope that you can, and will, do the talking for your, ah, industry."

Corbato sighed, a small sound, made a small movement of his shoulders. "The agreement is proving to be awkward and expensive to live by. As you know, simply to be here, to participate in this conversation, I have had to shut down the leadership cadres of seven segments of three cartels. In just this past month, I have seen to the, ah, early retirement of no less than Santos, Julio, Mendez and Jose—which is a major accomplishment."

"Indeed it is. But let's stop tiptoeing. The cartels in Medellín, Cali and Bogota have already been badly mauled, thanks to our combined efforts so far, both overt and clandestine, and now that those four have been taken out their leadership is demoralized and on the run. I must confirm my understanding that you are the sole remaining spokesman for the entire organization train, from individual farmers through the logisticians, the refiners, the shippers and pan-American distributor linkage, and that your acceptance of this deal is their acceptance of this deal. What I seek now is assurance that you have persuaded the remnants to accept the master plan, which grants complete control of the United States segment of the industry to the people I designate, and your personal participation in the settlement proceedings in Maryland at the end of the month."

Corbato sniffed: "My presence here is such assurance."

The sniff came close to pulling Richter's trigger. Over the years he had learned great respect for the decent, long-suffering, and hardworking people of Central and South America—gentle, amiable people who had endured centuries of pain at the hands of tinhorn tyrants. In his post-college years in Caracas and Lima he had found most of his one-on-one relationships with them—including even the most raggedy-ass peasants—to be marked by graciousness and wit. But collectively they seemed to have a curious, blind susceptibility to being led around by the nose, to shift this way or that when prodded by the swollen egos and senseless brutalities of creeps like this man here, who would grovel for the Yankee dollar, then whine about imperialism and fiefdoms and Yankee arrogance when they were expected to do something in return. This Corbato was a common murderer, and he'd be so rated in any nation on earth. It was difficult to sit in this lofty isolation and listen to the insolent sniffs of an individual who had caused more of those good people to be tortured and killed than anyone in recent times.

Well, forge on, Richter. Get off your soapbox and forge on. A social reformer you ain't.

"Which brings me to the second part of my mission here: to

narrow the gap between the amount you want for doing all this and the amount we're able to pay. And I emphasize the word 'able.' We have never disputed the amounts you cite as net income. I dare say we would be willing to pay that amount—even more—to accomplish our goals. But the fact remains, we have only so much money available for this thing and it falls short of what you are, ah, asking. So a key part of my mission is to see if there is any flexibility on your part."

Corbato stroked his thin mustache for a moment. Then he gave Richter one of his rare direct stares. "You say the upper limit of your applicable budget is thirty billion?"

"Twenty-nine billion."

"I remind you that, even in this falling market, my industry is grossing in excess of five hundred billion."

"I'm aware of that. But we are not talking industry gross. We are talking profit from the North American segment of your business. The amount left after all expenses, all overhead have been met. And it's readily apparent even to us, ah, Yankee outsiders, that these out-of-pocket expenses absorb incredible sums, all of them drawn directly from your industry's gross."

"The money you pay me, Mr. Richter, must in no way detract from U.S. foreign aid sums already being delivered—or promised—for social programs, legitimate agricultural subsidies, and so on. Your payment to me and, through me, to my clients, is clear and free, received without further accountability or political responsibility."

"Understood."

"Payable, on settlement at our projected Maryland meeting, directly to me in a lump sum."

"The lump sum aspect is what's been giving us a problem. It's extremely difficult to pass twenty-nine billion in cash clandestinely. We think we have that worked out now."

"But you must work it out for thirty-five billion. Not twenty-nine. Thirty-five."

"Thirty-five billion, to be divided among four men."

"Three men. You forget the shutdown of Jose."

Richter glanced across the room. Colt rolled his eyes, then gave a reluctant nod.

"And that buys us—"

"Complete control of the U.S. segment of my business."

"We have a deal, then?"

There was an interval in which the only sounds in the room were those rising from the traffic below.

Corbato shrugged and confirmed. "We have a deal."

They stood and shook hands. Richter said, "I've been asked to extend to you our sincerest thanks for the cooperation you and your industry have extended to us so far. We believe that both interests—your and ours—have benefited to a highly satisfactory degree. We want you to know we appreciate your contributions."

Corbato, showing a faint smile, demonstrated his talent for surprise. He said, "No doubt you have heard all the wicked things I've said about your nation and its people, Mr. Richter. That is the way of politics in these parts. But to you I apologize. As you no doubt know, I have spent many years in the United States, as student and as businessman. And, while many of my negative criticisms have been true, they are nonetheless far overshadowed and outnumbered by the attributes I've come to admire in your people."

Richter found he had nothing to say to this.

As they made their way to the parking center, Richter felt Colt's sidelong glance.

"Something bothering you, Colt?"

"What the hell happened to you in there?"

"I don't know."

"I mean, here's the deal of the frigging century, a deal we've been setting up for a year and a half, a deal that's going to make you and McKell and Corbato and me four of the world's richest men, and you not only make a last-minute try to knockdown agreed-on price, you also act as if you're doing Corbato a frigging favor to be in the same room with him."

"We got our deal, didn't we? So what's the problem?"

"Nobody, but nobody, treats Manuel Corbato like he's a subhuman creep—"

"I do. Because he is."

"You don't like him because he's trafficking in drugs? Well, hell, buster, don't get so choked up. After all, you're trafficking in drugs, too."

"To me there's a difference."

"What the hell's going on with you, for crissake?"

"I told you: I don't know."

CHAPTER 14

Richard D. Leonardi, being an incurable idealist, was uncomfortable in the Oval Office. The room was so majestic, so evocative of epochal events, so elegantly symbolic of the American continuum, that he felt vaguely offended by the idea of using it as a part-time political headquarters and campaign countinghouse. In his mind, factional scheming in such a hallowed place suggested a kind of defilement—Boss Tweed setting up shop in Independence Hall—so he took care to compartmentalize his binary responsibilities, doing his chief executive thing in the traditional rooms and confining party chores to the Roosevelt Map Room, the small, tastefully furnished chamber that had served variously since the 1800s as a cloakroom, a powder room, a Secret Service lounge, a wartime chart room and, as it was now, a kind of hideaway and study.

At the moment he was slumped in the Map Room's leather wing chair, brogans propped on an antique hassock, a yellow legal pad on his lap, and a leaden fatigue behind his eyes. Jenny Malone, his chief of staff, was on the sofa, expounding, in her clipped New England way, on the House leadership's drive to blunt the presidential initiatives in the drug war and then to step in and appropriate the accumulating successes as the majority party's own.

"No doubt about it, Mr. President: the drug thing will decide the next election. You've been making fairly good marks in some of the key domestic areas, true enough—educational reform, the value-added tax thing, nursing home subsidies lead the list—and you've been able to establish yourself pretty well as a savvy, cautious operator in the foreign policy arena. But it's the drug thing that preoccupies the voters, and it's where you're really beginning to shine—and we've got to do whatever has to be done to protect the gains you've made there. Pete Laubeck and Phil O'Malley are quite open about the importance they attach to drugs as the pivotal issue at the upcoming conventions, and they're marshalling the potshotters on their side of the aisle to blow you and your program out of the saddle, as it were." She coughed delicately and flipped a page in her notebook. "In the Senate—"

Leonardi sighed and waggled a hand. "Hey, Jenny, have a heart. We've been at this for twenty minutes now and you've essentially been saying the same thing the whole time. I get it, pal, I *get* it: I'm doing so well at the drug thing that it can get me reelected, and the Speaker and the Majority Leader are trying to see that that doesn't happen."

"Well—"

"I've been watching Pete and Phil, and they're very muscular, sure as hell. But so are we. I think that, with the polls heavily favorable to us and the Senate's willingness to continue its support for our drug program in exchange for our support for its task force on energy alternatives, Pete and his people are pumping mud."

Jenny shrugged. "Today, Mr. President. Today. But the conventions are nine, ten months off—an eternity. If it's all the same to you, I plan to keep plugging on ways and means to wind up the drug war before the conventions and convince the people that the credit's all yours."

"That won't be so easy if the people start listening to Randolph Ridenour."

"You mean his commentary yesterday?"

"He was very hard on my support of General Wallace and use of non-Regular troops. He thinks our sidelining of the Regulars not only exacerbates the armed forces morale problem but also is a transparent scheme to get paychecks to all those unemployed Guardsmen and Reservists and thereby boost Governor Gomez's political popularity. And he says General Wallace is an amateur, a dilettante, a boob who wouldn't amount to bean breeze if it weren't for the inspired advice and counsel he gets from Vice President McKell, the real brain behind our drug war successes."

Jenny sniffed. "Well, he's wrong on the morale thing and right on the Gomez thing. And since you assigned the drug war supervision to him, the vice president has been doing exceptionally well with it. General Reynolds is quite lavish in his praise—his public praise—of the leadership Brandon has brought to the mix. So how does that change the lie of our ball, Mr. President?"

"Many more voters listen to Ridenour than to General Reynolds, Jenny. Ridenour says I'm prolonging the drug war simply to help Gomez, a political ally, and that I'd be in deep doodoo if it weren't for Brandon McKell. If people start believing that—"

"All the more reason, Mr. President, why we should wrap up the drug thing as soon as possible. Even though Ridenour is the world's silliest ass, people do listen to him. And altogether too many of them think he knows what he's talking about. We'll have to admit, too, that such rave notices out of Ridenour deliver a heavy counterblow to all those media funny-boys who are giving Brandon such a hard time. Brandon's a good man, and Ridenour's raves and Brandon's very real contributions can appreciably strengthen our ticket next time around."

Leonardi gave her a tired glance. "Are you sure you and McKell can handle it? Do you need more help or anything?"

"No, Mr. President, you can leave the whole matter to me. I think the record shows that I know what I'm doing. I've mobilized all the drug war forces and put them to work in the best, least costly way possible under your vice president's management. Just continue to give me a free hand—make me your implementer—and we'll put egg all over the faces of the Laubecks and the O'Malleys. And we'll play the Ridenours like barroom pye-annas."

"Every day I realize more and more how lucky I am to have you around, Jenny."

"We go back a long way, Mr. President. And as far as I'm concerned—if I have anything to say about it—I'll be around for some time to come."

Jenny returned the notes to her briefcase and stood up. "I'll keep you tuned in on the House push-and-pull. And please don't fret about Ridenour. The drug war's all but over, and he'll be pumping mud, too."

Leonardi, already deep into the brief on another issue, shooed her out with an amiable flip of his hand.

Like the Oval Office, Jenny Malone made Leonardi uneasy, but for quite different reasons.

They had met in their salad days, when, as public relations trainees, they served as grunts in a regiment of lawyers and communications hotshots whose mission was to enhance the already excellent reputation of Exemplar Industries, a multi-product manufacturing corporation which even then boasted 214 plants and offices in a dozen nations. They were assigned to stateside company headquarters, and because they were fly-speck asteroids adrift among the PR department's quasars, they had only each other to lunch with. They found some common interests, traded *Mad* magazines and Virgil Parch cartoons, and, in inevitable reaction to the firm's resolute prissiness, became closet zanies whose crowning coup was to disrupt traffic in the executive men's room for an entire afternoon. Jenny acquired a female mannequin from a friend in an ad agency, and Leonardi surreptitiously placed it in such a way that the splendid calves, sheathed in nylons and shod with classy pumps, could be seen beneath the door of the director's favorite stall.

They were an unlikely pair. Jenny, for all her efforts to portray the sophisticated madcap, was in truth the stereotypical Boston prig. Worse, she would too often waver between pompousness and servility when in the adjacency of someone richer or higher in the ambient pecking order. But worst of all, she was brilliant, and, as one of the department nabobs once snapped, "She never tires of telling you so." In sum, she was the very kind of person Leonardi, an unequivocating realist, would ordinarily have worked hard to avoid.

Still, Leonardi had seen something poignant in Jenny's character—a kind of lonely, angry striving to escape the Brahminism in her maternal genes. Jenny didn't much like herself, Leonardi suspected, and was doing everything she could think of to make that fact more tolerable. And, in moments of deep, private honesty, Leonardi would admit that he was flattered by Jenny's open admiration; it was something, after all, for a second-generation American to be admired by the flower of a haughty family whose roots were in the Plymouth Colony itself.

So, partly out of pity, partly out of vanity, and partly out of the amiability generously endowed him by his Neapolitan forebears, Richard Leonardi, future president of the United States, became a friend of Jennifer T. Malone, and Jenny proved over the long haul to be a loyal and gifted personal advisor, aide, confidant, and gofer.

Jenny, resolutely single, lived in a house inherited from her grandmother and joined every civic club in sight while ascending the company's community relations ladder. But Leonardi, a second lieutenant in the Army Reserve, thanks to ROTC and some summer encampments, was invited to the Viet Nam gala, where, much to his own surprise, he rose rapidly to become not only a lieutenant colonel but also a bona fide hero, complete with a green beret, medals, and superficial bullet wounds in the gluteus maximus.

So he had metamorphosed from the narrow-tie, button-down corporate yardbird into the basic successful warrior, and he'd become so proficient at the trade that he was commandeered by the CIA for some post-Nam clandestine spectaculars in Europe, which resolved nothing in the world order but did heap additional raves in his resume.

It was here that coincidence reared.

While on terminal leave, he revisited his old corporate haunts and in the course of things, renewed his oddball friendship with Jenny, who by then had a corner office with drapes and two secretaries and had sold the inherited house in favor of a hulking pseudo-Tudor on a horse country hilltop.

They were having a drink at Jenny's country club when somebody mentioned that the local congressional seat was up for grabs; the incumbent was too sick to run again, and a gaggle of aspirants had no discernible appeal or competence.

"Why don't you go for it, Jenny?" Leonardi had asked, tongue-in-cheek.

Instead of laughing, Jenny had said earnestly, "I've thought about it. I really have. Trouble is, I like politics, but I don't have that something it takes to get elected to anything. It takes somebody like you."

Leonardi had scoffed. "Hell, I don't even live here."

"Oh, yes, you do. You never left. You kept this town as your permanent address. I know. I checked."

"You checked? Why?"

"For precisely this reason."

"Are you out of your frigging melon? I don't even like congressmen. Why should I want to be one?"

"For precisely that reason. You don't like them because you think they're not doing what they ought to be doing. Well, here's your chance to show them how it should be done. Besides, you're an ex-GI who needs a job."

"You are certifiably mad, Jenny Malone—"

"Maybe. But you are certifiably electable. A handsome war hero with a splendid Exemplar Industries background and medals and citations and bullet holes—"

"In his ass, Jenny. In his ass. How would *that* look in promos and posters, for crissake."

"Tell you what: get yourself an apartment downtown and I'll whomp up a campaign organization—gather some money for signs and promos and like that—and we'll file you as an independent and we'll *steal* that goddam seat. What say?"

"Why are *you* so fired up about all this?"

"Because I've got a snooty mother who resents me for not being a son she could see become president of the U.S. of A. In her Victorian eyes, the presidency is the height of respectability for man and family. So I tick her off, and she's always at me to make something of myself."

"Are you serious? You, your job, your house already look like a center spread in *Gotrocks Quarterly.*"

"Putting you in Congress and being your Washington strawboss would suggest to my dear, status-loving mother that her only child might not be a turnip after all."

"Shee-it."

"Come on, Rick—Let's do it."

"What if we lose?"

"We can't lose."

"I said, what if we lose?"
"Then Mother will have a stroke."
"Sounds like a good case for losing, to me."
"Hell, man, she's got all the money. Two hundred mill, inherited from her old man. You don't think I could live like this on the salary I make at Exemplar, do you?"
"I'll admit I wondered about that."
"Come on, Rick. Let's go to Washington."

And they did.
Three terms in the House, then election to the Senate.
A major party adoption, a debilitating economic recession, voters hungry for somebody new to lead them out of the wilderness, heavy-duty PAC support, his own left-of-center do-gooder idealism, a profile that looked good on billboards, a grin that played great on TV, a convention compromise, and *zap,* he was America's Main Man.
But Jenny Malone had changed.
She was no longer—likeable.
He suspected it had to do with Brandon McKell.
McKell, like everything else in this grotesque business, had derived from an expedient compromise.
The party's right wing, led by Frederick L. Randall, the archconservative real estate tycoon from North Florida, was suspicious of Leonardi's admitted openness to liberal ideas. Leonardi needed a bridge, a solid link between his own broad interpretation of the role of government, and the huge vote that inhabited the American underbelly and cherished the traditional values, from bubba trucks with enormous tires to white-columned mansions and minimal reliance on legislative solutions. The obvious answer was to find a running mate with an established conservative record who, as vice president, would represent the ballast to keep the Leonardi balloon from careening off on the liberal breezes generated by the House and Senate majorities.
Jenny and Abe Goldman, the national party chairman, had first suggested Randall himself, not only because he personified the conservative stance but also because he was a Floridian—a fact that promised heavy Leonardi support among the very vocal and burgeoning core of the senior citizen and Hispanic

votes. But Leonardi, who had a personal dislike of Randall and was repelled by such blatant kowtowing, insisted on a more subtle selection. Next up was William Logan, CEO of a Houston-based fast-food chain, as rich as Croesus, a lavish donor to the party's coffers, and widely recognized as "an enlightened conservative," a term coined by Randolph Ridenour on one of his "Sundown Symposium" things. Leonardi was tempted, but the senior vote was an attractive lure, as was the heavy-duty Hispanic influence shaping up in the Sun Belt, and so Brandon McKell was chosen.

A Jacksonville lawyer with a number of Florida legislative and appointive posts under his belt, McKell was a darling of the elderly and was said to have a wide network of influential friends in Central and South America. He was only middle-class wealthy, and therefore acceptable to the blue-collar vote. As icing on the cake, he had masterminded the election of conservative Miamian Jose Gomez to the Florida governorship. Four negatives: (1) McKell was virtually unknown outside Florida, (2) McKell had about as much personal charisma—read TV camera presence—as as a fire hydrant, (3) rumors, none substantiated, had McKell hobnobbing with members of the Miami–New York mob axis, and (4) Gomez had stolen the governorship from the incumbent, John Van Tanz, who was the brother-in-law of Randolph Ridenour.

A fifth negative, in Leonardi's eyes, was a severe problem: while all the party hotshots thought McKell as Leonardi's running mate was a brilliant compromise, Richard D. Leonardi though it was pure crap.

The fact was, he didn't like McKell. It was strictly visceral, from the moment of their meeting. Since McKell had given him no logical reason to feel this way, he had bent over backwards to get along with the man.

After the election, he had kept McKell at a distance, giving him all the usual ceremonials and the bread-and-butter chores, and asking Jenny first to filter and then to shunt to McKell all incoming stuff that involved party politics and/or domestic issues related to specific platform planks or campaign promises. "Have him handle them, Jenny," he'd instructed, "and then have him write me a weekly status report on what he believes to be the major ones. We'll lunch—it's important that he feels welcome here and has access to the president—and he can bring the reports to me then."

All of which put Jenny into a close working relationship with McKell.

And which had changed her. Instead of her having made McKell more likeable, as he'd hoped, McKell had made her more unlikeable.

He rubbed his eyes again and yawned. Aloud, he said, "There's always something to be uneasy about, buddy-boy."

CHAPTER 15

Dr. Oscar Schwenke, chief of weapons development under the DOD's Director of Defense Research and Engineering, made his home on the upscale side of Annapolis. His house was wide and low-slung, with generous slopes of shake-shingle roof, fat chimneys, cutesy windows bracketed by rustic shutters, and a broad lawn made mysterious by mature maples and expensive shrubbery. Its size and mood proclaimed that those who lived here were people of clout and substance, by God, and were not to be messed with (deliveries to the rear, please). Sweeney, arriving at sunrise, drove past it twice, first to check the general atmosphere, then to select a parking spot on the driveway where the van would be fairly well screened from the street.

He pulled into a turnaround walled by forsythia, shut off the motor, and, alighting, checked the doors. Freddie had loaned him the van with the provision that he would keep things fastened tight at all times; the rear hatch lock had been sprung, a legacy of the scumbags who had stolen the radio and radar detector during the last North East Water Festival.

Sweeney went to the side door and tapped lightly on the glass. He stood for a time, admiring a pair of cardinals splashing in the birdbath. He was about to tap again when the door was opened by Schwenke himself.

"Tom! What—Well, I'll be damned."

"Hi, Doc. It's been awhile, eh?"

"God, yes." Schwenke, his vest unbuttoned, his necktie hanging untied, a bandage plastered atop his bald head, waved his newspaper toward the kitchen. "Come in, come in. I was just having coffee before going to work. Want some?"

"Sure do. What's with the bandage?"

"A flatiron fell off a closet shelf, banged me a good one. No big deal."

"How's the missus?"

"First rate. She's visiting her sister in Denver this week. She'll be madder'n hell that she missed you."

Schwenke, a big man, narrow of face, with soft gray eyes magnified by his horn-rimmed glasses, carried a tray to the breakfast table, where he cleared away some crumpled beer cans, a dish full of peanut shells, and an empty whiskey bottle. He dumped the lot in a trash can in the pantry and returned to wave Sweeney to a chair in the sunny nook.

Schwenke poured the coffee, and they both sipped experimentally. The smell of stale beer persisted.

"How's Bert?"

"Great. He's doing high tech in Silicon Valley. Getting fat and rich. He'll be coming east for Thanksgiving."

"Tell him hi."

"Sure."

"You're wondering what I'm doing here at this weird hour. Right?"

Schwenke laughed softly. "Right."

"And you've heard I'm out of government, I suppose."

"It was all over the tube, the papers." Schwenke waited, his face a study in polite, restrained curiosity.

"I need to borrow your influence in high places, Doc."

"Like how?"

"I have a hardware shopping list. Things I have to scrounge for a special thing I'm doing."

"You mean weapons? Electronics?"

Sweeney nodded and sipped some more coffee.

"Well," Schwenke said, his gaze suddenly oblique, "I have to admit to some—confusion. If you're no longer in government, how can you—I mean, why would you, ah, want the use of GI stuff?"

"I'm not really out of government."

Schwenke's enlarged eyes showed instant comprehension. "Ah. The old intelligence razzle-dazzle." His hand traced an imaginary headline in the air. " 'War hero, pretending to be fired from spy post, goes undercover on secret mission.' "

"Something like that."

"So this shopping list has to be off the record, right?"

"Yep. Vouchers, memorandum receipts, all paper of any kind, fuzzied up and classified to the hilt."

"Hm. Dicey. There are checks and balances. Slow as hell, often inscrutable, but they're there."

"I know."

"Let me see your list."

Sweeney pulled the sheet from his jacket pocket and laid it on the table. Schwenke studied it for a time, his large eyes unblinking.

"Tall order."

"I'm afraid so, yes. Sorry to spring it on you like this, but things are moving pretty fast."

Schwenke humphed. "In your line of work it's never slow. It's always, 'Let me have it yesterday.' "

"Yeah."

"How much time can you give me?"

"Let me have it yesterday."

"It's going to take some setting up, Tom. I'll have to bury it in paper and computer smog. And, as you know, I'm not directly at the door of this closet. I have to slip this past an assistant director and a couple of supers. I can't just open the door, say he'p yo'se'f, then cover it with paper after the fact."

"How long do you think it will take?"

"Can you give me until the day after tomorrow? That's Thursday. Around noon, say?"

"Where should I pick it up?"

"All of this stuff is in various Fort Meade warehouses. I'll have it gathered and transshipped to the Humboldt Research Center on Thursday afternoon. You can make an intercept anywhere between that suits you."

"When it doesn't show up at Humboldt—"

"That's what paper and smog are all about. One manifest goes out at Meade, another is handed to the receiving foreman at Humboldt. The discrepancy won't be noticed for weeks—if past experience is any measure. Also going for us is the fact that your order, compared to the size of the shipments that usually travel between those locations, is infinitesimal."

"How about the truck crew?"

"They'll be guys who work for me. They'll be told to expect your intercept. What will you be driving?"

"That motheaten blue van out there behind your bushes."

Schwenke glanced out the window, craned for a better view, then smiled. "Motheaten is polite."

"I'll call you here tomorrow night to tell you what route the truck crew should follow. Okay?"

"Sure. I'm usually home by six."

"I'll also need a letter signed by you, Doc."

"Oh?" Concern showed briefly in the big man's eyes.

"You can seal it in an envelope and have the truck driver give it to me at the intercept."

"What should it say?"

" 'To Commanding Officer'—or whoever you think might suit—'of Aberdeen Proving Ground: The bearer is a representative of this office, currently assigned to a highly classified investigation, and it is respectfully requested that he be given every assistance. Should you have any questions about him and his mission, please call the undersigned directly, using Scrambler Code So-and-So.' "

"You're going to visit Aberdeen?"

"Yep."

"But what if the man calls? What do I say?"

Sweeney smiled faintly. "Just lay it on, Doc, and hide behind the Top Secret schmooz whenever you have to. Make me sound like Sean Connery."

"All right. Anything else?"

"Just one thing: Forget we've had this conversation. If you get in a crack over this stuff, blame it on your department's computer links. Or, if it gets really hairy, lay it on me. Say I held a pistol to your head. I can't be in more trouble than I am already."

"No sweat. Stuff's being lost all the time. That's the best thing about computers. They don't talk back when you blame them for screwups."

Sweeney pushed away from the table and stood up, holding out his hand. "You know how much I appreciate this, Doc."

"I told you before: All you ever need to do is ask."

"Hey—This doesn't have anything to do with Bert. This is something that—"

"Give me a break, Tom. You don't think for a minute that I buy that crap about your being on a secret mission, do you? So you're in some kind of trouble and need a little help. So I'm glad you came to me. It's the least I can do for a guy who dragged my machine-gunned son out of a rice paddy."

"And I told you before: You don't owe me anything. Bert would've done the same for me."

"I like to think so. Bert can be a huge pain in the ass at times. As his C.O., you must have known that. But he's a good kid, and he's mine, and you gave him back to me."

"Well, I have to go now. I'll call you about the intercept."

"Take care of yourself, hear?"

As he returned to the van, Sweeney's mind was busy with speculations, denials, guesses, denials, hopes, denials, and a general sense of uneasy confusion. All of which stemmed from the interval in which Dr. Schwenke had busied himself with the trash. Sweeney's gaze had followed Schwenke into the adjacent butler's pantry, a mellow and very expensive collection of woods and polished metals whose theme was cheeriness brought through the courtesy of off-white and light blue enamels. And there, at the extreme left end of the cheery cabinetry in the cheery pantry, was the built-in storage cabinet whose photo had been in the late Hank Nageler's wallet.

He headed for The District on Route 50, then drove the Beltway to Alexandria, where he went up Route 1 to a left that put him on Mount Vernon Avenue and eventually at the would-be Colonial building that housed the law offices of Lou Simon. Parking was impossible there, so he put the van in a garage and walked the two blocks back.

Brenda Larimore was at the reception desk, as usual, half hidden behind the stacks of papers piled around her like legal-size sandbags. And, as usual, she appeared to be mightily displeased with what she was reading.

"Hi, Brenda. I came to get my new checkbook and to look in on Lou. Is he in?"

Her blue eyes widened behind their huge glasses, and her frown gave way to a mixture of surprise and amusement. "As I live and wheeze. Mr. Simon's in New York today. But if this isn't a coincidence—Were your ears burning this morning?"

"Something was burning, but it wasn't my ears. Why?"

She leaned across the paper piles and squinted conspiratorially. "The *Washington Post* is looking for you. 'Seeking an interview,' the man said."

"Oh? Why did he come here?"

"He said he'd been trying to get you at your home, but no dice. He said he learned we were your legal representatives and thought we might know where you were."

"What did you tell him?"

"That we haven't seen you for months and have no idea where he can get hold of you." She chortled. "Which is no lie, sure enough."

"Did he have a name?"

She glanced at her log book. "Armand Francisco."

"Did he show you his press ID?"

"Yes indeedy."

"Did it have his picture on it?"

Her smile faded slightly. "Well, no. It didn't. Why? What's with the questions?"

"Armand Francisco is a sports writer who was badly bunged up when he was hit by a car last spring. He's still in a Silver Spring nursing home."

Brenda's face showed confusion. "You know this?"

"I'm a fan of his."

"Then who—"

"What did the man look like?"

"Small, wiry. Thick eyebrows. Dark eyes that—"

"Moved around a lot? Took in everything else while he was talking to you?"

"You got it. You know him?"

"Only by the name of Cummings. And then he was pretending to be a detective."

"Sh-o-o-oot. Did I do wrong?"

"You did exactly right."

"Whew."

"My John Meyers checkbook: Do you have it yet?"

"Sure do. Came in yesterday afternoon." She stood up and went to a file cabinet, where she rummaged in a drawer. "Ah. Here we are. Checkbook and some junk mail I picked up this morning from your P.O. box."

He fingered through the mail, then threw it into Brenda's wastebasket. Slipping the checkbook into his jacket pocket, he asked, "Could I use one of your phones, Brenda? Where I can talk sort of privately?"

"Sure. Use Mr. Simon's office. You want some coffee?"

"No, thanks."

He went down the short corridor, through the highly polished door and into Simon's office, a large room with high ceilings, thick carpeting, polished mahogany and floor-to-frieze bookcases. In contrast with Brenda's foxhole, Lou's desk area was a glistening expanse of wood whose only clutter was an elaborate phone set, a brace of pens in a sterling base, a notepad, and a banker's lamp with pull chain. He sat in the large leather swivel chair and punched up the German embassy.

"Mr. Kratzer, please."

The woman's voice was soft, friendly. "May I tell him who's calling, sir?"

"Armand Francisco, of the *Washington Post*."

"Thank you, sir. One moment, please."

There was a click, then a tiny pause.

"This is the public information attaché's office. Bernhardt Kratzer speaking."

"Tom Sweeney, Bernie. How are you?"

Krazter was a Heidelberger with a total command of the American idiom. "Tom Sw—where the hell have you been? I've been turning this frigging town upside down, looking for you. And what's with the Armand Francisco crap? He's sacked out in Silver Spring with a busted whoosis."

"You know him?"

"Not personally. Sports writers rarely call the embassy. But for my money, he's the best in town."

"You got anybody using his name?"

Kratzer laughed. "Hey, Sweeney—give me a break. I like to think I'm a bit more subtle than that."

"Just thought I'd ask."

"We've got to talk. I've really been looking for you. Very hard. Everywhere."

"Why?"

"I can't tell you on the phone. Where can we meet?"

"The Loose Goose."

"That dingy little watering hole?"

"Three o'clock."

He hung up and went to the reception area, where he blew a kiss and said, "Thanks, Brenda. You're a good soldier. Say hi to Lou for me."

"Sure will. Need anything else?"

"You don't happen to have your paste-on mustache with you, do you?"

She lowered her brows and darted glances from side to side. "No. It's my sister's turn to wear it today."

"Well, then, I'll just bare-face it."

"I'm glad. It's a very nice face."

"Remember: I don't do interviews."

She laughed. "I'll never forget it, Mr. Meyer."

"Meyers."

He retrieved the van from the parking garage and drove through The District to the Loose Goose.

"Hello?"

"Oscar Schwenke, calling as you asked."

"So?"

"Your hunch was right. He came to see me this morning."

"He was after hardware, I presume."

"Yes."

"Did he mention where he was living? Where he'd be taking the hardware?"

"No."

"All right. Keep in touch. I want to know everything he says and does."

"I don't feel very good about this. He's a friend."

"Life can be cruel, Schwenke."

CHAPTER 16

It was one of those neighborhood taverns that smell of old beer and new Lysol, where a tiny TV winks unheeded on a shelf above the backbar and where the bartender rubs tall glasses with a towel and stares out the window, remembering some kind of good old days. A woman in her fat fifties sat at the far end of the bar, sipping whiskey and reading a racing form. Two lovers, holding hands, traded whispers across a corner table. Both had beards.

At 3:02 Bernie came through the door, took off his sunglasses and stood there in his eight-hundred-dollar suit, blond and Teutonic, blinking into the gloom. Eventually he saw Sweeney and, after pausing at the bar to order a plain soda with a twist, joined him in the back booth.

"God, Sweeney, couldn't you pick a better place than this?"

"The Senate dining room is booked until Easter."

"What's with you, anyhow? I saw all the publicity on your leaving government and then, poof, you disappeared."

"Some people are trying to kill me. It wouldn't be you people, would it?"

Kratzer gave him a lingering stare. "Are you joking?"

"You don't see me laughing, do you?"

"Aside from the fact I like you and would hate the idea of causing you personal damage, I wouldn't kill you for an even more powerful reason."

"What would that be?"

"I need you."

It was Sweeney's turn to stare. "Now there's a droll idea."

"I'm serious—" Kratzer waited while the bartender ambled to the table with the soda and twist. When they were alone again, he completed the sentence. "—I'm serious about wanting to talk to you. Something heavy is moving, and my government wants to know what it is. I think you might help me get at it."

"Why me?"

"First, you have proved your reliability and determination many times over. Even our oldest hands say they can't remember working with an American who was more, ah, trustworthy. You watch out tirelessly for American interests, but when you cooperate, you cooperate."

"That's first. Is there a second?"

"Second, a strong anti-German sentiment is evident among the Americans today—especially in some sectors of the government. But you've never shown that you go along with the idea that all Germans are ungrateful wretches who are preparing to sabotage the world order. As a people we're not perfect by any means, but you seem to understand that our imperfections are the same imperfections everybody has, and you're willing to give us a chance to prove ourselves."

Sweeney held up a cautionary hand. "Hold on, pal. Before you get too gooey, I got to tell you: I'm not all that impressed with German reliability."

Kratzer's Nordic eyes narrowed. "Oh? Why?"

"I've had one of your cars for only twelve years and have driven it a measly quarter of a million miles, and what happens? One lousy little bomb, and it falls apart."

Kratzer's wariness turned into incredulous amusement. Shaking his head, he said, "Still the same old Sweeney, eh? I'm laying a superproblem on you and you make jokes."

"What's funny about a car coming apart?"

"Do you want to hear the problem?"

Sweeney shrugged. "Why not?"

Kratzer sipped his drink, made a face, and returned the glass to the table. "Have you," he asked slowly, "ever heard of 'die Pilze'?"

"Ah, yes, 'The Mushrooms.' Said to be a group of neo-Nazi businessmen that originated in Munich and has since spread through Greater Germany. Said to be headed up by the German everybody loves to hate, Hugo von Zoll, ace of industrial aces. Rumors only, nothing ever proved."

Kratzer nodded. "There's a lot of flame behind the smoke. Die Pilze, rumors notwithstanding, are becoming a royal pain to the German government. Chancellor Haussener is especially concerned about the way von Zoll and his consortium are moving into Siberia and other Asian oil centers—altogether legally, under bona fide contracts with the pertinent governments—and are positioning themselves to become the autocratic overseers of some of the world's largest undeveloped petroleum production and distribution sources. The wealth they stand to realize from that, coupled with their reputed long-term plans to elect a majority to the Bundestag and to infiltrate the civil service, will soon give them de facto control of Germany's legislature, its administrative bureaucracy and its technical infrastructure."

Sweeney took a pretzel from the bowl on the table and munched slowly, thinking.

"The world can't afford another Nazi government, Sweeney. It's already got a couple of fairly heavy-duty ones in the Middle East, several lightweights in Central and South America. But another Nazi Germany would tear it."

Sweeney gave him a wary look. "So what do you want of me? You guys in the Nachrichtendienst, in the German state police, in your slab of Interpol—hell, you're pros. You can break them up."

Kratzer shook his head. "That's just it. We haven't anything to nail them with. They always stay within German law. Under the law, they're allowed to politick. Under the law, they're allowed to meet and assemble. And so on."

"How about illicit manufacture and export of arms and war materiel? I hear they've been doing a bit of that."

"They're too cute to have a paper trail or an overt organization. No solid evidence. They learned to go carefully on that score after a couple of them were scorched for sending poison gas fixings to Iraq in the Gulf War. Everything they do these days, in terms of law, may really be garbage, but it's labeled perfume."

Sweeney sighed. "They'll make a bad move, make some kind of mistake sooner or later. All you have to do is wait and watch, then spring, break them up and send their leaders off to jail."

Kratzer sniffed. "Sounds easy enough, doesn't it. But we've been doing that for years and have come up with crumbs. They're like the Mafia: they're there, and they're crooks, but we can't legally get at them. We can't legally destroy their structure and power."

"So I ask again: What do you want me to do about it?"

Kratzer took a pretzel for himself. "They're up to something here in the States. We want you to help us find out what that something is. And if it's illegal in any way—if they can be proved to be violating any laws, American or German—we'll have them."

"How in hell can I do that? I'm out of government and virtually on the lam. What could I do that your legion of Nachrichtendienst agents aren't already doing?"

"The first thing you can do is agree to help me—us."

"Then what?"

"Come on, Sweeney. You've been in The Trade long enough to figure something out. Use your sources. Pull a trick or two. Hell, I don't have to educate you."

Sweeney did some more thinking, then asked the big one. "Why should I risk my buns for Greater Germany? What's Greater Germany going to do for me?"

"Ah, the good part. All equipment provided, all expenses paid. A flat fee of one million dollars in tax-paid cash—or its equivalent in whatever currency you name. Renegotiable, with provisions for a bonus, as a carrot for extra effort, or for extraordinary results."

"Who decides I'm worth all those bonuses and things?"

"I do. You will be working directly for me."

Sweeney asked, "When do you have to know?"

"Right now. A yes or no."

"How do you know I won't take what I know and sell it to the other people? The wrong people?"

Kratzer smiled. "It's a matter of character, of course. My

reading of your character says you are not likely to do that. You are basically an honest man."

"Still—"

"Let's put it this way: If you were to double on us, you'd pay the double's price. To the Nachrichtendienst, non-German agents are readily expendable."

"Like Hank Nageler?"

Kratzer's handsome face grew deeply serious. "You're not laying that trip on us, are you?"

"His possession of a Jagdmeister 500 made it an easy guess."

"Nageler was not working for us. But, even more emphatically, he did not get a 500 from us. We would never, ever, trust him with a 500. In fact, we were flabbergasted when we learned that he'd had a copycat set. It confirmed our suspicion that the plans had been stolen by you people."

"Why did you have Cummings kill Nageler?"

Kratzer shot him a quick, puzzled glance. "Cummings?"

"Cummings and Ames aren't your people?"

"I know no Cummings. No Ames."

"Scout's honor?"

"And I have no idea who killed Nageler. That's one of the things we expect you to find out. I didn't want Nageler dead—I wanted to interrogate him, for God's sake."

Sweeney smiled. "Cummings, eh?"

"Who *is* Cummings?"

"It's my guess you'll find him somewhere in your files. But, whoever he is, he's the dude who has persuaded me to accept your job offer."

CHAPTER 17

Richter hated late-lunch restaurants like this. High ceilings, drapes, filtered light. White linen, glittering silverware. A string ensemble, muttering show tunes. Pudgy men in dark suits and narrow neckties with tall, bored girls on their arms, waiting among the potted plants at the maitre d' station for permission to spend sixty dollars for two ounces of gin, two slivers of tasteless meat, two leaves of lettuce and four slices of dry bread—coffee or tea extra. Waiting to nourish, not their persons, but their personas, for the management, via exclusionary prices, a snooty ambience and a thorough understanding of the human ego, had fostered the illusion that only the rich and powerful broke bread here. Conversely, if one broke bread here, he must be assumed to be rich and powerful.

Thus the place was a salt lick in the Washington jungle, a capital-city game trap, made-to-order for those political and media predators who specialized in the snaring and exploitation of sycophants, climbers and snobs.

Ridenour sat facing the corner window, where his permanently reserved table was positioned so as to allow not only diners but also passing pedestrians to catch a thrilling glimpse of television's pope on those several days a week he granted audiences here. The guest chair was mobile; it would be placed according to the visitor's renown, with superstars and household words seated with their backs to the rubberneckers (thereby reducing chances that the guest might upstage the host) and with lesser lights and starlets deposited wherever their glowing delight at being in the presence of god would further illuminate the throne.

Richter decided that he must be one of the least of the lesser lights, since his chair was nearly side-saddle to Ridenour's. And (the afterthought ran) he must also be a disappointment, since this was not one of his better days and he felt anything but radiant.

"What are you drinking, Richter?" Ridenour asked without enthusiasm.

"Nothing today, thanks. I'm on duty."

Both Ridenour and the waiter, a burly fellow who looked slightly silly in his tight red jacket, showed displeasure.

"There are no civilized souls in all of the capital—not even our semicivilized policemen—who pass the noon without some form of restoration simply because they are on duty, my friend." Ridenour nodded the waiter away.

"You've just met the exception."

Ridenour's pout turned to a smile as he waved to someone across the room. "Learn something every day," he said between his beautiful teeth. "Your duty doesn't disallow lunch, does it?"

"I don't make much of lunch, actually."

Ridenour sniffed. "That makes you a very odd and dull boy indeed. This town runs on booze and lunch."

"That's one of its main problems."

"Nevertheless, you have accepted my invitation."

"Of course. How often is an obscure civil servant asked to this fancy hotel for a fancy meal by one of the most renowned and influential men of all time? It's an occasion I'll be able to tell my grandchildren about."

Incredibly, Ridenour showed no signs of recognizing the sarcasm. Instead, he showed his gorgeous teeth again and waved a modest, dismissing hand. "I wouldn't say that you're obscure, Richter. You are the public face of one of our government's most faceless and most powerful agencies. You personify the official secrecy that the American people and their Constitution find so repugnant. Besides, if you were really obscure you wouldn't have been asked to join me here today. Eh? Ha-ha."

"Gosh, that's true. I hadn't looked at it that way."

One of the three phones on the side table warbled politely. Without apology, Ridenour picked it up and asked the mouthpiece, "What is it?"

Lagalagalaga.

Ridenour's gaze traveled about the huge room and settled on the nearest chandelier. "I can't come to New York tomorrow. Didn't you tell him that?"

Lagalagalaga.

"I don't care if he *is* the network boss. I can't have the whole day consumed by a ten-minute meeting in New York. Why doesn't he simply fax me a memo, or something?"

Lagalagalaga.

"All right. Yes. Yes. Eleven o'clock, his office." Ridenour returned the phone to its cradle, his face pink and unhappy. "Damn."

Richter, munching an olive, asked, "Problems?"

"What is it about people who think that, just because they're president and CEO, they can pick up a phone and order somebody around?"

"Power corrupts, they say."

"The man came up through airlines and chemicals. What does he know about television?"

"He's probably somebody's brother-in-law."

The waiter brought Ridenour's vodka martini and after an exploratory sip the commentator's expression softened. "Ah, sanctuary." Warming further, he gave Richter another smile. "You're undoubtedly wondering why I asked you to lunch."

"I'm sitting on some information you need, I suppose."

"That's quite astute of you."

"Well, you're a famous journalist, and I'm a famous sitter, and I sort of put things together."

"Ah, yes. Well, I've been working on a little probe into some things for a future program, and in the course of that investigation the name of Harvey M. Wallace kept popping up. He's chief of the UIF in Florida, and I thought you, as head of an agency that works closely with the military and the DEA, might be able to give me a line on him—material that doesn't appear in his official bios and *Who's Who* entries and like that."

"I know who he is, but I'm not really tuned in on his personal frequency. I'm sure he has many friends who know a lot more about him than I do."

"Have you met him? Talked to him?"

"Several times. Why? Haven't you?"

"I've met him."

"Then why don't you ask him directly? Why me?"

Ridenour took another reflective sip of his martini. "I need to go into confidential mode now. Can you handle that?"

"It's my main thing, confidentiality. As you have so bluntly pointed out."

"Mm. But this is a shade different." Ridenour glanced over his shoulder and lowered his voice. "This is press stuff. You know—investigative reporting."

"Oh, wow."

Ridenour's eyes narrowed. "Are you putting me on?"

Richter, realizing he'd overstepped, summoned up a disarming smile. "You were so serious I couldn't resist a little kidding. It's a fault that got me in trouble as far back as grammar school. I apologize."

"Well," Ridenour said, obviously unable to decide if he'd been offended, "what I meant was, I want you to step out of your government shoes for a moment and serve as confidential source in a story I'm working on. You will not be quoted, or identified. You will, however, be paid."

"I'm not so sure government ethics would allow that."

Ridenour sighed, the sound of impatience. "Please, Richter, give me a break. I know all about your, ah, expensive tastes."

"What's that supposed to mean?"

"I employ investigators who help me build files on prominent people, my dear spymaster. And my investigators have told me about the lovely Valerie Moran in Falls Church. The Maserati. The chalet at St. Johann. Et cetera, et cetera."

"I like girls, cars and skiing. Nothing unethical about that."

"There is when they're paid for with unreported income."

"I don't follow you."

"Don't be tiresome. I've acquired copies of your IRS returns for the past five years, and there is no way that you could afford to live the way you do on the income you report. You not only follow me, my dear spymaster, you now are fully aware that I have you by the balls."

"I know one thing: I'm now not liking you more than I disliked you a minute ago. And that was quite a bit."

Ridenour finished off the martini. At his eyebrow's signal, the waiter emerged from the potted underbrush with a replacement perched on his dime-size tray.

When the man had retired to his post out of earshot, Ridenour said, "Now this is what I want you to do. I want you to provide me with your agency's dossier on General Wallace. I also want copies of your agency's analyses of the neo-Nazi trends in Germany and the reports and recommendations it has made to the president on that matter. I also want whatever you have gathered and recommended on the subject of von Zoll's exploitation of Siberian oil fields."

"All of which is very classified—most of it top secret."

"How about that."

"If you publish such information it will cause great damage to the United States."

"Who said anything about publishing it? I told you I'm working on a story. I didn't say what the story is about. The information I want from you is straight research—backgrounding—that will help me to develop my story more thoroughly."

"Even so, it's illegal to give it to you. And the risk to me would be enormous."

"Ah, but the risk will be worth it. I am keeping your secret life secret, so to speak."

"You're blackmailing me, in other words."

"One could say that, I suppose."

"If I don't cooperate, you will sing, and I'll go to prison as a tax cheat."

"Precisely."

Richter gave this some thought, staring out the window at the passing crowds, drumming the tablecloth with the fingers of his right hand. "This will take some time, some setting up, you know."

"Of course. You have until five P.M. tomorrow to have the material on my desk. Have it delivered by courier."

Richter eased back his chair and stood up. "Ciao."

"You're leaving so soon?"

"As I say, I don't make much of lunch."

* * *

As the limousine pulled away from the curb and made for Georgetown, Richter took up the car phone and pressed the buttons for SII Documents Library.

"Documents. Whitney here."

"Whit, this is Richter. Put your phone on scrambler."

"Yes, sir. All ready, sir."

"I have evidence that somebody has tapped that phony income tax file I set up with the help of Pete Liggett over at IRS last year. Will you punch it up on your computer? I want the name of the somebody and the date they requested the file under the Public Official Disclosure Act."

"Hang on, sir. I'll have it in a sec."

The driver made a smooth, magic left through an impossible traffic tangle, and Richter took a moment to relish the perquisites that allowed him the luxury of a chauffeured limo with dark, bullet-proof windows. *God, but it's good to* be *somebody . . .*

Whitney came back on the line. "All right, here we are, sir. According to Mr. Liggett, the planted file was summoned by PODA form 17A on twenty-two August, last, by a Lucy Saunders, ID'ed as a staff reporter and research assistant for the news department of Universal Broadcasting System."

"Nice work, Whit. Now I want you to call up the file on Randolph Ridenour, the UBS commentator."

"One moment, sir."

Another pause. Then: "Okay, sir, the Ridenour file is on my screen."

"Look in the index for an entry labeled, 'Affidavit, Corbato, Manuel.' "

"Got it, sir."

"Good. Make a printout of the whole file, with three separate copies of the affidavit, and deliver, Eyes Only, to my office. Then put the entire computer file on the Y System so that I can add some new material to it via the PC in my office. And buzz my secretary and tell her to order me some lunch and have it on my desk. I'll be there in twenty minutes."

"Yes, sir."

Richter hung up and sank into the backseat cushions of the

shiny black car, once again admiring the beautiful day beyond the tinted glass.

Aloud, softly, amused, he said, "You're such a frigging amateur, Ridenour. I'm going to show you how the pros play your lousy little game."

CHAPTER 18

Late on Friday afternoon, Sweeney had met the Fort Meade delivery at a truck stop on Route 301 near Bowie, where the sheer volume and clamor of business made the transfer of goods to the van a mere backwater eddy in a thundering cataract. He drove from there directly to The Orchards, arriving after nightfall, and, unloading with Freddie's and Cap's help, had set up the headquarters of what Cap called Sweeney's Ad Hoc Swat Team and Jiffy Gossip Center.

Cap's share of the loot included a computer with word processor and graphics software; three ultraspeed printers and modem ties with seven major information centers; a facsimile machine; a photocopier with color capability; an electric typewriter; a phone console with all the fancy whistles and bells; and a shortwave net with three car sets, one of which went into the van, another into her Mustang, and the third into Freddie's Ford. For himself Sweeney brought in a set of scuba gear; a set each of standard GI combat fatigues and black Special Forces night wear; a portable sonar; a pair of laser-assisted night glasses; a military camcorder with ten-mile laserscope capability; a remote phone bug set; a Gibbons electronic bug detector; a combination lock stethoscope; a set of jimmies and lockpicks; two Uzis fitted with folding metal stocks and thirty-two round magazines, and a case of ammo for each; two Beretta 92's with a case of ammo; and a case each of GI antipersonnel, concussion, and smoke grenades.

"Where are you putting all those guns and explosives?" Cap wanted to know.

"In your garage. Okay?"

"It's better than the living room. And who's going to wire up all these doodads?"

"I am."

"You know about phone lines and computers and parallels and interfaces and all that rigmarole?"

"Watch me."

"Where did you learn all that stuff?"

"The Amos L. Terwilliger Correspondence School for Appliance Repairs and Voodoo Theology."

"He's a former commando and spy kind a guy," Freddie explained helpfully. "They gotta know lots a things."

"Then maybe he can fix my broken toaster, eh?"

"Let's not get carried away now."

They finished up after midnight. Freddie left for his place in Elkton, and Sweeney, leaving Cap fussing with the computer, took a shower and went to bed in the upstairs guest room. When he awoke it was midmorning, and, from the top of the stairs en route to the bathroom, he heard the phone ring and saw Cap coming in from the patio to answer it. On a whim, he hurried back to his room, flipped open his briefcase, took out the remote phone bug, and tuned in for a test.

Washington, like all centers of political gravity, was actually kept functional by an amorphous corps of personal secretaries—those virtually anonymous civil servants who answered the phones and typed the letters and filed the papers and supervised the appointments and dried the tears of the mighty. There existed an underground communications network via which these well-groomed guerrillas kept very much in touch—checking up, counterchecking, referring to, cross-referring, buttering up, threatening, cajoling, and trading the gossip that oiled the federal machinery and eased the way for its operators. Cap needed only to dial a friend who was the friend of a Tina or a Margot who secretaried for a George Whoosis who was a whatsis at State or Defense or Commerce and, lo, information would begin to flow, or some special accommodation would be achieved. In the truly awkward or resistant cases, she had escalated, hinting that "the director will really be grateful for this," or "the director is abroad this month, but he's planning a Christmas bash at the Springs and he'll thank you in person then."

All of which had intrigued and amused Sweeney when he'd been her boss, but which had made her contemptuous of a system that operated via what she called "Xerox Machiavellis." Even so, she knew the game and how to push its buttons and flip its switches, turning herself at will into an authority on the human vulnerabilities that serve as the basic stuff of secret intelligence. (You want to know what's really going on at Defense, or who had said what to whom at Thursday's White House dinner party, or the real reason Admiral Frammus's wife was divorcing him? Ask Cap O'Brien.)

He set the bug's dial for thirty feet, inserted the earplug, flipped the switch, and sat on the bed to listen.

"Hello."

"Hi, Cap. Laurie Platt. I'm on my home phone, so we can talk. Did you get the package?"

"Hey, Laurie—I was going to call you this evening. It's just what I needed, and I'm really grateful."

"You're very welcome."

"Good news. I got a fax last night. It's part of a whole damn van load of office equipment a friend let me borrow."

"Some friend, eh?"

"I'll say. And so are you. Those staff reports are more helpful than you have any idea."

"Getting them to you was a bit hairier than I expected. There's some kind of lid coming down."

"How so?"

"Beats me. It's just that people I've been getting stuff from with no hassles at all are beginning to stiffen up—asking questions about who wants this, and why, and let's have a security clearance number, and like that."

"Oh? So how will you get me the staff reports?"

"I'll just give them my number, photocopy the docs, then bring the copies to my place here in Silver Spring and put them on my personal fax. If they begin handbag searches at the office exits, we got a beeg prob."

"Well, just don't expose yourself to real grief. I need the stuff, but not at your expense."

"No sweat yet. How's your novel coming?"

"Okay. It'll go a lot better with the stuff you're supplying."

"I was thinking, after all the time you've worked in The District, you should be able to write a love story about a GS-8 and her Pentagon G-2 guy off the top of your head."

"Well, it's not just a love story. There's a contemporary secret intelligence kind of subplot, and I've got to fill it with realistic details. But you wouldn't believe how many little things I've already forgotten."

"We sure miss you over at SII. That horse's ass, Aaron Richter, still hasn't replaced Sweeney."

"So I hear."

"So now we have to deal directly with Richter and that drizz who succeeded you—Rachel What's-her-face."

"Don't sell Rachel short. She's a darn competent woman. Her morale is probably shot to hell because Richter has given her my work on top of her own—with no pay sweetener. My guess is that, if it weren't for those two kids she's supporting, she'd have told Richter to shove it by now."

"There you go, Cap—always finding something good to say about somebody, no matter how crappy they are."

"You're not listening, Laurie. Rachel isn't crappy. She does the best she can under the circumstances. Richter runs a mighty bleak office."

"Okay, okay. All I can say is, if anybody ever badmouths me, I sure hope you're around to put in a word for me. Ha-ha."

"You can count on that. You've never let me down. And neither, for that matter, has Rachel."

"Well, like I say, we all sure miss you."

"Thanks. And I sleep better nights, knowing you and Susan and Lois are still the powers behind the Joint Chiefs throne. Long may you wave."

"Which brings up another reason I called, Cap. I need your advice."

"Ask away, dear heart."

"This job I have is—okay. Damn good pay and perks and benefits, retirement, and all that. And it's responsible stuff, too, you know, what with the national defense and the big picture and all that patriotic kind of thing. My boss likes me, and I've gotten the raises and all, and there's absolutely no good reason for me to give it up—"

"But you're thinking about giving it up. Right?"

"Well, sort of—"

"For what? What reason is better than no good reason?"

"I've been a little—itchy—for some time now. There's a kind of atmosphere. It's a downer. And it's not just the budget cutbacks and all the people leaving. It's that the people who still work here are—sour. They hardly ever laugh anymore, and the one up bit is very heavy, and there's a feeling of, like, cold anger, sort of. No more esprit de corps, no more I take care of you, you take care of me. Like that nice General Wallace from Florida. The JCs' Jaycees are so busy sucking up to that TV bastard, Randolph Ridenour, they're making General Wallace roll over and do tricks just to please him. In the old days the gang around here would form a circle around somebody like Wallace and tell Ridenour to go pee in his hat, but now they let the general be humiliated in hopes that Ridenour might someday say something nice about them on that godawful show of his."

"We're talking about the Wallace in Florida? The UFI honcho?"

"Yeah. Ridenour wanted to interview him, but Wallace told him to kiss off, he was busy, or something. Ridenour raised hell, and the Pentagon is making the general apologize to that slimer."

"Is Wallace something to you?"

"Oh, hell no. I was just using him as an example. He's a symptom of what's wrong around here, that's all."

"Okay, so you got the career blues. Big deal. Everybody gets those now and then."

"There's something else, Cap—"

"Ah. I thought so."

"My mom, she's an antiques dealer in Blue Ridge Summit, a little burg up near Camp David, and she's made a real good thing of it. Well, she's been wanting to take things easier now that she's getting along in age, and I've been helping her in the shop on weekends for five, six years, and, you know what? I love it. I love everything about it—the musty smells, the antiquity, the sense of history and Old America, and the people who come in to browse and buy because they get the same kick out of it I do. And, surprise! I turn out to be a hell of a good retail sales type. I'm a good buyer, a good seller, and I can read the hell out of customers and what they like and are looking for. And they like me, I can tell, and they buy from me like they enjoy it, sort of."

"And now Mom wants you to take over the shop full time."

"Oh, Cap, you are the limit, the way you can tell what people are thinking before they even say it."

"How's the pay?"

"Well, I'd be taking a whale of a cut, sure enough. And there are no fringes, perks, built-in security, and like that. It's living by your savvy and wits. On the edge. Pure talentsville—like show biz almost. But the shop's in a big old gorgeous rambling wonder of a house, with Mom living in a wing of it, and I'd have this darling apartment in the carriage house, and there are these huge shade trees and distant views and fresh air, and I'd save like mad on gas and wardrobe and rents and all the crap that goes with working the Washington scene."

"Go for it, Laurie."

"You mean—"

"I mean, do you want to spend the rest of your productive life kissing brasshat patoots, just to retire on a GI pension in Orlando's Shuffleboard Alley? Or do you want to smell the fresh mountain air and see people light up when you show them a seventeenth-century wrought iron smithereen and then some day drop dead, smiling, while you're standing under the trees and admiring the distant views? From what I hear in your voice, I don't think it's any contest. I think you'd be out of your gourd not to take Mom's offer."

"Still, there's the money, the security—"

"Oh, horse manure, Laurie. What the hell good are money and security if you aren't doing any laughing? If what you work at isn't what you are? If you spend your nights grumping instead of humping? If you look in your gold-framed mirror and find yourself wondering what your life's all about and will anybody ever know you were here—or care?"

"You sound like you know what you're talking about."

"Damned straight, I do. I spent ten years in government, making out great professionally and liking it, mostly. But then fate kicked me in the duff, and now I'm really living—flying my plane, writing, jogging, smelling the fresh air, seeing things I never saw before, giving myself to something truly important. And you know what? I'm starting to laugh. Not at things. About things."

"I'm glad for you, Cap."

"Run, dear heart, don't walk, to Mom's shop in the hills. And laugh your buns off."

"God, but you're good to talk to. I've never yet brought you a problem you haven't helped me with. I just wish there was something I could do for you."

"You're already doing it."

"Documents-shmocuments. I mean I wish I could do something real. Something, well, straight-up and caring, like you do all the time."

"You just did it."

Sweeney put away the gear, dressed, and went downstairs.

Cap had returned to the patio, where she sat at the table, bowed over a newspaper, considering an ad for winter dresses. The sun was bright, and it shone in her hair, and her face was aglow from the pages' reflected light. He stood quietly in the shadows behind the French doors for a time, watching. Then, unable to resist the rush of compulsion, he stepped behind her, bent, and kissed the top of her head.

She looked up, startled and flustered. "Well, now. What was that all about?"

"It was a gesture of admiration."

"What's that mean?"

"I'm not sure."

"You're weird."

"I'll say. But I sure do like you. I really and truly like you a bunch."

There was a suspended moment, a silence broken only by the distant calling of gulls, in which their gazes met and held. Then she blinked and said, "The coffee's fresh. Want a cup?"

"Do I ever."

CHAPTER 19

The Radimore Arms proved to be one of those residential hotel operations, with the upper two floors divided into apartments of several connected rooms and the rest amounting to a hive for quickie pollen-spreaders.

Sweeney stood at the registration desk and told the suet-faced little clerk that he needed a pad. The man's watery blue eyes took in the bandana on his head, the blue jeans, the sunglasses, the fake beard, guitar case and duffel bag. "How long?"

"Just a room, like. Makes nohow on big or little."

"I mean, how long you want it for?"

"Hey, man, how long do it take, eh? Ha-ha."

"We got one apartment left, by the month, first and last month payable up front. We got rooms by the hour at twenty bucks, or the day at a hundred. So what's your pleasure?"

"Switch-hitter, actually. A little leather, maybe. Group stuff now and then."

"I mean, which do you want—room or apartment?"

"Got a friend comin' from Philly but I don't know when, exactly. It's that way when they're married, eh, man?"

"Well, will she be here today?"

"He. He's a he."

"Is it to*day*?"

"I dunno. Looks like. Lemme in for now and I'll tell ya what else t'morra, okay, man?"

The clerk nodded at the register. "Put your name there and give me a hundred."

"You got one on the front, so I can see the street and watch for my friend?"

"Front rooms go for a hundred and twenty."

"Okay, man. He's worth it."

All hotel rooms depressed Sweeney, speaking as they did of wandering and loneliness, but this one was an E. A. Poe spectacular. It was slightly smaller than a beer can, with a single window that had last been washed to celebrate the news out of Appomattox. The adjoining "bath" was a niche featuring a stained sink, a hopper, and a bare sixty-watt bulb that jutted above a smoky wall mirror. There was a metal bed, two straight-back oak chairs, a small table bearing an art deco lamp, and a rotary-dial wall phone dating from the Prohibition years.

But it did have an excellent view of the street.

Which would be fine for staking out the building's comings and goings. At the moment, though, he was more interested in who was already inside, and so he opened the duffel bag, which Cap had dubbed Swami Sweeney's Magic Musette, and went into a personality change.

He took off the bandana and beard, exchanged a pair of work shoes for the dirty sneakers, pulled green coveralls over the denims, and settled a pair of safety goggles on his nose and a yellow hard hat on his head. Then he flipped the catches on the guitar case and took out the old Signal Corps lineman's tool belt provided by Dr. Schwenke. With this around his waist, he was ready.

The freight elevator took him to the basement, and the basement eventually revealed the hotel's main phone box. With a screwdriver and a dab of putty, he anchored a magnetized Irving interrupter behind a pivotal junction. After a three-second interval, every phone in the building went into an instant, maddening silence.

He took the rickety elevator to the main floor, and when he arrived in the lobby, the clerk was already in an arm-waving conference with an old geezer in overalls bearing the legend, *Building Maintenance.* As he crossed the battered parquet, tools and doodads jingling, they fell silent, their angry eyes on the phony phone dangling from his belt.

"Hi," Sweeney said. "You people got a prob, eh?"

The clerk rasped, "You from the phone company?"

"Yep."

"All our lines are dead, for crissake. I was just sending Sam to the pay phone to call you."

"Glad I saved you the trouble. We been doing some work on the cables down the street, and there's a general short. We think the problem's here in this building, somewhere on your top couple floors."

The clerk sputtered, "But—What the hell—You mean you gotta screw around in the apartments up there?"

"Well, I wouldn't call it screwing around, pal. You got a lot of very old phones in this building, and it's them screwing things up, not us."

"The phones in the apartments are all brand-new the last couple months, for crissake. The tenants put them in themselves—at their expense."

"Sure, but you got some real antiques on your lower floors, and the new lines are integrated with the old ones. Federal regulations, and like that. Specially in The District, you know. And the new stuff upstairs has thrown the old stuff downstairs into Blackout City."

"Oh, God—"

"Can Sam here take me around your top two floors?"

"Oh, God—"

A large man with one huge eyebrow and a flat nose emerged from the elevator and came across the lobby, fists clenched. "What the hell's with the phones, Lemke? Mr. Colt is havin' a shit-hemorrhage."

The clerk pointed to Sweeney. "This phone company guy says there's a general short, or something, and the trouble's in this building."

The man's eyes, like raisins in pudding, seemed not to move, but Sweeney knew he was being examined and spoken to. "So why'n hell don't you fix it?"

"I was about to go to the top floor and do just that."

"No way. Mr. Colt is havin' a meetin'. Nobody gets in for anythin'."

Sweeney shrugged. "No skin off my ass. So the phones in this neighborhood don't work for a week. I get paid anyhow."

"What you gotta do?"

"Test all the phone jacks up there. The phones themselves. Something you folks did has thrown the system into a short." He narrowed his eyes accusingly. "You folks did the installation yourselves, didn't you? You didn't have the phone company do it."

"Hell no. We didn't want no strangers comin' in, doin' our phones. The boss needs a lot a privacy. Besides, those guys charge an arm and a leg, and the boss didn't like the way they wanted to rip him off."

"And now," Sweeney said vengefully, "it's costing him a lot more than it would have if he'd paid for a pro in the first place. Which goes to show it don't pay to go cheap in anything, 'specially phones."

There was a moment of impasse.

The Eyebrow glared at Sweeney. Sweeney glared back. They both glared at the clerk. The clerk glared back. Sam looked bored.

The elevator door wheezed open and Aaron Richter stepped into the lobby, accompanied by Lieutenant Cummings and Sergeant Ames.

Sweeney said suddenly, and to nobody in particular, "Well, the hell with all of you. Fix your own phones."

And he marched out of the lobby, hard hat pulled low, making for the freight elevator. As he prepared to step aboard, he glanced back and saw Richter and Company pushing through the revolving door for the sun-washed street beyond.

Back in the basement, he removed the Irving interrupter, replaced it with a microdot for the remote bugging set, and returned the phone box lid. Then he took the freight elevator back to his floor.

In his room again, he activated the bugging base unit, set it on full recording, and affixed it to a bed slat. He sighed deeply, aware that his heart was thumping and he was sweating. Pulling off the coveralls, he flopped onto the cement-hard bed and lay staring at the ceiling.

Well, now. Close call. Too close.

But a very interesting turn of events.

So Richter and Cummings and Ames are attending meetings held by a man named Colt.

Richter and Cummings and Ames: The oddest of couples, plus one.

And who is Colt?

31° 11′ N

81° 09′ W

The night was very dark due to a cloud sandwich, high and low, due north of Jamaica. They had been flying since lift-off on integrated HUD and HDD.

For Capt. Jeremy Knight, who was a traditionalist, this was a personal pain. He equated the system, for all its ingenuity, with a thirteen-dollar video game cassette. Much of the fun had long since left the artful science of aviating, thanks to the fact that so much was given over to electronics, even in the best of weather. Flying was especially dull at night, when one had to lash oneself to a constant watch of an amalgamation of a windscreen Heads-Up Display and a lapboard Heads-Down Display. At first it had been fascinating to deal with a moving topographical terrain map—fed and augmented by forward-looking infrared, low light-level television, radar, TV, sonar, and alphanumeric data—but eventually came the sense of being less the fighter pilot and more the supersonic Nintendo player. Even the F-107-A "Picket" of Bud Littleton, his wingman, cruising invisibly in the blackness at five o'clock high, was on the screen, a green wedge precisely positioned and slavishly loyal to the movements of the glowing T that represented his own ship.

He felt a weary annoyance. He and Bud could fly to Jupiter and back without ever having to look out the canopy.

They were in a gentle curve to north by northwest 225 miles south of Bermuda when Bud's voice was in the earphones. "King Two to King One. Over."

"King One. What's up, Bud? Over."

"King Two. Did you see that squizzer at six o'clock high, about one-nine-oh miles out? Over."

"King One. Nothing registered here. Over."

"King Two. It was just a flicker of something. Something pretty big and very high. Over."

"King One. Probably an aberration. Theater Command has nothing in that area, according to the poop I have on my patrol leader's brief. Over."

"King Two. Roger. I'm not sure I even saw anything. It was more like an impression—a flicker at the edge of my board I saw out of the corner of my eye. Over."

"King One. Clouds do some queer things now and then. Maybe it was all this crapola around us—"

"There! Did you see that, Jerry?"

"Sure did. Not very well, but there was something, all right. Right at the very edge of our probe capability."

"Could it be something like a Bear? Those Soviet Bear recons used to pop in and out like that in the last days."

"King One. Back to procedure, please."

"King Two. Roger. Sorry. Over."

"King One. Whatever it was, I'll shunt it to Homestead. If they want somebody to investigate, fine and dandy. Out."

His fingers danced across the keyboard, and the possible sighting was on its way to the great Tactical Data Analysis Board in Florida.

They flew on for a time.

"King One to King Two. Homestead's answering. Are you reading? Over."

"King Two. Sure am. 'Friendly AWACS,' they say. How come our briefing data doesn't reflect the presence of AWACS in our sector? Over."

Captain Knight thought about that. AWACS, acronym for "airborne warning and control system," was usually carried aboard a four-engine airplane with a crew of up to seventeen communications technicians who kept watch on everything that went on, in the air and on the surface, over a radius of some three hundred miles. The ship's powerful surveillance radar and a grandma's attic of sensing and data-processing systems with state-of-the-art display panels enabled the crew and its ground command station—as the CG, Harvey Wallace, liked to put it—"to follow the progress of a flea on a hound dog's back." So if Homestead knew about, and was using, an AWACS in this part of the Atlantic sky tonight, why didn't little old Jerry Knight know about it?

"King Two to King One. I'm picking up a surface blip at eleven o'clock, coordinates AE seven and CC six. Do you read? Over." There was excitement in Littleton's voice.

"King One. I've got it, Bud. It reads out as a small boat, moving fast on a course of three-five-five. Am descending to three thousand and have activated the heave-to-and-be-recognized tape. Stand by. Out."

The lapboard showed the boat-blip enlarging in precise scale, creating an image that conformed to what he would have seen under visual flight conditions. He was about to arm the two Snapdragon ASMs under his wings when suddenly the blackness ahead was lit by the sparkling of incoming tracers.

"Holy hell!" Littleton's voice crackled. "They're shooting at us, Jerry! The board shows them zizagging, too. Hey, man, this is a first. We got combat going here."

There was a pause filled with the radio's busy silence.

"Go on, Jerry, you're on the money. Take them."

He punched the button, and the sky lit up with the missiles' flaring, and in less than a minute there was no trace of the boat on the board and only a diminishing glow on the midnight sea below.

"Nice shot, Jerr-baby."

There was another interval, and then Knight heard himself say, "I never even saw the poor bastards. Not once."

"They never saw you, either. And before you get all gooey remorseful, it could be you and me burning down there on the water, pal. Just remember that."

Another silence. Then: "King One to King Two: Proper radio procedures, please. Out."

CHAPTER 20

Pop Cooley had sold his Aviles Street shop and was retiring after forty years as a tailor, and Harvey and Millie Wallace had been invited to a small dinner party in Pop's honor at the Comachee Cove yacht club. The general was a big man with a tough body, but, as he liked to say, shapewise he had been born a squash in a world that admired rake handles. To camouflage bulges that were in the most awkward and unmilitary places, he would submit his uniforms, from Class A's to fatigues, to Pop's talented needle and scissors. Over the years they'd grown quite fond of each other, and the dinner invitation had certified that fact. The food had been great and the conversation mellow, but after the thank-yous and good nights and horn-blowing and hand-waving, they had driven all the way to the traffic light at San Marco in silence. There, as they waited for the green, Millie said, "That was a nice evening."

"Sure was."

"Maude Cooley is such a lovely person."

"Yep."

"She and Pop go so well together."

"Yeah."

"It was good to get away from the military shoptalk for a change. And you look smashing in that blue suit."

"Good."

"I'm very proud of you, you know."

"Oh?"

"You're—consistent. You're as amiable and genuine with the Cooleys and their little family as you are with the muck-amucks from Tallahasee and Washington. There aren't many men like that, and I'm proud to be married to one."

"How about that."

He turned south on San Marco, which at this time of night was relatively clear of the Winnebagos and camper top trucks and vans of invading snowbirds. Only the fast-food joints and convenience stores showed signs of life, and even they seemed somnolent.

"Harve?"

"Mm?"

"What's wrong?"

"Wrong? Nothing. Why?"

"You seem so—distant. Distracted."

"Sorry. I am wrestling with something, and I guess it shows a bit."

As they entered the Avenida and its curve at the ancient coquina fort, she said, "Hey. Let's stop here and sit on one of those benches on the seawall."

He glanced at her. "Are you nuts? This is mugging time."

"Oh, come on. There isn't a pedestrian for blocks around, and the town's asleep, which means the muggers are all busy burgling. And how could we not be safe? The big honcho of all the armed forces in Florida is right here."

He laughed softly and shook his head, signaling a skeptical surrender. "Okay, we'll give it a whirl."

They sat on a bench close to the fort, listening to the black restlessness of the Matanzas and, beyond its tossing and washing, the distant pounding of the sea. A wind had risen, fitful and redolent of oncoming rain, and the palms and high oaks of Davis Shores swayed, their shadows making small signal lamps of the remaining lights there. The Bridge of Lions was a graceful, sparkling arc, and to its south, the mastlights of moored boats waggled like busy fireflies.

"Warm enough, Millie?"

"It's beautiful, and exciting, and I'm with my guy. What means warm enough?"

"You didn't want to sit here for the view. You wanted to get me where I might open up on my problem. Right?"

She smiled. "Boy, are we *married.*"

"You're a hundred-caliber pistol, you are."

"So what's the problem?"

"The problem is that I can't name the problem."

She waited.

"Something's going on, and I have this nagging feeling that I'm being played for some kind of patsy."

"Give me a for instance."

"Boots Franklin. Remember him?"

"Sure. The Air Force colonel who runs things down at Homestead, or something. He was at Fürstenfeldbruck when we were assigned to Wolfratshausen. You always spoke well of him, seems to me."

"The other day Boots sent me a personal and confidential note by overnight Fed Express, of all things. He could have faxed it, he could have TWX'ed it, he could have sent a courier, he could even have phoned me, for that matter. But he went outside the structure to send me this note. And in it he said that something screwy was going on and he wanted to talk to me about it—could we maybe get together where we wouldn't be in the center of things, sort of."

She waited while he paused, thinking.

"So I returned a note the same way, and Boots rented a Piper at Miami and flew to Daytona this morning. I drove down and we had lunch at a little joint near the airport."

"So that's why you were wearing civvies when you left this morning."

"Boots told me that there was an action over the Atlantic three nights ago. A routine two-plane patrol discovered and eventually destroyed—after a very brief shoot-out, by the way—a fast boat running the drug blockade. And—"

"A shootout? Isn't that unusual?"

"Sure is. First recorded armed resistance, actually. But that wasn't what bothered Boots. What bothered him was the fact that just before the action our patrol leader reported the presence of a large aircraft at the perimeter of his surveillance capability—a presence also reported by two Navy picket ships off Jamaica. That represented three independent reports of an aircraft presence, entered and plotted on the master board at Homestead, with Boots as duty officer approving the posting. The report simultaneously and automatically went upstairs, first to Eastern Sector Tactical Air Intelligence and then into the Master Continental Strategic Computer. The MCSC is maintained by the Joint Chiefs of Staff, and collects and digests all information gathered by all ancillaries of the National Directorate of Intelligence for daily reports to President Leonardi. But the report also went upstairs with Boots's request for advice and clarification, since his data from ESTAI told him that nothing big—foreign, civilian, or U.S. military—was flying out there at the time. So what kind of advice and clarification did Boots get from MCSC in Washington? 'The sighting was an AWACS. No action required. Delete posting.' That's what he got."

"An AWACS—one of those super recon planes?"

"Yeah."

"So what's wrong with that?"

"Two things. First, if there was an AWACS out there, it should have been clearly established for, and tracked by, Boots's people. Since it wasn't, it was either a fundamental glitch in the system or an outright withholding of information by somebody at ESTAI in Washington. And second, no matter what it was, glitch or secrecy, I should have been told of the incident. I was not. I had to hear about it from an Air Force colonel under my command who had to tip me off by way of a civilian delivery service and a lousy ham-and-cheese on rye."

They listened to the wind for a time, feeling the dark and sleeping city behind them.

"Do you," she asked quietly, "think somebody in the Regulars—topside in Washington—is trying to fix your wagon because you're a Reservist?"

"I've considered that, and Boots asked the same question. But my hunch tells me it's bigger than that—that some stupendous game is under way and I'm not even a player."

"Some pretty stupendous things are done in the name of jealousy. The—"

"Hell, the Regular–Reservist rivalry has been going on ever since Valley-damn-Forge. The Regulars have always looked down their noses at the citizen soldier—and if the great work done in the two world wars and Korea and the Gulf and all the other police actions didn't dispel it, I don't guess the 'weekend warrior' image will ever go away. Or ever, in the final analysis, keep hotshots like your Main Man from holding sensitive positions at every military level. Inter-service jealousy just ain't heavy-duty enough to carry what's going on here, you ask me."

"What, then?"

"I don't know. It's just a feeling. The same feeling I had when I was in Washington a couple of weeks ago for that mysterious bull session with the JCs' Jaycees. When those weirdies, Donnelli, Grubb, Hoff and Benson, were asking their weird questions. When that ass, Reynolds, ordered me to apologize to that super-ass, Ridenour. I felt then, and still feel, that they were using me somehow."

She pulled her jacket closer against the wind. "I thought you were real high on the Joint Chiefs—"

"I am, Millie, I am. The Chiefs themselves are the best of the best, and I know for a fact that they respect me. I know each of them—have for years, as corporate president and soldier—and I'm certain that the chairman, General Willard himself, personally, recommended me for this current command. I don't have a problem with the Chiefs. I have a problem with those special assistants of theirs."

She sighed. "I don't understand anything about the military anymore. The Chiefs never used to have special assistants like those guys—"

"Hell, Millie, everything's changed since the Communist meltdown and the post-Gulf reorganization and the belt-tightening. Instead of being ready to fight World War Three with the Soviets, we suddenly discovered that we had to be ready to be the world's beat cop, because there simply isn't another country with the clout or moxie to face down tinhorn tyrants and neighborhood bullies. Now, instead of being prepared to fight a worldwide military threat, we're actually fighting a hemispheric epidemic. Now, instead of carrying the freight, assisted by citizen troops, the Regulars—cut to the bone by economics—have been forced into the assistants' role. It's easier and cheaper to federalize civilian soldiers on a selective special-need basis than it is to maintain a huge force of Regulars ready to handle big threats that never materialize. Mark my word, the Reserve is going to be more and more important to the national defense in coming years—the most important it's ever been. Meanwhile, the entire military-industrial mechanism has been so enormously changed, so convulsed, there's no recognizing it anymore."

Millie sighed. "Well, all I can say is, if an oily opportunist like Reynolds is in a key topside role, anything can happen—and it probably won't be good."

He gave her a lingering, sidelong glance.

"Why are you looking at me like that?"

He felt a smile forming. "Millie, you're something else."

"Why? What did I do?"

"It's what you said."

"What did I said?"

He sat, squinting into the wind—quiet, thoughtful.

"Harve? Do you still have a pulse?"

"Look at it this way." His hands began drawing boxes in the air. "You have the president on the top as commander in chief. Under him, you've got the the National Security Council. And as co-equals with the Council you have the Joint Chiefs and the National Directorate of Intelligence. The Council, along with the JCs, oversees the whole defense structure, from the Secretary of Defense down to the Army infantry squad. And the Council, along with the Directorate of Intelligence, oversees the entire intelligence-gathering machinery, from the CIA and the State Department and the space spy satellites on down to the guy in the trench coat in Lower Bowel, Slobbovia. You put a twister, or a group of angle-shooters, in a key spot, say, between the National Council and its co-equal boxes, and you could pull off all sorts of cute things. You could have the major portion of the defense establishment thinking you're doing one thing while you're really doing something else. You could have the entire intelligence system gathering information presumably for one purpose when the big, real purpose is altogether different. Then you could tell the National Security Council and the president what you bloody well wanted them to know, not what they ought to know. Right?"

"You mean Reynolds and his pals might be doing something like that?"

"They're weird, and they're ambitious, and I don't like them much. But for all that, I don't think they're high enough on the pole to pull off something of the dimensions I'm talking about."

"High enough? Only the JCs are higher. And you say they're straight arrows."

"I'm talking high-powered civilians. Bureaucrats. Politicians. People with enough clout to influence the National Security Council."

"That narrows it down, I'd say. There just aren't a lot of people with that kind of clout."

He gave her a lingering, thoughtful stare. "And that, pal, is what scares me. It scares the hell out of me."

"What are you going to do about it?"

"I don't know. I don't even know if my hunch is right."

"Well, there's one thing you've got to do right away, and that's to take me home. I gotta go."

They returned to the car, and as he unlocked the door, Millie asked, "Just why did Boots Franklin write to you? Why you, of all the people he could have contacted?"

"I asked him that. He said it was because he trusts me."

"He doesn't trust anybody else?"

"He said he doesn't know who to trust anymore. Except me. He said if something rotten's going down he was pretty sure I wasn't part of it."

"That Boots Franklin: he sounds like my kind of guy."

When they got back to quarters and Millie had disappeared upstairs, he hung his jacket in the hall closet, pulled off his necktie, and went into the library for a nightcap. Only after he had settled into his favorite chair did he notice that the answering machine's call-recorded light was blinking.

He pressed the button.

The first call was Amy Harris, telling Millie that the Friends of the Library board would start the planning of this year's book-and-author dinner at Thursday's special meeting at Susan Blanchard's house.

The second call was a sorry-got-the-wrong-number.

The third made him sit forward in the chair.

"Hi, Bojo. This is Gutbucket. Give me a call on my unlisted at code three-oh-one, five-five-five, thirty-two oh-one. And use your scrambler. It's important."

He listened to the message twice—astonished, amused, pleased and puzzled.

A voice out of the past, speaking names of once top-secret significance.

Sweeney, of all people.

Sweeney.

Of course. The perfect answer.

Good old Sweeney.

CHAPTER 21

Jenny Malone had arranged to have McKell speak before the Delaware Business Club at the Hotel Du Pont in Wilmington. She had advised President Leonardi that further steps should be taken to counter the media's escalating mockery of Brandon McKell—leading columnists had begun to call him "Vice President McDull"—and that Delaware was a good place to start because, despite its small geographical area, it contained an enormous reservoir of financial and political clout. Leonardi had agreed, with the provision that she accompany McKell; if Delaware was so damned important, it should be schmoozed with a higher octane than McKell alone could deliver, and not only was her current media popularity soaring but she was also regarded highly by Delaware's industrialists as one of their own.

Even so, it would certainly receive nothing better than cursory mainline media attention, since it was a routine appearance featuring a speech by McKell. Which was an advantage in Richter's eyes because the humdrum would also desensitize the hungry free-lance reporters—those American "paparazzi"—who had begun to cherish the long-shot hope of catching McKell meeting with somebody crooked, bizarre, sexy or otherwise exploitable in the supermarket tabloids. The trip, Richter decided, offered an excellent opportunity for one of their confidential meetings.

In a phone call, Richter had reminded Malone that "Leonardi's hard-nosed restrictions on Administration use of government aircraft means that you'll have to make the Wilmington trip by train or bus. But when you figure the security hazards and the cost of protection, neither would save the taxpayer a hell of a lot of money. So why not use McKell's limousine, with the regular Secret Service detail escorting in another car? Not only would that be economical, it would also solve the problem of absurd juxtaposition."

"What the hell is that?"

"You're a realist. McKell is very close to being torn to shreds by the media as a stuffed-shirt, airhead playactor who never had a real idea in his life. He's becoming the frequent target of late-night TV comedians; the capital's in-crowd lunchtime smart-asses are making him their favorite joke. Hell, he's on his way to being a staple in the Doonesbury strip. I guarantee you, Jenny: It's getting so bad that no matter how public or obviously innocent the circumstances, any consultation between Brandon McKell, vice president of the United States, and Aaron Richter, director of the sinister Special Intelligence Initiatives, would be picked up by media hotshots like Ridenour, or Polk, or Ludman, and dubbed 'Stan Laurel meets Grigori Rasputin.' Preposterous. Absurd. And therefore very high profile, very alluring for the professional funny-fellas. Which would be very bad at this particular time. Our negotiations with the people abroad are climaxing, and any undue attention right now could very well throw things out of balance and destroy a year's work. See what I mean?"

"I see it better than you do, pal. Why the hell do you think I took so many pains to persuade the president to let Brandon handle the drug thing? If Brandon ends up being a hero of the drug war, the smart-asses will have to look elsewhere for a punching bag. If he ends up being a yuk, we've all got problems."

"We're in no disagreement on that. You and I are especially heavy-duty Administration soldiers, and it's to our interest to keep the Administration intact. That's precisely what I'm talking about."

"So what about this trip, then?"

"The three of us can use the cheap ride to Wilmington behind the limo's dark-tinted glass to catch up on things. Without our meeting becoming the centerpiece skit on 'Saturday Night Live.' "

"I'll set it up, Aaron."

McKell had presided over the Senate that morning, so Richter and Jenny met the limo in the Capitol Building's high-security parking garage and the convoy left from there. They took Route 50 and the Bay Bridge to 301 because the Secret Service guys didn't like the Baltimore clutter and all the tollbooths and overheads on I-95. Which pleased Richter because this route was much more scenic and the day was beautiful, with a cobalt sky and bright autumn foliage.

Once the cars were up to speed, McKell sealed off the driver compartment and poured three coffees from the built-in thermos. "You realize, Richter, that the three of us meeting like this is especially dangerous. Reporters would love to know just why the vice president, the president's chief of staff, and the head of the SII are taking a long automobile ride together. Have you thought about that?"

"It had occurred to me, yes." Richter avoided Jenny's amused eyes for fear he might laugh.

McKell went on. "So to maintain security and keep us from looking too much like intriguers, I suggest you stay in the limo while Jenny and I are in the hotel. In those cabinets there's lunch, TV and videocassettes, newspapers, phones—that sort of thing. But whatever you do, stay out of sight."

"You worry too much, Brandon. Relax. It's a nifty day, and we've a few hours to do some serious talking."

McKell glanced at Malone. "Let's start with you, Jenny. Anything to report?"

She opened her notebook in that fussy way so dear to comedians and cleared her throat delicately.

"The president continues to be delighted with the progress being made in the drug thing. He measures its success not only by the military reports but also by the efforts of those on the other side of the aisle to minimize his personal role in the success and to credit themselves for how things have gone. 'There is no greater flattery than usurpation,' as he puts it."

Richter laughed quietly but said nothing. McKell obviously didn't get the little joke.

"He still approves of the way I'm handling things?"

"Absolutely, Brandon," Jenny confirmed.

"It's most important, you know. I have the distinct feeling he doesn't like me very much, and I have to do everything I can to persuade him to keep me on the ticket next time."

"Well," Jenny crooned reassuringly, "you're not without your own power base, Brandon. There's a huge bundle of right-wing money in the country that wants—demands—that you be on the ticket. So it's really irrelevant whether Leonardi likes you or not. If he wants to be reelected himself, he'll simply have to have you along for the ride. Unless you screw up somehow. And that's why Aaron and I are here. To help you to avoid screwing up."

Richter stifled an urge to laugh.

McKell and Jenny went on for some time about congressional politics and developing national campaign issues and likely candidates for the opposition slate. Richter tuned them out and enjoyed the spectacular day. He sipped coffee and munched a Danish and lazily watched the Delmarva countryside roll by. And wondered: What would it be like to be born and to grow up and to work and die in a big old red-brick country house like that one there? To spend your lifetime at the center of distant lavender horizons, surrounded by the smell of hay and the rustling of cornfields, and shaded by those tremendous maples?

Was he missing something?

"What do you think, Richter?" McKell was asking.

"Eh? About what?"

"Do you think Corbato will perform as we hope at the Azalea Manor meeting?"

"Of course. All this was his idea in the first place. He could see the handwriting on the wall: the hellish pressure from the combined military actions; the incredible climb in the industry's overhead and related costs; the inevitability of death or prison for the principals. Those countries are fed up with the drug royalty rolling in luxury while everybody else rolls in dirt and sweat. They're fed up with the law's applying to everybody but the men in the dark glasses and stretch limos. In us, he sees a way to have his cake and eat it, too. He wants this thing to come off as badly as we do, so he'll perform, all right."

Jenny broke in, "And so will von Zoll and his people. To take over Germany, they're going to need enormous piles of money, and Corbato's plan is so good they can't possibly do anything but embrace it. That's the very root of our caper—the reason it was established—and I see no reason to alter that sanguine view of things."

Richter agreed. "From the very damn beginning die Pilze have been warm to our overtures, especially now that they've had so much difficulty in keeping a lid on their thing with Iraq. With its oil industry dead and its other assets under the UN thumb, Iraq needs everything die Pilze can send them by way of weapons and money if it's to keep Iran and Syria from dominating the Middle East. But the UN heat and the German government surveillance are so intense, von Zoll and his people are very happy to consider another, equally lucrative, but much safer arrangement on this side of the world. Why wouldn't they listen to Corbato? He's offering them one of history's biggest gold mines, with us Americans—you, me, the others—taking almost all of the risk and doing all the coolie labor for a modest percentage of the action."

McKell looked at Malone. "Anything else, Jenny?"

She brushed some crumbs from her skirt. "My problem is, and has always been, an inability to trust Colt. After all, he's a renegade Nachrichtendienst agent who went sourly native after years in South America. He's the rankest kind of opportunist, and I'm never sure just which side of what line he's going to come down on. At first I simply couldn't believe that he was in fact Corbato's go-between. I'll have to admit that the man has delivered as promised, and I have no right to doubt him further. But, damn it, I do. He's just too damned—sleazy."

Richter laughed. "Hell, Jenny, you're as snooty as that mother of yours. Any drug mechanic is bound to be sleazy."

She laughed, too. "You're right, of course, Aaron. Von Zoll is obviously very hot to make a deal, no matter what Colt is or isn't. He'd be a fool not to, what with the long-term money hunger he's got to feed."

McKell adjusted the knot of his silver gray necktie. "How about Corbato? Is he still on stream?"

"Mm. We're planning to fly him to Aberdeen on one of the C-one thirties. He's all primed, anticipating life as a hugely rich fellow free of blood, sweat and tears."

"And the first payment—?"

"At the settlement at Azalea Manor. Subsequent payments after my signal to our banker in Bern."

"So really, then, Colt is in the driver's seat for the time being."

Richter shook his head. "Colt's never in the driver's seat. Colt is our contract orchestra conductor, making sure all the instruments are playing the tune we've composed—harmonizing and on the beat."

"Well," Jenny Malone said uneasily, "no matter how you put it, we've got a lot riding on Colt right now."

Richter said, "Sure. But he's just an agent, working for the cleanest incentive there is—a guaranteed percentage of a huge gross. He stands to become an exceptionally wealthy man who can live to a rich, ripe old age if he does his job for us well. If he doesn't—if he rats or turncoats for even more money—he won't be around to enjoy it. He knows that."

They rode for a time, considering this. Then McKell patted his gorgeous hair and asked, "Anything else before I go over my speech?"

Jenny said, "Not for now. I've got a few other things, but they'll keep until the ride back."

Richter shook his head.

It wouldn't do, he'd decided, to tell McKell about the problem in Florida. If he heard now about the growing flap over the so-called AWACS sighting, he'd be delivering his speech in damp trousers.

The Stearman taxied along the grassy fence line and ruddered crisply into the wind, snorting and rumbling, as if it were on rails; then, without the slightest hesitation, it raised its tail and skimmed the turf, jouncing with a kind of polite glee, to leap over the trees and head for the high blue. Sweeney, having survived uncountable takeoffs in his travels, had learned to recognize pilot authority—a brisk sureness in the way the airplane responded to the controls, on the ground and in the air—and it was obvious now that Cap O'Brien had it in bushels.

Nested in the front cockpit with his gear, he was in the shadow of the top wing, but the rearview mirror showed her awash in sun brilliance, highlighted against the receding autumnal bay country. She was smiling faintly, and her eyes were alert—considering the instruments, glancing about the plane itself, watching the sky around her.

"Lord, you even look like the Chartreuse Countess," he said into the intercom. "What's with the antique helmet and goggles?"

"Army Air Corps issue in nineteen forty-one."

"You weren't alive back then."

"I got them from an Aberdeen military surplus store the day I soloed. I was a teenager, all knees and elbows and freckles, and I wanted to look like a hotshot aviator. Now I wear them because they're comfortable."

"You don't have freckles."

"Want to bet?"

"On your face, I mean."

"They've relocated."

"Then it's a bet. To win you got to show me."

"Here? Who'll fly the plane?"

They laughed together.

The Susquehanna Flats and the perimeter towns of North East, Perryville, and Havre de Grace appeared almost at once beyond the shimmering propeller disc, being no more than fifteen air miles from their takeoff point. Cap set the throttle at the minimum necessary to a slow climbing spiral, gaining a comfortable altitude while conserving fuel, which, she had grumped earlier, "cost more per gallon than Scotch damn-old whiskey." He'd reminded her that she'd be reimbursed for any flying she did for him, but she'd made a face that showed she didn't believe him.

As the Stearman curved higher, its engine chortling, he thought about her and how important it was that she did believe him.

No. Make that how important she was becoming to him.

Their little exchange on the freckles thing was a case in point. In other times, with another woman, he would have read her easy banter as the opening of a dialogue whose concluding lines would eventually be whispered in the sack. And he'd have begun plotting his campaign at once. But here and now, huddled in the vibrating cockpit of a thousand-year-old biplane, he understood in some unspecific way that he would always see her, deal with her, at a level above and beyond the usual. His involvement with her was much more than raunchy infatuation, much less then veneration.

It was— Well, hell, *what* was it?

Her voice was in the earphones. "So here we are, circling serenely above the sun-dappled waters of the majestic Chesapeake Bay, at one with the angels. What do you want to do now, angel?"

"I want to get some shots of the current layout at the Proving Ground—road network, building placement, bunker locations, what's on the artillery range. That kind of stuff."

"Well, you know the problem. If we get too close, it's Air Police City."

"According to Dr. Schwenke, with the laser-magnified oblique camera I have here, I don't have to get close. I just have to look normal. So what's normal? What do you normally do when you come flying along thisaway, Countess?"

"Aerobatics."

"Say what?"

"I usually do aerobatics when I'm over the headwaters of the bay. In case something goes wrong and I have to bail out, chances that the airplane falls on people and property below are minimized. Know what I mean?"

"Sheesh."

"What does that mean?"

"It means, 'Can't you just do a few lazy-eights and look normal?' "

"A few lazy-eights is not what those watchers at the Proving Ground have learned to expect from this here yellow bird. So check the buckles on your parachute and dig in."

"How the hell am I supposed to get pictures when I'm hanging upside down on my buckles?"

"Don't ask me. I'm just the cabbie."

"So all right. You do your stunts. But also do me a favor. As your last trick, turn southeast, descending to about a thousand feet as you pass the Turkey Point light. Then beyond Grove Neck, turn west along the Sassafrass River and, when you're back over the bay, drop to fifty feet and turn northwest, full throttle, straight for Spesutie Narrows. Fly due north along the Narrows and don't grab altitude until you reach the mouth of the Susquehanna."

"What's with all this fifty feet business over a military restricted area? You're *trying* to get us shot down?"

"According to Schwenke's T.O. and E. for the Proving Ground, it isn't rated a high-intensity security zone. It's mainly a testing area for modified line equipment and ordnance. Which means they don't have anything particularly deadly by way of surveillance and protection. Which further means that if we come straight in, fast, with our wheels just above the water, we're going to surprise whatever watch they may have mounted. I'll have the high-speed strip camera anchored on the portside cockpit rim and we should get a useful low-level panorama of everything the Army's got showing over there."

"Sweeney, for cripes sake," she protested. "A yellow Stearman is a yellow Stearman. Besides, they probably logged my serial number ages ago."

"So what are they going to do—put out a contract on you? Sue? Protest to the United Nations? Relax. The Army has more to do than get into legal hassles with a fun-loving local pilot who flew over a corner of its turf."

"Damn it, you're a dangerous guy to be around."

"I like to think so. Meanwhile, let's do some waltzin', Matilda."

The Stearman's shadow, racing across the blur of water below, seemed close enough to touch.

The machine was at full voice—a baritone symphony of blaring exhaust ports, thrashing propeller, singing gears and humming struts and brace wires. A stiff crosswind had risen, and Cap had to hold a hard set of rudder to keep the nose fixed on Spesutie Narrows, a narrow channel that made the Proving Ground's easternmost terrain a separate offshore isle.

About a mile south of the lighted buoy that marked the eight-foot channel leading into the narrows, Sweeney said,

"Hold her as steady as you can, Cap. The camera's starting to track everything a hundred and eighty degrees to port."

"It's not so easy, pal. We're picking up a lot of turbulence."

"I'm talking direction, not attitude. The camera adjusts for that."

Ahead, details came and went, magic vignettes that flickered momentarily in the onrushing: a sailboat, leaning into the chop, girls in bright colors, waving; a motor yacht, riding sedately among the whitecaps; a pair of fishermen in a bobbing outboard, hunched over their poles like priests contemplating the verities. Red and yellow trees; military buildings, dots of white against the land; spindly radio towers; a water tank; small boats, docks.

"Sweeney—Over there, to your left front. By the hangars on the airfield there—"

"I see it. A chase chopper, winding up."

"That's the kind that has guns all over."

"Yep. Just keep going."

"They're going to chase us and shoot us down."

"No way. It looks like a tied-down test-bed chopper, a ship they use to try out new gear."

"But—"

"Just keep going, damn it. Fast. Low. Then, when you get to the bridges, climb to five hundred, turn due east, and make like a bat out of hell for home. We'll have a nice tailwind going for us."

"Then what?"

"Sit us down as quickly as you can and make us some coffee."

Cap made a quick, low turn into the wind, set the Stearman neatly onto the meadow, and then, with short blasts of power, walked the ship to the flight line and let it tick to silence in the blue shadow of the hangar. While Sammy tied the ship down, Cap swung to the ground and helped Sweeney with the cameras.

"God," Sweeney moaned, "I'm getting too old for this kind of stuff."

"You mean you didn't enjoy your flight?"

"It was great, except that my knees and elbows are black-and-blue from bouncing around in that shoe box, except that my face feels torn off by the wind, except that I kept wanting to throw up, and except that I've had to go to the bathroom since the very first barrel-roll."

"Cap'n Eddie Ricketyback, that's you."

They drove to the house in Cap's Mustang, not saying much, and when they got there, Freddie Dilworth was waiting on the patio.

"Hi, Freddie. What's up?"

"Just a couple things I want to tell you about. They could be helpful."

Cap said, "I'll go make the coffee."

"Just a sec, Cap," Freddie said. "Some of this has to do with you."

Sweeney sighed. "Make it fast, if you can. I'm in no condition to dawdle."

"I was at my store, like usual, late last night, doin' books and cleanin' up a bit, when some dude knocked on the door. He said he was an insurance adjuster, lookin' into the bomb thing that took out a citizen and the Mercedes he was in. I told him the kid worked for me, odd jobs, and that I didn't know a lot more than that. And he said did I know Thomas Sweeney, owner of the Mercedes, and I said sure, but not very well, and he asked if I knew where you're living now and I said it beats the hell out of me. Then he asked me if I knew Veronica O'Brien, and I said I did, and he wanted to know where she lives and when's the best time for him to find her there. He said the deceased had given O'Brien as a reference."

Cap glanced at Sweeney.

Sweeney asked, "How did you answer that question, Freddie?"

"I told him Miss Cap was living in a little house on George Street in Chesapeake City."

Cap said, "What? Chesapeake City?"

"I own a little house there. An investment, sort of. It's a rental, fully furnished. Only right now I ain't got a renter. I put you in it on the spur of the moment, sort of. I figured you wouldn't want snoops coming around here, seeing all the computer stuff and all."

Sweeney smiled. "Freddie scores again."

Cap wasn't so pleased. "Heck, he'll visit me there—"

Freddie shook his head. "Nope. I told him you were in Europe. On one a them bicycle hostel tours, where it's harder than hell to get in touch with you. I told him I should know, because you're two months behind in your rent."

Sweeney laughed with unreserved delight. "See Cap? I told you Freddie Dilworth was a blinking genius."

Freddie blushed. "I think you ought to give me some of your clothes so I can hang 'em in the closets over there at the little house, though. Somebody might check up on my story. Know what I mean?"

"A Class-A, wide-gauge, hundred octane, fuel-injected, Kansas City cut of genius." Sweeney laughed again. "So did this dude say anything else, Freddie?"

"He just gave me his card and said I should call him if I spotted you and that there would be a reward or something if I got him in touch with you."

"You got that card, Freddie?"

Freddie handed it over. "All it says is 'William Adams, insurance adjuster,' and then a Baltimore phone number."

"What did the guy look like?"

"Small, thin, sort of, but tough. You know. Dark eyes that made him look nervous all the time. Thick eyebrows."

"So this Adams gave you his card and left. Is that it?"

"Well, there's a little bit more. When he drove off in a rented Taurus, I followed him. But all he did was check into Traveler's Rest, that Elkton motel."

"Is he still there?"

"I don't know."

"Well, as the man says, ya done good. Anything else?"

"A few minutes ago, when I was waiting for you, Cap's unlisted phone rang and I listened to the recorder. Some guy named Bojo returned your call and says he needs to talk to you bad."

"You're a sterling chap, Freddie, m'lad. I'll call him when we get back."

"We? Where we going?"

"After my little trip to the loo here, you're going to drive me to the Traveler's Rest. I want to do a recon on this Adams, and I need you to watch my flanks."

CHAPTER 22

The afternoon had become dull and metallic in hue, and to the southwest the sky was clotting into towering black clouds whose centers flickered redly. Freddie steered the Ford into the shadows of a convenience store adjacent to the motel and parked so as to give them a full view of the green Taurus sitting at the door of No. 3, alone in that melancholy featurelessness that seems to be a standard in rental cars. Setting up watch, Freddie and Sweeney shared a quart of beer and a large submarine sandwich.

"Cap tells me you two were fired from your jobs down there in Washington."

"We were asked to resign. It's the same thing."

"Is that why you're doing all this running around? You're mad, and you're trying to get even with somebody?"

Sweeney bit off some sandwhich and chewed thoughtfully for a time. "I've wondered about that myself, Freddie. I ask myself, 'Just what the hell are you trying to do, Sweeney?' And I answer, 'Trying to save my butt, that's what. Somebody's after me, somebody's got a real hard nose for me and wants to do me in, and I ain't gonna let that happen.' And then I ask, 'Why, if you fear for your life, don't you just run to the police, or the FBI, or the Home for the Elderly Abused and ask for help, for sanctuary?' And I answer, 'Somebody leans on me, I lean back.'

'Oh, yeah?' I hear myself sneering. 'Don't give me that macho crap, pal. A Schwarzenegger you ain't. You're not even a John Wayne. You're over the hump, and you get scared out of your eyes, and you want to pee in your pants when you hear a gun being cocked.' Then I say, 'It's bigger than me—something's going on that's against the national interest, and I've got to find out what it is and warn the president.' And I hear myself laughing and saying, 'So you're the whole goddam U.S. of A. national defense system, eh? Who needs a CIA, who needs an Army and an Air Force and a Navy and the Marines when you're around, eh, pal?' And then I come to the final—the only—explanation: 'I do what I do because that's the way my dials are set. I do it like I blink, or breathe. I'm Popeye: I yam what I yam, an' tha's all I yam.' And then I keep on going, wetting my pants all the way."

Freddie took a swig of beer and burped gently. "You always been like that?"

"I suppose so. All I know for sure is that I was better at conning myself in the earlier years. I was much more ready to believe the macho crap, to bury my real self under a lot of glamorized horse manure. And so the only answer to your question is, I guess, that no, I'm not running around trying to get even; I'm not trying to prove through lone-wolf heroics that my boss was a horse's ass for firing me. I'm running around like this because I don't know how *not* to run around like this."

Sweeney fell silent. Then: "What makes you so interested in what makes me tick, Freddie? It seems to me you're doing a bit of running around yourself."

"That's why I want to know what makes you tick. I can't decide just why, exactly, I'm sitting here, gassy with beer and watching some goddam hole in the wall. I thought maybe you might know."

"What would you be doing if you weren't sitting here?"

"Watching TV and feeling guilty."

"Guilty?"

"I can't watch TV without feeling that I should be doing something else. Not that the TV's all bad—some of it's damn good, actually—but it's a feeling I get. The tube reminds me that I'm watching, not doing. I'm spending my life in the grandstand, instead of being on the field, playing. I ain't doing, I ain't thinking. I'm letting somebody else do my doing and thinking. Know what I mean?"

"Yep."

"My life's half gone, and I ain't done anything with it yet. Nobody'll know, or care, I been here."

"You have kids, a family. They'll know."

"Maybe. But families grow up and drift apart. Know what? After all these years I can hardly remember what my old man looked like. He was good to me, important to me. But I grew up, and grew apart, sort of. And then, finally, even the memories faded away, like. Now, he's only a nice guy I once knew, and I don't have the least idea what he was all about, what his life was all about."

"So that's why you're here, gassy with beer?"

"Here I'm out of the grandstand and on some kind of field."

"Welcome to the team, Dilworth."

They traded glances and began to laugh.

It was then that Cummings-Adams came out of No. 3, accompanied by Ames, he of the tinted glasses. The two climbed into the Taurus and, after backing around, voomed south on the highway.

"Tallyho, Freddie. We got ourselves a bonus. Let's see where these guys go, eh?"

Freddie was reaching for the ignition when two .45 Colt automatics came through the open side windows—one to press against Freddie's head, the other against Sweeney's.

A deep voice said, "Leave it off, pal. And both of you keep looking straight ahead. Pat 'em down, Lou."

The left rear door opened and the car tilted slightly under a third man's weight. A quick, deft hand removed the Beretta from Sweeney's shoulder holster. A similar search of Freddie's jacket came up with nothing.

"This pistol is all they got topside. Move them out of the car so I can see what they got down below."

"All right," the deep voice said. "Both of you ease out backward, put your feet on the ground and your hands on the car's roof. Easy, now."

When the pat-down was complete, the man said, "Okay,

walk to that stretch Caddie behind the billboard over there. Keep your hands in your pockets. They come out of your pockets, or a fast move of any kind, gets you dead."

Sweeney, struggling to think, sent glances right and left, looking for an out, for a person—any person—who might spot the situation and sneak a call to the cops. But the dark clouds had arrived, and there was a burst of wind, a swirl of rain spittle, and those few people in sight were scurrying, heads down, for shelter.

"Get in the backseat. Lie on the floor, facedown, with your hands behind your heads."

They did as they were told, and in less than a minute the big gold-colored car was moving fast, its tires sizzling on rain-spattered highway. One man drove, with a second in the front passenger seat. The other two were in the rear, shoes planted solidly on Freddie's and Sweeney's backs, .45s held inches from their napes. The car smelled of cheap whiskey.

Sweeney estimated they had been driving about ten minutes when the deep voice said, "Turn right there—up ahead there."

The car slowed, made the turn, and began to jounce on the ruts of what had to be a farm lane.

"All right, Zeke, turn around, facing the highway, and then stop by that fence there. Leave the motor running."

"They're gonna kill us," Freddie said suddenly, his voice muffled.

"Easy, Freddie. Keep your cool."

"Shut up, you two."

Sweeney felt a flash of anger, a totally irrational surge of outrage so strong it smothered his rising panic. "Up yours, you son of a bitch. What are you going to do if I don't shut up? Shoot me sooner?"

The car came to a halt, and the voice said, "Everybody out and stand by the fence. Except you, Zeke. You stay beside the car."

The lane was a miserable, puddled channel in a vast sweep of corn stubble that seemed to have no ends, no horizons. The car had stopped beside a post-and-rail fence in a weedy defilade made murky by the misty rain.

Sweeney felt a peculiar calm, a sensation that seemed close to quiet anticipation. As he was shoved against a fence post, he looked about, and everything had a special clarity, a kind of commanding beauty: the shredded corn, the puddles reflecting the low gray sky, the browns and grays and blues and reds and greens and all the shades between. The cool of the rain, the smell of distances and the high, lonely call of a bird.

"Are you all right, Freddie?"

"Sure. I'm fine. It has to end sometime, doesn't it?"

"Yep. And you played a damn good game."

The three men, pistols pointing. The fourth, leaning against the car, smoking a cigarette. It became suddenly important to Sweeney that he see their faces, but, oddly, their features remained blurred, indistinct.

The shots sounded like sticks swept across a picket fence. Rapid, staccato.

Sweeney stared, and the faceless men with the pistols collapsed into the mud, and the man with the cigarette spun around, twice, like an inept ballerina, then slid slowly down the gold Cadillac's riddled flank to form a spread of rags in a spread of puddle.

"Jesus," Freddie choked. "What the hell happened?"

Sweeney heard his own voice: "Somebody shot them."

"Who?"

"I don't know."

A motor whirred into life, a distant sound in the mist, and the car's sounds dwindled rapidly, leaving only the hissing of the rain in the shifting wind.

"Let's get out of here, Sweeney."

"Wait'll I get my Beretta back. And their wallets."

"I want to go home and hug my wife. I haven't hugged my wife for a long time."

"Get in the Caddie. I'll drive this time."

CHAPTER 23

They returned to the Ford, left the battered Caddie in the convenience store parking lot, then drove directly to Freddie's bookstore-garage. Freddie, with no further word, went inside, walking stiffly, as if each step hurt.

A week earlier, Freddie had retrieved the Pontiac, left idling in front of the Happy Hour Motel, after convincing the police that it had been stolen from his garage by the man found jack-handled in the shower stall. The car was now alone and dirty in the weedy lot. Sweeney took the keys off the mechanic's rack, sat in the front seat, and went through each of the wallets he'd retrieved from the bodies in the farm lane.

He was trembling badly, and his teeth wanted to chatter. He sat back, waiting for the spasm to pass, and he saw his face in the rearview mirror. The shock and fear had left no discernible traces there. It was all inside—the fluttering, the nausea, the understanding that he had peered into the pit, and that someday there would be another go at it, and there would be no coming back. It was there. Waiting. Shifting through papers, struggling to concentrate, he saw for the first time that inevitability was no philosophical abstraction. It was definable, measurable, implacable, a tangible force that ruled him as surely as he was ruled by gravity.

Harold Donly. Louis McIvey. Ezekiel Crane. Arthur Grimes. Names on Pennsylvania driver's licenses. All claiming Philadelphia as home. There were licenses from at least a half-dozen states, and on each license there was a different name. (Will the real murdering bastards please stand up?)

Phony papers and Pennsylvania were a combination that evoked Fatso Dominic.

A ten-wheeled son of a bitch, Fatso was.

But he was also a place to start.

Sweeney drove to Wilmington, calming himself by re-creating as he went 1991's Operation Squid, in which he had first learned of Dominic. Fatso was one of the East Coast's major purveyors of criminal talent, illegal weapons, burglar tools, passports and visas, assorted licenses and disposable motor vehicles. Fatso's hardware inventory was ingeniously warehoused in an innocuous wedge of row houses just off Church Street, near the rusted riverfront mills, while his caper cars and vans were disguised as a used-car lot beside the railroad in Edge Moor. All transactions were strictly cash and carry.

His trembling had subsided by the time he went into the little grocery store that served as Fatso's business entrance and bought a package of lima beans from the tiny white-haired woman behind the counter.

"I want to see Fatso."

"Whatcha gonna do them beans?"

"Cook them with a ham hock."

"Need two packs for that."

"Okay. Give me another." He handed her five quarters.

As she rang up the sale, her bony thumb pressed a button under the counter rim. A very large black man with a very large bulge under his jacket came through a door at the rear of the store.

"Who you?"

"Ham hock and five quarters say I see Fatso. They do not say I answer the doorman's questions."

The man eyed him carefully, not at all pleased by his findings. "You don't look right."

"My mother thought I was cute."

"And you got an attitude problem."

"Do I ever."

After a thoughtful interval, the man said, "Three minutes. Then you're outa here."

"Suits me."

Fatso was also very large, a condition obviously abetted by spaghetti, a mountain of which he was now in the process of consuming. He sat behind a table adorned by a checkered cloth and an absurd little vase of plastic forget-me-nots, and he was slurping with unrestrained enthusiasm. "How you find me, pal?"

"Vinnie Caruso, of the South Philly Carusos."

"How come Vinnie dint call me first?"

"You know Vinnie never uses phones."

Fatso nodded. "Okay. You know the answers. Whatcha want?"

"Contact with a couple of dudes."

"I don't deal in personalities."

"Vinnie tells me otherwise. Vinnie says you're a talent agency for very special, hard-to-reach clients. Vinnie says that for a price you would tell me how to contact Elvis."

Fatso grinned widely through a mouthful of spaghetti "That's Vinnie, all right. What a joker, eh?"

Sweeney shrugged. "You want to do business or not?"

"Who the guys you wanna contact?"

"If I knew, we wouldn't be having this conversation. All I have is what Vinnie gave me from his file: driver's license photos and some phony Philadelphia addresses." He spread the documents on the tablecloth.

Fatso and the black man studied the photos for a full thirty seconds, then traded amused glances.

"You sure you wanna talk to these guys? These guys is meatballs. Very slow lane," Fatso said.

"I want to talk to both high and low brackets. My daddy always told me, 'Never take the low bid, never take the high bid. Find out what they are and divide by two.' "

Fatso smiled, openly disdainful, like a new-car dealer considering a trade-in. "These guys is all free-lancers out of Marcus Hook. You hire 'em like you hire day labor on the street corners. If they ain't drunk, that is. Low bid? These guys is it."

"Let me have their names."

"I take my percentage off the top, you know."

"For what, exactly?"

"Real names, real addresses. That's all. I don't take no responsibility for no deals, no matter the hit's made or not. Specially that."

"Naturally. Your clients: Do I tell them you sent me?"

"They wouldn't talk to ya if ya din't."

"And they pay you for the referral?"

"That ain't none a your biz, pal."

Sweeney nodded. "I guess not. So how much is low? From my, ah, consumer's point of view, that is."

"For these guys, five hunnert a name. Two thou, on this tablecloth. For top-a-the-line quality, five thou a name, or twenty thou on the cloth."

"All right. It's a deal for these cheap guys."

Fatso wiped his mouth with a huge checkered napkin. "Can I see your green, mister?"

"Certainly." Sweeney opened his wallet and flashed his invalidated SII special agent's badge, bronzed and presented to him as a keepsake. "Consider the two grand to be a contribution to the safer, more sane world so diligently sought by those in charge of our wonderful government."

"Shee-it! You a Fed?"

"Yep."

The large black man made a move for his shoulder bulge, but Fatso waved a pudgy hand. "Hold it, Sam." His stare fixed on Sweeney, he asked, "This a pinch?"

"Of course not. I simply need to hire some hitters. We have to take out some foreign spies, and, as you know, the government forbids its people to do hits. If you cooperate, if you make this contribution, you stay in business, no questions asked, no interference. Like it's been until now."

"Spies, huh? I hate them foreigners."

"They're taking over everything, all right."

Fatso put down his napkin and pushed away from the table, his appetite obviously dulled by this extraordinary development. He and Sam exchanged long, thoughtful stares.

Sam broke the silence. "I can't believe Vinnie told this fuzz about us, Boss."

"Yeah," Fatso said, regarding Sweeney again. "How about that, pal? Vinnie never talks ta nobody. Specially Feds."

Sweeney answered with the partial truth. "Right now Vinnie's in protective custody. He helps us stymie the foreign spies in return for our ignoring certain of his personal federal tax violations. But outside that basic agreement, he has another major incentive. He is cooperating with us because one of the prime aims of the foreigners is to take over American rackets. Vinnie's bonus agreement is, he helps us at the political and military espionage level, we look the other way in certain of the Mob's, ah, commercial areas. You and your operation, for example."

Sam was unconvinced. "I think that's a crock, Boss."

"Look," Sweeney said irritably, "it should be obvious to you both that, if I know this much, I know everything. And, knowing everything, I could have brought a regiment of Feds to blow the walls out of this craphouse today, instead of just little old me wandering in to buy lima beans. Right?"

Stares were traded again.

Sweeney saw the wavering and bored in. "Besides, what the hell you got to lose? You give me the contacts, you stay in business and collect your agent's fee from your four clients. You don't give me the contacts, I hire some other hitters somewhere else and you get the whole Federal government down on your little grocery store like a hundred tons of wet noodles."

Fatso nodded. "Okay. We deal. Consider your two grand paid."

Sweeney took out his notebook and pencil. "Go ahead."

"These guys is"—Dominic's fat forefinger began to tap the photos in sequence—"Spuds Morfey, Al Lingo, Pete Burns and Luigi Mansini. You hire 'em through me. If I can find 'em and they's sorta sober, that is."

Sweeney nodded. "Good. Now I need to know who hired them today."

"No way am I gonna tell ya that."

"Oh, yes, you are. Believe me. You're going to tell me."

"It was some guy in a hurry. Name of Adams, stayin' in a Elkton motel. He had ta cool some heat, r-i-i-ght now."

"Okay. Now I want the name of the absolutely best shootist

in the Middle-Atlantic States. The shootist that the rich and famous in Washington, Philly and New York are in the habit of hiring. I don't care what his fee is."

"It ain't one guy, it's a firm. Warren Stiegel, Billy Yates, Michael Lorenzo, and Ray Plummer. They's a firm that operates under the name, Stiegel and Company, Public Relations, an' their main office is in the penthouse of Willoughby Towers, that new high-rise just off I-95 in Chester. You tell the girl at the reception desk that I sent ya. That's the way it works with them."

"I have a better idea. You call her now and tell her John Parker, Mr. Stiegel's new CPA, will be there"—he glanced at his watch—"in an hour."

"She closes up at five."

"Tell her to wait. And tell her that I'm to be given every consideration."

The receptionist at Stiegel and Company was an amiable little woman in her midthirties who wore her brown hair short and her white smile wide.

"So, then, you're the Mr. Parker Mr. Dominic called me about. The new CPA. Mr. Dominic is such a nice man, don't you think?

"He certainly is."

"Mr. Stiegel just thinks the world of him."

"I can see why. And as for you, young lady: you have my sincerest apologies for keeping you after hours. But my schedule has been hectic today. Absolutely hectic."

"Not to worry," she said good-naturedly. "I have to work late tonight anyhow. I'm Dottie Fitzgerald. So what can I do for you?"

"First, are any of the firm members in town tonight?"

She laughed. "Oh, no, sir. They're all on trips for clients this week. It's a very busy time for us."

"Darn. I was hoping at least one would be around if I have to check on anything. Mr. Stiegel has authorized me to do a quick audit of the second- and third-quarter books. There's a possible tax break of major proportions, and he called Mr. Dominic and asked him to get me on the job, posthaste, because

I'm a loophole specialist and the deadline for this loophole is tonight at midnight. Naturally, your bosses want to beat the taxes any way they can."

"Oh, my, I should think so. The ledgers are kept in the file cabinet in Mr. Stiegel's office. He handles those matters himself, which is a break for me, because the couple of times I saw those books they looked like Russian phone books, know what I mean?" She laughed, jolly and guileless.

"I hope they don't look that way to me."

They laughed together at this.

"Come on down the hall, Mr. Parker, and I'll unlock the office for you."

There were two sets of ledgers, both of which, as he read, he photographed with his low-light miniature Minox. The overt one, presumably legitimate, was kept in the file cabinet's top drawer and dealt entirely with "public relations accounts." The other, which was encased in embossed leather and bore the legend, *The Bible, Revised,* was retrieved from the top shelf of a floor-to-ceiling bookcase after a broad, conspiratorial wink from Miss Fitzgerald, who managed to show a lot of thigh in climbing and descending the library ladder.

Entries in *The Bible* suggested hieroglyphics. But Sweeney had done a lot of time in cryptoanalysis. With the portable electronic decode wheel provided by wonder-worker Oscar Schwenke, he had, in less than an hour, learned that Stiegel and Company had contracts with some exceptionally wealthy and prominent individuals and firms.

One entry literally took his breath away: Stiegel and Company had been paid $35,000 on October 9 to "pursue the Sweeney project."

The sum had been paid in full, and in cash, by Aaron Richter, of Washington, D.C.

He was compelled to sit down while dealing with the shock.

He was the target of two malevolent forces: the mysterious Cummings-Adams, a man in a hurry on the cheap, and Aaron Richter, his former boss, who was paying top dollar for quality shooting.

Gathering himself, he followed a sudden hunch. He returned to the *The Bible* and rechecked the entry for *Ridenour, Ran-*

dolph, which further advised him to see the folder labeled, *Ridenour, Randolph—Current* in the open PR file cabinet. It contained some network promos, a few pictures of the Great Man, a contract for "direct mail promotions, non-network," and, slid almost haphazardly between two promo bills, a fax sheet of a paper dated a year earlier and headed, *Affidavit.* He read this carefully, twice, then photographed it before returning it to the file.

On the way out, he smiled at Miss Fitzgerald and said, "You're really a great soul to be so patient with me. The least I can do is take you to dinner. What say?"

"Wouldn't you know. My chance to go out with a darling-looking man and I'm nailed to my word processor. What rotten luck. Thanks a bunch anyhow, Mr. Parker. Rain check?"

"You bet. Any time."

"This has been the grossest kind of day for me."

He patted her hand, then went into the foyer and punched the elevator button. As the door opened and he entered the car, he glanced back at the reception area, where, through the expensive glass wall, he could see Miss Fitzgerald busily typing away.

A flicker of memory showed him the bodies sprawled in the muddy farm lane, and he said aloud, sadly, wearily, "You don't know what gross is, dear heart."

"Hello."

"Mr. Richter?"

"Yes."

"Warren Stiegel here."

"Good evening."

"There was a try on Sweeney today. Four hoods from Marcus Hook took him and that backup guy of his into a cornfield. The hoods bought it, and Sweeney and his friend were rescued."

"The four bodies?"

"Removed without trace."

"Where is Sweeney now?"

"The man's like smoke. He evaporates."

"What about Cap O'Brien? She might know."

"We checked her out. She's in Europe."

"Well, keep looking. We've got to find him before there's another try. I don't want him killed before I can talk to him."

"We're working on it."

"All right. Thank you for calling."

CHAPTER 24

Harvey Wallace took three days of his months of accrued leave time, and he and Millie flew Delta to Baltimore. There, he had told his staff, Millie would visit her ailing mother and he would sneak away for a little fishing on Chesapeake Bay. Actually, he didn't know one end of a fish from the other, and it was only sheer luck that he had qualified as a small powerboat sailor during some temporary duty years ago at Fort Monroe. But the arrangement called for his presence off Turkey Point at noon on Thursday, and there he would be, by God, silly hat and lures and poles at the ready.

He rented the gear and a seventeen-foot runabout at the Shelter Cove Marina on Hance's Point. The boat was more than he needed; an outboard rowboat—maybe a canoe, even—would have done the job. But the runabout was the only small craft immediately available, and besides, its lines and luster were sort of classy and he didn't want to show up for this reunion looking like some kind of rube. So he paid the fee and stocked up on ice for the fish lockers and ham sandwiches and Coke for him and coursed down the east channel past Bull Mountain to Rocky Point, where he reduced power and, riding the easterly wind and the outgoing tide, drifted onto the Flats. Where the charts showed a four-foot depth at mean low water, he dropped anchor, lifted a pole and made like a fisherman.

The gentle motion of the boat and the wind's whispering made him drowsy, and so he wasn't sure how long he'd been sitting there when a voice at his right elbow said, "Hey, dummy—Don't you know that it's so shallow here the fish have wheels?"

Sweeney, his face framed in scuba black, the mask on his forehead sending out shards of reflected sunlight, grinned up at him from the shimmering water. "And where the hell did you get that nutty hat?"

"Careful, boy. This is high style in Saint Augie. And who are you calling dummy? I'm the one who's riding across this pond. You're walking."

"Good to see you again, Harve."

"Same here. Want to come aboard? Or will that diminish your dramatic effect?"

"Hey, man, I'm not standing on this muddy bottom and hiding behind your boat just to be dramatic. I've been eyeballing the shoreline across the way, and it's been a long, lazy swim for no reward. Right now I want you to look like you're alone to whoever might be glassing you from Aberdeen."

"So who gives a damn about what they think at Aberdeen?"

"That's what I want to talk about. But you first. So what do you want to talk about?"

"You mean I've got to talk while you keep bobbing in the water like that?"

Sweeney laughed. "No. Take your boat to the cove behind the big driftwood pile over there to your right. The water's deep enough for an anchorage. See the stairway on the bank there?"

"Yes."

"Well, don't take it. Climb the bank through the trees directly to the left of it. My house is on the bluff. It looks unoccupied, shut down. But the cellar door's open."

Sweeney had changed into a sweater and slacks, and he and Wallace sat in the library, sipping Scotch and staring at the sun-sparkles on the bay.

"This is a pretty damn nice place for a guy who can't keep a job in Washington, where nobody ever gets fired for anything," Wallace said.

"I wasn't fired. I resigned. It said so, right on all the networks."

The general smiled. "Tell me, do you always receive guests in scuba and keep your house looking shut for the winter?"

"Only when people are watching, waiting to find me and kill me."

Wallace's smile melted into somberness. "I'm assuming that you'll tell me what the hell you're talking about."

Sweeney poured the general another Scotch. "I had a couple of reasons for calling you. That's one of them. To tell you about it. But it's going to take awhile. It's pretty involved."

"Begin with the beginning. I've got the time."

Sweeney told Wallace everything he knew—from Nageler's death to this morning's reconnaissance of the Proving Ground waterfront. He finished by confessing, "Actually, I was putting you on about the long swim, Harve. Freddie Dilworth took me upstream in his runabout and I just dropped over the side. After my recon he picked me up downstream and brought me back to where I caught you dozing."

"You really lucked into it with Freddie and Cap O'Brien, didn't you."

"Premium-grade godsends."

"But why would this Cummings hire four small-time hitters to do you and Freddie? Why would Richter pay thirty-five big ones? And Ridenour: He doesn't need to hire his killing done. He's got the three deadliest tools known to man: a huge ego, a mean mouth, and a microphone. Believe me, pal. I've met the guy."

"That's another reason I called you. The grapevine told me about The Great Television Shootout and how the brass has decided you owe that horse's ass an apology. And that's the reason I got the idea to look up Ridenour in the records of the Famous Person's Hit Man Company. And that's the reason I called this meeting. It struck me that anybody who ticks off Ridenour has just got to be a dearly wonderful person to spend an afternoon with, pumping information from and soliciting the help of."

Wallace nodded. "And that's why this dearly wonderful person came all the way to Maryland. He wants to pump some information out of you. Or at least see if you have any ideas."

They exchanged smiles—long-separated friends, remembering what had made them friends in the first place.

Wallace picked up the binoculars and examined the Proving Ground shoreline. "So what do you think is going on over there, Sweeney?"

"All I know is, they're flying something in, or they're flying something out, or they're doing both. With C-one thirties that come and go like commuter trains. And I'm getting ready to penetrate the base to see if I can find out what the something is. Meantime, I was sort of hoping you'd have some suggestions. But obviously, being an Army Reserve officer, you don't know nuthin'."

The general, moving the glasses through a steady traverse, said, "Up yours, Swooney."

"Seriously, Harve, as UIF honcho, maybe you can find out what the shipments are all about—and also get some kind of line on what Nageler could have been looking for over there. Bernie Kratzer and the Nachrichtendienst don't know, the CIA and the National Security Council don't know—if they did it would have shown up in the presidential daily briefings—and, most assuredly, I don't know. Folks in your daisy chain might know and not even know that they know, if you know what I mean."

"I've got a few buttons I can push." Wallace lowered the binoculars and set them carefully on the coffee table. "Meanwhile, though, your crack about the Reserve Corps—it was too close to the bone to make me laugh. And it's precisely why I'm here to talk to you. Maybe you can find some buttons to push in my behalf."

"What's your problem?"

"I think that, as an activated Reservist, I'm being used. I think somebody's setting up something, and they need a soldat outside The Pentagon Establishment to make it work."

"What kind of somebody? Military, or political?"

"My hunch tells me it's both. But that's what I want you to find out. I honest-to-God can't trust anybody else to do it."

"So what appears to be going on?"

Wallace sipped his whiskey, his gaze on the afternoon, as if there were answers in the distant blue hills across the bay. "Things are going too well. Things are too good to be true."

"Say what?"

"How familiar are you with the drug war mechanism?"

Sweeney shrugged. "The Pentagon's daily digest sheets. The tube. The newspapers and magazines. My schtick was the Eastern Hemisphere Desk, strategic military intelligence, and whatever narcotics figured in my projects were small-scale—the occasional exploitation of a high-level addict, setting bribes and payoffs afloat on the drug-money stream now and then. That kind of tangential stuff."

"Well, to understand how things are going too well, you need some context."

"So lay it on me."

Wallace finished his drink and sank back in his chair. "In the beginning there was the Drug Enforcement Agency, a purely civilian operation that was no more than police-type track-and-bust stuff by handfuls of agents who had to get permission to go to the bathroom. After the Gulf War and the Communist meltdown, President Bush, faced with a drug epidemic that wouldn't go away and a military machine with nothing to do, put the two together, authorizing the Pentagon to use U.S. military forces to backstop the DEA with hardware and skilled personnel. That's when the Army set up the Southcom Counternarcotics Operation Center at Quarry Heights in Panama, and American Special Forces troops and the U.S. Air Force, supported by the Navy at sea and the Coast Guard in domestic waters, began clobbering the druggies' import efforts in the arc from Venezuela to Florida. But even that wasn't enough, so there was a huge diplomatic push that resulted in the 1992 Treaty of Acapulco and the internationalization of the war. U.S. forces, at the invitation of the relevant South and Central American governments, moved into the field and began rousting the druggies in their lairs."

The general paused, thinking, and Sweeney waited for him to gather the strings.

"But Congress began to stew about a Viet-Nam type involvement and a backlash among the South Americans who saw Yankee Imperialism in the works. This, along with the hellacious cost, mandated a restructuring. Leonardi had been elected president by then, and his solution was to keep the Air Force and the Air National Guard and the Navy and Coast Guard on the interception job in the air and at sea, as before. But he removed the Army combat infantry divisions and their support units and turned over the whole on-the-ground campaign to South American troops, abetted by select mercenary units under the direction of the special assistants to the Joint Chiefs—the so-called 'JCs' Jaycees.' And to lower the Pentagon profile even more, the drug war was 'civilianized'—a rotten little word for shutting down Quarry Heights, moving the control center to Homestead at Miami, and putting the whole shebang under the command of the UIF, personified by yours truly, the quintessential weekend warrior." He took a ham sandwich from the cooler he'd brought up from the boat and bit into it, chewing pensively.

Sweeney continued his silence.

"That's when everything turned weird, everything started going great. All of a sudden the farms began shutting down under the pressure of Colombian and Peruvian troops, thanks to up-to-the-minute intelligence fed them by our Special Forces and CIA satellite surveillance. Our air and sea interceptions, aided by universal radar, AWACS, and balloon radar pickets, began to nail smugglers in numbers you wouldn't believe—it was shooting fish in a barrel. Then as a knee-jerk fallout, criminal drug distribution in the U.S. began to dry up, and street prices soared to the point that users, forced out of the market, began showing up at all levels and kinds of domestic treatment centers. I kid you not. Everywhere I look, at all strata of command, it's now Big-Successarama."

Sweeney placed his empty glass on the coffee table. "So what's the beef?"

"As I say, it's too good. Every boat and plane—and there's been damned few of them left to run the risk these days—has been picked up by our air and sea screens and blown to hell. Not one prisoner. Not one craft taken. Not one body recovered. Nothing but splinters of boats, planes, drug packages and people found floating on the sea. Meanwhile, the ground units have destroyed entire networks of labs and processing plants, interdicted overland shipments of raw and finished goods, and burnt huge areas of farmland, and now we have a virtual shutdown of the whole goddam machine."

"Well?"

"So why—when all the combined armed forces of the United States, led by crackerjack Regular officers operating out of the most advanced computerized headquarters known to military history, were unable to do it—have a tenth of the forces, led by a Reserve Corps general, been able to shut down the drug cartels? How come our interception of blockade runners has approached one hundred percent? How come these runners, like lemmings, fly or sail unswervingly and without resistance to their doom under our guns? How come I have the impression that I'm given reports out of Homestead and the Pentagon that are incomplete or fudged? Why do I feel compelled to come a thousand miles on a phony vacation to talk about these things with a busted intelligence bigwig who is free-lancing for the Germans, of all people, while not busy trying to keep his own ass from being blown off?"

Sweeney gave him a look. "Okay, so why did you come? What tore it for you?"

"An AWACS that didn't exist. The runners have finally begun to fight back, and on the first engagement, our planes and a couple of picket boats spotted a big something at the rim of the action. The report was checked with the Jaycees and they said it was an AWACS. Only no AWACS was either scheduled for that night in that area or—according to my own, private questioning of the Air Force people in charge—actually sent on patrol. They said there was no apparent need, what with the thin runner traffic and the blanket laid by the balloons and universal radars. So the big question is, why would the Jaycees lie to me?"

"Not a lie, maybe. Maybe a simple mistake?"

"Then why not admit it? And, if it was a mistake and there was no AWACS, what the hell *was* that thing flying on the rim and why wasn't it plotted on the board?"

"So you expect *me* to find out?"

"I don't know who can be trusted inside. And whoever I get to help from the outside has to be familiar with the ways things work topside. That, pal, spells Sweeney."

They each attacked another half sandwich.

"Want me to make some coffee?"

Wallace shook his head. "No, I'm fine."

Sweeney said, "So, here we are: two guys asking questions. One, on the inside, needs somebody on the outside he can trust to chase down answers. The other, very much on the outside, needs somebody he can trust on the inside."

Wallace sighed. "That says it, all right."

Sweeney thought some. Then: "Do you have any connections at the National Communications Registry?"

"No, but one of my guys does. Why?"

"A guy named Schachtel at CIA is my only route to a copy of any transmissions Hank might have made on his DKK. But Schachtel's out of town. Can you maneuver a copy for me?"

"If it's there, I'll get it to you."

After another interval Sweeney said, "In all this schmeer we've got one thing in common, Harve."

"What's that?"

"Ridenour. He tries to do a number on you. He deals with the firm hired to kill me. He links my questions to your questions. He makes my questions your questions."

"Meaning my answers will be your answers?"

"Sure looks possible, doesn't it?"

"Yeah. I'd say so."

"Let's think about that some, eh?"

"Millie had an interesting idea about my—our—problem. Actually, she just gave words to something I'd been thinking all along."

"Vot's dot?"

"What if somebody at the Jaycee or NSC level was, well, editing the reports that go to the president? What if somebody was telling Leonardi only what they wanted him to know?"

"Why would somebody do that?"

"To give him one idea of what's going on in the drug war when something else was really going on."

"Like cornering the market for their own benefit?"

"Something like that."

Sweeney nodded slowly. "I think Millie's onto something there."

"But who? And who's really doing what?"

Sweeney said, "That, my boy, is what you and I are going to

find out." He paused, thinking. Then: "I assume you've already apologized to Ridenour."

"Of course. I'm an officer and I follow orders. But he hasn't used it yet."

"Ah. I didn't think so. The grapevine told me about the incident, and I've asked Cap to monitor Ridenour's shows so we'd have a record of what you said. So what happened?"

"He sent it back to me, saying I had to redo it. I wasn't being apologetic enough. He said that I sounded as if I don't really mean it."

Sweeney laughed, shaking his head in disbelief. "That guy is a thousand-horsepower squid."

"You've noticed that, eh?"

"And we're going to blot up a little of his ink."

"What do you mean?"

"When are you due back in Baltimore?"

"This evening. When I get there. Millie doesn't expect me until late."

"Okay. You're going to return your boat to Shelter Cove. I'll meet you there in, say, an hour. From there you'll follow me in your car to The Orchards. We'll have Cap videotape your new apology. And I'm going to be producer, director and script-writer."

CHAPTER 25

If things kept going this way, Cap thought, she would have to add an ell to the house. It wasn't that bad, of course, because most of the information had come in over the modems and was now stored on floppies, all carefully alphabetized and filed in cardboard boxes that she had stacked neatly along the wall adjacent to her computer desk. The rest—faxes of position papers, bios, PR releases, speeches, news clippings, along with pirated videocassettes and tape recordings that had been shipped by her pals via overnight parcel services—were kept in a row of tin file cabinets Freddie had dug up at an auction in Chestertown, of all places. Her complaint to Freddie just the day before: "I have built here either the world's largest small library or the world's smallest large library."

"What's in it?" Freddie wanted to know.

"A panorama of the most recent two months in the life of the planet Earth, as witnessed and documented by The People In Charge."

"Oh, wow. What's it for?"

"It's for the convenience and edification of our beloved Führer, Thomas F. Sweeney, of course."

"Yeah, but what's it do for him?"

"Feeds him. Think of strategic intelligence as one of those creatures that catch food, chew it into manageable, digestible, nourishing consistencies and then feed it back to their young. All around the world, every hour of every day, the intelligence creature's many tentacles gather up information—the fundamental food—and send it up ten basic chains of command and responsibility until it gets to Washington, where it's centralized, coordinated, evaluated, condensed into nourishing portions, and then fed to the government's separate parts in the amounts everybody hopes will keep the nation healthy. An abbreviated menu, or a kind of daily dietary chart of what's been taken in and redistributed over the past twenty-four hours, is sent to the president and his staff through the National Security Council. We've tapped into the organism's main food processing system. We've not only reproduced the dietary charts for the past sixty days, we've also got a pretty good picture of what the president has done and said after reading them. Sweeney's been studying the material, looking for patterns that might give him a clue as to what Nageler was working on and what he wanted Sweeney to warn President Leonardi about."

"No wonder the government's so lousy. It's probably got a hellish case of indigestion, what with all that chewin' and spittin."

She smiled wryly.

"Godamighty, how'd you do all this, Cap?"

"I called in a lot of markers. I also cussed a bunch."

"But it's so damn—complicated."

"Well, it wouldn't have been possible without computers. But with the right computer equipment and access codes, and if you've been doing this kind of thing for ten years and know where and how to poke the tender spots, it isn't too big a deal."

Freddie had left, muttering that nothing was wrong with Washington that a dozen shiploads of Digel wouldn't fix, and soon after that the phone had rung and it was Sweeney, wanting some personal background material on Randolph Ridenour. She knew she had nothing about the man in her own files so she dialed the code that gave her Rachel Ramsey, her successor in SII, and asked that the SII dossier be put on the confidential M wire and routed to Oscar Schwenke's terminal, where an access code number provided by the good doctor enabled her to call it up on her own screen here at The Orchards. No soap, according to an advisory put on her screen by Rachel: the dossier was now locked into the personal computer of Aaron Richter and was temporarily unavailable to staff inquiries.

She considered calling Audrey Blum, an archivist at the CIA, but these days The Company was so carefully policed and so publicly scrutinized such a call would most assuredly be, to use Sweeney's expression, pumping mud. Audrey had always been damned helpful, but nowadays The Company itself could no longer admit that it kept dossiers on prominent American citizens. The IRS and the FBI? Of course. The Library of Congress? Certainly. The Census Bureau and the Statistical Abstract? Indeed. But the nation's largest and single most important intelligence-gathering machine? Uh-uh. Not as long as congressmen needed a whipping-boy that was guaranteed to get juicy headlines back home. So she punched up access screen calls to pals in each of the CIA's peer organizations—the DOD, the State Department, the National Security Agency, the FBI, the Defense Intelligence Agency, Treasury, Energy, and Army, Navy and Air. She even tried the Voice of America and retried in the lower ranks of the SII itself. But all these sources managed to put on her screen was baby-formula bio material, so paplike, so antiseptic, it could well have been pumped out by the publicity mill of Ridenour's network.

She told Sweeney all this two hours later when he walked through the door with General Wallace in tow.

"Aaron Richter?" He traded glances with Wallace. "Why would Richter want to read up on our favorite TV star?"

Wallace shrugged. "A curious coincidence, I'd say. Maybe he's plugged Ridenour into this thing like we have."

Sweeney's face showed doubt. "I'm not so sure about that," he said politely. "And there's a bigger question: If Ridenour is in the business of hiring hoods, and Richter is in the business of meeting with hoods in cheap hotels, who's to say Ridenour and Richter aren't in cahoots? And if they are in cahoots, why would Richter be studying the dossier of Ridenour? One would assume, wouldn't one, that Richter would be quite familiar with Ridenour's background."

"Yes, one would assume that, one would."

Cap, annoyed, said, "Are you guys for real?" She held out her right hand. "General Wallace, let me introduce myself, since our esteemed leader apparently can't handle the social protocols. I'm Cap O'Brien."

The men made a business of being apologetic, and Cap pretended that she'd been kidding. Which irritated her even more, since she was a lousy pretender and had never given much time to playacting for any reason, for anyone. Looking at this, she realized that she was dealing with a derivative of jealousy. Sweeney had shown more interest in what Wallace thought about her explanations than he'd shown in the explanations themselves, and as the one who had been the first to lend him a hand in this schmeer, Sweeney's taking her for granted ticked her off mightily. Which had raised her into another level of indignation. She had many vulnerabilities, but jealousy wasn't among them, and so it was preposterous, this pouting like a schoolgirl over something so inane, so ridiculous. Why the hell was she *being* like this?

Come on, Cap, went the sudden, silent admission, *you're conning yourself. Sweeney's your problem.*

Sweeney had not only moved into her life, he'd taken it over. Just by being there, by being who and what he was, he'd seized the fabric of her life, shaken it, tossed it, broomed it, and hung it on a line, where its hues were daily altering under the intensity of his light.

He was tough, tenacious, wily, resourceful, adaptable as a chameleon and outrageously masculine. He never simply went somewhere—he marched. He couldn't even butter a slice of bread without its suggesting a saber attack. He had a gift for singleminded cerebration under heat; he could even, she was willing to bet, simultaneously rub his stomach and pat his head while mentally solving the *Times* Sunday crossword puzzle. He was, in sum, insufferable.

And yet—

There was that continuing, unmistakable hint of the little boy in it all. A smart-ass little boy, to be sure. But with an indefinable, underlying winsomeness, even so. There were times, even when she was the most furious with him, she wanted to smooth his hair and straighten his tie, for cripes sake.

Last Tuesday night, in rebellion, she had gone to dinner at the Kitty Knight House with Jon Moore, the marina owner and state legislator who had made a considerable effort over the years to add her to his trophies. The evening had been a disaster, with Jon epitomizing all the things she found to be so dreary in Today's Man. He was fragrant, he was elegantly manicured, he had an absolutely darling hairdo, and he was mindlessly, hopelessly in love with himself. All of which would have been more tolerable if there had been any substance to his conversation, but he'd chattered along like a P. G. Wodehouse airhead, his most profound subjects being duck decoys and his favorite movies.

And, worst of all, Sweeney had dominated the evening, because she'd kept comparing Jon to Sweeney, and between cocktails and dessert Sweeney had seemed to become less the High-Tech Huckleberry and more the Ivy League Ivanhoe.

"Cap? Yo, Cap. Are you listening to me?"

"Certainly I'm listening to you. What did you say?"

"I said we're going to make a videotape of General Wallace. Would you please take the copy as I write it and put it on the scroll-screen so he can read it?"

"Sure. Where are we going to shoot this epic?"

"I don't want any identifiable background."

"How about the picnic table, with the woods behind? Woods are woods, and the light's good there, too."

"That should be okay. Harve, do you by any chance have a uniform in that Hertzmobile of yours?"

"A full set of Class A's. I always have them with me on trips because I never know when I might need them."

"Good. While Cap and I are setting up, put them on. I want you looking as ferociously military as you can get."

They shot the thing several times. The first two were busts because Wallace was stilted and uneasy, too obviously reading his lines. The third go was just about perfect, despite the general's tendency to squint.

"Mr. Ridenour, I have, at your request, remade this videotape, in which I was to apologize to you for my behavior during your recent attempt to interview me in Saint Augustine. You rejected the first version because you felt the apology failed to convey true contrition.

"This version will also be unacceptable to you, I'm sure,

because now I not only categorically refuse to apologize but I also put you on notice that I have documentary evidence of your having engaged in, first, a grossly unethical agreement to lobby for Manuel Corbato, a Cartagena drug lord, and, second, a contract in which you engage, on a monthly basis, the services of a public relations firm that is the cover for a team of professional killers. I am also in possession of extensive information about other, perhaps even more heinous, crimes and misdeeds calculated to further your professional television career.

"The intent of this recording is to warn you that, if you persist in your attempts to defame me, to damage my professional reputation, and to harrass me in my earnest attempts to serve my country, I, in turn, will feel entirely justified in defending myself by turning over all of my files on your transgressions to the appropriate law enforcement agencies. This is my last direct communication with you. Please address any further comments to my attorneys."

Sweeney clapped his hands lazily, softly.

"That'll do just fine, General."

"I have my own little problem with it, though. I'm using blackmail to halt his harrassments. Doesn't that make me just as rotten as he is? Using one crime to stop another?"

"Yep, it shore do. But remember the old saying I taught you in Munich all those years ago: 'When in an alley fight, fight like an alley fighter.' You had a lot of stars in your eyes in those days, and you almost got your buns shot off as a result. Don't tell me those stars are coming back."

"Hell, Sweeney—"

"Besides," Cap put in quietly, "Ridenour isn't about to cry foul. Who's he going to complain to—the police? Not when we can show an affidavit in English, addressed to whom it may concern and signed by Manuel Corbato, that authorizes Ridenour to represent Corbato and his 'interests in the United States.' Not when we have a copy of a bill, marked paid in full, that proves Ridenour's patronage of a firm that specializes in murder."

"But this other crap—this claim of knowledge about his other transgressions. What transgressions?"

Impatience crept into Sweeney's tone. "Hey, man. You don't remember a hell of lot about what I taught you during our little do as Bojo and Gutbucket, do you? Remember that son of a bitch Kugel, the neo-Nazi in physician's clothes? Remember how we shut him up and got him out of the way?"

"Well, we told him we knew about him—"

"Right. We never had to mention the word Nazi. We had only to tell him that we knew about his 'secret sin.' There he was, Herr Doktor Respectability, with a practice that reached from Munich to Salzburg. Herr Doktor Wonderful, he was, in the eyes of German High Society. And I told you then, and I'm telling you now: Every person alive has something in the background, some private, deeply hidden shame. All you have to do to control or defang somebody—anybody—is to convince him you know his shameful secret. You don't have to do a thing yourself. His own guilt and shame and fear will do the work for you. That's what we did with Kugel, and that's what we'll do with Ridenour. Between the documents and your knowledge of 'his personal shame,' the bastard will be out of your face for good."

There was a stilted silence, which Sweeney broke with the obvious question. "Just what is it," he asked softly, "that Ridenour's got against you? Your secret sin, maybe?"

"You can't guess how many times I've asked myself that question, Sweeney. And I honest-to-God can't answer it."

"You'd never met before?"

"Not that I can recollect."

"Well, there's got to be a tie, a rationale, somewhere."

"Why? Maybe it's just chemistry. We detested each other at first sight."

Sweeney shook his head. "Nope. He's going to too much trouble, complaining to your bosses and all that, for a simple case of dislike. No, it's much bigger than dislike. That Corbato affidavit: does that suggest anything to you? Have you ever been in contact with Corbato or any of his people for any reason?"

"Hell, no. What reason? The son of a bitch is my enemy."

Sweeney waved a hand of surrender. "Okay, okay. Just asking."

"I thought for a time during and after the interview that Ridenour was trying to use me as a device to get at Governor Gomez. Sort of like he had a plan to depth-bomb the governor—a political antagonism thing—and he saw me as a medium for that. But now I'm not so sure. The more I think about it the more I'm convinced that the pings were really bouncing off my hull."

After a supper of Cap's famous tuna salad and Mrs. Smith's famous apple pie, the general drove into the sunset with a wave and the earnest promise to keep in constant touch via scrambler.

Sweeney and Cap sat on the patio and watched the twilight take possession of the bay. It was one of their few quiet times, and he had a momentary, poignant vision of them as Gramma and Gramps Sweeney, settling in for the night, together, but drifting silently and privately between sentimental recollections of the beginning and elemental speculations on the end. Eyes half closed, he studied her profile, a composition of delicate arcs and shadows against the lavender sky, and he was suddenly awash in yearnings that were ethereal and nameless.

He said, "You weren't yourself today. What was eating you?"

"My weariness. I was tired of everything."

"Well, you've got the right to be. You've been hitting it pretty hard these past few weeks. You've done a fine job, and I'm grateful."

"Thank you."

What was this tension, this stiff correctness? He'd grown comfortable with her air of amiable aloofness, the suggestion that everything she saw about her was madness and that she liked it anyhow. But today—now—this quality he liked in her so much had been replaced by a sullenness, a tacit but unmistakable resentment.

"I meant to ask you: How was your date the other night?"

"Great."

"He seems like a nice enough guy."

"He's all right, if you go for the flaky playboy type."

"He said or did something to tick you off, though."

He felt her quick glance. "What do you mean?"

"You've been sore ever since he brought you home."

"I'm not sore."

"And I'm not a Sweeney."

"What ever gave you the idea I was sore?"

"Never mind. It's none of my business."

"You got that right, buddy-boy."

"See? See the way you snapped at me just then? That's the sore I'm talking about."

"You have yourself to thank for that."

"Oh, so now it's my fault—"

"Damn straight, it is."

"How the hell come?"

"Oh, stick it in your ear."

"Come on, now. What's this all about?"

"You come into my life, into my home, you take over, you make me work seventy hours a day, and then you don't even give a crying hoot that I go out with some self-adoring ass who spends the whole evening telling me the difference between a mallard duck and Marlon Brando."

"Well, shoot, I thought you liked the guy. He's got real cute hair—"

"Oh, forget it."

"And it was a good test to see if you're being watched. You aren't, obviously."

"So you not only abandon me to a dweeb, you use me like I'm some kind of damned fish lure."

"Dweeb? Fish lure? I'm not exactly clear on just what the hell we're arguing about here—"

She rose from her chaise and brushed down her skirt with angry sweeps of a hand. "Well, if it's any comfort to you, I'm not sure either."

He stood up, too, confronting her. "I realize that I've been a rotten imposition, and that I've sure as hell thrown your life into a big-time wobble. I'm really very sorry about that. More sorry than you could ever guess. You're an absolutely wonderful person, and you're the only person in the whole world I care about pleasing, and I kick myself every day for what I've done to displease you. I've disrupted so much of your life I had absolutely no right to pick up that guy by his paisley cummerbund and kick his tailored ass all the way to Baltimore, like I wanted to." His own anger began to build. "Where's the sumbish get off, coming around here and messing with my woman?"

"*Your* woman? Who said I was your woman—"

"I did, goddamit. You're my woman, and you know it."

They came together in a gentle collision then, and they stood there, holding each other close and struck silent by the understanding that all the years and all the miles had led inexorably to this peculiar, unifying turbulence.

Toward dawn, she turned and, closing against him, peered at his face through the dimness. "Are you awake?"

"I'll say. My mother said this would be the most beautiful night of my life, and I'm not going to miss a minute of it."

She sniffed. "The old bride joke. I heard that one in high school, pal."

He kissed the end of her nose. "Aren't you glad I'm not as old as my jokes?"

She yawned. "What time is it?"

"Time to be getting out of this here sack and onto hossback. We gonna ride down Aberdeen way t'day. You're going to drive the van while I make like one of Oscar Schwenke's itinerant inspection technicians."

"Can't we just stay in bed the whole day?"

"You've talked me into it. We visit Aberdeen tomorrow."

She was sleeping again, but he lay awake, staring out the casement at the rain-pebbled bay. The sky was lowering, and the wind was picking up, cold and restless. A good day to lie abed.

His mind would not let it go.

The question: What did they signify?

What had Nageler been trying to say?

H, L, N.

H, L, Z.

H, C, Z.

H, V, N.

H, V, Z.

H, V. Z?

Hugo von Zoll?

The president is in danger from Hugo von Zoll?

Metaphorically possible, if you believed what so many newspaper and magazine columnists were writing these days about the clear and present danger of a new Nazi Germany.

But hardly the kind of screaming, immediate, personal danger that warranted the lifting of both hopper lid and seat.

No, the letters stood for something else. Something urgent and filled with great danger.

But what?

CHAPTER 26

It was the poet's bright blue October day, and Richter sat, turned slightly sideways on the hard board seat, so that the sunlight fell fully on his face. The artillery range, an undulating prairie dotted with thickets showing the variegated hues of autumn, spread southward from the bleachers and seemed to shimmer in the beautiful morning. A gentle easterly breeze came off the bay, filled with the scents of sparkling water and distant forests.

It struck him that all this military activity for the benefit of no more than four bureaucrats provided a kind of elemental, theatrical answer as to just why it is men seek political power. To know that by simply lifting a phone you could energize a huge Army base and drain the national coffers of inestimable amounts was almost as exhilarating as sex. But Richter's curse was that, unlike most aspirants to domination (or those already enjoying it) he could never truly stifle his awareness of political power's bitter counterforce: vengeance, and its supreme expression, revolution. He was continually, naggingly mindful of the fact that every prerogative has its cost—every Louis XVI has his Madame LaFarge—and in his most private moments he would see that his driving need to excel, coupled with an innate gift for scheming and opportunism, had made him the very sort whose head would be among the first to roll. Now, sitting in the sun, eyes half closed in the amiable warmth, he perceived the comfort to be derived from being entirely, mindlessly bad. The purely evil person bore no burdens; Aaron Richter, the unprincipled but basically well-intended angle-shooter, paid a daily price in suppressed guilt and remorse. His problem, in short, was that he was sinning more and enjoying it less.

He glanced at the arrogant General Reynolds, sitting pompously erect, eyes slitted, jaw jutting in the proper military mode; at Colt, looking gaunt and hard and bored, like a banana country assassin at a PTA meeting; at Cummings, the steely little Bavarian (He wondered what the man's name really was—Kummings? Von Kommen?), with doctorates in political science and languages and the personal morals of a Pithecanthropus, watching the proceedings with dark, darting eyes.

Just what did they measure on the satanical scale?

Well, he thought morosely, *whatever they are, I'm one of their gang.*

The lieutenant colonel wearing a chest mike strutted importantly to the front and center of the bleachers. He crooned, "Good morning, gentlemen, and welcome to Aberdeen Proving Ground and our demonstration of the Model Fourteen A-One experimental target drone, code-named 'Hammerhead.' The commandant regrets that the logistics conference at the Presidio makes it impossible for him to join you today, but he has asked me to convey his compliments and his complete understanding of General Reynolds's requirement that the device and this demonstration be kept under the tightest security. For this reason, only I, your expositor, and the team of five technicians required, are in your company here. Now—"

General Reynolds held up an interrupting hand, and it was immediately clear to Richter that the general, who already knew all the answers, was playing to the one-man gallery represented by Cummings. "A question, Colonel: this device is essentially an aircraft. So how can you keep security on a machine that will be buzzing through the air for a surrounding population of many thousands to watch at will?"

The colonel smiled serenely, his manner verging on the condescension that comes with having answered such questions uncounted times. "This base has been testing weapons of all sorts—many of them airborne—for a number of years, General. The surrounding population, including base personnel and the residents of the many towns and housing developments nearby, have become quite inured to our activities. Explosions and the sounds of aircraft are, you might say, a way of life in this part of Maryland. Local residents take no more interest in our fireworks than, for instance, Manhattanites take interest in traffic sounds."

Reynolds wasn't about to let him off that easily. "I'm not talking about housewives, cabdrivers and furniture salesmen, Colonel. I'm talking about espionage agents who might be watching from boats, or those hills over there."

"They might see, sir. But it's unlikely they would understand what they were seeing. When we're testing a new artillery shell, say, a spy might see and hear a large piece discharging. He would have no way of knowing precisely what had left the barrel and exploded downrange."

Cummings shifted on his hard seat and said, "Could we just get on with the demonstration? I'm due back in Washington for a lunch thing."

General Reynolds nodded at the colonel. "Carry on."

"First, gentlemen, the show part of our show-and-tell." The colonel cleared his throat. "To your left front, just above the horizon, you will make out a small airplane cruising in a lazy clockwise circle. That orange dot is actually a single-engine Cessna, a type favored by many civilian sports fliers; it's seen by the hundreds in Eastern U.S. skies each day. Now please watch what happens when I actuate this preprogrammed computerized command kit." He knelt beside what resembled a plastic tackle box, opened a panel lid on its flank and touched the red button there.

Squinting, Richter saw that the tiny dot had broken away from its circling and was now descending and growing steadily as it came directly toward the bleachers.

"You will notice, gentlemen, I am standing free of the command kit, arms folded. I will explain the significance of this in a moment."

The airplane began to take shape, its wings a shallow V, its fuselage a central orange blob, its engine a faint drumming. It came lower, and eventually its shadow darted across the tree line marking the horizon, and the humming had become a snarling. In what appeared to be the central visual point of the great prairie, there came the ragged, tearing sound of machine guns, and tracers cascaded from the plane's belly mounts, churning a swath of dust fountains across the arid reaches of the range's impact zone.

"Hot damn," Colt enthused.

The orange machine lifted skyward in a blattering arc, the sunlight glistening on its surfaces, then, as it was full into its vertical climb, additional fire poured from a tail-mounted gun.

"Absolutely goddam wonderful." Colt laughed.

At the apex of the screaming upward rush, just before the faltering stall-point, a machine gun opened fire from an emplacement on the grandstand's right flank. Tracers rose to flicker briefly in the plane's vicinity, and then, as it turned belly to the sky, the Cessna vanished in a clapping roar and a cataclysmic smear of incandescence and oily smoke.

"Beautiful," Colt said, grinning widely as the shredded wreckage came tumbling down in a ghastly, fiery hail.

"Holy hell," Richter heard himself saying.

There was a taut, suspended moment, and then the colonel began prattling of computerized radio controls, sound sensors, vectors, azimuths and adjustments for wind and weather deviations. The four men in the bleachers sat staring silently at the angry bonfires scattered across the terrain.

Finally General Reynolds turned his gaze on his three companions. "So much for the AWACS problem, eh?"

"It's bloody marvelous," Colt said. "The ground crew needs to do no more than preset the airplane's behavior on the computer and send it off. No escort ship required."

Richter said, "I suppose the plane was programmed to blow up when its receiver detected nearby gunfire. Which naturally leads the interceptor crew to believe their fire destroyed it. Right?"

The general nodded, his face a study in satisfaction. "You got it."

There was another pause, during which the three turned their attention to Cummings, who had been wordless throughout the demonstration and who was, after all, the most important reason for its having been arranged.

"So," Colt said in his unabashed way, "what do you think, Mr. Cummings?"

Cummings did not answer immediately. Instead he took a moment to make some notes on his wallet pad.

"I think," he said at last, "it will do."

Reynolds and Colt traded pleased glances. Richter watched the bonfires and the drifting smoke.

"What's delivery time, and how many will be available?" Cummings wanted to know.

"We have three of these advanced models ready right now," Reynolds said. "Three more can be delivered by the middle of next month."

"I'll buy the three at once, and I'd like to have them utilized as quickly as possible. I'll buy the other three if, and as soon as, their use becomes advisable."

"How much were you able to get?" Cap asked.

Sweeney sighed and returned the VCR to its carrying bracket on the van's sidewall. "Not a hell of a lot. Just the zoom and the explosion and the fallout."

"What was it, for Pete's sake?"

"It was pretty far away, but it looked to be some kind of target drone. Much larger than usual. A full-size plane, is my guess. And target drones don't usually blow up. They just come drifting down on a parachute after they've been hit. So I don't know what the hell it was."

Cap steered the van onto a paved road leading west through a nest of squat concrete structures that Dr. Schwenke's map had designated "adits to underground ammo storage bunkers." She drove in silence while Sweeney spread the map and marked the site of the drone incident.

"That was a demonstration of some kind," he muttered. "The map says that's a demo range over there."

"How about the listener we dropped off in that grove of pines near the instrument landing approach hutch? That couldn't be too far from where all the shooting took place."

He patted her knee. "You're reading my mind. Let's go back there and scan its tape. It might have recorded something other than machine guns and plane crashes, eh?"

She made a quick U-turn and, when they reached the crossroads, turned north on the dirt lane.

"That must be it," Sweeney said. "They were having a VIP demonstration. That's why they were all so fiercely nice at the main gate when we went through. It just seemed too easy. Show a paper, show an ID, show Schwenke's letter, and slap-crack-salute, welcome to APG."

"Makes sense."

"Turn left up there."

"Got it."

They pulled behind the pine screen and Sweeney retrieved the tape. He put it on the player, but it had kicked in too late in the demonstration, because only the air action and crash noises, plus a few lines of conversation from some adjacency, were audible.

Voice 1: "—the delivery time, and how many will be available?"

Voice 2: "We have three of these advanced models ready right now. Three more can be delivered by the middle of next month."

Voice 3: "(Garble)—three at once, and I'd like to have them utilized as quickly as possible. (Garble) —and as soon as, their use becomes advisable."

Voice 3: "What say we go get a cup of coffee? (Background noises, car motors starting)

Sweeney reinstalled the tape and they drove off for the main gate. He spent the time in the rear of the van, closing cases, buckling straps, making a list of the listening equipment they had stashed around the Proving Ground. He photocopied this and clipped it to his marked-up map.

Cap called over her shoulder, "What do you think of that conversation?"

"There's not much to think about. It sounds as if somebody put in an order for whatever was being demonstrated. Who and what and why is anybody's guess."

"Maybe we'll learn more when we come back next week."

"Maybe."

It was even easier to leave the post than it had been to enter. The MP at the gatehouse, an Alp in olive drab and ribbons and hash marks, simply took their visitors' pass, threw a highball straight from The Professional Saluter's Handbook, and forgot about them instantly. As they made their way north through the town of Aberdeen on Route 40, Sweeney said, "Pull into that diner ahead of us there. I want to call Bernie Kratzer."

"Why now?"

"It's noon. He said he'd be available any noon hour."

While Cap went into the diner to order lunch for them, Sweeney entered the outside booth and dialed Bernie's special 800 number. After three rings the phone at the other end lifted.

"Ich weiss nicht was soll es bedeuten."

"So sagt Heine. Aber ich weiss."

"Farmer."

"Dell."

"Hello, there, Sweeney. What's up?"

"That Jagdmeister you loaned me. I've put it on auto and have it beamed at a target area. When I tested the playback this morning I got a nice video of the recording period but not a peep of sound. What am I doing wrong?"

"Are you using batteries?"

"No. Household current. It's plugged into a wall like a ten-dollar toaster."

"Did you turn on the audio switches?"

"Switches? Plural? I turned on the audio on the face panel to the right of the screen."

"There's another switch on the main frame next to the AC/DC external power adapter plug. That has to be in the 'on' position when you're using an external power source."

"Now you tell me."

"I also told you last Monday, when I brought the thing to you at the Loose Goose. And remember: When all else fails, read the frigging manual."

"Sorry to bother you with this, Bernie. I should have figured it out."

"No problem. So how are things going otherwise?"

"Slow. But I think we're making progress. I've just made a swing through the Proving Ground, did a recon and dropped some listeners. I've also got the five-hundred trained on the unloading ramp at the airstrip there. I'll have a written report for you by the weekend."

"Is the five-hundred in a secure location?"

"Yeah. Under the deck of my place at Turkey Point. Somebody would have to be looking very hard for it, and even then they might not see it."

"Sounds good. Remember, the five-hundred is a very choice item."

"It's the cat's ass, all right."

"So okay. Anything else?"

"Just a word of thanks."

"Thanks? What for?"

"The tail you've put on me. The backstop team. They've probably already told you about the cornfield incident, and I just wanted you to know that I'm grateful. You always were a careful thinker, a looker-ahead. And I'm damned glad. If you weren't, Freddie Dilworth and I would be fish food about now."

"Well, I'm very glad you feel this way. There's only one thing you ought to know. I haven't put a tail on you."

"Say what?"

"There's no backup team. Leastwise none I've assigned."

"Then who in hell put the cool to the four shootists who were about to do the wet stuff on Freddie and me? The guys in the gold Cadillac—"

"Seriously, Sweeney. This is all news to me. If you have some guardian angels, they sure aren't mine."

"Okay, Bernie. I'll be in touch."

He hung up and went into the diner.

He ate the hamburger Cap had ordered for him, but he didn't taste it.

CHAPTER 27

"Yes, Irma—What is it?"

"A call for you on Line One, Mr. Richter. It's Mr. Randolph Ridenour, and he wonders if he might have a word with you."

"For God's sake, Irma, why don't you just say 'Randolph Ridenour is on Line One'?"

"I don't understand, sir. I just said that."

"Never mind. Put him through."

"Richter?"

"Yes."

"Randolph Ridenour here."

"So?"

"Remember our lunch last week?"

"Of course. What about it?"

"Well, I've been thinking things over—reviewing our conversation, so to say—and I've decided that you were right."

"In what particular way?"

"You said you didn't think it would be such a good idea for me to do a show on General Wallace. Or to poke into the German thing. I've thought about it and have decided you're right."

"Oh?"

"Yes. It wouldn't be in the country's best interest."

"I'm glad you agree. What made you change your mind?"

"I'm as patriotic as the next man. My being a journalist doesn't mean I'm not patriotic. Journalists are just as patriotic as anybody."

"I see."

"That's why I'm not going to do a show on Wallace."

"I must confess to a bit of confusion. In our conversation at the lunch you said you wanted the Wallace and German files for research—that you didn't plan a show on the subjects. And now—"

"Well, television is my business, and everything I do is calculated to fit into the business. So—"

"So you were lying to me. Is that what you're saying?"

"Not lying, exactly. I hadn't made up my mind as to whether to balloon the research into an actual show. Now I have. I'm just dropping the whole idea of doing anything on Wallace and I have no further interest in seeing your files on the German thing."

"You expressed interest in my personal affairs, too. Where do we stand on that?"

"I've had second thoughts on that, as well."

"You mean you are no longer interested in my IRS file? My car, my chalet—that sort of thing?"

"That's right. It simply isn't newsworthy."

"I see."

"I thought I'd call you to let you know of these decisions. I'd hate to have you sitting around, resenting me, worried maybe, waiting for the other shoe to drop."

"Oh, I'd never do that, Mr. Ridenour. I'm not the worrying kind. Besides, something told me you wouldn't go through with your plans. I have a keen intuition."

"Mm."

"Well, then. Anything else?"

"No. That's it."

"So it's good-bye, Mr. Ridenour. I appreciate your call."

"No hard feelings, then?"

"Not here, Mr. Ridenour. I'm a strong believer in that old admonition, 'Don't get mad, get even.' "

"Yeah. Well, I thought I ought to call."

"Good-bye, Mr. Ridenour."

* * *

"Irma, get me the Stiegel PR people in Chester, Pennsylvania, will you? Put them on Line Three."

"Yes, sir."

"Stiegel and Company, Public Relations. Miss Fitzgerald speaking."

"This is Aaron Richter. Is Warren Stiegel in?"

"One moment, please."

"Hi. What's up?"

"I just got a call from Ridenour. Nice work."

"It came off then, eh?"

"Yep. He's decided to drop everything."

"You're an artiste, Mr. Richter. You just don't get some countergoods on a blackmailer and then lay it on him. You plant it so some other victim will find it and lay it on him. Ridenour to Richter to Stiegel to Sweeney to Wallace, then back to Ridenour. Zap. Artiste is the word."

"Well, in a sting like that you have to have a Sweeney. It doesn't work without a Sweeney."

"It's almost creepy, the way you figure what he's likely to do. I wouldn't have bet a penny that he could be led to my files and make sense of them. But he did just what you said he'd do. Again."

"It's no big thing. I know he's around. I just never know where, and that's why I need you. I know he needs tools, and there's only two places to get them: from the government or the mob."

"And when you're ready to shut him down—"

"Again, that's why I need you."

"I'll be kind of sorry when you give me that nod. I'm getting to like Sweeney. He's a card-carrying dilly, that guy."

"Sorry? You should see it from here, Mr. Stiegel."

CHAPTER 28

It was just after noon when Sweeney and Freddie left the van and the Ford in the parking garage and made their way to the Radimore Arms. The pasty-faced little clerk with the weepy blue eyes was on duty as usual, wearing his shiny brown polyester suit as usual and appearing to have the world's largest case of heartburn, as usual. He gave Sweeney's bandana do-rag, sunglasses, beard and blue jeans his customary disdainful examination, then turned to do the same for Freddie, whose ensemble consisted of a black, broad-brimmed felt hat, a Genghis Kahn paste-on mustache, a Miss Piggy T-shirt, a paisley jacket, and pink leotards and cowboy boots.

Eyes fixed on Freddie but speaking to Sweeney, Lemke, the clerk, said, "So then, Mr. Flugel, your long-awaited friend has finally arrived."

"Ain't it so. You ever see anybody more arrived than this beeg, be-ootiful hunk?"

"Will he be sharing the room with you, Mr. Flugel?"

"Will he ever. We may be out by Memorial Day. Ha-ha."

"I'll have to charge you extra for the double occupancy, of course. And I'll need a name."

"What's the matter with Lemke?"

"I mean I'll need your friend's name."

"Ludwig-Friedrich Karl-Heinz Engelbert, Ritter von und zu Frammersdorf-Rottweiler. 'Ace,' for short. His great-granddaddy was a German ace in World War One. That's why everybody calls him 'Ace.' "

Lemke, mouth puckered as if dealing with a lemon, made a note on his pad. "Does Mr. Ace have luggage?"

"It's still in the Avismobile. I wanna show him the room first.

The clerk cleared his throat. "I'm curious. Does Mr. Ace ever say anything? Or does he speak only German?"

"Hell, he don't speak nothing at all. He's a moot."

"I see." The desk phone rang then, and Lemke, seeming to be almost tearfully grateful for the rescue this represented, became instantly engrossed in whatever was being said by whoever was on the line.

Sweeney led Freddie across the lobby to the rickety elevator and they were in the room and retrieving bug tapes just as the clock in the tower down the street bonged noon.

"God," Freddie said, shuddering, "I can't wait to get out of these dumb clothes. Did you see the way that fatty on the desk was staring at me?"

"Can you blame him? You look adorable."

"Shee-it."

Sweeney pulled on a headset and handed another to Freddie. He held a finger to his lips, signaling silence.

Freddie mouthed his question. "Why?"

Sweeney took a magic slate from the bureau drawer and wrote, "First lesson, espionage: Assume your room is bugged. Make no noise you don't want somebody to hear." He lifted the film and the note disappeared.

He activated the first tape, labeled *Top Floor A*, which proved to be a disjointed mishmash of phone conversations between the man Sweeney identified as The Eyebrow and assorted service people—a dry cleaner, a grocer, a car rental agent, a food caterer, and a call girl madam. *Top Floor B* offered little more, the only difference being a call from The Eyebrow to a 900-number heavy-breathing, dirty-talk phone service in L.A. *Top Floor C* contained some chew: an incoming call asking for Colt, answered by The Eyebrow, then turned over to a voice whose German creaked like a hawser under strain.

"Colt here. What's up, Mr. Cummings?"

"I want a meeting with you and Richter to finalize the arrangements for the Azalea Manor meeting."

"No problem with that. Although Richter's pretty hard to nail down sometimes. When would you like to do this?"

"Your suite, tomorrow, early. Say oh-eight-hundred hours."

"I'll get right on it."

"Also, I need to know if Corbato will be bringing people with him to the Manor and, if so, how many."

"I know for a fact that he will have his mistress with him. But who else, I'll have to check."

"All right."

"If there are any problems with tomorrow, I'll call you. Will you be at your place in Wilmington?"

"Yes. But let there be no problems. This is extremely important."

"I understand."

"Until tomorrow, then."

The remainder of the tape belonged to Colt's leaving for the day and The Eyebrow, who, according to his sound tracks, was not only security supervisor, troubleshooter, and gofer, but also resident satyr, since he saw to it personally that the maids who serviced the suite were themselves regularly and robustly serviced.

When the tapes had been heard in their entirety, Sweeney replaced them with fresh cassettes. Then he picked up the magic slate, held it so Freddie could watch, and scrawled:

"You stay, get videos of Richter, Cummings, whoever else arrives tomorrow's meeting."

Freddie took the slate and wrote, "Where will you be?"

"Cap's, reviewing Aberdeen stuff and 500 data. You come soonest with pix. You need something, use outside phone or shortwave in Ford."

"What the hell do I do the rest of today and tonight?"

"Be ready at window with telephoto. Monitor all tapes. Important as hell to learn where Azalea Manor is, when meeting will be held there. Listen to everything. Bring used cassettes with you, replace here with fresh."

"I hate listening to that little pig's grunts and squeals."

"Spy work can be tough."

Sweeney returned the slate to its drawer, pulled on his denim jacket and went to the door. Aloud, he said, "That was clean out of sight, Ace. You're a real Kool-Aid dynamite trip."

Freddie showed his teeth and shook his fist.

Cap pretended busyness at her computer, but she was merely rearranging files, a routine process designed to camouflage her sidelong inspection of Sweeney. His face was showing unmistakable signs of fatigue; his eyes, narrowed over the charts and photos and printouts he had spread on the dining room table, were heavy-lidded and strangely oblique, and he seemed pale, and, well, gaunt. Yet the fire was there, as always—the air of a man about to charge the heights, swinging his sword and urging his troops onward—and so she tempered her concern with a silent reminder that for one who worked as hard as he did there was the right, perhaps even the duty, to sag a bit around the edges.

And then the other, larger thought obtruded:

So this, then, was her man—the pile of bone and muscle and hair and breath and soul that in some ineffable way manifested her own completion. She'd never been aware of waiting, or of searching, but it was clear to her now, and had been since their first intense embrace, that she had been doing both for years. Looking at him now, she knew with indefinable certainty that the searching had ended, that there would not be another Sweeney—another anyone—ever. There simply couldn't be two of what he represented: a macho, insensitive horse's patoot at Point A who, at Point B, would be whispering a gentle word and administering a tender touch; an egocentric chauvinist gump who could suddenly be funny and ineffectual and altogether sweet and giving and self-effacing; an exciting, fast-lane sophisticate one moment, and a bumbling, world-class village idiot the next. A dude with a face you wouldn't look at twice who still managed to be more gorgeous than anybody on the planet. He could get up from that table right now, and walk out that door there and never come back again, and she would know for the rest of her days that, in him, Cap O'Brien had already had all she could ever possibly want—or handle—by way of masculine fulfillment.

So this was what they write songs about, eh?

What a pain in the ass.

Impulsively, she broke the silence. "How are you making out over there?"

He glanced up. "You should ask yet. There's not a durn thing on these Aberdeen listener readouts that tells me what I don't already know. There's grass over there, and trees, and they make noise in the wind. They have cars and trucks over there. They got guys who stand beside cars and trucks and talk about girls they'd like to get into the grass, or under the trees. They got airplanes that come and go. They got all kind of noisemakers over there. Ain't that the living nerts?"

"How about the five-hundred?"

"I'm getting to that now."

The silence resumed, and she decided to get truly busy.

First she went page by page, column by column, through the week's Elkton, Wilmington, Baltimore and Newark, Delaware, dailies, the Cecil *Whig* and several other Eastern Shore weeklies, and even a clutch of neighborhood ad freebies. Confirming Sweeney's initial findings, she too saw no mention of the cornfield shooting—no reports of bodies found or inquiries launched. She saw complete ignorance of an incident that ordinarily would get at least a paragraph in even the most jaded of metropolitan newspapers. Earlier, with less than half the media scanned, Sweeney had made a call to the Cecil County Sheriff's office, suggesting that he was a reporter for the *Philadelphia Inquirer* and asking if there were any truth to rumors that there had been a gangland-style massacre in a rural area outside Elkton. The public affairs officer had been openly amused by the very idea. Sweeney had been puzzled and vexed by this universal unwillingness to acknowledge the fact of four bullet-riddled corpses in a country lane and an abandoned stretch limousine at a major highway convenience store.

Next she scrolled through the criminal ID material piped to her by Peggy Trumbull at the National Study of Organized Crime in Bethesda. Halfway through the roster, a new thought came to her.

"Sweeney?"

"Mm?"

"That stretch limo. The one you and Freddie drove back to

Elkton from the cornfield. What do cops do with cars like that?"

"The normal procedure is to red-tag it, and if someone doesn't pick it up within forty-eight hours of tagging, it's hauled away. The numbers are traced, registered letters are sent to the owner and lienholders, and if they don't pick it up, it's sold as salvage. But limos are usually rented, so this one will be retrieved in time."

"But what about all the bullet damage? Won't the cops do something about that?"

"Sure. Especially with that hood's blood all over the fender. They'll put out a BOLO, too. But with no bodies, no claimants, well—it's sort of Dead-End City."

"BOLO?"

"Be On the Look-Out. It alerts other police agencies that this car has been found and maybe it'll fit into something somewhere else."

"Well, it was just an idea."

"It was good thinking."

Her gaze still on the scrolling screen, she said, "If you liked that, you're going to love this. 'Corbato, Manuelo Gonzales, age fifty-four, Colombian national with at least ten years' residence in the United States, present whereabouts unknown; confirmed ID as one of the most wealthy and powerful of the Colombian drug chieftains; suspected of organizing and directing one of South America's largest narcotics manufacture and distribution cartels. Wanted by DEA in connection with three drug-related slayings in Los Angeles in 1991, and—' It goes on and on here."

"Would that be the Corbato who signs affidavits and pops up on our tapes and is preparing to attend some kind of meeting with assorted bigwigs, including our former employer?"

"Who else?"

"Are you sure? Are there any other Corbatos?"

"None here."

"That's a very interesting turn of events, in light of these still frames from the five-hundred surveillance of the past thirty hours. Come here and take a look at these."

He had spread four outtake instaprints, fanlike, under the

glare of the halogen desk lamp. She peered at them for a full minute.

"Okay, four photos of four similar-looking airplanes with four similar-looking soldiers unloading similar-looking cartons from the planes and placing them in four similar-looking trucks. Right?"

"That's what you're seeing, all right. Those are U.S. Army C-one-thirty transport planes, and each is parked on a hard stand at the southwest corner of the Aberdeen airfield. See these numbers along the bottom of the frame? They say at what time of what day the situations depicted were caught by the five-hundred. This first one was taken at oh-two-thirty-five hours three days ago, when I first set up the instrument. This one was the next day at oh-one forty-six hours—the plane landed a bit earlier that day. The third one was caught yesterday at oh-two twenty-seven hours and is the first shot taken after I learned how to set up the five-hundred's laser-guided X-ray spectrograph function and zero it in on the aircraft hatch. The fourth was taken this morning at oh-two thirty-one hours, also with the spectro operating."

"What's all that mean?"

His smile suggested a form of queasy triumph. "The five-hundred can't photo the contents of a package, but thanks to its integral X-ray spectrograph, it can disperse the light radiation of the contents and record the resulting spectrum photographically. Which, in turn, can give a reliable reading on the composition of the contents."

"So?"

He held a paper to the light. "This is a reference table. These columns are spectrochemical keys, in this case profiling controlled substances—drugs, to you. You take the numbers established by the five hundred machine, here, and compare them with the spectroanalytical keys listed here, and voila, you done got yourself in the know on the what."

"So what's in the cartons, for cripes sake?"

"Our U.S. Army C-one-thirties, my dearest friend, have been delivering, almost like a scheduled Amtrak freight train, cartons loaded with pure cocaine."

"Cocaine?"

"Yes indeedy-doody. Cocaine."

"From where, for cripes sake?"

"South America, is my guess."

She sputtered. "But—but—Where do the trucks take the stuff? Does the five-hundred tell us that?"

"No, because I have the five-hundred on a fixed mount, zeroed on the one-thirty hard-stand area, and it can't pan. But our Listener eighteen at oh-two fifty-seven hours today picked up sounds that place the same truck motor, along with two voices matching those picked up at the plane, in the immediate adjacency of Explosives Bunker thirty-two." He slid the map under the light and tapped a finger. "Right here. On each of the last four nights, the bunker doors were opened and shut within half an hour after the planes' landings. Which has to mean that the cartons were taken from the planes and stored in an ammunition bunker, right there on dear ole Aber-damn-deen Proving Ground."

She gave him a lingering stare. "Is this what Nageler wanted you to tell President Leonardi? That at Corbato's request Ridenour contacted U.S. military officials to arrange a deal enabling GIs to use military planes and bases for drug-trafficking?"

He shook his head. "I don't think so. It's probably a significant part of it, but I don't think it's the all of it. No way is it the all of it."

"Why are you so sure?"

He sat down on the drafting stool and rubbed his eyes. Then, blinking, he returned her stare. "It's the context, Cap. The scope of things, the cast of characters, the chronology, even. Consider:

"A notorious free-lance espionage agent is wiped out while in possession of equipment available only to the highest level of German national security forces. Then I am suddenly a target for assassination, because the blighter died in my bathroom, leading any number of persons unknown to believe—correctly, I'm sad to say—that he left me a message they don't want to go any farther. Subsequently, as I tried to find out where I am and how I got that way, I, along with this gorgeous former co-worker who gets the hots for me and just can't stay out of my bed, am chased, bombed, shot at, and otherwise put on the lam. I discover that my old boss, Richter, one of the highest totems on the U.S. security pole, is having meetings with shady characters, among them some Germans who have been trying to wipe me out. When I confront Bernie Kratzer, head of German intelligence in the U.S., he's as confused as I am, worries about neo-Nazis trying to set up something here in the States, and hires me to be his loose cannon end-runner in his attempt to find out what's going down. Meanwhile, another German, or set of Germans, takes me and Freddie to a cornfield for a wipeout and they're wiped out instead. Only there's no official report of the incident or any open hint that the shooting ever happened at all—which has got to be one huge high-level law enforcement and security coverup if I ever heard of one. Now we learn that there's to be a big meeting of the shady Germans and Richter, et al., at a place called Azalea Manor, and that the American military is importing cocaine to Aberdeen all the while our pal, Harvey Wallace, is winning the goddam drug war in South America."

Cap sighed. "A pretty complicated batch of wildlife."

"Yeah."

"So where do we go from here?"

"I think the first thing we absolutely must do is to find out where Azalea Manor is and who's going to be meeting there with Corbato. And why. I suspect the 'why' is what we have to get to our presidente."

"Do you think Richter is dealing?"

"It sure looks that way."

"I'm not surprised. The man's a born angle-shooter. He always made me uneasy.

"Hell, Cap, everybody's an angle-shooter these days."

"Well, I'm not."

"The hell you ain't. Look at all the angles you shot just to get my warm and tender body into the sack."

"Oh, stick it in your ear."

They traded smiles, and he pulled her to him. After a time, he raised her face gently and peered into her eyes, saying softly, "Now that you and I are grooving good, I want to ask you to do something special for me. Something that's, well, sort of out of the ordinary. That's not usually done by the vast majority of American women—"

She blushed deeply, and her stare wavered. "Well, I— You— You've seen that I'm no prude, that I'm a pretty uninhibited type, and all that, but—I'm not into the really far-out kinky, Sweeney—"

"I don't see what's so far-out kinky about putting in a phone call to Saint Augustine, Florida. I realize that most American women don't do that every day, but heck—"

She pushed him away, made a fist and punched his chest. "You rat!"

"Ouch. What did you do that for?"

"You were suggesting—"

"Hey, don't get on *my* case. *You're* the one with the dirty mind."

They were laughing openly, loudly, then, and he ducked when she threw a pencil at him.

"Damn you, Sweeney, those fool jokes of yours are going to get you brained one of these days. Probably by me."

"Enough of this lovemaking. Call Harvey Wallace for me, will you?"

"Harve, Sweeney here. Are you on scrambler?"

"Sure am. What's up?"

"I'm trying to develop a clue. First, a question. Do your aviation people videotape interceptions? I mean, is taping a standard part of the standard drill?"

"Certainly. Why?"

"I'd sure like to have copies of the next several intercepts. Could you arrange to have them sent to me?"

"After what you did for me, I'd get in the air-e-o-plane and make the sumbishes myself, Sweeney. I owe you a real bunch."

"What did I ever do for you, pal?"

"Randolph Ridenour doesn't think I'm newsworthy anymore. I bore him to death. And it's all your fault."

"So you've heard from him, eh?"

"A very hat-in-hand phone call."

"Did he say anything about your documentary evidence, linking him with drug lords, paid assassins?"

"Not a word."

"Then that means we've got him right where we want him."

"All I know is, I've got you to thank for getting him off my back."

"So that means you owe me, buster. And your first installment will be tapes of a little experiment. I want you to tell your gunners to fire their initial bursts close to—not at—the target vehicle—boat, plane, whatever. And I want videos of what happens."

"No big deal. But why?"

"You do it, and I think you'll see why."

CHAPTER 29

Richard Leonardi opened the agenda folder before him and, with a quick glance at the others seated around him at the long table, let it be known that the session had begun. The low-key, amiable chatter subsided, leaving only the muted sounds of distant traffic and a fitful autumn rain at the windows.

Leonardi was an admirer of Harry S (no period) Truman, thirty-third president of the United States, and as he gathered himself for the afternoon's sparring, Truman's words scrolled across his mind:

A president has to know what is going on all around the world in order to be ready to act when action is needed. The president must have all the facts that may affect the foreign policy or the military policy of the United States. Of course he must know what is going on at home, because the attitude of the people of the United States, who, in the final analysis, are the government, must be favorable to any action he takes.

Determined to see that the United States would never again be surprised by an enemy's military action, Truman bulldogged the National Security Act of 1947, and the National Security Council, a creature of that legislation, had met regularly in this room every year since to provide, in Truman's language, "a running balance and a perpetual inventory of where we stood and where we were going on all strategic questions affecting the national security." And now, as he always did when seated here, confronted by the NSC's five mighty, haughty, and incredibly knowledgeable members, Leonardi felt a rush of stage fright.

There was Kowalski, chairman of the recently established Universal Intelligence Directorate, which amalgamated and condensed for the council—and therefore the president—all the latest thinking of the CIA, the FBI, the SII, and the myriad lesser agencies constituting the intelligence community.

There was Anderson, secretary of state, who had a traveling salesman's intimacy with the world's back alleys.

There was Ackerman, secretary of defense, Patton in a pinstripe suit.

There was Pomeroy, chairman of the National Security Resources Board, who knew everything about everything; and General Romano, chairman of the Joint Chiefs of Staff, a business tycoon in olive drab.

Together they represented some 150 years of experience in world-class commerce, industry, finance, government, diplomacy, and military affairs. They were the Holy High Sachems of Clout, and in their presence, Richard D. Leonardi, president via a personal ambition abetted by public whim and indifference, felt Lilliputian in both accomplishment and intellect.

So now, like a drunk who looks for someone drunker in order to feel more worthy, his gaze went across the table to the sixth member: Vice President Brandon McKell, in attendance not by executive order, not at the president's pleasure, but under a provision—make that "mandate"—resulting from the Senate's fine-tuning of the root Security Act of 1947. McKell was there, a half-century later, because Harry Truman's Senate, stung by Truman's initial clumsiness and embarrassing unfamiliarity with the view from the Rooseveltian throne, had decreed that the vice president would attend all sessions of the National Security Council so that he wouldn't be caught flatfooted by any incapacitation of the chief executive.

The media of any era loved to bash the vice president, but in this case, Leonardi knew, McKell truly deserved it. He was a ward-heeling horse's ass. Therefore it helped to remind himself that, while he was a beanie-wearing freshman in the company of these towering, Phi Beta Kappa seniors, Brandon McKell was a kindergarten brat.

He was not the dumbest guy in the room.

And, by the goddam way, these hotshots, too, pulled on their pants one leg at a time.

"Before we get into the agenda, gentlemen, I'd like to lay out for you the things that are heaviest on my mind these days, and to give you a head start on the policy proposals I want you to submit for my consideration at the next session. I'm particularly anxious to get your points of view on where we should be going now that"—he nodded slightly toward McKell—"Brandon and Jenny Malone and General Romano have brought the South and Central American narcotics invasion to a relative trickle. With the Soviets having torn themselves apart, and with the Communist disintegration in general causing spectacular realignments around the globe, the ebbing of the drug threat puts more pressure on us to cut our military expenditures to even more drastic minimums and to redirect the focus of our national security policies, with emphasis on hemispheric economic and military stability. The Treaty of Acapulco, that great enabler in our struggle against the narcotics pestilence, along with the economic cooperation agreements with Canada and Mexico—those already in place and those impending—put us in an excellent position to achieve an unprecedented tranquility from the Arctic Circle to Tierra del Fuego. A reading of the Congressional tea leaves suggests that the majority of the American people believe this, and so do I. Therefore I'd like this body, in the next several months, to evaluate our national security needs in light of this strong-running current and give me its recommendations. What do we need to protect ourselves and our neighboring nations in an era of extraordinary hemispheric collaboration? I want to know what you think about this, and I want you to make proposals.

"I also want you to think about nuclear terrorism.

"In the Middle East, despite the heavy rethinking among Arab power centers following the chastening of Saddam Hussein, certain theorcratic sects continue to see violence and terror as the means by which to discourage, and eventually evict, American and European interests and investments in the Arabian Arc." He nodded toward Kowalski, honcho of the UID.

"Sam tells me that in the past four weeks he has gathered direct evidence of German-developed nuclear weaponry and related technologies being delivered piecemeal into Iran, Iraq, and Libya, the nations in which these terror groups make their clandestine bases." He glanced at the secretary of state. "Arlen Anderson says his diplomatic people in Germany make no bones about the source: the so-called 'Mushrooms,' the underground neo-Nazi industrial network established and directed by Hugo von Zoll. Chancellor Haussener tells me that von Zoll operates scrupulously within German law and that there is nothing the German government can do to stop the legal export of legal machinery and parts, even when it's obvious that they are destined to be modified and incorporated in nuclear devices. The Bundestag is readying legislation that will make such exports impractical and unrewarding, but von Zoll's political and economic influence is extensive, and so such legislation faces difficult going. Making matters even worse, von Zoll's cartel has just this week struck even stronger deals with the Russian and Commonwealth governments and, as a consequence, now stands to control a new and major source of oil. If the Middle East is nuked by German-supplied terrorists, if our own domestic and hemispheric oil sources are nuked, von Zoll and his Russian sponsors will be in the energy catbird seat. I personally see von Zoll, his Nazis, and nuclear terrorism as our major national security problem, and I want you all to give me your recommendations soonest." He paused. "Any questions or comments at this point?"

Pomeroy held up a hand, pencil waggling. "Mr. President, I have a question for Sam."

"Let's hear it."

"Your people report, Sam, that the Nachrichtendienst is especially active here in the States at the moment, presumably chasing down rumors that von Zoll is spreading his activities into the Western Hemisphere. To your knowledge, is the Dienst—and therefore the German government—aware that von Zoll has launched a secret effort to buy a controlling interest in the United Broadcasting System? That von Zoll wants to build a major U.S. information and entertainment empire centered on his control of UBS?"

Kowalski shook his head. "No. The German government

intelligence service is not yet up to speed on von Zoll's corporate raiding and general acquisition programs. He has bought up important pieces of real estate in Delaware, Maryland, Virginia, and Pennsylvania. His front people have taken over at least a dozen small- to medium-size newspapers in the Southwest, and on the Coast, most importantly in the Seattle area, he has acquired several independent radio and television stations. In Germany itself, our agents have not yet reported a single indication that these von Zoll maneuverings are known to Chancellor Haussener's government. Von Zoll is superb at establishing fronts to keep his dealings secret, and the only reason we know as much as we do about these activities is that the CIA has turned around one of his agents, a stock analyst in New York."

Vice President McKell cleared his throat and spoke for the first time. "How come the CIA is turning von Zoll's agents? I thought Aaron Richter of SII was supposed to have responsibility for the neo-Nazi thing."

The others stared at McKell as if he had just developed a third nostril. After a strained pause Sam Kowalski said softly, in the manner of a patient schoolteacher, "Well, Mr. Vice President, there's a lot of overlapping and networking in the intelligence business. No single agency can ever hope to have—or, indeed, want to have—exclusivity in a certain information area. We take our intelligence where we find it. Aaron Richter is one of our most highly skilled intelligence-gathering technicians, and as such he helps me—and the nation—enormously. But he would be the first to welcome assistance from any quarter, no matter how unlikely."

"Well, it makes me uncomfortable when there are so many spoons in any given stew. It makes for confusion and error."

Leonardi said, "As an old intelligence hand, Brandon, I can assure you that intelligence turfs can't ever be exclusive. In my soldiering days I knew and worked with Aaron Richter, and he's very fast-lane. But I've never yet seen him turn down help, even if it floats in over the transom. Please, take Sam's word for it."

McKell fell redly silent.

Leonardi asked, "Are there any other questions or comments, gentlemen?"

General silence.

"So, then. Let's get on with the agenda. Arlen, what are your proposals for our dealing with the human rights issues in sub-Saharan Africa?"

As Secretary Anderson opened his notebook and adjusted his spectacles, Leonardi closed his eyes briefly and stifled a sigh.

The thought: *It's going to be a long day.*

The afternoon's rain had become a midnight storm whose hissings and clatterings were loud in the darkened room.

She pulled away finally, and considered him through half-closed eyes. He was on his back, staring at the ceiling through the lightning-laced gloom.

"What's the matter, Brandon?"

"Matter?"

"You're not your, ah, vigorous self. You've been a hundred miles away all evening. Is something wrong?"

"I don't know."

She made a small, amused sound. "Well, if you don't know, who does?"

"I'm bothered, Jenny, but I can't get a real handle on the reason. I have a feeling things aren't what they should be. It's just a—feeling."

"Things? What things? You mean us? Our ducking the Secret Service for fun and games in this—what's the brochure say?—'cozy wayside inn with an infinite view of the majestic Chesapeake'?" Her laughter was muffled by her pillow.

"The NSC meeting this afternoon. It had—undertones."

"How so?"

"It was an atmosphere. The discussions were entirely routine, a lot of stuff we'd been over many times before. The drug war's ending, the hemispheric trade and security mix, the German problem, the Middle East nuclear thing, human rights in the Third World, what to do about China, et cetera, et cetera. But I had this feeling that Leonardi was watching me."

"Hooboy. What do you mean, 'watching'?"

"It's the only word that comes close to fitting. He was deliberately not looking at me because he was really watching me. Know what I mean?"

"Well— No. I don't know what you mean."

"I wonder if Leonardi has tumbled to what we're up to?"

She rose up on her elbows, staring intently at him through the restless shadows. "No way. There's absolutely no way he could have tumbled to anything without my knowing about it. I am his chief of staff. I run his office, screen his calls, read his mail, approve his appointments calendar, boss the White House office personnel—Hell, he doesn't even have a wife or a girlfriend he can talk to because he lives like a celibate. And not only that, I have bugged the phones in his private quarters. The man's practically a priest, the way he goes about the presidency. No fun and games, no card games with the guys, no hanky-panky. His mind is totally on the job, and when he's not in his office he's preoccupied with personal privacy, with correctness, with all the proprieties. That's one of the main reasons we're able to pull off this caper—his strange form of stiff-necked isolation from the slam and bang. Compared to Leonardi, Cal Coolidge was a trade show greeter."

McKell sighed and rubbed his eyes. "I guess all this started with something he said today. Somebody mentioned Aaron Richter, and, while he said some favorable things about Aaron, I'm not sure he meant them. He alluded to his young days, and how he had worked with Aaron, and the way he spoke gave me the impression that he didn't much like Aaron—didn't really trust him, or something. I can't fully explain it."

Jenny sniffed. "Hey, boy—if Leonardi didn't trust Aaron, Aaron wouldn't be head of the SII, I guaran-damn-tee you that. I've listened to some of their conversations, and, while there's sort of a formal tone about them, I also detect a lot of mutual respect. I grant you, Leonardi talks to all us hired hands that way, but if there was any real dislike or distrust, I sure would have picked it up. I'm a very intuitive person, and that's what I'm paid for: to use my intuition, full-throttle, all the time."

"Strange, isn't it," he said, his voice low, philosophical, "how you get one thing handled and something else pops up to give you the heebies."

"Life has a way of doing that, all right."

"Here I was, feeling a lot better now that Sweeney is no longer around to cause problems, and what happens? Leonardi starts staring at me."

"Come on, Brandon, knock it off."

"I think Leonardi really plans to do it. He really plans to drop me from the ticket the next time around."

Her voice became severe. "No more talk like that. Between this caper and the money tree in the South, you'll be too big for him to kick around. He'll be in no position to do anything about you—negative, positive, bad or good."

They lay quietly, thinking about these things.

"Well," he said finally, "I admit I feel better now that I've talked to you about it. I guess all the tension of the past few weeks has me seeing spooks."

She reached out. "Come here, dummy. In a few minutes I'll have you seeing stars."

Throughout the gentle combat, her mind was elsewhere, racing, filling with options and alternatives.

When he was finally deeply asleep, she eased into her robe and slippers and went down to the library, where she phoned the Radimore Arms extension.

"Ames?"

"Well, hi, there, Your Ladyship. You're up late."

"There's something I want you to do. Immediately."

"Your wish is my command."

"Fetch me the close-out material. At once."

"You serious? Sort of ahead of yourself, ain't you?"

"That's none of your business. Get it and bring it to my place without delay. I'll be waiting at the gatehouse."

"Well, whatever you say. It'll take me at least an hour, though."

"I'll expect you in an hour."

CHAPTER 30

It was raining again, a bitter, wind-driven downpour that seethed in the trees, formed swirling halos around lampposts and made clamorous cataracts of the streets. It was a good night for break-ins, what with all the racket to cover the sounds of crowbars or whatever, but Sweeney earnestly hoped that there would be no need for the forcible-entry option. It was just too damned wet and cold to be tromping through shrubbery and splintering wood and cutting glass, and talking with friends was a lot better than tearing up their property.

He nosed the van into the driveway with high beams blazing and parked in the familiar turnaround. He gunned the motor before turning it off, slammed the door a couple of times and made a general fuss out of his arrival. By the time he had dashed through the storm and stood at the front door, punching the bell button, either the Schwenkes were ready for company or he could be sure that he had the place to himself.

Lamps went on in the dim interior and the door opened.

"Tom—my God, don't you know enough to stay home on a night like this?"

"Hi, Doc. I hope I haven't come at a really bad time."

"Not at all." Schwenke smelled heavily of alcohol. "I was just dozing over Tuesday's Move at the Nighties. Come in, come in. Let me take your coat."

When they were seated in the den and the TV had been turned off, Sweeney asked, "Where's Louise? In bed already?"

A shadow seemed to move across Schwenke's smile, but then his face brightened again, too much. "No, she's still visiting her family out West. I'm still bach-ing it."

Things came together for Sweeney. A darkened house, dust, unwashed dishes on the coffee table, scattered newspapers, an absent wife, false ebullience and the reek of booze: a case of terminal loneliness; suicide by the ounce.

"Want a drink, Tom?"

"No, thanks."

"Mind if I have one?"

"Heck no."

"Takes the chill away."

"Yeah."

Schwenke lifted a square bottle from the floor beside the sofa and splashed whiskey into a finger-smudged glass. The first gulp down and working, he smiled again. "So, then: What's up?"

"I need some more help."

"You got everything I put on that truck?"

"Oh, yes, and I'm much obliged. This is something else, and I don't even know if I'm wasting your time or if it will lead to anything, or what. But I had to drop by and lay it out for you."

Schwenke waved the glass in a gesture of ready understanding. "Sure. Let's have it."

Sweeney, groping for a way to ease the melancholy that goes with the exploitation of a friend, began with, "I suppose quite a few government types come to you for help with their special equipment problems, don't they, Doc? I mean, I'm not the only one, I'm sure."

"Not so many. I am head of a rather large research and development operation. Most of our patron departments, our in-house clients, so to speak, follow established channels when dealing with us." Schwenke, seeming to relish this tiny moment of self-importance, took another gulp from the glass.

Sweeney nodded. "But there are a few. Could you give me an example or two?"

"Oh, no. Sorry. Whenever I deal directly with individuals who have special device problems it's understood that we enter a condition of mutual confidentiality. You, for instance: Would you want me to mention to someone else that I provided you with a truckload of goodies? Hell, no."

"Well, you got that right," Sweeney agreed, "but I'm just talking generalities here. I don't want you to tell me anything specific, like Hank Nageler coming to you and asking to borrow the lab copy of the Jadgmeister five hundred you built from the plans SII stole from the Germans."

Schwenke grinned crookedly. "Borrowed, hell. Rented. For a bundle. Up front. No questions or deals. Cash on the table. Not everybody's a freeloader like you, Sweeney. Ha-ha."

Sweeney laughed to show he appreciated the joke. "Well, I was never told that my department could rent things from your department. It was never—"

"Ha. Departments don't rent from departments anymore. Don't be ridiculous. The individual rents from me. I'm the guy needs money. The government doesn't need money—it's got everybody's money. Then it gives everybody's money to all the tinhorn grifters and brass-button nabobs in those little countries you can't find on the fuggin map and our own cities are rotting and our kids can't read or add, and the government taxes us more so that it can give more to the Russians, for God's sake. We spend half of a goddam century, spend half of our goddam national treasure to keep the goddam Russians in their cage, and then when their stinking system falls apart around their Commie ears, old Schwenke and Sweeney and all the working people in the land have to cough up to bail the Commies out because the sumbishes don't have anything left but babushkas."

Schwenke poured and tossed off another three-fingers of bourbon, his eyes hot and restless.

"It doesn't make much sense, sure enough."

"Well, tell you one thing, pal: my government screws me, I'm going to screw my government back. They've done it to me enough. I won't live long enough to see any replay of the French Revolution, pal, but as sure as God made little green apples, there's going to be one right here in the U.S. of A., because there's a hundred million Oscar Schwenkes who are mad as hell and like the guy on TV, they ain't going to take it any goddam more."

"You're one of the lucky ones, though, Doc. This big house, the beautiful wife, the educated kid, the nice cars—hell, you're crying all the way to the bank. Right?"

"Wrong-o. Everything you see around you here is mortgaged up to my bald goddam scalp. Everything you see is owned by some fuggin S and L that I can't pay back because I'm so far behind in my taxes, and my beautiful wife is leaving and I don't know where she put the extra car keys or the insurance policies or my winter sweaters, and I swear to God I think I'm going nuts because I don't know who I am anymore, or if anybody even gives a shit about me now that I'm getting old and bald and funny-looking and can't do anything useful, like mowing the lawn and putting the kids to bed. You didn't know that Bert wasn't my only kid, did you, Tom. We had a little Maggie, but she fell into the pool one day and my wife didn't say anything for six months but just sat and stared at me because I had left the pool house door unlatched when I went to the super for another six-pack and little Maggie was floating facedown for—oh, Jesus Christ—for a whole hour—"

Schwenke, his unblinking eyes on the storm beyond the casements, didn't bother with the glass this time, but tilted the bottle and took a long draw.

"How long ago was Maggie, Doc?" Sweeney asked gently.

"I don't remember."

"How long has Louise been gone?"

"I don't remember that, either. She never told me where she put the extra car keys."

Sweeney sighed a silent, inner sigh. Here was his opening. Why did he feel so rotten about using it?

"They're probably in that left-hand cabinet in the pantry. That blue-and-white job with all the drawers. That's where most folks would be likely to put them."

Schwenke sneered. "Shows how much you know. That's where that asshole Nageler is keeping the peashooters. He says to hide something, you should put it in plain sight or in a drawer with the kitchen matches and barbecue forks. There isn't key one in that cabinet, pal. Only twenty bucks' worth of matches, twine and thumbtacks—and twenty grand's worth of peashooter in a kid's wooden pencil box."

"Pretty expensive peashooters."

"One peashooter. I haven't made the second one yet. Twenty grand apiece isn't much when you consider how tricky it is to make one of those little bastards. You wouldn't believe the rigmarole I had to go through to be sure I wasn't going to kill Louise and that yippy little fleabag Peke of hers."

"What was so tricky?"

"Have you ever tried to encapsulate toxic acids in a cellar goddam workshop, for crissake? It isn't like making a milk shake, you know."

"Nageler ordered two, but you made only one. Why?"

Schwenke yawned noisily. "Insurance. As long as I'm needed to make another shooter, I'm safe. And it wasn't Nageler. He ordered it for a client. Hell, Nageler is like you and me and all the other errand boys in this freaking town—up to his ass in debt and loneliness and no way out. Everything we do is always for bigshots or institutions that keep us in some kind of debt so we can't find a way out of their control. Well, buster, by not making the second peashooter I keep a little control of my own."

"And only Nageler knows where you keep the thing?"

"Only Nageler, the client and I. And now you."

"What if you aren't here when Nageler comes to pick it up? Do you have a drill on that?"

"He has a key to the house. He collects keys. You wouldn't believe the key ring that sumbish carries in his car. I bet he has a key to every lock in every building he's ever been in. I used to kid him. 'Why don't you get a set of burglar jimmies and go lightweight?' I'd say, and he'd just laugh and tell me it was his hobby, collecting keys. You ever hear of anything dumber than that?"

"People are weird, all right."

Schwenke's head swayed to one side, and his eyes rolled briefly. He started, sitting up straight, and blinking.

Sweeney glanced at his watch and stood up. "Well, I guess I'd better run along."

"Hey—You never told me what you want. You said you want some more help—"

"I've changed my mind."

Schwenke yawned again. "All the talk about money scare you? Hell, Tom, for you it's always on the house."

"No, it's not that, Doc. I just thought of another way to handle my problem. But thanks. Thanks a lot."

"Sure you don't want a drink? A nightcap, maybe?"

"I'm driving. Thanks anyhow."

Schwenke nodded, elaborately somber. "Remember, if you drive drunk, it's best to have a car. Hee-hee."

As Sweeney made his way to the hallway coat closet, Schwenke muttered, "Louise'll be sorry she missed you."

Sweeney returned to say good-bye, but Schwenke was already asleep, snoring softly, the empty bottle on his lap. So Sweeney went to the pantry and opened the drawer. There were matches, all right, and twine and thumbtacks. In the back, behind a map of California with a crayoned arrow and a note in Bert's handwriting that said here was where he was working now, he found the schoolkid's pencil box.

Raising the lid, he counted three battered pencil stubs, a broken ballpoint pen, and five paper clips. No peashooter.

And the lid was damp.

Damp?

He stood, motionless, thinking about this.

There was only one explanation. Schwenke the Sozzled Snoozer had had another visitor this dark and stormy night. A surreptitious, rain-dripping visitor.

He felt a stirring of uneasiness—indefinable, vague. Something just this side of alarm.

He turned off the kitchen lights and on the way out paused in the den to pick up a tweed jacket that lay on the carpet. He took the bottle from Schwenke's lap, set it on the table and then draped the coat over the slumping shoulders.

At the door he turned to look once more on this sodden unhappiness, dealing with the fact that his old friend was already deep into a kind of death.

"Louise has missed a lot of things, Doc," he said softly. "And so have you."

CHAPTER 31

"Yeah?"

"This is Randolph Ridenour."

"So?"

"There's something I'd like you to do for me."

"I'm pretty busy these days. Cummings has got pretty much of an exclusive on my time."

"This will entail a mere overnight to Saint Augustine."

"Which overnight?"

"Tonight. Then back tomorrow afternoon. Cummings won't even miss you."

"Why should I go to Saint Augustine?"

"The plan isn't working as I'd hoped. The Man is simply not showing any signs of weakening, giving in. Quitting."

"You promised Cummings you'd have that guy out of there."

"The Man's a lot tougher than I thought he'd be."

"And you want me to fix that. Right?"

"Well, yes. We've got to get him out of the way so Brandon McKell can take personal charge. He's not getting out of the way."

"I'm a busy man, Ridenour."

"Oh, I expect to make it up to you. Ten thousand dollars for an overnight job isn't bad pay, the way I see it."

"Twelve grand is better."

"All right. Twelve then."

"I'm calling the airport right now. Good-bye."

CHAPTER 32

The tape was running a second time because Harvey Wallace wanted to be certain of what he had seen on the first run-through. The officers around him—his own headquarters staff and the delegation from the National Guard's 125th Fighter Interceptor Group at Miami's Homestead base—seemed again frozen to silence by the raw violence. This was no mere gun-camera exercise stuff, with practice tracers groping outward in deceptively lazy arcs for artificial targets; it was a High Noon shootout in the middle of Drug Alley, in which people were maimed under the glare of a subtropical sun.

Major Pete Crowley, A-2 for the 125th, served as narrator, and his voice sounded dry and strained in the screening room's murk.

"What you see here, gentlemen, is an Aeronado seventeen, a low-wing, single-engine, four-seat aircraft of Brazilian origin which was introduced in the mid-nineteen eighties as an entry in the private and sport-flying market. The machine was never a great success, and those that did reach the market were used mostly for commutation by small manufacturing companies and mining operations. The aircraft seen here, flying at five hundred and sixty feet on a north-by-northwest course above the Atlantic, was picked up by our picket balloons at oh-seven hundred thirty-four hours today. Two F-sixteen interceptors, modified to accommodate side-shooting combat camcorders, were dispatched by Homestead. The intercept was made two hundred fifty-eight miles southeast of Puerto Rico, and the Aeronado was first laser-marked for missile targeting, then tailed for the forty minutes it took to summon and place two National Guard Rasper assault choppers. We see one of the Raspers cruising a mile to the starboard of the suspect machine."

General Wallace said, "Freeze there, please. Am I right when I say I see two people in the cabin of that Aeronado?"

"Not exactly, sir. The shadow here"—the spot from his light-wand moved to the cockpit area—"represents the pilot and, in the right-hand seat, the copilot-navigator who also, it's now assumed, suggests the gun-controller."

" 'Represents'? 'Suggests'? What are you saying?"

Boots Franklin, seated at the far end of the table, held up a hand. "If I may, sir: I've been curious for some time now as to why the pilots we've intercepted have been so, well, stoical in the face of armed challenge and sure attack. In this exercise I placed a K-seventeen laser-lock personnel detector aboard the close-in camera chopper so that we might confirm just how many people were aboard whatever aircraft we intercepted."

"I've never really trusted those damned things."

"Their reliability has been ruled satisfactory by our weapons research people—not to the point of authorization as a regular-issue device, of course, but satisfactory. We really have improved on the Norwegians' air-to-surface antiship missile heat-seeking system, and not just in the miniaturization. It's keen enough to pick up another soldier's body heat a mile away—even when he's inside a moving vehicle. It's not perfect yet, and I'm not willing to bet the family jewels on our reading in this case. But the reading said there were no people at all on that Aeronado."

"None at all?"

"None at all, sir."

"All right, Pete. Proceed."

"The helicopter that made this tape is here on the west, or port side of the suspect aircraft. It has made its standard radio challenges to no avail and now closes in for a visual inspection. As is standard procedure, the starboard-side chopper hangs off, running its own wide-angle video of the general action scene." The tape went into freeze-frame again and the wand-light waggled across the Aeronado's expanded image. "At these locations are rather primitive mountings for what appear to be the old-style thirty caliber Browning aircooled light machine gun—one in each wing root and one in the tail cone. As weaponry goes, it's very basic, actually. But, as we've seen, very dangerous, too."

General Wallace broke in: "When we get to the corkscrew inspection—when the chopper is flying over, around and under the Aeronado—freeze it so we can get a good look at the belly and the underside wing panels, will you, Pete?"

"Yes, sir. That'll be about—right—now. There we are. As you can see, the aircraft is quite orthodox on its underside except for these podlike structures under the wing root. These appear to be ammunition pans, appended to accommodate the gun installations. And these slots, in the wings, here, and the tail cone, here, are obviously ejection chutes for spent cartridges. We estimate there's no room in each of the pans or in the tail cone for more than a belt of two hundred fifty rounds. Want to look at it some more, General?"

"No. Carry on."

"Our camera ship backs off to port. All the protocols have been satisfied: challenges radioed, lack of current aircraft license established, no ID or aircraft available on the masterboards at Homestead. This inset of the pilot's heads-up display shows an arming of the chopper's underside chain gun only—no missiles are involved, per your instructions, General. Now the chopper pulls steady and settles in on a course parallel to the Aeronado's and about one hundred yards to port, and, again pursuant to your orders, General, the chain gun fires a fifty-round burst whose stream and pattern are straight ahead, never closer to the Aeronado than the one hundred yards. Almost simultaneously, the Aeronado peels away violently in a climbing turn to starboard—so—with its tail gun firing—the stream seems to be almost all tracer ammo—and—here—there is a heavy bullet strike in the chopper's starboard canopy—note the ruptures and debris—there—and, as the screen image degenerates we assume that it is here that the gunnery officer has been hit and—here—at the—blackout—the chopper is seen to be entering a wild spiral. Then, in this rough splice to the tape from the other chopper, we see here, at the left, the camera chopper recovering just above the sea's surface and banking to the northwest. The Aeronado, meanwhile, is executing a series of what appear to be senseless maneuvers, with all three of its guns spraying tracers in all directions. And then, coming in from offscreen to the right, the fire streak that denotes the escort chopper's laser-guided LOAL missile which—here—strikes the Aeronado amidships. This pan shot follows the Aeronado's wreckage and fireball into the sea, where there is a secondary explosion."

"How do you account for that secondary, Pete?"

The ceiling lights went on and Crowley faced General Wallace, squinting against the glare. "We believe it was a charge the airplane was carrying."

Wallace sat silently thinking. When he spoke, his glance took in the intent faces around him. "It looks as if we've just watched the rather outlandishly clumsy performance of a jerry-rigged, computer-controlled drone, whose crew was a pair of mannequins. Wouldn't you say, gentlemen?"

There were murmured sounds of agreement, and Crowley said, "During which, General, gunfire rigged purely for audiovisual effect hit our chopper's lightweight, nonrefracting camera canopy by sheer chance, severely wounding the gunnery officer. That's exactly what we think."

Wallace said, "Which further leads me to believe, gentlemen, that we've been subjected to a con all along. A con in which externally controlled aircraft, cruising like decoys, were set up to make us think we were shooting down manned smuggling craft."

"And," Crowley added, "this Aeronado was strictly an attempt to allay our growing wonderment over the lack of action and reaction from the drones when challenged. The Aeronado was rigged to open fire as soon as fired upon, and it carried a charge that assured its destruction during the ensuing exchange of fire."

Wallace regarded his old friend, Colonel Franklin. "Do you agree with this assessment, Boots?"

"With every word, sir. That accounts for what we thought was an AWACS, too. The controllers were using a rudimentary radio-control mechanism for their earlier drones, and that required a mother ship. That's what our pickets saw on the perimeter. Now, with this new setup, all they need is enough fuel for a one-way flight and some computerized aerobatics, enough ammo to make some cosmetic fireworks, a computer setting that flies the plane into our picket line, and voom, we shoot down a ship that puts up a scrap and we go home feeling better about killing smugglers and wondering less why they never fight back."

"Anybody have any ideas why the drug people would go to all this trouble?"

A long silence followed the general's question.

Boots Franklin said eventually, "I have an even bigger question, sir. Why would Washington tell us the mother ship was an AWACS?"

This pause was even longer.

Wallace cleared his throat and said, "I'm going to come right out with what we're all not saying: somebody Topside wants us to think we're destroying drugs while we're not. Somebody doesn't want us to know they're really being slipped through in another place."

Exasperated, Fred McIntyre rasped, "But where? How?"

"Surface craft?" George Cannon ventured.

"Not likely," Wallace said. "The Navy has an absolute full-Nelson on all seagoing vessels of any size. Our chopper and flying machine fellers have an absolute surveillance of all small boat traffic. Our DEA and Coast Guard people have put major bungs in the U.S. port system."

McIntyre then came up with the obvious, the unacceptable suspicion. "The only vehicles moving with impunity and regularity over the whole arena are our own military supply planes. Mainly Army C-one thirties."

The statement hung there, a great, silently reverberating indictment.

Wallace said softly, "We have a pressing, practical question to deal with: Why would somebody go to all the trouble, risk and expense of flimflamming UIF? Why so much effort to *persuade* us that we've won the goddam drug war? Why so much effort to keep us patrolling the goddam oceans between

East Nowhere and West Nohow? Why all the fuss and blow to keep our attention centered on South and Central America?"

"We can only assume, sir, that either we still pose a problem to them somehow, or the success of whatever they're up to turns on the con job."

Wallace smiled faintly. "Right-on, Boots. Either way, we still worry them a lot."

"What do you think we ought to do about it, General?"

"The first step is for all of us here in this room to keep this discussion most secret. Only I should be allowed to reveal this matter at a time and place I deem appropriate. Anybody have any problems with that?" He waited. Then: "Since I hear nothing to the contrary, those of us here will consider this matter classified 'Most Secret' until I personally notify each of you that the classification is reduced or lifted. Is that understood?"

"Yes, sir."

Wallace checked his watch. "All right, it's almost one, and I have to make a phone call. You are dismissed."

As Wallace made his way to the door, Boots Franklin touched his sleeve. "Pardon, sir, but could I maybe interest you in some lunch? I owe you one on our little Series bet."

"Sorry, Boots. I really am, since I had lost all hope of you ever paying off. I haven't the time. After my phone call I'm due at the Avenida Manor for a meeting of the Saint Augustine Commerce Club. I'm to be the guest speaker, and after reading the press advances I can hardly wait to hear what I have to say."

Franklin feigned elaborate relief. "Great. That takes me off the hook for another year."

"Sweeney? Harve Wallace here."

"Hi. What's up, Harvé-meister?"

"I saw the tapes of the intercept. And I see what you mean. Somebody's been putting us on."

"Okay. We're both riding the same wave, then. So you keep your eyes open there and I'll do the same up here, and between us we might find out just what the living hell is going on and why so many people have gone to such obvious trouble to make idiots of you and me."

"Call me if you learn anything, eh?"

"Count on it. You're one of the few friends I've got, Harve-baby."

"Okay. Got to run. Bye."

It was a beautiful day, with the Matanzas sparkling under a brilliant sun and a soft breeze stirring in the palms along the waterfront. The Avenida Manor, a hulking gray coquina mansion dating from the early Spanish colonial period, was located on the bayfront near the central cathedral plaza, only a few blocks from Wallace's headquarters in the Government House. One of the things he liked most about St. Augustine was the closeness of things—the proximity of so many quirky but useful places. It was a walker's town, and so he took advantage of the fact as often as possible.

As he walked, he was unable to define his feelings. Recent weeks should have been filled with elation, a sense of accomplishment, of duty done well; instead, he'd been continually uneasy, depressed by a sense of paying a hidden price for something he really didn't need. Sweeney's drunken pronouncements, uttered one rotten night during the bleakest of those terrible weeks in Munich all those years ago, returned to his mind in this most unlikely of moments: "Knowing the truth can hurt like hell, sure enough. But not nearly as much as not knowing the truth. If you know the truth, my dear Bojo, if you know exactly why it's necessary, you can hang by your thumbs indefinitely. The trouble is, in this world nobody knows for sure what is true, or exactly why things are necessary, and so our days, our nights, our lifetimes are filled with an everlasting, silent scream."

He'd had incredible, unreal, success in his role in the drug war but could never say exactly why. He had somehow made all the right moves, but just why they were right had eluded him. And so he'd been screaming Sweeney's silent scream. The new knowledge that he and all his wonderful men and women had been patsies in some enormous flimflam hurt, to be sure, but not nearly as badly as the *not*-knowing had hurt. Now the question was what to do about it. The entire system was suspect; to whom do you run, whom do you warn, when the king himself could be a crook?

God, what a crummy world.

Was it time to retire? Take his pension and let somebody else worry about it all?

He thought about that—squinting in the sunlight, breathing the briny air, listening to the call of the gulls.

In a pig's valise, pal. Lash up my thumbs and let me swing. If they want me out of this job, they're going to have to throw me out.

He headed east across the plaza for the traffic circle at the foot of the Bridge of Lions, keeping to the shade of the huge oaks. A group of historical reenactment types, locals costumed in tricorns and colonial English uniforms, practiced a manual of arms, their huge bayonet-tipped muskets glinting in the autumn light, their leader's commands clear above the traffic sounds and the gabble of tourists in goofy hats and raunchy T-shirts who slurped ice-cream cones on the nearby benches. Some of the crowd applauded and whistled when they saw Wallace's Class A's, with the shiny shoes and the brass and the ribbons and the stars, and he threw an answering salute when Ozzy Detweiler, the reenactment director, called his colonials to attention and ordered a present-arms.

At the gazebo, Wallace turned right to follow the tabby path that led toward the maritime museum on King Street, and it was at that moment the day began to come apart.

His peripheral vision, sharpened by years of soldiering, showed him that, to his right, a black BMW sedan was easing away from the curb near the corner of King and St. George. It was moving slowly, its dark-tinted driver's side window sliding down. Contrasting with the steady traffic movement, the car's seeming lethargy was a discord, and Wallace gave it a direct, hard look.

Now resting on the BMW's windowsill was the classic tube-silenced automatic pistol, and the muzzle was pointed directly at him. The old campaigner's reflex permits the human body to drop and flatten with catlike speed. Even so, Wallace, dropping and flattening, felt the slam of hot, explosive wind close against the left side of his head.

The assassin, obviously, had not reckoned on Ozzie Detweiler's troops, because the car, the shot, and the general's dive for cover were witnessed by eight musket-bearers and their saber-waving officer, who, energized by some primal sense of outrage, chorused an ungodly rebel yell and plunged into a wild charge, in which at least three bayonets and a sword pierced and destroyed the BMW's left-side tires.

The pistol snapped again, three times, sounds virtually lost in the traffic buzz, and Ozzie and his troops hit the deck in piles of blue, buff and glittering silver and brass. The tourists, shrieking, fell back in an expanding circle of panic as the assassin, a tall redhead wearing gold-framed tinted glasses, leaped from the disabled car, swinging his pistol, and broke into a full sprint east on King.

Wallace was running then, cursing, in unthinking pursuit, and the man saw him coming. A second snicking sound, and again Wallace felt the hot shock wave against his face.

As if it were far off, Wallace heard his own voice shouting the supreme idiocy: "Knock it off, goddam you!"

He leaped over a concrete bench and closed the gap, his legs and arms pumping, his breath raling from exertion, anger and fright.

A carriage, one of those ornate, high-wheeled jobs, stood at the corner of King and Charlotte, across from the Fiesta Mall, unoccupied except for the driver, who apparently had been waiting for fares among the funny-hats now sprawling and wailing on the grass. The assassin fired another shot just as he dashed past the horse, and the animal, neighing with fright, reared in its traces, forelegs churning wildly.

In the lunge, the horse sideswiped the gunman with a force that tossed him like a rag doll to the sidewalk and sent his pistol spinning into the street. But Wallace, too, was thrown off stride when the carriage lurched backward into his path, giving the fugitive time to recover and resume his lead. Now, however, the man appeared to be hurt, limping as he ran and holding his right arm close.

Horns clamored and brakes squealed as the pursuit left the plaza and careened across the busy intersection where King crossed the Avenida and began its climb to the bridge.

Ahead, up the rise, blinking lights, lowered barriers and sirens signaled that a draw-span repair crew had begun another of the seemingly never-ending tinkering sessions that had belabored the city since 1992. Wallace, his eyes bleary, his chest aching, his legs agonized, was aware of angry shouts as he and his quarry clambered over the hoods of those idling cars that had already begun to choke the mainland approaches and the bridge's western half.

From somewhere in the distance came the warbling and hooting of police cars.

The two-lane bridge, under heavy repair for the past week, had been closed to a single lane of traffic, with the westbound lane choked with supplies and maintenance vehicles and the eastbound lane given to alternate flows governed by a pair of uniformed county police deputies. The man with the tinted glasses, once clear of the west-end jam, continued his eastward run up the centerline, staggering between the waiting cars and the maintenance clutter, pushing his way though the hardhats who had gathered about a tailgate water cooler. And Wallace saw then that he was going to try a jump across the gap between the bridge's slightly raised central draw sections.

His own voice, rasping, still sounding remote and alien: "Stop right now, you son of a bitch—You aren't going to make it!"

The man slowed as he approached the gap, and Wallace, struggling to shoulder his way through a knot of ogling pipe fitters, could see that the gunman, too, was having doubts.

The decision came quickly. After stooping and pulling a small caliber pistol from an ankle holster, the gunman danced sideways, crouching, to where a female deputy—slender, pretty, puzzled by the commotion—stood beside a flatbed truck. He seized the woman and, closing his left arm around her neck and pressing the backup pistol to her head with his bleeding right hand, he half lifted, half dragged her to a position at top and center of the incline. He teetered there, holding her as a shield and glaring at Wallace.

"Okay, soldier-boy, end of the line. One more step and I blow this molly away."

"Let her go. This is between you and me."

"Between you and me, hell. The only thing between you and me is that you're going to fetch me a car. And when I'm in the car, driving up I-ninety-five with no tail in sight, I'll let her go."

A large policeman, service pistol leveled at the man in the glasses, appeared suddenly to Wallace's left. "All right, hot-shot. Let the lady go and we won't have no more trouble."

The gunman dealt with this by turning quickly, the woman shielding him from the policeman's pistol, to fire a single shot.

The big cop, peering down at the blood wetting his shirt below the badge, sank slowly to his knees, saying softly, "Shee-it-oh-dear."

But Wallace used the interruption as the kind of break Sweeney had taught him to exploit all those years ago. During the tiny interval in which the man had turned to deliver his shot, Wallace had stooped and snatched up a length of half-inch scrap piping that lay at his feet. It was no jack handle, but it would have to do.

As the man glanced back at him, Wallace made his throw. The hurtling pipe cartwheeled lazily, as Sweeney had assured him such a weapon always would, then it neatly bisected the tinted glasses, and the gunman reeled—a grotesque, blood-spouting unicorn—to topple out of sight over the lip of the draw span.

The woman swayed drunkenly, then, beyond balance, also fell away, whimpering and turning over twice before making a second splash in the swift green currents thirty feet below.

Wallace, for the thousandth time in his life cursing his inbred, tyrannical sense of responsibility for others, kicked off his shoes and went after her.

It seemed eons before he struck the water and even longer before he could become oriented in the dark swirling. He could see nothing but murky water and passing flotsam, but, when surfacing for a gulp of air, he saw the woman's white face just before she sank once again. A few quick strokes and he had her, and, holding her head above water, he let the incoming tide carry them toward the city pier a hundred yards to the south.

"Are you all right, young lady?"

"I'm scared out of my mind. I can't swim."

"Relax. This swim's on me."

CHAPTER 33

"Hi, Cap. Laurie Platt."

"Well, well. The ole antiques lady. How the heck are you?"

"Not the ole antiques lady yet, sorry to say. Still plugging away at the Joint Chiefs code room. But comes the turn of the year, you won't see me for tire smoke."

"I bet your mom's pleased you've made the decision."

"Yeah. She's getting the carriage house ready for me already, for Pete's sake."

"That's what moms are all about."

"I guess so."

"So what's going down?"

"I called to see if you're still needing material on that weirdo, Randolph Ridenour."

"I can always use more. You have something?"

"Just some bits and pieces. I don't know if they'll help you, but I thought I'd call anyhow."

"Good. Let me have them."

"Well, I was working codes and decodes for all-service radio traffic on the midnight trick. They asked me to do this overtime; it's cheaper than having a field grader on straight duty."

"Budgets, budgets, budgets."

"Yeah. So I was taking a stack of flimsies to General Reynolds's office when I passed the priority mail desk, where I saw another pile of red-tagged letters for the general. I added them to my stack and took the lot to his office. On the way, the memo on top caught my eye."

"So? What did it say?"

"It was the CIA's confidential daily advisory to the JC chairman and his staff sections. A very routine piece of mail. It's mainly stuff you're likely to see sooner or later in the *Wall Street Journal.* You know: who's the new CEO at Gismo Corporation; what Horsemanure Inc. paid for its new fertilizer plant—that kind of stuff. Only this one had a mention of Ridenour on its first page."

"Which said—what?"

"I'll read it to you: 'Interrogation of CIA source in New York confirms imminent sale of United Broadcasting System to an unidentified German cartel. Source says Randolph Ridenour, UBS news commentator, has agreed to head the network's news and special events department upon completion of the deal. Other details to follow.' "

"Very interesting, Laurie. I don't know what its importance is, either, but every little bit helps, I always say. Anything else?"

"Only one little thing. A friend of mine has this guy who owns a farm over on the Eastern Shore—I don't know how near to you—and she was telling me at lunch that his nose was all out of joint last weekend because his neighbor's horses keep busting a fence or something, and the neighbor is a real snooty pain in the ass who won't do anything about it. The neighbor is, guess who, Randolph Ridenour."

"Hot damn! Good, good stuff, Laurie."

"Really?"

"Oh, boy. Does Ridenour's place have a name?"

"Yeah. It used to be the Llewellyn House. But Ridenour calls it Azalea Manor. It's off Route two-thirteen south of Chestertown. He's hardly ever there—it's sort of a superprivate retreat or something, apparently—but it's a real nice spread, my friend says."

"Laurie, you've just earned a steak dinner on me."

"I have?"

"Is that it, then?"

"I guess so. Oh, by the way: have you heard the news?"

"What news?"

"Somebody tried to assassinate that nice General Wallace today—the guy who heads up UIF in Florida."

"My god. Really?"

"Mm. Some man tried to shoot him, but—get this—the general chased him out on a bridge, where the guy grabbed a woman cop as a shield. The general killed the bastard with a pipe or something, then jumped into the river where the cop had fallen and saved her like a teenage Atlantic City lifeguard. Isn't that the limit?"

"My god."

"There was quite a buzz about it around the Pentagon."

"I should think so."

"It's already on the tube, too. They're calling the general a big hero, and like that. Have to run now, Cap. I'll be calling again."

"Thanks a bunch, Laurie."

"This is Freddie Dilworth."

"Hi, Freddie. Cap."

"Hello, there, my friend. Did you catch the news about that general who was just here? How somebody tried to shoot him?"

"Yep. Some deal, eh?"

"He's pretty frisky for a guy his age, you ask me."

"I'll say."

"So what can I do you for, Cap?"

"Have you heard of a place called the Llewellyn House down near Chestertown?"

"Sure. I know it. Why?"

"This is very important, so drop everything and get right at it, please. I want you to run down there and get as many photos of the place you can."

"That won't be easy. It sits real far back off the road, being a big old manor house, and the new owner, whoever that is, has posted the property and set up real tight security, according to Bob Billings, the deputy in Chestertown who goes hunting with me and Al Jacobs whenever their wives let them out of the house."

"How about the entrance—gates, walls, that kind of thing. The perimeter fences, or whatever."

"That's a lot of perimeter. The place covers about two hundred acres."

"Well, do what you can. And get me the photos and a map marked with the house soonest."

"Okay. I'll bring them to The Orchards tonight. I have to come down there anyhow, because I have the pix Sweeney asked me to get in Washington."

"How did it turn out? Did you get good stuff?"

"I think so. But Sweeney'll have to decide that."

"See you tonight, pal."

"Hier Kratzer."

"Ich möchte über ein Märchen sprechen."

"Was für ein Märchen?"

"Aus alten Zeiten. Wie Heine, zum Beispiel."

"My god, Sweeney. You're lucky you caught me in bed, seeing as how it's only three thirty-five in the morning."

"Sorry Bernie, but this couldn't wait."

"What's up?"

"Do you have a good fax handy?"

"It takes special dispensation from Berlin for German embassy personnel to wear facsimile machines in their pajamas. But there's a good one in my office downstairs. Why?"

"I have photos of two people I'd like to run through the Nachrichtendienst and Interpol registries. If I fax you these shots, could you fax them to your ID people in Berlin? There's reason to believe that the pix are of German nationals—an idea strengthened by the fact that tapes made by the photographer have them speaking German."

"That's a good reason to believe they're Germans, all right. Are you ready to send now?"

"Sure."

"Give me ten minutes—eight in which to wake up and pull on some pants, two for getting to the office and turning on the damned machine."

"Call me on my unlisted when you're ready to receive."

"Kratzer, Sweeney."

"Well, well. Good afternoon."

"Berlin ID'ed the people, as you requested, and I'm putting

the pix and the Dienst's comments on each on the fax. Are you ready to receive there?"

"Sure. But tell me now. My curiosity is killing me."

"Picture A, the man you ID as Cummings: That's Dr. Hans Schneider, formerly a detective inspector of the Bavarian State Police, highly educated, much traveled. Tried and convicted in nineteen eighty-five for various extortion schemes. He did three years, after which he was hired to set up a bodyguard and security system for the industrialist Hugo von Zoll. He is still with von Zoll, and is said to be the tycoon's most trusted personal friend.

"Picture B, your ID, Colt, first name unknown: That's Heinrich Baum, a former agent of the Nachrichtendienst, who specialized in counterintelligence and served for many years in Mexico, Peru, Colombia, Chile and Argentina. His reputation is terrible. He is suspected today to be a free-lance wheeler-dealer with many connections in the South American drug trade."

"That's good stuff, Bernie. I really appreciate your help on this one."

"Where were these shots made?"

"At the Radimore Arms in Washington. They were there yesterday. My bugs tell me they were fine-tuning plans for a meeting to be held the day after tomorrow in Maryland with Manuel Corbato, the Colombian drug bigwig, and assorted types from the U.S. of A."

"How's Corbato getting to Maryland? He's too hot to go through Customs."

"He's being flown into Aberdeen on a U.S. Army C-one thirty, no less."

"You've got to be joking."

"Nope. God's truth."

"What's the Maryland meeting about?"

"I don't know. But I'll find out."

"How?"

"I'm going to attend it."

CHAPTER 34

The Stearman's engine drummed softly, evenly, fragrantly in the silky night sky, and the stars seemed to be mirror images of the twinkling habitations bordering the great black spread of the Chesapeake. In the rearview mirror he could see Cap's face, softly aglow from the reflected light of the instruments arrayed on the cockpit panel before her. It was a beautiful face, despite the grotesque goggles and the constrictions of the leather helmet, and he studied it for a long interval, relishing anew the understanding that she was his and he was hers.

"I've been plotting on my knee chart, Cap," he said into the intercom, "and I put us over Betterton."

"Right. That's the Sassafrass River under our tail. The cluster of lights to our left front is Still Pond, and beyond that, Kennedyville. In the darkness off our left wing is a private airstrip owned by the Bellanca family."

"The famous aviation Bellancas?"

"Yep. And off to the starboard, across the bay, is Middle River and Glenn Martin's beeg, beeg factory."

"How much are you charging for this tour of the homes of the rich and aeroplaney?"

"I'm metered by zones. For every ten miles, an hour of sack time."

"You're a randy wench."

"Why is it I get the most randy when I'm buckled into this flying machine?"

"Because you are a pree-vert. A seducer of minors. Minor bureaucrats, that is."

"Correction: Only one minor *ex*-bureaucrat."

He recognized that they were making chatter to keep the anxiety-adrenalin factor at a manageable level. They had spent the entire afternoon and much of the evening going over Freddie's photos and tapes, studying the Geodetic Survey's topographical map of the real estate comprising and surrounding the two hundred acres of Azalea Manor. They had made an overlay, and to this Sweeney applied key azimuth intersections to establish benchmarks that would keep him oriented during the mission. The target area was flat to rolling country, with patches of forest and open fields bounded on the north, east and south by county roads. On the west was the bay, and for a man with twenty-nine combat paradrops to his credit, plus a dozen special mission jumps for CIA, such a well-defined, well-manicured drop zone under the brilliant stars of a mellow night would seem to be a piece of cake. But he was older now, and flabbier in both body and spirit, and the prospect of plunging through the night for a soundless pinpoint landing in a very unfriendly backyard was less than soothing.

Cap, too, was uptight, not only because the jumper was her Very Significant Other but also because her VSO was entirely dependent on her orchestration of timing, direction, altitude, windage, barometric readings and plain old steady flying to establish the precise moment when he must step into space.

"One thing going for us," Cap said in his earphones. "We're tootling along the edge of some of the busiest air traffic in the world. I'm flying under VFR tonight—if ever a night was made for visual flight regulations, this is it. But here we are, in the wee hours, and you wouldn't believe the radio traffic. We're on the outer fringes of ATCs at Philly International, Balto International, Washington National, Dulles, umpteen military airfields, and the Restricted Zone Monitors in and around good old D.C. The sky is full of gabby airplanes of all sizes and shapes. The Azalea Manor guys aren't likely to notice a tired old Stearman. Not among all the GI Joes, the red-eye commuter specials, and the rich cardiologists flying home to Mom in their little six-million-dollar Aerojets after a week of examining breasts at Whoosis Casino in Vegas."

"Why didn't I fall for a rich cardiologist, instead of a wordy, indigent, flying schoolmarm? Or is it, an indigent flying-school marm?"

"No, it's a marm-flying indigent school."

"By the way, you said something about D.C.'s Restricted Zone Monitors. Is that what you flying machine drivers call the Scud-Busters on top of the Washington Monument, and other ordnance bristling around the center of town?"

"Yep. And we take it seriously, too, buddy. Those ground-to-air missile launchers are designed to shoot first and ask later. You want hot crosses in your buns, pal, just fly too low over thirteen hundred Pennsylvania Avenue."

"I'm glad you noticed it. I'm one of the security honchos who set it up. I'd hate to think you're ignoring us."

"Sudlersville below. I'm at seven thousand now, and I'm making our turn southwest for the Chesapeake Bay Bridge. I'll finish the climb there and make a U to the northeast. We'll begin your countdown then. Remember, I'm master control on jump time, but I'd appreciate your backstopping me."

"Is the wind holding?"

"Yep. A sweet afton, blowing gently at six miles per hour out of the south."

"That's 'sweet Afton, flowing gently.' Afton ain't a breeze, it's a creek."

"Oh, God, how did you ever get so smart?"

"I'm an old Afton fan, is all. Spent many an hour fishing for green braes there."

They picked up Route 301 and followed the highway to the bridge, which appeared as an arching ribbon of stars linking a pair of minor galaxies. He felt the Stearman ease out of its climb and then, minutes later, the subtle dropping of its right wings as Cap entered a gentle turn to starboard. He made still another check of his gear: chute buckles, wrist altimeter, weapons and utilities satchel, flashlight holster, map case, compass, night glasses, and helmet straps.

The engine racket fell off to a muttering as Cap cut throttle and began a long, flat, downwind power glide.

"Time to get out on the wing, pal." Her voice was cool, businesslike.

He flipped off his lap belt and, pulling on the upper wing handhold, raised his bulk free of the seat and swung his left leg over the cockpit rim. The slipstream, even under this reduced throttle setting, was formidable, fluttering his coveralls and flattening his cheeks. When his right leg was free, he crouched on the lower wing root walkstrip, clutching the center-section struts, facing rearward, squinting at Cap, whose stare was fixed on the cockpit clock. She held up a forefinger, signaling the standby, and shouted, "Rock Hall below—Mark reference!"

He checked his watch, and, after his confirming nod, her upheld hand began to chop the air in rhythmic little arcs, marking the ten-second countdown.

At her final wave he felt the plane's tail rise, and he shoved himself down and into the clear.

The Stearman's noise fell away to a soft drumming, and he stabilized his fall by rolling into the prone position and bending his arms and legs slightly so as to minimize speed and maximize control. He popped the chute after an eight-second fall, and once the inertial stresses had subsided, he was floating through the whispering night, high and alone above the blackness and scattered twinklings of the rural Delmarva Peninsula.

Most of his military jumps had been traditional, made at low level with "vanilla cones," as intelligence people liked to call standard chutes with circular canopies of nylon. But tonight's high jinks called for a protracted, gliding descent—a kind of flight, actually—from where he had left the plane to Azalea Manor, which lay in the darkness a mile below and two miles ahead between the pools of light marking the Allenby chicken-processing plant and the grain silos and loading sheds of the Rawley Corporation's Kent County facility. So he was riding a "waffle"—the new type of backpack clandestine-entry chute with a rectangular, double-layer airfoil canopy, which, with proper handling of the control toggles to allow for the present mix of altitude, visibility, wind speed and direction, would enable him to float, to spiral, to descend as smoothly and precisely as if he were riding thermals in a sailplane—and to land quietly, stealthily, long after the sounds of his transporting airplane had dwindled to silence.

The benign weather forecast had decided him on this precision penetration. Aerial photos that Cap had acquired from an Elkton surveyor showed Azalea Manor to be roughly a parallelogram, with one of the shorter sides bordering directly on the bay. The bayfront was bulkheaded with a combination of riprap and pilings, and a floating dock extended from this wall. On the northeast corner of the parallelogram was a small grass airstrip with a shed-type hangar and an adjoining fuel storage yard. Freddie's shots from the state road showed an electrically controlled, ornamental iron main gate, and his telephoto stuff from a windmill on the adjacent farm had shown two aircraft parked on the landing strip—an obsolete, tadpole-shaped Model 500 helicopter that appeared to have been modified for crop spraying, and a Henschel "Dagger," a single-engine turboprop sportster used widely in the Third World as a catchall, cliche machine used for everything from short-haul personnel commutation, through military reconnaissance, to low-level counterinsurgency fighter missions.

According to the Radimore Arms tapes, Cummings, Richter and Colt had established midnight as the time of the official meeting. Corbato and his mistress were due at Aberdeen at 2030 hours and would be driven to Azalea Manor, arriving early enough for a rest and a change of clothes before meeting with the others. They would return to Aberdeen for their flight to Cartagena the following afternoon. Cummings had asked some uneasy questions about the security at Azalea Manor, but Colt had reassured him, pointing out that this was the United States, not some war zone, and the mansion was a walled island in a large, well-fenced farmland tract that was forbidding to trespassers. And the house was invisible to passersby.

Freddie, ever the waterman, had suggested an approach from the bay, but Sweeney had argued that activity around the waterfront and dock, which was quite close to the house, was likely to be noticed. Besides, to meet the timetable they would have to use a powerboat, and boats were time-consuming, fussy, and noisy at night; moreover, the gliding-plane-and-parachute combination was not only faster and cleaner but also so unorthodox it was more likely to go undetected.

Sweeney's original plan had been for a straightforward drop onto the far end of the airstrip at 2200 hours, followed by a twenty-minute hike to the inner wall and a rope climb that would put him into the ornamental gardens of the main house by 2330. The remaining half-hour would be used to select a position and set up his surveillance gear. But the good forecast and excellent graphics had persuaded him to eliminate the hike by dropping within the inner wall at its southeast corner, where, some five hundred yards away, he would be amply screened from the mansion not only by the darkness but also by a tree line and a cluster of hay barns.

"How are you going to get out of that place?" Cap had wanted to know.

"I'm going over the wall on my rope, here"—he had tapped the aerial photo with the pencil—"and I'm going to follow this creek, here, southeast to the fence line along the state road, here. You, Freddie, will park your Ford in this copse beside the road, here, at oh-thirty hours and wait as long as it takes for my stalwart form to emerge triumphant from the gloom of night."

"Sheesh."

It went even better than he'd hoped.

At two hundred feet on his illuminated wrist altimeter, he let out the line that lowered his equipment satchel five yards, creating a separation which would reduce his chances of being torn up by his gear in a rough landing. But the wind was easy and manageable, the glide angle was precise and steady, and, with the help of his starlight intensification goggles, he needed to toggle only one turn of a spiral to glide over the darkened airstrip and drop inside the inner wall, touching down in the meadow grass with no more commotion than a step off the front stoop.

He gathered in the chute and equipment satchel and, crouching, scurried to the deeper darkness at the base of the towering sycamores, where he lay for a time, listening.

No voices, no barking dogs, no car noises. Only a lethargic night breeze wandering a sleeping land.

He stashed the chute in a nearby drain culvert, slung his equipment, and set out briskly along the cover of a hedge line, feeling slightly smug until, turning the corner of the hedge, he virtually collided with a man in dark coveralls who was about to treat himself to a swig of coffee from a thermos cup.

There was no time for thought, nor for the man to react. Sweeney's karate move sent him careening backward in a shower of coffee to slam against a plank fence, from where he toppled, facedown, like a felled pine.

Filled with sudden alarm, Sweeney crouched beside the prostrate guard for a full minute, listening for reactions, the sounds of curiosity from nearby security people, or dogs, maybe. There were none. He went through a pat-down. His penlight showed him a wallet containing four dirty pictures, a packet of condoms, eighty-four dollars and seventy-three cents, three credit cards and driver's licenses and ID forms in the name of George Johnson, with permanent home addresses in Chicago, Duluth, Indianapolis, Philadelphia. All had a business address at, of all places, Dominic's Grocery Enterprises, Wilmington, Delaware.

He used a length of his satchel line to tie the man's hands behind him and his ankles to a fence post. A piece of cloth torn from the fellow's own coveralls served as a gag. He slid the guard's Uzi silently into a drainage ditch, keeping the two ammo magazines for his own use.

Obviously Cummings, uneasy about security, had brought along his own little army. This man suggested some kind of outer security perimeter, and with the first ring so far from the house, the going was sure to be much more difficult near the doorstep. Worse, there was the possibility that the guard system had a mobile checkup routine. If so, with the discovery of the trussed-up link, there would be a general alarm and the whole thing would be blown.

He made the wall without further incident, and was over and beyond the obstacle, standing in the shadows of the ornamental garden's huge gazebo, rewinding his rope and stowing its grapple, at twenty minutes before midnight.

He inched toward the house, step by step, breath by breath, spotting and evading two silent, motionless guards en route. The driveway turnaround was occupied by a panel truck whose flanks heralded the Savory Favors Catering Company and whose crew, four liveried Muscle Beach types, relayed trays of hors d'oeuvres through a service entrance. At the foot of the balustrade fronting the huge, elevated patio, he had his first piece of luck.

The house was an enormous and faithful reproduction of the Tudor style, with broad sweeps of tile roof, looming chimneys, leaded casements, and meticulous brickwork. Central to its long axis was an ell whose east face, which jutted into the flagstone patio, was given almost entirely to a towering window of cathedral proportions. This was, obviously, intended to provide a monumental frame for the pastoral view beyond the gardens. And it was also a meeting room; Sweeney could make out walls lined with bookcases, a large conference table surrounded by high-back, leather-trimmed chairs. Two of the liveried men bustled about the table, adjusting the lie of notepads and pens, placing crystal water bottles and tumblers at convenient locations, and fussing with the floral centerpiece.

The second piece of luck was even better. Bracketing the patio and its central balustrade was a pair of giant cedars, whose foliage proved to be even denser that the photos had suggested. After another full minute of reconnaissance via his nightglasses, Sweeney moved to the base of the cedar on the left and quietly made his way upward through the prickly tangles. The quickening breeze, damp and heavy with the smell of the needles, helped to disguise whatever rustlings his movements generated, and at seven minutes to midnight he was invisibly ensconced, with his Jagdmeister 500 fully trained on the great window and the room beyond.

A sentry came across the flagstones to stand directly below him, Uzi slung, hard eyes giving equal time to the library and the shadowy gardens. The sentry lingered for two minutes; then he moved off, his soft-soled shoes making hardly a sound on the stonework, to disappear in the shadows to the north.

At precisely midnight, there was movement in the great room, and Sweeney, pulling on the monitor headset, flipped the switch that put the 500 video recorder silently to work.

CHAPTER 35

Richter looked about the cavernous room and was saddened by the contrast between the exquisite architecture and the ordinariness of the men who had gathered to use it. Cummings and Corbato faced each other from chairs on each side of the table "above the salt" (as his mother would have put it), thus suggesting equality, and he sat in a kind of regal isolation, like an umpire separating contestants, in the ornate armchair at the table's head. Colt sat down-table from Cummings, and across from him was Randolph Ridenour, whose house this was and who looked pale and nervous, as if he would rather be anywhere but here. Colt, gaunt, slow-speaking, wary; Corbato, expressionless, blandly malevolent; Cummings, furtive, watchful. The faces of evil. The faces of greed. Of distrust. Chicanery. Egocentrism. Willfulness. Mankind at its worst, gathered in a place whose beauty and elegance were testimony to mankind at its best.

Richter. How did he himself fit into this sorry incongruity?

Too well.

To counter a sudden inner eddy of something akin to remorse, he went immediately to business. "Gentlemen, this meeting is somewhat like a real estate settlement, in that we'll be applying our signatures to a formal description of a verbal agreement made earlier. A business is being sold, and here's where the principals and their agents will apply their signatures to the document that officially describes the transaction. But first, I think we ought to have a summing-up, a comprehensive look at where we were, where we are, where we're going, and how those things each of us has been doing interlock with the whole."

"What the hell for?" Colt broke in. "We all know what we've been doing and why. Pass out the copies and let's get to signing."

Richter turned his gaze, slowly and deliberately, to Ridenour. "Correction, Mr. Colt. Security has required a certain amount of compartmentalization, and not all of us have been completely in the know at all times."

"Who are you talking about, Richter? Hell's ass, we couldn't have pulled this off without everybody being completely in the know."

Richter shrugged. "That's not entirely so. Jenny Malone has withheld certain pieces from most of us. Not many pieces, to be sure, but some. Because of this, and because she wasn't free to be here tonight, she's briefed me thoroughly and has asked me to do the same for all of you."

Colt's eyes narrowed angrily. "Pieces? What pieces? You mean I haven't been playing with a full deck?"

"You, of course, are the exception, Colt. You've always been completely informed, for reasons that will be made clear in a moment. But—"

Ridenour, who had been slumped in his chair, pale and miserable, stirred and sat erect. "May I say something?"

Richter nodded. "Of course."

With his gaze fixed on the table before him, Ridenour said, "I don't know how much the rest of you people know, but I found out the hard way that I've been kept in the dark on some pretty important things. For instance, until he showed up at my door this evening, I had no idea Mr. Richter was a member of this team. No idea at all. And because I wasn't aware of this fact, and because I was trying very hard to do my job for this group by making General Wallace look lightweight, politically motivated and militarily inept, I unwittingly offended Mr. Richter. I'd like to offer him my most sincere apologies, right here and now. And I'd also appreciate being filled in on the big picture so that I don't risk doing something else to make an ass of myself and jeopardize my appointment as UBC news chief."

His gaze moving about the group, Richter inserted an explanation. "Because of his very high public profile and an occupation that calls for loquaciousness, and because of the rather limited scope of his assignment in this matter, Jenny Malone thought it best to keep Mr. Ridenour pretty much on a need-to-know basis."

"So then why does he need to know now, for crissake? He'll still get his cut—"

Richter held up a hand. "That's enough, Colt. Jenny's asked me to chair this meeting and to give a summary. And that I'm going to do." He glanced about. "Are there any more objections?"

Cummings leaned forward, elbows on the table. "I think a summary is in order, but I want to say straight out that I resent Ridenour's hiring one of my best men to make an unauthorized try at that general down in Florida. It got my man killed and made a media hero out of the frigging general, and I don't like it one damned bit."

"And I apologize to you, too, Mr. Cummings," Ridenour said. "My attempts to discredit General Wallace had been going badly. Your man seemed eager to earn some extra money in a slack moment and I thought we'd all benefit if the general were simply to be shut down. It didn't turn out well, and I'm sorry."

Corbato shifted in his chair, annoyed. "Could we please cut out all this crap and get on with the purpose of the meeting? Let's hear your summary, Richter. And then let's sign the papers. I'm tired and I want to go to bed."

Richter gave him a cool, level look. "Very well, I'll begin with you. Because it all began with you."

Regarding the others then, he fell into the expository mode—a commander debriefing troops, a professor reviewing a course. (And, a wisp of lugubrious thought suggested, a preacher sermonizing on the fantail of the *Titanic*.)

"Señor Corbato is a first-class businessman"—Richter nodded affably toward the impassive face across the table—"and he saw the handwriting on the wall a year or so ago. For him and his fellow cartel leaders, the hemispheric international agreements, the treaties and military cooperation, the assaults from all sides, were making narcotics manufacture and distribution—especially to the United States—more expensive and dangerous by the day. In its heyday, the worldwide business was grossing up to six hundred billion or more a year; last year it was down to two-twenty billion, with the U.S. gross dropping to an all-time low of forty billion. Making things even worse from Señor Corbato's point of view are the renewed and much more stringently applied extradition agreements which make it more likely that South American druggists will be arrested and tried in the United States, where punishment is a hell of a lot stiffer than anywhere else.

"Señor Corbato saw that if he could gain absolute control of the remaining major South and Central American manufacturing and distribution cartels, becoming The Boss instead of being one of the few most powerful bosses, as he was, he could end most of the bloodshed and misery while permitting the principal participants to continue enjoying important rewards. How would he do this? By cutting a deal that would be economically and politically advantageous to all sides concerned in North American trafficking. This was possible because each of the several remaining major cartels was a dictatorship, and if you threw out the dictator and took over the dictatorship you became, in fact, the undisputed owner of that cartel. And if you were the owner, you would decide who you'd do business with and on what terms.

"His plan had several major steps. First: as the new Big Boss, he would set a price for that part of his operation that trafficked in the United States. Second: he would contact the decisionmakers in the U.S. government and, for the established price, shut down all hemispheric operations involving the U.S. market. Third: to make sure it stuck, to counter any concerns about cheating, investigators and accountants of the U.S. Drug Enforcement Agency would be given continuing access to his books and the right to make unannounced spot inspections of manufacture and distribution. Fourth: the American DEA representatives, on-site or elsewhere, would not concern themselves with Corbato operations in other countries. Fifth, and finally: the United States would continue, and sweeten importantly, all aid programs and trade agreements it had already made with official hemispheric governments so as to pick up the slack resulting in those economies that have had to rely on drug trafficking to remain solvent. In other words, the U.S. treaty with Corbato would not affect its existing treaties with Latin American nations.

"The result of all this? Señor Corbato would get his price, like any businessman, for selling a piece of his business. The United States, on the other hand, would cut off the flow of illicit drugs into its streets for a fraction of the cost of continuing the seemingly endless effort to control hemispheric drug smuggling. It could then concentrate its resources against the awkward, expensive and dangerous operations that have long frustrated Japanese and other Asiatic druggists who aspire to a high-volume American narcotics market. Drought-enforced rehabilitation of the addicted would follow, and the Americans would have won their drug war at what would amount to a one-time-only bargain price."

Richter paused. Then: "Would you say that's a fair description of your thinking, Señor?"

Corbato nodded, but said nothing.

Richter's tired eyes turned toward Colt. "This is where you come in, Colt. Why don't you tell us in your own words how you saw and dealt with things?"

It was a good move. Colt was obviously pleased with this recognition of his importance—his centrality in the scheme. "I was conducting business in Cartagena at the time, and Señor Corbato brought his proposition to me because he knew that I had excellent contacts in the American government and that I frequently served as agent, or intermediary, in delicate international deal-cutting of this sort. I saw at once, of course, the weak point in his otherwise sensible idea. And that's the fact that the American government dotes on its posture of morality, which would make it difficult, if not impossible, for it to embark on what its Greek-chorus moralists would decry as 'government trafficking in drugs.' But I learned long ago that many American government people are 'moral' only so long as it benefits them personally or gets them good media exposure. Otherwise, they suffer their humanity as do you and I." He paused here, apparently expecting some chuckling reaction but getting none. So he went on.

"Soon afterward, Ridenour came to Cartagena to do a TV series on the drug war. Being as I am, I knew what very few people in the world know: Ridenour has a very special relationship"—he raised an eyebrow impishly and the others, all but Ridenour, of course, smiled to show they got the joke—"with Jenny Malone, President Leonardi's chief of staff. I suggested to him that, if Señor Corbato's offer could be picked up without the knowledge of Congress, hotbed of American pseudomorality, and paid for with already appropriated funds, supplemented by private contributions from the president's high rolling supporters, not only would the drug war end but the Administration could—with adroit politicking and media management—make the president a hero of the drug war and guarantee him a second term and a party in high favor for years to come. Intrigued, and armed with a secret affidavit naming him Señor Corbato's emissary, Ridenour took the plan to his dear friend and confidante, Jenny Malone, who quickly saw the possibilities."

Colt glanced down the table. "Does that adequately describe your role in all this, Ridenour?"

Ridenour shrugged.

Colt went on, openly relishing his limelight role as interlocutor. "As for Ms. Malone, she knew that in these days of lean budgets and legally limited private political contributions it would be impossible to divert enough appropriated money or to drum up enough private gifts to pay Señor Corbato his price without Congress, or the General Accounting Office, or the FBI and IRS eventually catching on. And under American law, such diversions are just plain illegal—as the Ollie North flap, whatever the truth behind it, has shown. Noodling all this, Ms. Malone came up with an audacious idea: Why not kill several birds with one stone and keep the price of the stone to a minimum?

"Her solution was rooted in the German situation. According to the SII intelligence reports she'd been reading, Hugo von Zoll, the industrialist who is the guru and bankroll for Germany's far right wing, known as 'die Pilze,' or 'The Mushrooms,' was looking for investments that would bring in the heavy-duty money he needed to finance his group's move to dominance in German national politics. But his problem, too, was one of law—German law. His politics, seen as neo-Nazi by the German establishment, were under heavy scrutiny. So money infusions would have to be legal, or, if illegal, carefully laundered.

"Ms. Malone called in the SII chief, Aaron Richter, here, who knows more about the Germans than the Germans do, eh, Richter?"

Richter's smile was polite. "You always did have a gift for hyperbole, Colt."

"Anyhow, 'Aaron,' she said, 'how do I get in touch with Hugo von Zoll? How do I tell him that he can buy into the humongously lucrative worldwide narcotics trade at a low, low going-out-of-business price—provided he keeps his drugs out of the U.S. market?' And Aaron told her to talk to yours truly, old man Colt, who was a personal friend of von Zoll. And I talked to Hugo. 'Hugo,' I said, 'you will buy stock in certain American companies. The management of those companies, anxious to reelect Leonardi as the American president who won the drug war, will, through a system of cutouts, bribes, phony manifests, and all the other laundering techniques, use your money to create a lump-sum secret account in a London bank in the name of Manuel Corbato. You will, in effect, have bought a kind of co-ownership in Corbato's highly lucrative worldwide narcotics trade—less America, of course, ha-ha—for a bargain price. You will have passed the test of German law, which is extremely severe on illegal narcotics trade, because you've invested in legitimate U.S. businesses that pay you huge dividends. What German law won't know is that these sums are, in fact, the return from your investment in narcotics, which will help you dominate German politics and the German government. And, as a huge bonus, you will have very important friends in the top echelons of the U.S. government, because your money will have helped these individuals to create and sustain the illusion that Leonardi had won the drug war. An illusion heightened by spectacular—albeit phony—interceptions of smuggling airplanes and powerboats and infantry firefights in the Andes and on the South American north coast.' That, friends, is what I told Hugo von Zoll. And Hugo von Zoll has accepted the proposition and assigned his trusted lieutenant, whom we know as Mr. Cummings, to represent him in this closing and to oversee the 'Mushroom's' narcotics operation once it has begun. Is that a fair statement, Mr. Cummings?"

"Quite fair."

Richter sensed it was time to regain control of the meeting. "There's another dimension to all this," he said, "a further refinement Jenny has made in the Corbato plan. Since President Leonardi is already highly regarded for his considerable successes in the drug war, and since Vice President McKell needs to shuck a media-created image of bumbling and ineptitude, she has prepared a public relations program that will reveal McKell to have been the mastermind behind the drug war victory. With the help of Mr. Ridenour and certain ambitious Pentagon officers, she plans to show the world that Leonardi assigned McKell and General Reynolds to head the drug war campaign from behind the scenes because he feared General Wallace, who is to be portrayed as a political sop to certain party megacontributors, was not up to the task. But, as Mr. Ridenour has just pointed out, we've had a bit of trouble with that one, since General Wallace has yet to show he's the least bit cowed."

Colt broke in again. "And, finally, we come to Aaron Richter, who, as head of SII, was asked by Ms. Malone to watch over general American interests as this overall arrangement was forged and brought to its realization tonight. His presence, his role in all this, is therefore essentially monitorial. Would you say that's an adequate description of your role, Mr. Richter?"

Richter smiled coolly, ignoring Colt's sarcasm. "That should do it." He consulted his watch, then asked, "Does anybody have anything else they want to say at this point?"

After a somewhat awkward silence, he lifted a briefcase from the floor beside him and said, "All right, then, here we go: Mr. Cummings, representing Hugo von Zoll, will put up the cash to pay Señor Corbato the money he wants to cease all narcotics smuggling into the United States. In return, the United States, represented here by yours truly, Aaron Richter, will authorize the transhipment by C-one thirty aircraft to the U.S. Air Force Base at Rhein-Main, Frankfurt, those tons of narcotics delivered this month by Señor Corbato as a good-faith binder and currently stashed at Aberdeen Proving Ground. That tonnage will be trucked from Frankfurt by civilian carrier to von Zoll's Eureka Kompanie in Munich. Further, Mr. Cummings will, for the sums agreed to here, take ownership, in behalf of Herr von Zoll, the areas of future international enterprise assigned him by Señor Corbato and described in detail herein."

Richter took five folders from the briefcase and dealt them out. "It's short and sweet, gentlemen, a document almost like a deed. Take a few minutes to read it, and if all is satisfactory, Mr. Cummings and Señor Corbato will sign, and the rest of us will sign as witnesses."

Richter gave five minutes to the reading. Then he coughed dryly and said, "I've heard no questions or comments, so I assume nobody has any problems with this document. Right?' "

Another pause followed. Then: "All right, gentlemen. It's signature time."

There was the sound of pens scratching, after which the folders were returned to Richter, who slid them with care and a kind of mock reverence into the briefcase. Smiling faintly, he said, "History has been made, eh, gentlemen?"

As the others pushed back their chairs and prepared to leave the table, Richter held up a hand and said quietly, "Just a moment, please. There's one more thing."

The others stared at him, waiting.

"I'd like to announce that you're all under arrest."

CHAPTER 36

Had Sweeney not been so snugly installed in a snarl of cedar branches and needles, he might have fallen to the ground. But his tight spot served as more than a safety harness—it also kept his jump of astonishment from jostling the Jagdmeister 500.

Richter's startling announcement was followed almost instantly by the appearance of the four liveried caterers, only now they were brandishing Uzi submachine guns. They demanded that everybody freeze, because they were DEA agents who would blow everybody's balls off if they didn't comply. The men at the table rose from tipping, clattering chairs, arms extended, eyes wide, mouths open, staring not at the Uzis but at the .38 snub-nosed revolver that had magically appeared in Richter's right hand.

"Easy, gentlemen," Richter said smoothly. "Nothing fancy, please."

Sweeney, watching but hardly seeing, knew instinctively that he would never be able to sort out the series of events from that point without playing and replaying the videotape. What seemed to happen first was a kind of weird dance around the table; Corbato, Colt, and Ridenour backed away, almost in step, from Richter and the caterers who had formed their own advancing line. Next, the archways opening into the adjacent foyer were suddenly crammed with men in dark jumpers, who sprang into the room with their own Uzis blazing.

"Jesus God!" Sweeney heard the words in his head.

The four caterers went down like reeds before a scythe, machine guns bouncing on the thick carpeting, their creamy jackets spouting red fountains. Richter spun about and got off two quick shots before he, too, staggered against the table and rolled into a heap. Colt stood fast, arms raised high. Ridenour ran in a complete circle, hands to his head, squealing like a frightened child, before running full tilt for the foyer. Behind him, with slow deliberateness, Cummings raised a .45 caliber automatic and fired a single booming shot that sent the TV personality into a series of somersaults. The mad rolling ended in the clattering collapse of a potted palm and a glittering ornamental suit of armor. Ridenour's body lay still.

"Mama mia, I'm *gone,"* Sweeney said aloud. "Right *now* I'm gone."

He pulled the headset down around his neck, threw the 500's sling-strap over his head, and dropped into a caroming fall—a grotesquely laden pinball in an evergreen machine. The cedar's tangled branches and their clustered needles tore at him, stinging his face and hands. Then he was on the ground and leaping for cover against the base of the balustrade, praying that none of the dark-suits had seen him. As he waited, the seconds passing like years, he opened his gear satchel, withdrew his Uzi, unfolded its metal stock, and inserted a 32-round magazine. He put a shrapnel grenade in each of his side pockets and an extra magazine in the chest pouch where he carried the Beretta.

He knew he should turn for the retreat to the garden wall, but he could not do it.

Richter, the stuffed-shirt horse's ass who had fired him, had stood toe to toe with the enemy and was now a gunned-down, stuffed-shirt, heroic horse's ass.

He might still be alive.

Well, he won't be alive long if I get suddenly dead.

You have to check.

Why?

Because that's the way you are, goddamit.

He raised his head and peered across the patio. A voice, hot, angry, seemed to be coming from the foyer. The words were muffled, unclear, but the voice sounded like Corbato's, and it was not pleased.

Sweeney pulled himself up and over the balustrade and sprinted across the flagstones to the garden door next to the library that he had seen in the photos. It was in shadow now, and surrounded by a wall of ivy, and he had a time finding the knob.

It was open. He pushed through into what appeared to be a kind of pantry and wet bar. Beyond a doorway was the library.

The bodies were strewn about, inert. The dark-suits had disappeared.

He knelt beside Richter and searched for a neck pulse.

Richter opened his eyes, and one of them winked. "Where the hell—were you—when I needed—you, Sweeney?"

"Are you all right?" Sweeney whispered.

"What a jerk. I've got—two, maybe—three bullets in me—and I'm expected—to be all right?"

"Come on, I'll get you out of here."

"No way, meathead," a voice above Sweeney snarled. The muzzle of an Uzi pressed against his skull. "You goin' to put your piece down and you goin' to lay on the floor there, face-down, aside your buddy. And you won't move." The man called, his voice heavy with South Philly inflections, "Yo, Cummings! Here—in the liberry! They's anudder one!"

There was the drumming of running feet, and then Sweeney was hauled erect and spun around to face seven men—Cummings, Corbato, Colt, and four gunners in dark coveralls. He heard Colt mutter, "I'll be goddammed. Sweeney, no less."

Cummings seized Sweeney by the collar and shoved him against the table, holding the .45 muzzle under his chin.

"How many more of you are there?" the soft, inflected voice demanded.

"Four airborne divisions."

Cummings banged the pistol barrel against the bridge of Sweeney's nose. "How many more? How *many?*"

"Just me," a voice said from the pantry–wet bar doorway.

All eyes, startled, turned to the source as the man there opened up with a rapid series of shots from a Remington 870 pump-action scatter-gun. The room was filled with thunder and yelps and the clattering of falling gunmen. Cummings dived and rolled out of sight through the archway into the foyer. Corbato and Colt followed, running hunched down, and Corbato was shouting in Spanish, "Rosita! Rosita! Run for the car!"

They were alone then, except for the silent bodies and the twitching, moaning bodies.

"Freddie?"

"Come on—hurry. We gotta get movin'."

"How in the hell did *you* get here?"

"I saw sentries near the road where I was waitin'. Too many of 'em. We hadn't planned on that many bein' around, so I figured I better provide you with a rear guard, sort of. So I got out my rope and blunderbuss and followed behind you."

"You're something else," Sweeney said, picking up Richter's briefcase and handing it to Freddie. "This case is very important. Don't let it get away."

"Okay." Freddie unbuckled his musette strap and looped it through the briefcase's handle.

"Now help me with this guy."

"Who is he? And how we gonna help him? He's been shot, for crissake."

"Come on, Freddie. Just lift him onto my shoulders, will you?"

"Where we goin'?"

"Out through that pantry—the way we came in—then across the patio, down the steps and around the house to the driveway. There's a panel truck there. Quick!"

A burst of Uzi fire tore through the room from the pantry, and chunks and splinters erupted from the meeting table's polished expanse.

"Damn it, they've found the garden door," Sweeney said.

"Yeah, and the only other way out is through the foyer, and at least five guys is waitin' for us there."

"Okay. Stand aside. I'll clear things up a bit." Sweeney took a concussion grenade from his jacket pocket, pulled the pin and tossed the grenade through the door and into the pantry's gloom. There was a bright flash, a jarring thump, and a burst of smoke and debris.

"That should do it, Freddie. Go through the pantry now and see if the patio is clear."

After a cautious peek around the twisted doorjamb, Freddie

hurried through the lingering smoke and dust to the garden door at the far end of the shattered room. "Two guys knocked out in the pantry," he called. Then he pointed the shotgun out the garden door and fired twice. "Two more down on the patio. Come on now. It's clear."

Staggering under his burden, Sweeney wobbled through the pantry and followed Freddie to the balustrade, where, under the cover of Freddie's shotgun, he lowered Richter as gently as possible to the shrubbery bed below. Then he went over himself. Lying on the ground beside Richter, he unslung the Uzi and made sure it was ready to fire. "How're you doing, Richter?"

"Not quite—ready for—handball yet."

"Well, hang in there. A few more yards and we'll be at the panel truck and we'll get you to a doctor."

"Watch the—approach to—the main gate. Cumming's had—a machine-gun—crew there. May still be—"

Freddie thumped to the ground beside them. "Okay, let's move it."

A long burst of gunfire raked the shrubs and pocked the stonework just above their heads. The fire had come from the gazebo area, and Sweeney took a moment to send back ten Uzi shots. Somebody out there cursed loudly.

Freddie barked, "You go ahead, Sweeney. I'll do the shootin' for our side."

"I'll shoot if I goddam well feel like it. Who are you—Audie Murphy, or something?"

"Don't—fight, kids— I have—a headache—"

They trotted, scrabbled, staggered, waddled and, in a narrow strip between the garage wing and the driveway turnaround, crawled to the truck. Freddie threw open the rear doors and Sweeney rolled Richter onto the floor.

"Here are the keys," Freddie said, tossing a ring to Sweeney. "I took 'em on the way in. You drive."

"What'll you be doing?"

"I also got the keys to that Olds over there. You head down the driveway and I'll follow in that. When we get to the narrow cut between the big sycamores, I'll jam the Olds sideways across the road. Whatever other cars they got to follow us in will be held up a spell."

"Okay. I'll wait for you there."

Sweeney started the van's motor. Renewed shouting and indiscrimate gunfire came from the house. These intensified when Freddie backed the Olds around and, tires squealing against the macadam, took position behind the careening, accelerating van.

It went as hoped. The Olds proved to be a formidable roadblock, just long enough to cram the driveway between the steep clay banks of the cut through a tree-shrouded ridge of lawn. They could hear other cars starting up back at the house. Freddie hopped into the van's front passenger seat and they were off, making about fifty as they descended the long slope to the main gate.

Sweeney handed Freddie his two grenades. "Watch on the right side up ahead. There may be a machine gun near the gatehouse—"

A burst of fire took out the windshield.

"You mean *that* machine gun?"

"That's the one, all right."

"I pull this pin here and then throw the thing, right?"

"You got it."

Freddie's arm made an arcing movement outside the right window, and as the van screeched around the final turn there was a flash and a heavy thump in the bushes there.

"I did it."

"Next time, please do it so the frigging grenade doesn't go off when we're alongside. It makes my ears ring."

"That gate up ahead is closed."

"What gate?"

The speedometer read sixty-five when the van hit the wrought iron barrier. There was a hellish banging and clanging, and Sweeney fought to keep the careening vehicle from overturning as it plunged through and, seconds later, swung onto the northbound lane of the state highway.

"Wee-hoo," Freddie said.

"Anybody behind us? My rearview's gone."

"Nobody yet."

"Your Ford's hidden about a quarter-mile ahead, right?"

"Yep."

Sweeney let the van decelerate. "Tell you what: We'll put

Richter in the Ford and you drive him ahead in that. I'll decoy with the van."

"I got a better idea. There's an all-night Farm Family Care Clinic just outside Galena. You drive him there in the Ford and drop him off before he bleeds to death. I know those medics, and their drill will put Richter in the county hospital by daybreak, and you can count on it. Those bastards behind us won't be lookin' for a Ford, so you'll be okay. Meantime, I know all the back roads in these parts, and with this vittles wagon as bait, I'll sucker whoever shows up into a goose chase. We'll meet at Cap's place."

"All right. But you be careful, hear?"

"I ain't let you down yet, have I?"

Sweeney gave him a sidelong glance. "No, you sure haven't."

Freddie freed the briefcase from his musette strap and handed it to Sweeney. "You'll be wantin' this."

"Will I ever."

They made the vehicle switch, and as Freddie prepared to drive off in the battered van, Sweeney held his satchel aloft. "How about taking some of these grenades with you?"

"I won't need 'em. 'Sides, they make me nervous."

Freddie had been gone for about two minutes when Sweeney, making Richter as comfortable as possible in the Ford's rear seat, heard a car coming from the south, fast. Watching from his forest cover, he saw a black Mercedes sedan, long and low and brutish, sizzle past in an angry flare of headlights and glittering steel.

"Good luck, Freddie, you wonderful, amazing man."

CHAPTER 37

When Cap was a kid, and her father had been out on the bay all day, tending nets or setting traps or duck hunting—whatever he did out there on the great wide water—the hours before sunset would be a time for pacing. Her greatest fear as a child had been that he would not return, leaving her alone in a world that had none of his tenderness and understanding. And the lower the sun, the deeper the shadows, the more her mind would evoke the pale lostness of schoolmates whose watermen fathers had simply not come home one day, their only legacy a drifting oar, a sodden hat, a capsized boat. The images would set her to pacing—back and forth on the dock, up and down the stairway, through and around the rooms, across the lawn and among the trees—her gaze hardly ever leaving the bay.

Then, one dreary, long-ago February, it had happened, and she'd blamed herself, as girl and woman, for having conceived, witchlike, a self-fulfilling dread.

And now she was doing it again.

She had become abruptly aware of weariness in her legs and back, her shoulders and neck, and it was only then that she realized she had been pacing. Back and forth on the patio, always moving, always watching the driveway and the state road beyond, struggling against visions of a world without Thomas F. Sweeney, making a silent plea to whatever force governed the universe that she wouldn't have to suffer that kind of loss again.

In the dawn light, a flicker of headlights, the distant sighing of tires on dewy macadam.

And then he was there, slamming doors, wrestling gear from the trunk, muttering to himself. As she came down the walk, eyes brimming, he turned and smiled.

"Hi, there."

"Hi."

"Give me a hand with this, will you?"

"Sure. This is Freddie's car, but where's Freddie?"

"He'll be along. Meanwhile, I need a cup of coffee."

"It's making. Are you all right?"

"A bit tired."

"Well, you're home now, and I'm glad."

They were holding each other then, and they stood for a long time in the morning mist, unable to pretend—to feign nonchalance—a single moment longer.

After a shower, a plate of ham and eggs and four hundred gallons of coffee, Sweeney rested back in his chair and gave her another fond inspection. "You look great this morning. What have you been doing to yourself?"

"Well, I brushed my hair."

"You should do that a lot. It's very becoming to you."

She sat in the chair across from him, put her elbows on the table and leaned forward to glare into his eyes. "If you don't tell me about it this instant, I'll sue for a divorce."

"We ain't even married."

"What's that got to do with it?"

He shrugged. "I went in on the chute, landed as planned, got some gorgeous audiovisuals of the Cocaine Summit, and, with Freddie's help, managed a rather noisy, impolite and undignified departure."

"Good. Now fill in the gaps."

He described the whole thing, from touchdown to the vehicle switch and Freddie's driving off in the riddled van. "And so,

Richter by now is reeking of iodine under a mountain of nurses at the Kent County General Hospital, and Freddie's playing hide-and-seek with a black Mercedes filled with hoods."

"Don't you think we ought to find him and give him a hand?"

"Nonsense. Having watched Freddie Dilworth at work, I can assure you that Cummings and his hoods are the ones who need help. Freddie will be here soon. You'll see."

"And then what?"

"It's off to Washington with our video recording and our briefcase full of signed documents."

"You got those, then?"

"Of course. Why do you think Cummings, et al., are giving such heated chase? I have papers that will send them to jail through the twenty-first and twenty-second centuries."

"And we're just sitting here, gabbing?"

"Well, we have to do something until Washington raises its blinds and opens its doors. Besides, I have to figure out just which shop we're going to first."

"How about taking the video and documents to President Leonardi? From what went on at Azalea Manor, it's pretty clear that his staff has become a narcotics ring and that he faces political disaster. Isn't that what your friend, Nageler, was trying to say?"

"The only thing tougher than getting to see the president of the United States is finding a plumber on Sunday morning. Besides, we don't know the whole story yet, and I don't think we know yet what Nageler was really trying to say. There's something missing in all this."

"Something *missing?* My God, man, you've got a White House chief of staff, a director of a top U.S. intelligence agency, several advisors to the Joint Chiefs of Staff, and a South American drug lord conspiring to set up a Nazi with the funds he needs to take over the German government—all with the intention of keeping the vice president on the next election's national ticket, when the president is guaranteed to be reelected. The only thing missing from that mix, pal, is Angela Lansbury, working it all out between commercials."

Sweeney was about to answer when there was a popping and a snorting in the driveway, and they hurried to the window. There he was, Freddie Dilworth, chugging up the gravel lane in a caterer's van that looked as if it had come out the far side of a kitchen sink disposal. They ran out the door and helped him from the driver's seat.

"Yo, Freddie. You okay?"

"Sure. A little tired, but okay."

"Where's the Mercedes full of hoods?"

"The Mercedes is up to its sunroof in quicksand. The two hoods—Cummings and Colt—are tied to the workbench in Miss Cap's air-eo-plane hangar until you tell me what you want done with them."

Sweeney and Cap traded glances. "I'm afraid to ask you how all that happened," Sweeney said.

Cap said, "Come in the house, Freddie. I'll get you something to eat."

"Eat? My God, Miss Cap, I'm about to bust my seams." Freddie nodded at the van. "Do you have any idea how many teensy-weensy sandwiches and cakes that thing had in it?"

Sweeney laughed. "Come on in anyhow."

While Freddie was in the upstairs bathroom, cleaning up, and Cap was fussing in the kitchen, Sweeney went to the spike Cap called "The Message Center" and riffled through the notes pinned there. One of them stirred instant interest: "Sweeney: General Wallace has dug out Nageler's radio transmissions. See file, Nagell3, and accompanying cassette."

He inserted the cassette in the player, then sat at the computer and booted up, his curiosity at full throttle as he tapped into the file and the words came on the screen.

Wienerschnitzel to Apfelstrudel. On station, everything okay. Fine, let's hear from you, eh? One code name calling another, then a little exchange so workaday, so utterly comon, it, too, would be code. Then, later, more code, heavy with suggestiveness:

The hot-pants—queen has—screwed us. Quick. Some garbling, and a passage that dealt raggedly with somebody getting even with somebody. Then: *Smash her—Rifle? Box?* Which? The word "Büchse" could be either one. In this context the first choice could be military, the second could be sexual slang. But if the entire passage was indeed code, none of it meant anything to Sweeney.

Then the anguished call to his pal. Open. In English.

Silence from the pal, Apfelstrudel.

Open English derision from someone who sounded like—had to be—Ames, the redhead with the gold-rim eyeglasses.

End of transmissions, the screen said.

Sweeney sat for a long time, staring at the amber words. Reading. Rereading. Playing the tape. Listening. Listening again. Trying various constructions; trying absolute literal translation; trying wildly loose, rock-culture invention. Groping for parallelism, inference, nuance.

Wait.

What if—

How about—

"My aching ass!"

Cap, at the sink, looked over her shoulder. "Did you say something?"

He sat, staring at the computer screen, unmoving.

"Yo, Sweeney: You there?"

He gave her a quick look. "Is the Stearman gassed up?"

"Certainly. Why?"

"You're going to fly me to Washington."

"Just like that?"

"Yep. Call Sammy on the intercom and tell him to start up the plane. Tell him to be sure it's ready for a hop to Washington."

"Well, for Pete's sake, you make it sound like you're Lindbergh getting ready to fly to Paris. Washington's less than an hour away—" She went to the wall-mounted box and pressed the button. "Yo, Sammy. Roll her out and start her up, will you? We're going VFR to Washington National, but I want all the IFR people to know it, so advise the ATC. Sweeney and I will be there in a minute."

Sweeney went to the foot of the stairs and called, "Hey, Freddie. Watch the fort. Cap and I are going to Washington."

Freddie's answer came drifting down. "Okay. Don't get bent."

Picking up the videocassette and the briefcase, Sweeney made for the door. "Hurry, Cap. I have a feeling we don't have a hell of a lot of time."

"Why?"

"I don't know why. I just have the feeling."

When they got to the hangar, Sammy was lying on the floor, cussing up a storm and rubbing his head, which had blood on it.

"Sammy!" Cap ran to him and knelt. "Are you all right? What happened?"

Sammy waved a feeble hand. "Those two beauties Freddie brought in this morning—They got loose somehow and belted me a good one."

Sweeney, looking about angrily, rasped, "Where did they go? Which way?"

Sammy wobbled to his feet and pointed vaguely northeast. "Toward the highway, runnin' like hell. And you know what? The bastard with the heavy eyebrows? The sumbish had the nerve to use the friggin phone before he left."

"What did he say? Did you hear?"

"How the hell do I know what he said, my ears fallin' off and him snappin' around in some for'n language."

"Well, intercom Freddie at the house. He'll give you a hand with that cut on your head."

Sammy glared at Sweeney. "Cap, I told you first time I laid eyes on him he was trouble. *Trouble?* He's a freakin' disaster."

Cap nodded. "Yes, Sammy, that's true. But he's not always at his best like he is today. Get to know him, you'll see he has his downside, too."

Sammy stared at her, trying to sort that one out.

CHAPTER 38

Cap kept the climb even—not too shallow, not too steep—and over the mossy slabs of Middletown's roofs she made an easy one-eighty turn for the southwest. The approaching winter was being announced by a lowering overcast that rode a stiff wind out of the Pennsylvania hills to the north, and the lead-colored bay ahead—so glassy only hours before—was lacy with whitecaps. The engine bellowed steadily, sending back the bouquet of rich exhaust, and below the goggles her cheeks tingled, flat and taut, in the icy propwash.

Sweeney had said nothing since he'd climbed into the front cockpit, and, recognizing that he was wrestling with something, she kept her own silence, losing herself in the little fussings of flying.

They were at fifteen hundred feet, with Crystal Beach off the lower right wingtip, when the sky filled with the sound of dry sticks breaking—a raucous noise whose suddenness literally lifted her off the seat cushion.

"Holy baloney! What was that?"

Sweeney's voice was in her ears. "We're being shot at. Get down on the deck and head for Aberdeen."

She craned her head right and left in alarm, searching for the attacker. "Where is he? What is he?"

"He's making a turn under us and is coming back for a belly run. It's a Henschel 'Dagger,' a low-wing, single-engine turbo-prop thing. This particular one was parked at the Azalea Manor airstrip when I went in last night. You can assume Cummings heard you on the intercom with Sammy and that he called one of his people to get up here and stop us. It's fast and tougher than hell, so go down and go slow and get over populated land."

"Slow? Are you nuts? We need all the speed this critter can manufacture."

"Wrong. See how wide his turns are? He's too fast for efficient attacks on this old crate. Not only that, but he's not a very good pilot and he's a lousy marksman."

"What the heck do you know about it?"

"Watch it. Here he comes again."

"What'll I do?"

"Make a bad target by showing how good you fly."

As they skimmed the water, missing boats by inches, there was another racketing, and gashes showed in the yellow fabric of the right lower wing. The Henschel, true to Sweeney's promise, went tearing past, close overhead, and the Stearman wobbled in its propwash.

"That guy's really starting to bother me," Cap grated.

"That's the way to talk. That's the Chartreuse Countess I know and love. Fly the bastard's pants off."

"Why over Aberdeen?"

"The guy's shooting may make the Army and the state police mad enough to send somebody after him."

"Why not just land, get out, and run?"

"We're in the middle of the bay, for cripes sake."

"The Army airfield. And there's lots of pastureland over there, too."

"Sure. And that's when he'd really nail us—gliding in on a straight path, rolling our wheels in the grass. No, just keep moving and keep dancing and hope the sumbish runs out of ammo."

"What do I do after Aberdeen?

"When you pass the Proving Ground, turn southwest and zigzag along the Pennsy line, keeping your wheels just above the overhead power lines, all the way to Baltimore and Washington. That way, he won't be able to get under you, and all that voltage will make him nervous."

"Well, it'll sure make me nervous, too. Not only that: do you realize that by flying down that railroad line we'll be heading straight into a huge jungle of prohibited areas and military defense zones?"

"Exactly. If we ran down the bay route, we could be shot down without anybody ever knowing why. This way, the whole goddam Eastern Defense Command will be watching us and clearing the way ahead of us. And that's why I want you to get on the horn and tell anybody who'll listen that we're on our way to deliver the president some documents crucial to U.S. security. Kick up as much fuss as you can. Make everybody know we're coming, make everybody make way."

"How about the people on the ground? That nut is shooting real bullets. Somebody'll get hurt."

"Maybe. But if we stay over the railroad, how many moms hang washes on the Pennsy? How many kids ride tricycles there?"

She looked over her right shoulder. The Henschel was in a near-vertical bank over the Turkey Point light and leveling off for a straight, behind-the-tail pursuit that promised to close within the minute. She placed the Stearman's nose on the Proving Ground's checkered water tower and turned her radio to the Phillips air base traffic control frequency of 126.2.

"Phillips ATC, Stearman one-zero-zero-three Alpha, at five-zero feet VFR on one-eight-oh. Request clearance emergency vector for Washington National. We are being pursued by armed un-ID'ed Henschel single turbo presumably flown by terrorists. Please clear ATA and alert law enforcement."

Her altitude was too low for reliable transmission and reception, but she'd had to make the effort. Surprisingly, the voice came back, belabored by interference but understandable.

"Stearman one-zero-zero-three Alpha. Is this some kind of stunt—a prank? Over."

"Phillips ATC, stick your head out the window and see how this grabs you."

She had been watching the Henschel in her rearview mirror. The other machine closed to virtual point-blank range just as they leapfrogged Spesutie Island and went blattering across the airfield. With the sound of the first shots, she kicked the Stearman into a wrenching vertical bank to the right that took them in a tight, thundering, deceptively lazy 180 turn with the air base control tower as the pivot. Eruptions of concrete and turf formed wildly scattered trails across the runways and taxiways, and she was aware of a scrambling of tiny running figures and frantically circling vehicles. Her earphones were suddenly cacophonous as the tower rattled off orders to the Stearman and the Henschel to "cease and desist and land at once for consultations."

Cap punched the button again. "Phillips ATC, Stearman one-zero-zero-three Alpha. Please clear to Washington National Special VFR. This is an emergency—a national emergency."

The Henschel was coming around again, but she tried to ignore it. If she didn't sort out the traffic-control problem, they could end up in more danger from near-misses and military intercepts than from the madman in the Henschel. When it came back on the line, Phillips ATC was cool, collected, and obviously the beneficiary of some quick advice from God and the FAA.

"Stearman one-zero-zero-three Alpha is cleared out of Phillips-Aberdeen Control Zone to east, then southwest to NAS Patuxent River, maintain Special VFR conditions at or below three thousand feet. You are reminded that central Washington is a prohibited zone."

"Negative, Phillips ATC. Your clearance will guarantee destruction of one-zero-zero-three Alpha and national security documents aboard, destined eyes-only for the president. Request Special VFR your zone via Middle River, Baltimore, Fort Meade, and Washington National, with special clearance all prohibited zones. Please advise all agencies that the terrorist aircraft is firing live ammunition and may very well cause damage and personal injury on the ground. Urge all agencies to make maximum effort to intercept and destroy terrorist aircraft, a red-and-black Henschel 'Dagger.' I'm going to be very busy now, so this will be my last transmission."

For emphasis she lured the Henschel into another gunnery run while she virtually floated around the air base ATC, and she could imagine all the soldier boys diving for cover as little fountains of debris and shattered glass spouted from the tower's facade.

"Hey, Cap," Sweeney grumped through the intercom, "why are you screwing around here? Let's get the show on the road, damn it."

"I've been having a lot of unproductive talk with some air controllers. So I have just gone incommunicado, and if they want to shoot us down they'll have to wait in line."

"So let's go, then."

She headed southwest, so low over the railroad that one of the Pennsy's silver streamliners seemed to catch up with them and match their ninety knots. The Henschel made a wide turn over Churchville, so far off it looked as if it might be headed for Canada, then, its wings glinting in the pewter-colored light below the overcast, it came for them in a long, descending rush. As the other craft closed, Cap booted the Stearman into a shallow, diving turn that put it into a virtual head-on collision course. This not only ruined the Henschel pilot's range-setting but also forced him to voom aloft in an almost-vertical climb.

"Way to go, kid," Sweeney said. "Ruin his aim and his timing, he won't shoot at all. He's got his problems, too, especially the limits on his ammo and gas. Thank God the nut isn't carrying air-to-air missiles. We wouldn't last a minute."

"Well, we may not have to worry about missiles, but we do have to worry about the weather. It's starting to turn stinky on us. The ceiling's coming down, I'm feeling rain on my face, and the crosswind is so stiff I'm practically breaking the rudder pedals to compensate."

"Keep at it. Baltimore's just ahead."

The Henschel pilot also took note of the weather, apparently, since he began to attack more urgently. Cap managed to give him a good run, but three of his machine-gun bursts connected solidly, tearing away an interplane strut, shredding the upper right wing, and smashing Sweeney's windscreen. Two bursts that missed sent flickering tracers ahead to tear up a line of boxcars on a siding and to knock out some windows in a signal tower.

But then they were over Baltimore, where the Pennsy did a lot of its work in deep cuts and tunneling. Cap kept the ship on its heading, but held one eye on I-95, which was roughly going her way and was easier to watch in all the hullaballoo than the instrument panel and its compass. The Henschel pilot seemed somewhat awed by so much big city so close below because the rearview mirror showed him to be wheeling wider on his turns and getting higher in the sky, both of which, happily, reduced the shots coming the Stearman's way.

Cap said, "That guy seems to be even more inexperienced at this kind of thing than I am."

"Right-o. We may be dumb, and we may be doing all the wrong things, and we may go to jail for a hundred years, but that guy is a mile ahead of us in all respects. He doesn't know his ass from a bass bassoon."

"I wonder why that doesn't make me feel better."

A rattling hail of fire ran across the lower-left wing aileron and took out a pair of landing wires. The Stearman was growing sluggish, and she thought she caught a miss in the Lycoming engine's beat.

She picked up the Pennsy tracks as they emerged from the southside tunneling. Throttling down to just above stalling, she settled the wheels about four millimeters above the power line spaghetti and began to wallow for the misty blob of Washington, twenty-five miles ahead.

The Henschel made two more passes, the first of which turned the Stearman's horizontal stablizer to flapping junk, blew away the baggage-hatch lid behind Cap's cockpit, and riddled the top wing anew. The second came between Beltsville and College Park, and it turned Cap's windscreen to an opaque tangle, bisected a center-section strut, and set the Lycoming to coughing and throwing brown smoke.

"Are you okay, Sweeney?"

"My pants are wet."

"Hold on. Washington National is out. I have to set this baby down."

The Stearman barely cleared Union Station and made a wobbling turn along Louisiana Avenue with the Henschel close behind. And then Cap lost track of chronology and precise circumstance, knowing only that the end began when the Henschel passed overhead, a shadow that screamed. She had no awareness of watching, but she must have, because her mind registered the Henschel's mad climb over the Capitol, a darting of fire and smoke from the ground somewhere, and the red-and-black machine's dissolution in ballooning flames and whirling debris. She felt, rather than saw, the insane rolling, over and over, that coursed down the sky to conclude in a tower of spray in mid-Potomac.

And then they themselves were down, benumbed in a welter of wrenching and splintering and tearing. The wreckage seemed to have a mind of it own, determined to slide as far as possible along the great wide way of Pennsylvania Avenue, committed to sending cars over sidewalks and pedestrians shrieking into doorways, over walls, and up trees.

A silence. Deep, total.

Then a pattering of rain. Heavy drops, wet, splattering on the torn fabric and steaming metal.

Sweeney's voice: "Did you bring an umbrella?"

CHAPTER 39

After his bedside visit with Aaron Richter, the Secret Service people had escorted Leonardi to the hospital's VIP sitting room, where, the moment the door had closed behind him, he shed his jacket, kicked off his shoes and stretched full length on the sofa. With the rheostat he dimmed the lamps; with the remote button he opened the drapes; and with heavy eyes he gazed at Washington's midnight skyline, yearning for sleep but locked in the wakefulness that accompanied defeat and sorrow. He had always hated waiting, but this wait, a mere twenty minutes or so while Jenny and McKell said their hellos to the patient, would surely be among the most onerous and difficult of his lifetime.

He sought to think of happy times, the good old days, but for all the effort the happy times eluded him and the good old days defied definition or recognition. Good old days? When had they been? Not in his boyhood, belabored as it was with the child's ever-present and seldom-satisfied hunger for love and reassurance; not in his teens, an endless stretch of anxieties and disappointments; not in his manhood, an eternity of physical drain, mental traumas and spiritual deterioration suffered in the name of "ambition"—the American euphemism for socially acceptable avarice and plunder. He had grown up in a home oppressed by an immigrant father's losing struggle to cope and belong; he had scrambled and kicked and connived and bootlicked to win a college degree; he had endured and barely escaped personal entrapment in the self-righteous, priggish money-madness that permeated Exemplar Industries, Inc.; he had survived a war and its attendant insanities; he had plunged, absurdly naive and idealistic, into the presidency, where he had discovered, on a cosmic scale, that he was not nearly so smart as he wanted to be and not nearly so stupid as he feared he was. And now, here, tonight, the most painful of all rejections: betrayal by friends. *Good old days? What good old days, for crissake?*

He was drifting in filmy recollections of his first car—an antediluvian Ford coupe with faded whitewalls and a horn that played the opening bars of "Dixie," which he'd bought with two hundred and ninety dollars saved from his after-school job with Bleeker's Nursery and Lawn Service—when the intercom warbled.

"Yes?"

"Charlie Morris on the door detail, sir. The vice president and Ms. Malone are here."

"Okay. Show them in, please."

He turned up the lights, closed the drapes and pulled on his shoes and was once again a delight for all to behold when Jenny and McKell came through the vestibule and waded through the outrageously thick carpet to take his hand.

"You look very tired," Jenny said solicitously.

"That I am."

"Can't you steal a week or so and lie on the sunny sands of Florida?" McKell said jovially.

"That I can't."

After an awkward pause, Leonardi waved at the easy chairs. "Sit down, you two. What do you think about Aaron? Did he give you any idea of just what happened? Of how he managed to get himself shot? All I could get out of him were platitudes and evasions."

Jenny shrugged an elegantly tailored shoulder. "Nothing more than we've already got from the DEA people. He says he was with a narc team scheduled to bust Randolph Ridenour and some friends for possession and trafficking. There were some intelligence nuances in the case and he wanted to be in on the raid and subsequent interrogations to confirm or refute his informants. He says it was strictly routine."

"Didn't he tell you anything at all, Mr. President?" McKell asked, elaborately earnest.

"I sense there's a lot he isn't saying, and it ticks me off. When the president asks for a report, the president should get a report. Aaron just smiles wanly and says he'll fill me in later. I assure you he'll do just that."

"Well, after all, he was pretty badly hurt, it seems, and he isn't feeling up to snuff yet."

"Mm." Leonardi nodded somberly. "And neither of you can throw any more light on this incident? I mean, you both are in charge of our drug war campaign and you have many sources. Haven't any of those sources contributed any further understanding of the contretemps at Azalea Manor?"

McKell shook his handsome head. "Not a thing, sir."

"But we're still working on it," Jenny put in.

"I need some coffee," Leonardi said suddenly. "Jenny, buzz Charlie and ask him to have some coffee and Danish sent in for us, will you?"

Although their flight had ended within five hundred yards of the White House, three days passed before Sweeney saw an indication that the White House was at all interested.

The three days had been marked, of course, by great consternation over the circumstances of their arrival. The period began with Sweeney's and Cap's extraction from the Stearman's sorry mess by at least a platoon of Washington's metropolitan police, who, in minutes, had been joined by the Capitol Police, themselves augmented by uniforms and badges Sweeney had never before seen or imagined. By noon, the lot had been upstaged by men with narrow eyes and narrow neckties who were fond of announcing, through clenched teeth and to all and sundry, that they were the FBI. And by nightfall there had begun a parade of people whose tailoring was increasingly tasteful and expensive and whose credentials revealed that they were from NSC, JCS, DCI, SII, CIA, DOD, DIA, NSA, NRO, USA, USN, USAF, G-2, ONI, A-2, NORAD, BMEWS, SLBM, SPASUR, and, probably, AAA, AMA, BBDO and MGM.

By noon of the second day the visiting delegations had begun to include members of the House and Senate Intelligence Committees, the Armed Services Committees of each chamber, and an assortment of entirely irrelevant legislators and satraps who had perceived this to be a marvelous photo-op. The game was to be photographed while severely questioning Sweeney and Cap, who had taken on, however illogically, the aura of an airborne Bonnie and Clyde. This absurdity had been triggered by two developments: first, the wonderful footage of the Stearman and its tormentor as they wobbled into disaster—acquired, shared and run incessantly by the major television networks—that had been shot by a teenage tourist from Altoona, PA, from atop the Washington Monument with his birthday videocam and long-range zoom; and, second, the announcement by Ted Turner that he had engaged, for unprecedented sums, Superstars Roscoe Feigenheimer and Louella Zik to play the leads in the movie version.

Truth and substance had been lost in all of this, of course, because, in essence, nobody could divine the truth or find any substance in Sweeney's and Cap's flat-out refusal to talk to anybody but President Richard Leonardi.

Neither the fact that Sweeney had worked with many of these individuals and had, indeed, done the town with some of them, nor the fact that he was a highly respected war hero and a former high-level intelligence official seemed to carry any weight with anybody. He and his beautiful former secretary (who was now reputed to be his mistress) were big-time drama, big-time news, big-time charisma and, best of all, photogenic as hell. And that's all that counted to anybody, from Murgatroyd Silverspoon to Joe and Gert Bubba.

Sweeney's primary concern was not the hullaballoo and his newfound wicked-celebrity status but the fact that the briefcase containing the videotape of the Cocaine Summit and its derivative documents had disappeared from the crash-site. In one of their few moments together he'd asked Cap if she knew what happened to the case and her answer, obviously shaded by the strain she'd been under, was that she didn't even know what had happened to her and as far as the briefcase was concerned she hoped that President Leonardi would take a moment in his Oval Office to shove it up his oval orifice.

At the end of the third day, around ten P.M., actually, the

burly SP ensign who superintended the restricted officers compound at Anacostia came through the door of Sweeney's quarters—a room slightly smaller than a shower stall—and told him to put on his pea jacket and come to the street, where a car was waiting to take him "into town."

The night was cold and starless, and the wind carried the promise of more rain, maybe snow. Sweeney and the ensign climbed into the backseat of a gray Navy Plymouth and the driver, a gob with no smiles left for anybody ever, drove them north through The District to Walter Reed Hospital. Nobody said a word the entire way.

He was led through what looked to be a side door of an annex and taken to an elevator which, after a hissing ride to somewhere near the moon, opened onto a glistening floor, a corridor subtly lighted by parchment-shaded lamps, and walls covered with pictures of presidents and government luminaries of the past. At the double doors at the end of the hall, two very large men in dark suits held a whispered conversation with the ensign, who then saluted and returned to the elevator.

"This way, please," one of the big men said, holding open the door.

More subtle lighting, more elegant tiling, everything shiny, shiny, squeaky-clean, and then Sweeney found himself in a huge and fancy sitting room whose central semicircle of easy chairs contained President Richard Leonardi, Vice President Brandon McKell, White House chief of staff Jenny Malone and Cap. Sweeney noted that McKell and Malone appeared to be surprised and uneasy, while Cap looked pale and angry.

"Hello, Sweeney. Long time no see."

"Mr. President."

"Have a seat." Leonardi waved toward a wide, deep, brocaded settee. He was neither amiable nor hostile. Neutral. Like the colors in the fancy room.

The president explained to the others: "I understand Mr. Sweeney has been trying to contact me, so I've invited him and his friend and compatriot, Ms. O'Brien, to join us here for a chat. Coffee, Sweeney?"

"No thanks."

The president considered McKell and Malone somberly, but when he spoke his tone was conversational. "As I've told you,

Aaron Richter hasn't yet thrown any real light on what happened to him and the others involved in that Maryland thing the other night. But I've learned some things from another source, and I think it's time for me to share them with you."

McKell licked his lips nervously, but Malone remained her cool self, her gaze alert and interested.

"I've learned," Leonardi continued softly, "that what was going on at Azalea Manor was the culmination of a humongous international sting. An elaborate, secret collaboration between certain elements of the duly elected German government headed by Chancellor Erich Haussener and certain elements of the duly elected American government headed by yours truly. The idea was to suck in and destroy the neo-Nazi movement headed by Hugo von Zoll. It was also a scheme which serendipitously was supposed to throttle the drug lords and save our nation from death by narcotics—in the process reelecting me and the vice president and establishing our party for decades to come as the can-do party."

Sweeney's glance met Cap's, and he winked.

"There were two major flaws in the scheme, however," Leonardi was saying. "First, it was illegal as hell, both in Germany and the United States. Second: neither Chancellor Haussener or I had the foggiest notion that it was going on. We knew nothing about it because our zealous staffers knew we would never permit such a gross violation of law and ethics."

Sweeney felt the intensifying shock and surprise gathering in the room.

Leonardi sipped his coffee. Over the rim of his cup he said, "I've asked you and Ms. O'Brien here, Sweeney, because I'm going to highlight what the Secret Service guys found in the briefcase they took from the wreckage of your plane, and I'd like you to straighten me out if I wobble. Okay?"

"Yes, sir."

"Here goes: Things were getting too hot for Manuel Corbato, the drug lord, so he decided to consolidate the South American drug industry and offer to sell to the Americans that section of his business that derives its income from the United States. Corbato asked a free-lance German agent named Colt to persuade the Americans that if they were to buy him out they could control the epidemic sweeping the U.S. scene. Colt saw that the idea, if sold to the right people in Chancellor Haussener's government, could earn him additional fat go-between fees by setting up the ruin of von Zoll and his neo-Nazis, whose crimes were always just beyond the chancellor's legal reach. Colt's plan: first, induce von Zoll to buy the American share of the drug business—which the Americans would be only too glad to sell him, thanks to the difficulty of sliding their own participation past Congress and other watchdog agencies. Next, arrange to catch him at it, red-handed, and present the German government with documentary evidence of his trafficking in drugs. Von Zoll would then go to jail for a long time, his Nazi movement would be thoroughly discredited, and fat fees of gratitude would be forthcoming from both governments for this combined sting and drug war wrap-up. How am I doing, Sweeney?"

"Couldn't have put it better myself."

"The problem," Leonardi said, "was that the plan called for breaking the law to set up a lawbreaker. It would be entrapment on a cosmic scale. So the need was to keep both governments officially in the dark about the the U.S. buyout and the German sting."

McKell, nervously fingering his necktie, was speechless, but Malone asked in her unruffled way, "My God, Mr. President, where are you getting all this baloney?"

"Let me finish. Colt arranged to have Corbato's offer brought to you, Jenny, by your lover, Randolph Ridenour, and you at once saw the U.S. domestic political possibilities. We could buy out the drug enemy with Nazi money and claim that Vice President McKell's inspired leadership had brought victory in the drug war. McKell would gain new respect and our party would reign supreme for hell knows how long. So you persuaded me to turn over the drug campaign to Brandon and you, and you, with the help of Aaron Richter, General Reynolds, and a group of von Zoll's Nazi agents, set up the sleight-of-hand in Florida and the South American countries that would make it happen. It all might have worked, too, if it hadn't been for Tom Sweeney and Ms. O'Brien. They saw through the plot and broke it up. Isn't that right, Sweeney?"

"So far, yes."

McKell broke in, sputtering, "My God, Mr. President, do you realize what you're saying—"

"Of course I realize what I'm saying. I'm saying that you and Jenny have violated the law. I'm saying that I am, here and now, demanding your resignations. I want them on my desk the first thing in the morning."

"But how do you know this?" McKell was actually whining.

"Tom Sweeney eyeballed the meeting at Azalea Manor. He videotaped everything that was said and done there. Not only that, he provided the documents of agreement, all signed by the principals. He and Ms. O'Brien were flying them to me when a von Zoll plane shot them down over Pennsylvania Avenue. You and Jenny are identified with the plot by the plotters' own words. And you're both finished."

Malone, still cool, said, "Not so fast, Rick. Our resignations would set up an immediate media uproar, and when the public found out that you suspected two of your key people of some kind of shenanigans you would be on your own way out. You can't dump us without explaining why, and the explanation would inflict hellish damage on yourself and the party."

Leonardi considered her with open incredulity. "You are truly amazing, Jenny. Don't you have any remorse at all?"

Malone patted her tidy coiffure and cleared her throat delicately. "Remorse? Why should I feel remorse over a plan that virtually guaranteed the solidification of your political gains as a drug war leader? That would dramatize Brandon McKell's contributions as the one who had done the real fighting—the foot soldier who carried out your orders with skill and intelligence? Neither I nor Vice President McKell had any idea that the proposal, presented to us by Aaron, was violating any law, here or abroad. I admit that I plunged into the thing with great enthusiasm because it seemed to be such a wonderful way to accomplish so much. I should have known it was illegal, but I did not. My intentions were the best. I am guilty mainly of incomplete research due to wishful thinking, born of my blind support of my president and his vice president."

Sweeney held up a hand. "Tilt! The idea wasn't brought to you by Richter. You enlisted Richter, who agreed to set up the arrest of Cummings and get the goods on von Zoll so that Chancellor Haussener's government could legally prosecute, convict and imprison as many Nazis as possible. And I don't give a damn if he was breaking the law or not—he saved my heinie. I fell into the schmeer by chance and Hank Nageler's dying effort to get revenge, and Richter spent one hell of a lot of time keeping me from being blown away by Cummings and his Nazis. So I won't let you lay it all on him, babe."

Malone ignored Sweeney. "You can make all this go away, Rick. You can win your second term and go down in history as the man who beat the druggists. You can leave your party with unbeatable strength for decades. All you have to do to accomplish these great things is to keep your mouth shut. Say nothing. Do nothing. Stonewall the media and the political opposition on Sweeney's Paul Revere plane ride. Do those things, Rick, and the future is yours."

Leonardi stood up and went to the big window, from which he gave nighttime Washington a testy inspection. He stood there for a time, deep in thought, and the room was silent.

"Well," the president said eventually, "here's how it's going down: Along with the McKell-Malone resignations, I'll be asking for Aaron Richter's as well, since it's obvious he knew from the beginning that what he was trying to do was entirely unethical, if not felonious. Second, I'll place General Reynolds on early retirement, since the nation can't afford high-ranking officers in responsible positions who fail to apply sound ethics to questionable situations and procedures. Third, I'll give Brigadier General Harvey Wallace his second star, a promotion he hugely deserves for his dedication to the highest principles of military service and for his much-publicized personal bravery in the face of great hazard. Fourth, I'll appoint Thomas F. Sweeney to the post vacated by Aaron Richter, making Mr Sweeney director of SII. Fifth, I'll see that Ms. O'Brien's airplane is either restored or replaced at government expense. Sixth, I'll arrange a television talk on all the networks, in which I'll explain every last thing that happened in this gross matter and accept personal responsibility for it. I will not have the American people duped this way, and when the crew deliberately, calculatingly, endangers the ship of state, the passengers—the citizen voters—deserve a full accounting from the person responsible, the captain on the bridge. I would rather not be president if it means I must cover up the misdeeds—even the unwitting, well-intended miscalculations—of my staff and my Administration. The people deserve an accounting in this mess, and, by God, I'll see that they get it."

Malone showed anger for the first time. "You're throwing everything away. You're an idealistic idiot."

Leonardi turned from the window then and said quietly, "I'm going back to the White House now. I'm tired and I have to do some more thinking." He glanced at Sweeney. "I've covered everything, haven't I?"

"Except for the most important part."

"Oh, God. You mean there's more?"

"Yep. Your impending assassination."

It was like that child's game, statue, in which, when somebody calls a word, the kids all freeze, holding the pose they were in at the moment of the call. The room was suddenly filled with statues.

"My *what?*"

"I did not come tearing down here in a wheezy antique airplane, risking the life of the woman I'm going to marry and getting thrown into the movies, just to tell you about some weirdo plot to kick out some Nazis and get the junkies off our streets. I could have written you a letter about that. I could have UPS'ed the video and the documents. But what I couldn't do was risk your life further. I could not ignore the warning, written with john seats and in his own blood, left by our old sneaky-time pal, Hank Nageler."

Leonardi's face was a study in purple. "Go on."

"Do you remember what a raised john seat *and* lid meant?"

"Who can forget something like that?"

"Hank raised them at my house before he died. And he wrote on the wall—in his blood—the three initials, *HCN*. I had trouble with that until I learned from Dr. Oscar Schwenke, designer of special weapons, that Nageler, acting for a client, had asked Schwenke to make a pair of prussic acid peashooters. HCN is the chemical formula for prussic acid—one of the deadliest of poisons. When it's sprayed in the face of a victim, it provides a perfect imitation of a heart attack. The HCN peashooter—a favorite of political assassins everywhere. Nageler had ordered two, but Schwenke made only one, knowing that he was safe only as long as the client still needed his services. Insurance, he called it.

"Which was more than Nageler could arrange for himself, because he was expendable once the client had made a deal with Schwenke. Tapes of Hank's last radio call made it clear that he realized he'd been set up—sent on some ostensibly important surveillance mission that was really a ploy to position him where he could be made to vanish. He was being removed as a witness, as a link to Schwenke, if ever the authorities suspect assassination instead of the heart attack the assassination is supposed to look like."

Leonardi asked the obvious question. "So who is the client we're talking about here?"

Sweeney sighed. "Hank Nageler's final radio sending to his helper ashore—whoever it was may never be confirmed, but his bandaged head suggests it was Schwenke, knocked silly by Ames—said, in essence, 'The eager-beaver queen has conned us. Get even. Smash her box.' The peashooters were to be stashed in a pencil box in a pantry drawer at Schwenke's home. What other box could Schwenke be expected to smash? Who is the equivalent of a queen in the American equivalent of a royal household? Your chief of staff, Jenny Malone. Jenny Malone, who wants her lover, the Veep, to be president. So that she, herself, can become president."

The Malone and McKell statues blinked.

Leonardi gaped. "Say again?"

"When Ridenour came to her with Corbato's offer, Malone saw that, while the idea itself could bring some useful social and political results, it also offered her a vehicle by which she could maneuver herself into the presidency. Nail down McKell's vice presidency in your second term by making him hero of the drug war. Then, squirt you into an HCN 'heart attack' just before the end of your second term, which makes McKell president until the oncoming election, in which his straight-out election—with her as his chosen running mate—is almost guaranteed by the huge sympathy vote. Once McKell's in office and she is vice president, another 'heart attack' can be arranged and, voila, look who's president."

Cool, even-voiced, unabashed, Jenny Malone stated the absolute truth: "Sweeney, you must be out of your mind."

"I won't argue that."

"There is no way you can prove any of that garbage."

"There are two ways, as a matter of fact. One is to see what a jury makes of Schwenke's testimony. The other is to look at the contents of that briefcase of yours."

"You're insane—"

"Probably. But nuts or not, I'm willing to bet that the Azalea Manor hullaballoo has accelerated your schedule. I'll bet you a Coke that you plan to waste Rick at the earliest possible opportunity. Why wait? A dead Leonardi moves you a notch closer and gives you time to rework your plans to replace a President McKell. Right?"

"Rick, for God's sake— Are you going to let this madman slander me this way?"

Brandon McKell seemed actually to quiver, and his pallor was spectacular. "Goddammit, Jenny— You planned to kill me, too?"

"Shut up, you stupid son of a bitch. This character hasn't a shred of proof—"

"You were sleeping with Ridenour all the time you were planning to kill me, too."

"Shut your goddam mouth! Don't say another word!"

Another word was not said, by anyone, for a full minute. It was as if a plug had been pulled, a disconnect, or a short circuit had interrupted all motion, all sound. Then Sweeney said, "Mr. President, as the new director of SII, I have police powers of investigation and arrest, do I not?"

"Of course," Leonardi said irritably.

Sweeney held out his hand. "Ms. Malone, before the president and these other witnesses, I'm telling you that I suspect the presence of a deadly weapon in that briefcase of yours. I plan to search the briefcase. Give it to me."

"The hell I will, you crazy bastard."

Sweeney tore the case from her hand, flipped it open, and peered inside. A brief groping, and he produced a long, thin tube with what appeared to be a spring-loaded compressed-air cylinder at one end.

Malone, chalky, eyes glazed, seemed to sway.

Sweeney pocketed the peashooter. "Your move, Mr. President."

Leonardi coughed gently and, reaching, pressed the intercom button. "Charlie, come in here, will you? Sweeney's just made an arrest and I want you to take the suspect downtown on a bunch of suspicion charges."

"Right away, sir."

Leonardi pulled on his jacket and made for the door. Over his shoulder he said, "Brandon, I want your letter of resignation on my desk by eight o'clock tomorrow morning. And I'm ordering you to remain in The District pending further investigation of Sweeney's claims." Giving Sweeney a lingering glance, he added, "And I want you at your SII desk tomorrow at eight. Understood?"

"Yes, sir."

Sweeney and Cap waited until everybody had left, then made their way to Richter's room.

"Hi." Richter smiled weakly from a conglomeration of bedding, bandages and tubes. "How did it go in there?"

"Has anyone talked to you?"

"Just the orderly with the bedpan. And the president, who, after congratulating me on my survival, told me I was fired and would be lucky to escape criminal charges. And also that you would succeed me."

"I wasn't after your job, you know."

"Of course you weren't. But I'm glad you got it. You'll make a hell of a director."

"That was a very ballsy thing you did at Azalea Manor—making a DEA drug bust so that the German government could have documentary cause to arrest von Zoll. Even when you had to know that Cummings had a small army on hand."

"Not so ballsy. Cummings was going to be my escape hostage. And knowing you, I was pretty sure you'd be lurking in the woodwork, listening. That's why I insisted on giving that detailed summary of the case. So that you would know what was going on if I happened to get blown away."

"I'm sorry your career had to end this way."

"No big deal. I was about to quit anyhow. I was feeling too much guilt, too much sorrow, too much everything. Not good enough to join the choir, not bad enough to enjoy the mud. As a Class-A burnout, I'd have made a premium-grade booboo anyhow, sooner or later."

"Well, for a burn-out you sure pulled some classy moves. Especially when you kept Cummings thinking you were trying to nail me when you were really trying to keep him from nailing me. Slick City. And much appreciated here."

"You're welcome."

"Well, I hope you don't fry in fat that's too deep. And, since I owe you one, I'll help you all I can."

"Okay. Now get out of here. I'm tired."

The phone rang then, and Richter picked it up. He glanced at Sweeney. "It's for you."

"Hello?"

"My achin' back, Mr. Sweeney, I been tryin' to find you for three days now. I called the White House and I called the War Department and I—"

"What is it, Freddie?"

"I got them fellas Cummings and What's-His-Face chained in the cellar of my Chesapeake City house. What in hell do you want me to do with them?"

"You found them, then, eh?"

"They was hitchhikin' on Route two thirteen. I gave 'em a lift."

"Well, keep them where they are. I'll send some people to pick them up tomorrow. Meanwhile, are you okay?"

"First rate."

"You sure are, buddy."

Hanging up, he patted Richter on the shoulder. "I'll check in with you tomorrow."

"Appreciate it."

As they waited for the elevator, Cap said, "Busy night."

"Well, you sure as hell weren't saying much in there. Where was your big mouth when I needed it?"

"Hey, back off, pal. How am I supposed to say something when you and the president of the U.S. of A. are hogging the stage and making all the speeches?"

"Careful. I'm now an agency director, and you've got to show more respect."

"Did you mean it when you said I'm the woman you're going to marry?"

"Not for a while yet."

"How come?"

"I've got a very tough morning in the office tomorrow. So you've got to give me at least until noon."

EPILOGUE

New lead national elections,
from wire services and staff:
(Page 1 banner, with deck, all editions):

IT'S LEONARDI AGAIN—BY A LANDSLIDE

TICKET-MATE WALLACE TAKES VICE PRESIDENCY IN BIG, EASY WIN

President beats odds against reelection; loses only 3 states

Last year's apology for staff malfeasance applauded by voters

WASHINGTON—Richard D. Leonardi won his second term as president yesterday as the nation's voters, cramming polls in unprecedented numbers, showed that they love him anyhow.

"Miracle?" the president asked at his victory celebration. "Nonsense. It shows the American people value candor and an earnest individual's determination to play fair and square."

Also a big winner was Harvey M. Wallace, a retired reserve corps major general, widely acclaimed hero, and former commander of the hemisphere's anti-drug forces, who was named to the ticket as vice presidential candidate by party acclamation at last summer's convention.

Wallace was suggested by Leonardi after the former vice president, Brandon McKell, resigned under a cloud. The same scandal, which Leonardi revealed in his famed "mea culpa" TV speech of last winter, brought the ouster of his chief of staff, Jenny Malone, who has also been indicted by a grand jury on as-yet undisclosed charges. The main prosecution witness in the case, Dr. Oscar Schwenke, former Defense Department weapons design chief, is undergoing therapy at the Betty Ford Clinic.

Leonardi and Wallace and Wallace's wife, Millie, after a jubilant victory celebration at party headquarters here, flew in Air Force One to Florida, where they will spend a holiday with close friends, including Thomas F. Sweeney, director of Special Intelligence Initiatives, and his wife, Veronica, and Mr. and Mrs. Frederick Dilworth, of North East and Chesapeake City, Md.

Meanwhile, national chairmen of both parties—

(NOTE TO DESK EDS: Pick up here, first edition body text)